Sweet

ADDICTION

Sweet

ADDICTION

NEW YORK TIMES BESTSELLING AUTHOR

J. DANIELS

For my love,

my amazing husband,

who puts up with my craziness.

Chapter
ONE

"SHIT. SHIT. SHIT. JOEY? I need you!" I'm flustered and running late as usual, frantically trying to zip up my new black strapless dress and failing miserably. "Damn it, Joey."

Throwing my hands in the air in frustration, I step into my favorite black pumps and run downstairs into the bakery, my bare back completely exposed. Joey, my assistant and dear friend, is leaning his tall, perfectly tailored, suited frame against the doorway and watching me, clearly amused. A winning smile spreads across his face, and if I weren't so rightly irritated, I would have stopped to appreciate just how handsome he looks.

"What the fuck? Can you zip me up, please, so we can go? The cake should have been delivered over an hour ago."

He pushes off the wall and moves toward me, his expression softening. "No, dear, it's already been delivered."

My back straightens as the cold metal of the zipper slides up my spine. "What? No it hasn't."

"Yes, it has." His hands grip my shoulders and spin me. "I dropped it off myself because I knew you would be freaking out up there getting ready and making us late."

"Really?" I ask, staring up at him unconvinced.

He nods. "Really, cupcake."

Smiling and reaching up, I kiss him quickly on his freshly shaven jaw. "You're the best, you know that right?"

"I know." His eyes run down my body and I feel my cheeks heat up. "You look *amazing*, Dylan. Seriously," he wiggles his brows at me, "if tits did anything for me…"

I hold up my hand to stop him, but teasingly mold my breasts and plump them up. "Yeah? They do look fantastic right now, don't they?" He smiles down at me, his one dimple sucked in tightly.

"You ready for this?" he asks as he brushes my hair off my shoulder. "We can still back out. I'm all for ditching this shit and going bar hopping instead." His brow arches as he searches my face, waiting for my response.

I exhale forcefully and grab his arm, leading him toward the door. "No, we can't ditch. Juls will be pissed if we don't show up. Besides," we halt at the door and I grip his massive shoulders, "I thought you wanted to do bad things with men we'll never see again?" Slutty wedding sex awaits and I am more than ready to experience it.

His eyes quickly light up with mischief. *There's the naughty Joey I know and love.* "Oh, fuck yes. Let's do this, cupcake."

ஒ

FAYETTE STREET IS BUZZING WITH people, all wandering in and out of shops on this beautiful June day. I lock up and spin around, seeing Joey stomping his foot irritatingly in the direction of our transportation.

"Seriously, Dylan? Do we have to take the van? This suit is *way* too nice for that thing, and you know what kind of cars those rich bitches will be rolling up in." He motions to his outfit with a sweeping hand as I walk toward the driver's side.

"I'm sorry, but do you have another suggestion? Your car is in the shop and this is my only mode of transportation at the moment." I open the door and step in, standing on the ledge and looking over the roof at his scrunched up face. "And be nice to Sam. He's been through a lot lately."

He lets out an exhausted breath. "If I ruin this nice suit… and please explain to me why you named this stupid thing. Who names their delivery van?" I ignore his last comment and start it up, glaring at him as he climbs in to ward off any further insults.

"Don't make me put you in the back," I warn as I pull away from the curb toward an evening of inevitable awkwardness.

ᘒᘓ

"HOLY SHIT. THIS PLACE IS fantastic!" Joey shrieks as I pull onto the driveway leading up to Whitmore Mansion, following a long line of expensive vehicles. I wince and rub the steering wheel, preparing Sam for the looks he will undoubtedly receive. "Oh, for Christ's sake. See. I fucking told you we would stand out like idiots. Do you realize we're sandwiched between a Mercedes and Lamborghini. A fucking Lamborghini."

I swallow loudly. Joey's right. My delivery van, which is adorned with swirls of cupcakes and icing splashes on both sides, is completely out of place here. I'm fairly certain we will be the only non-luxury vehicle in the parking lot. My ringtone startles me and I quickly pull my phone out of my clutch, hitting the speaker phone button.

"Hey, Juls."

"Are you here yet? I'm dying to introduce you to Ian and his entourage of insanely hot friends. HEY. What are you doing? You should be rounding up the groomsmen. Jesus, do I have to do everything around here?"

I giggle at my best friend as we slowly inch closer to the parking attendants. She's usually very calm and collected, until it's close to show time.

"Please, for the love of Christ, tell me one of Ian's ridiculously hot friends prefers cock to pussy. I need to get laid, and I needed it to happen yesterday." Joey is practically bouncing in his seat as I chuckle at him. There is nothing he likes more than a wild, no strings attached hook up, and weddings offer the best situation for such thing. Especially weddings where there is free booze.

"Actually, his friend Billy didn't once glance at my boobs when I was leaning over Ian, so you might be good to go there, JoJo." With that information, he pulls his visor down and begins fixing his already perfectly coifed blond hair.

"We're at the valet guys now, so we'll be right up." I hit end and stop in front of three young boys who eye up Sam questionably and glance between the three of them, silently asking who wants to drive it. I step out with my purse and walk toward them. "Here, the clutch sticks, so don't be afraid to be rough with him." Tossing the keys to the one closest to me, I loop my arm through Joey's and watch as the two boys who don't have to drive Sam snicker at the one with the keys.

"It smells like cupcakes in here."

My head falls back and I laugh with Joey at the valet attendant as we follow the crowd into the venue.

To describe this place as beautiful is an extreme understatement. Entering through rustic doors, the floor plan opens up to a massive foyer with dim lighting given off by Tiffany-inspired glass chandeliers. Stained glass windows surround both doors, and antique furnishings and artwork fill the room. Guests are making their way down the hallway, which leads into another large room, most likely where the ceremony will be taking place. A grand staircase, wide enough for ten people to walk side by side, leads up to a second level, and as I inhale, the scent of old wood and calla lilies fill my lungs. *Damn it.* This wedding is going to be beyond chic.

"There you are. Holy shit, Dyl, you look incredible. Is that dress new and when can I borrow it?" My beautiful best friend is adorned in a navy dress with an empire waist, her dark chocolate brown hair pulled back into a chic bun. "Justin is going to shit a brick when he sees you," she whispers against my ear as she ends our hug. I'd prefer it if he just dropped dead at the sight of me, but I'm not that lucky.

"Thanks. You look amazing as usual. How's the bride?" Her fingers fluff my blonde waves that fall past my shoulders, and she leans in and gives Joey a kiss on each cheek.

"Annoying. Come on, you both need to find seats and quickly. We're about to start." She grasps my hand in hers and I pull Joey behind me as we walk straight back and into the room labeled The Great Hall.

"Okay, where are all the hot boys at?" Joey searches the room, practically bouncing on his feet. The boy is on the hunt and has a predictable, one-track mind.

I shake my head at him. "Could you please try and keep it in your pants during the ceremony? You are technically *my* plus one, and can wait to get all freaky with some lucky man at the reception."

"I make no promises, cupcake." He smoothes his suit and wiggles his brows at me as Juls extends her hand, pointing toward the left side of the room.

"See the man sitting five rows back on the end, with the ponytail?"

I laugh and her eyes widen. "Ponytail? You didn't say Ian had a ponytail."

"Well, he does. And he lets me tug it when I'm coming."

"Hot damn. Get it, Juls!" Joey begins fanning his face and I know I need to do the same. My cheeks suddenly feel like they're on fire. Although, I shouldn't be that surprised at my best friend's comment. Between the three of us, we're all entirely too obsessed with the male appendage.

"Anyways," she continues with a tone, "the three equally delicious looking men next to him are all his colleagues. And Billy," she meets Joey's anxious eyes, "is the one next to the two empty seats. You guys better hurry up and grab them before someone else does. Oh, shit." She glances down at her watch and pushes us forward into the room. "Sit. Hurry." She clicks away on her heels as I stare down the center aisle where the bride will be walking down any minute. *Shit. I can't walk down that aisle to my seat. That has to be some kind of weird karma to walk where the bride of your ex-boyfriend is about to walk. No, thank you. I do not need that kind of bad luck.*

"Come on." I grab Joey's sleeve and pull him with me toward the left side of the room, walking quickly up the rows of chairs until we stop at the fifth row. Ian, Mr. Ponytail, glances up and smiles at me. *Ooohhh, he is cute.* "Excuse me," I say softly. I step between his long legs and the chair in front of him, trying to quickly make my way to the two empty seats. There isn't much space to wiggle through, and I inwardly laugh at the thought of my six foot two, muscly assistant doing the same shimmy right behind me. The lights start to dim, indicating the ceremony is about to start, so I move faster, Joey pushing up against my back.

"Oh, shit." My heel slips on the arm of a suit jacket that is hanging on the back of a chair and I fall backward, crashing straight into the lap of the man sitting two seats down from Ian. His hands quickly grab my waist and I gasp at the contact. *Oh, great. Good job, Dylan.* Glancing down slowly, I see the sexiest pair of hands I've ever laid eyes on. They're big, and his long fingers tightly grip my hips. Slightly tanned skin contrasts beautifully with my black dress, and I hear a few muffled laughs coming from behind and both sides of me. My eyes flick up to meet Joey, who is grinning widely and glancing behind me amusingly at whoever's lap I am sitting in. I stand up quickly and spin, getting the first real look at the man my ass is now acquainted with. "Oh, shit," I gasp, seeing a small smile form at the corner of his perfect mouth. *Oh, God, I want those lips on me.* Full and pink with a predominant slit running down the middle of the bottom one. His tongue darts out and slowly licks it. *Whoa.*

"You already said that, love." *Holy fucking shit, that voice. Are you kidding me with that voice?* Low and sweet, I can almost taste it. My eyes quickly scan the rest of his face as Joey nudges me in the back, urging me to move forward. *Fuck him. He can wait a second and allow me to marvel at this spectacle in front of me.* His body is fit, built, and definitely makes good use of a gym membership. Perfectly disheveled, dark brown hair that is slightly grown out, striking green eyes that are glued to mine and a strong jaw. *Jesus, is this guy for real?* He could be a fucking model with these looks.

"I... uh... I... sorry." Swallowing loudly after my poor attempt at a sentence, I move quickly and fall back into the chair closest to the aisle, my chest heaving rapidly in my dress.

"What the fuck was that?" Joey whispers as he sits down next to me, blocking my view of the hottest guy I have ever seen in person.

"I don't know. I fell."

"You are such a whore; you did that on purpose. Christ on a cracker, he's hot." Joey leans back a bit and I meet the man's eyes briefly before I drop my head, my cheeks instantly flushing. "Did he get hard? Is he huge? He looks huge."

I cover my mouth after a loud gasp escapes. "Jesus, you have zero filter. Thank God, we aren't in a church. He does look huge though, right?" We giggle and make crude gestures at each other as the wedding party music begins to play.

"I bet he's bigger than Justin," he teases and my eyes widen.

"Are you serious? The ring bearer is probably bigger than Justin."

His mouth falls open. "I fucking knew he had a little dick. You never admitted it."

"Yup." I wiggle my pinky finger at him and he cracks. "We should have gotten Sara a dildo as her wedding gift. She's gonna need it."

Oh, my God, Joey mouths as I glance up to the front of the room. My eyes instantly fall on Justin, who is now standing next to his groomsmen. *Fucking hell, he looks good. I was hoping he got fat.*

"You okay?" Joey whispers and I nod, slowly turning in my seat so I can see the bridesmaids walk down the aisle. They're all wearing peach-colored dresses that sweep along the floor with each step they take. I smile at the flower girl as she sprinkles petals along the path and settles up front with the rest of the party. The room is beautiful, everything in white and coral. Tall crystal cylinders line each row of chairs and small, lit votive candles float in the water they hold. Calla lilies are spread throughout the room in vases, on tables, and each bridesmaid clutches one. With the change of the music, the guests all rise to their feet and turn their heads toward the back of the room. My eyes meet Juls' immediately as she stands by the door.

"You okay?" she mouths.

"Whatever," I reply. She steps up and opens the double doors, allowing Sara to walk through with her father.

I spend the rest of the ceremony staring down into my lap at my fingers. They are freshly painted a deep plum color and I smile at the sight of frosting, which is smudged on my left ring finger knuckle. Popping it into my mouth and sucking, I moan softly at the sweet taste of sugar as Joey weeps like a baby next to me. To my surprise, I'm not emotional at all. Weddings usually turned me into a blubbering idiot, but today, at this particular wedding, I'm emotionless. I guess a part of me should feel a bit sad. Not because my ex-boyfriend is getting married to someone other than myself, but because I wasted two years of my life on a relationship that almost broke me, and seeing him again is a reminder of all that time wasted. An annoying reminder. *Why the hell did I even stay with him for that long?* It definitely wasn't because of the sex. Sex with Justin was bland and boring. He never once brought me to orgasm. Not once.

I would have to finish myself off after he rolled out of bed and stalked into the bathroom. Of course, I always let him believe he got me off. I had to give the guy something. Raising my head, I glare at his profile. *You're welcome, dick.*

"And now it is with honor that I present to you, for the first time ever, Mr. and Mrs. Banks. You may now kiss the bride." Everyone stands up and cheers and, of course, I follow suit. It would be rude not to, and I'm not bitter, so, whatever, I cheer. Justin and Sara share a lingering kiss and earn a few whistles from the audience. I feel Joey's hand squeeze mine and I glance up into his big, blue eyes.

"I cannot *wait* to go drink my weight in booze," I whisper to him.

He bends and presses his lips to my ear. "And I can't wait to get my hands down the pants of this playa next to me. Maybe play a little just the tip."

"Jesus. You would." Everyone is watching the bride and groom walk down the aisle, but I'm lost in silly conversation with one of my closest friends. I'm giggling so hard that tears are starting to fill my eyes. And these will be the only tears shed from me today.

"Come on, Dylan, you know you want to slip off into a dark corner with your mystery man whose lap you accidently fell into. Maybe do a little something else in that lap of his."

I raise my eyebrow and lean back, seeing piercing, green eyes flick to mine instantly. A small smile pulls at the corner of his mouth. *Sweet Mother, he is gorgeous.* I quickly lean forward and try to play it off, but fail miserably as a wicked grin smears across my face. "Hell yes, I do. I fucking love weddings."

Chapter
TWO

T HE GUESTS FILE OUT OF The Great Hall and up the grand staircase
to the second level. Once Joey and I reach the top, we stand there
a moment to take in our surroundings. The entire second floor is
the reception hall, and ridiculously decked out in coral and calla lilies.

"Holy hell. Are those ice sculptures?"

My eyes follow Joey's gesture toward the right side of the room.
"Isn't that a bit over the top? Ooohhh, there's the cake."

"Told you I delivered it. I feel you doubt my capabilities as your
trusted assistant."

I nudge his shoulder as we walk to the place card table. "And I feel
you really love Sam and are just afraid to admit it."

Tilting his head back, he laughs loudly. "How badass would it be if
we started doing our deliveries out of a Lamborghini."

"Badass and extremely impractical. Maybe when we make our first
million we'll splurge on a luxury delivery vehicle." I grab our place card.
"Come on, we're table twelve."

I don't really care what table we're at, just as long as we aren't in
direct view of the bridal table. Justin still hasn't made eye contact and
I'm hoping to keep it that way, and with this many people in attendance,
avoiding him shouldn't be a problem. Round tables cover three sides of

a large wooden dance floor, the bridal table elevated on a platform and overlooking the guests. The tables are draped in white linen with coral ribbons running along the edges and beautiful calla lily filled centerpieces. The DJ is already playing music and a few people are dancing while others mingle around the tables, talking and enjoying themselves.

"There you two are." Juls comes skittering over to us in her dangerously high heels and grabs onto our forearms as we admire the sculptures. "How was it? Be honest." I cock my head to the side and scrunch up my nose as Joey rubs the back of his neck, seemingly in pain. Juls panics, her eyes bug and her fingers immediately rub her temple.

"It was brilliant!" I yell as relief washes over her, followed by a stern *I'm going to kick your ass* look.

"As usual, you are one badass bitch, Juls. If I ever get married, you'll be running that show." Joey rubs her bare shoulder and she winks at him.

"Well, I only have a few minutes to spare before I have to get the bridal party lined up to come in so," she steps in between us and loops her arms through ours, "let's go introduce you to some hotties." *Oh, shit. I almost forgot about hot lap guy. Almost.*

"Oh, my God, Juls, you missed it," Joey says through a laugh.

I lean back and hiss. "Shut up, Joey."

"What? What did I miss?" She flicks her head back and forth between the two of us as I stare him down.

Don't you dare. I'm still your boss and will fire your ass right here. He must have read my thoughts because he never finishes his sentence, or maybe it's because we're now standing in front of the hot, Chicago, man candy club. The four of them are standing near a table conversing amongst themselves, but all conversation comes to a halt as we walk up. All of them, and I mean all of them, are way too attractive to properly function around, and now it's suddenly feeling a thousand degrees hotter in this room.

"There's my girl." Ian reaches his hand out and Juls steps into him, placing a quick kiss on his cheek before she steps back. I keep my eyes on Ian, not wanting to drift to the man whose eyes I know are on me. I can feel them burning a hole into my profile.

"Boys, I would like to introduce my very best friend, Dylan." Her hand grabs mine and pulls me forward as I glance up and run my eyes down the row of men, stopping on the one closest to me. *Damn, he keeps getting better looking.* "And this is Joey, the hottest gay man in Chicago."

"Oh, please, Illinois, bitch. Let's not downplay my sexiness." Joey straightens out his tie as I try not to laugh. My assistant has no modesty.

Juls glances down at her Tiffany watch and her eyes go wide. "Crap. Ian, will you finish the introductions? I need to take care of some shit."

"Sure thing, babe. Be quick though." He holds onto her hand tightly, making her tug away playfully before his smile lands on me.

"Christ, you're so pussy whipped." The blond man standing next to Ian says softly. I glance at him quickly, smiling at the idea of Ian being completely caught up in my best friend. The two of them started dating a few months ago and she's already head over heels for him. Due to our busy schedules, this is our first time actually meeting, and from what I can tell by the way he looks at her, he seems just as infatuated.

Ian glares at the blond who laughs around his drink before he turns back toward me. "Dylan, it's nice to finally meet you." He holds out his hand to me with a genuine smile as I shake it. Ian is tall and built, very muscular with nearly jet black hair that is barely long enough to pull into his pony. His brown eyes regard me kindly.

"Yeah, you too, Ian. I've heard such lovely things from Juls."

He shakes Joey's hand and exchanges some pleasantries while my eyes strain to not look at the man standing directly to my left. "And these are my work associates and mates, Trent, Billy, and Reese," he says, motioning down the line of men. *Reese. Of course that's his name. A guy looking like this wouldn't be named something not sexy, like Ted or Joe.* I shake Trent and Billy's hands as they say how nice it is to meet me. Trent, who made the pussy whipped comment, is the shortest of the group with almost white blond hair that curls at the ends. And Billy, who only has eyes for Joey at the moment, has sandy blond hair that is kept super short, and diamond stud earrings in both ears. I begin biting the inside of my cheek as I turn my body toward Reese.

"Dylan, I believe we've met briefly." He extends his hand and I place mine in his without hesitation, feeling his callused fingers tickle my skin. I have to look up into his stare, even though I'm wearing one of my tallest pair of heels. He's got a torso that stretches on for miles, one I'd like to wrap myself around. His perfectly tailored, dark gray suit frames his hard body almost unfairly, and as he smiles, the tiniest little lines appear next to his eyes. I sigh. His attractiveness is a bit unnerving.

"Yes, briefly. I'm so sorry about that." *Not really.*

Still holding my hand, he leans in a bit, his breath warming my face. "I'm not. Let's go get a drink."

I stumble a bit at the closeness of his face to mine, but somehow manage a quick nod in agreement to his request. Finally dropping my hand, I meet Joey's eyes and he winks at me before I turn and walk side by side with Reese to the bar. I want to reach out and slip my hand back in his, but I don't. That would be weird. *Stay strong. Resist the urge.*

"What can I get you?" the young bartender asks and I realize, after a long silent moment, Reese is waiting for my order, staring at me with an amused grin.

"Oh, umm, jack and coke please."

Handsome next to me raises his eyebrows at my drink selection. "No girly drink for you?"

I shake my head and brush my hair behind my ear. I've never been the type of girl who orders martinis and fruity drinks that cost eight dollars apiece.

"I'll have the same." His fingers strum the counter as I try not to stare at his profile, which is an extremely difficult task. The man is too beautiful *not* to stare at. I'm handed my drink and immediately take a large sip. "So, I don't think I've ever met a woman named Dylan before. And I *definitely* don't think I've ever had a Dylan fall into my lap." His lips touch his glass and I stare a bit longer than I mean to as the liquid slips into his mouth. *And I am now suddenly jealous of his beverage.*

I shift on my feet, flicking my stare back up to his eyes. "Oh, um, my parents were a bit obsessed with the singer. They had picked the name Dylan before finding out the sex and decided that no matter what, that was going to be the name. So, here I am."

He smiles. "Yes, here you are. Do you like any of his music?"

I think for a moment before replying. "I like that American Girl song."

Smiling slightly, he leans against the bar, his tall frame towering over mine and the bartender's. "That's Tom Petty," he corrects me, his lips curling up in amusement.

"Oh, then I have no idea if I like any of his songs or not." I wrap my lips around the tiny straw and his jaw tightens, a small twitch appearing at the sharp angle of it. He clears his throat and runs a hand through his hair, making it even more of a perfect mess. *God, even his hair is sexy.*

"So, bride or groom?" I ask, watching his confusion turn into realization.

He smiles behind his glass. "Bride, sort of. I don't really know Sara, but I've worked with her father. He invited the four of us." His hand motions toward Ian and Trent who are sitting together at their table. I shake my head as I realize Billy and Joey are already missing. *Predictable Joey. We've been here for a whole five minutes.* "You?"

I roll my eyes. "Groom, unfortunately."

He steps closer, brushing his suit jacket against my bare arm and tilting his head down toward me. "Really? Why, sweet Dylan, does it sound like you *really* know the groom?"

Sweet Dylan? Oh, my. I glance up into his eyes. "Because I *really* know the groom. He's my ex."

His eyes widen and he leans back. "Seriously?"

I nod. "Cheating ex to be specific."

"Fuck. That sucks. I mean, isn't this awkward for you? Why are you even here?"

I laugh slightly and point through the crowd toward the dessert table with my free hand. "Do you see that beautiful, five tier, deliciously constructed, wedding cake?" He nods and searches my face. "I made that. That's why I'm here."

"No shit? So, you're a baker?"

I proudly smile as the DJ softens the music.

"And now, ladies and gentlemen, I ask everyone to direct their attention to the front entrance. The party has arrived!" The crowd cheers and whistles as each bridesmaid and paired groomsmen line up at the door. I feel a pair of lips brush against my ear and freeze, my pulse instantly racing.

"You interested in watching this?" His face is dangerously close to mine and I almost stumble at his scent, which is now filling my lungs. He smells like citrus and I have a sudden urge to bury my face into his neck and inhale him deeply.

"Not really," I softly reply, glancing up into his green stare. Nodding once, he grips my elbow and pulls me through the crowd, stopping in front of the dessert table.

"So, what do we have here?" He tilts his glass and takes a sip as we both admire my work. I smile and beam at my creation. It really does look fabulous.

"Well, the cake itself is an orange sponge cake with Grand Marnier whipped cream and marmalade filling," I gesture toward the peach colored pearls and calla lilies cascading down the side, "and the little dots and lilies are made of sugar so it's all edible."

Leaning forward, he admires the flowers with a furrowed brow, studying it closely. I greatly appreciate his interest, considering they were a bitch to make, and can't help but giggle quietly at his look of deep thought. I've never even seen a groom react this curiously to a cake I made.

"Wow. I thought the flowers were real. You can really eat those?"

I smile proudly. "Mmm mmm. They are insanely sweet and practically dissolve on your tongue once the heat of your mouth touches the sugar."

He raises an eyebrow at me as he straightens up. "Christ. You make that sound so dirty," he says with a low raspy voice. I shrug as if to silently portray I always made things sound dirty, which seems ridiculous even in my head. *No big deal, just how I talk.*

"So what do you do, Reese?" I take a generous sip of my drink and watch his eyes go to my mouth, my teeth clamping down on my straw.

After a moment's hesitation as his eyes linger, he replies, "I'm a CPA with Walker and Associates."

Nearly choking at his admission, I clear my throat as his eyes widen. "Get the hell out of here. You're an accountant? You?" *He must be joking. Beautiful and highly intelligent? I feel like I've found a unicorn.*

He simply nods and studies my face with a small grin. "Does that surprise you?"

"Yes. The guy that does my taxes has psoriasis and looks more like my father. There's no *way* someone as hot as you is an accountant." *Jesus, Dylan.* I close my eyes and shake my head, hearing a small chuckle from his direction. When I open them, finally, I lock onto his curious stare, his lips slightly parted as if he's about to speak. The DJ comes over the speaker system and halts him.

"And now it's time for the bride and groom's first dance."

I turn my body toward the dance floor, which has suddenly opened up to allow Justin and Sara into the center. Sara looks beautiful in her strapless gown with intricate beading and Justin looks decent in his suit. Okay, maybe a little better than decent, but that doesn't say much. I've always thought all men look better in a suit, no matter what they looked like before they stepped into it. A familiar song softly plays overhead and I cringe.

"Jesus Christ. You have *got* to be kidding me." I down my drink and place it on the dessert table as Reese steps closer to me.

"Do you not like this song?" he asks. Everyone is watching the couple adoringly and I'm staring at Justin like I want to punch him in the throat. *What a tool.*

"No, I love this song. I loved it so much that I made it *our* song two years ago." I laugh. "Of course, I shouldn't be surprised Justin failed to be original here. He was never one for change or originality, especially when it came to our sex life." My eyes flick to Reese who is now sucking on a piece of ice. He bites it hard and lets it slide down his throat as he leans down, his nose brushing against my temple. I freeze.

"Really? Tell me." I swallow loudly and close my eyes, wanting to block out everything around me that isn't him in this moment. It's only his breath on my face, his scent, and the slightest contact of his skin against mine. "Did the two of you ever sneak off at a wedding and fuck each other's brains out?"

Holy hell. Did he just say that? My eyes shoot open and my mouth drops. *Can I honestly respond to that? Would he like it if I told him exactly what I want to say, which is I only want him to fuck my brains out at this wedding, or any wedding for that matter?* I shift on my feet and search my head for the appropriate wording when Joey appears at my side, out of breath.

"Cupcake, I need a moment." He grabs my hand, smiling flirtatiously at Reese and pulls me toward our table, planting me firmly in a chair.

I glare at him. "This better be an emergency for me to allow you to pull me away from *that* conversation. He just basically insinuated he wanted to fuck me into tomorrow, and I'd very much like that." My eyes flick back to Reese who is talking to one of the bridesmaids now, her hands playfully pushing at his chest as he speaks. *Oh, please, you look so desperate.*

Joey straightens his tie and pulls his jacket off, slipping it on the back of his chair. "Good lord, he's direct. But back to the important matter at hand, Billy just gave me the best blow job of my life."

My eyes narrow at his beaming face and he shrinks a bit in his chair. "Seriously, Joey? *That's* what you had to pull me away from Reese for? You couldn't have waited until *after* I had an orgasm to tell me this?" I lean forward and his eyes widen. "And for shit's sake, what guy hasn't blown you that you aren't quickly trying to give the title of best mouth in Chicago to?"

"That's not all I needed to tell you." He moves in closer to me, his hand brushing my hair back to reveal my ear. "On our way to our secluded hook up spot, I saw the bride with her lips wrapped around the best man's dick."

"WHAT?" I clasp my hand quickly over my mouth as I feel hundreds of eyes on me. "Are you fucking serious?" I manage in a much more appropriate tone. He nods just as Juls storms up to our table.

"You two bitches are so fucking loud. What's going on?"

"Nothing," Joey and I say in unison.

I'm not sure we should make Juls aware of the situation just yet. I'll let her get paid first, and then drop that juicy bomb in her lap. She'll want to rub it in Justin's face how he got what was coming to him, and that might result in a canceled wedding reception and a loss of her commission.

I brush my hair off my shoulder and smile sweetly at her. "Are you done with your wedding planning duties now?" I ask, wanting to change the subject.

"Yes, finally." She rolls her eyes. "That fucking wedding party was a disaster. I'm pretty sure they were all in some giant orgy back there before they walked into the reception." I meet Joey's eyes and we both try to keep a straight face. The music picks up and Juls jumps on her heels, reaching out for our hands. "Ooohhh, I love this song! Come on. Let's go show these rich snobs how we shake it in downtown Chicago."

"You know it, girl," Joey says as I shuffle quickly behind them.

She makes a quick stop at Ian's table and my eyes lock on to Reese who gives me a playful smile behind his drink. The other boys are talking amongst themselves. "Wanna dance, babe?" Juls asks before Ian grabs her and pulls her into his lap, kissing her passionately in front of everyone. I can't help but blush and glance quickly at Reese, who notices and winks at me. My heart beats roughly in my chest at the gesture. *Relax, it was just a wink.*

"Jesus Christ. Get a fucking room," Joey says, pulling me in the direction of the dance floor.

"Wait." I pull my hand out of his and quickly walk around the table. I stop in front of Reese and lean down, pressing my lips to his ear as he lifts his face to mine. His fingers curl around my arm and the contact makes me momentarily dizzy. "Keep your eyes on me," I say, and he sucks in a breath. Our eyes are locked and our faces inches apart.

"How could I not?" he replies softly. I straighten and see the lingering intensity in his stare as Joey reclaims my hand and pulls me out onto the floor, which is now packed with guests.

Beyoncé's "Naughty Girl" is bumping through the speakers, the bass vibrating through my body as I begin to move. Joey and Juls dance next to me, the three of us trying to out dance the other. My hands move up my body, brushing over my stomach, up my chest and up around my neck as I close my eyes and let the music take over. I love to dance, especially with my best friends. My hands run through my wavy hair and I feel the hem of my dress rise a bit, brushing the middle of my bare thighs. "Go girl!" Joey squawks and my eyes flash open to see him spinning and twirling around me, as only Joey can do. For a man so tall and muscular, he can move his body as if he were professionally trained. I sway my hips and move in the most overly flirtatious way possible, hoping and praying Reese is watching me, but not having the balls to glance over and know for sure. I squeal with Juls as Rihanna's "S&M" comes on overhead. A pair of strong hands wrap around my tiny waist from behind, and I still, feeling hot breath in my hair.

"Don't stop, Dylan." Reese's voice sends a chill up my spine and goose bumps along my exposed skin. His hips move against my back as he pulls me against him, his hands slipping around my stomach. Juls' eyes widen and she goes to reach for me when Ian appears by her side and grabs her hand, spinning her into him and dipping her for a kiss. I close my eyes and feel his hands move up my rib cage, his thumbs brushing along the bottom of my breasts as I rub my ass against his crotch. I haven't danced like this with a guy in years; in fact, I don't know if I've ever enjoyed it this much before. My pulse is hammering in my throat and I can feel my face heat up from the contact. We're moving together in perfect rhythm as I reach up and around his neck, feeling his breath on my bare shoulder. His hands spin me and my chest presses against his.

"This dress is killing me," he says, brushing my hair out of my face and tucking it behind my ear. We continue to move against each other, his impressive erection digging into my stomach and my hands gripping tightly around his neck while he holds on to my hips. Our lips are so close — open as our ragged breathing brushes each other's face, sharing the same air. If either of us were to move in slightly, we would be kissing.

"Were you watching me?"

"Depends. Were you dancing just for me?" I lick my lips and nod. His eyes widen before he drops his hands from my waist and grabs my hand, pulling me away from the dance floor. *Holy shit. This is it. I'm actually going to have slutty wedding sex with the hottest guy on the planet.* I inwardly high-five myself as we move quickly between the guests.

I follow closely behind him, my heels preventing the faster walking I would have preferred as we move down the staircase and down the hallway that leads to the bathrooms. My chest is rising and falling rapidly and my nervous energy has kicked in, causing me to practically bounce on my feet. He pushes the men's room door open and drops my hand.

"Wait here." Disappearing behind the door, I stand outside the men's room and pray to God no one is in there. I'm so wound up right now, I can't imagine what would happen if we didn't follow through with this. I've never felt this turned on in my life.

I lick my dry lips as he opens the door and smiles. "You don't mind a bit of an audience, do you?"

My eyes widen and I swallow loudly, seeing a small smirk form on his lips. "I hope you're joking." *I'm not having sex in front of people. No fucking way.*

"I am. Come on." He grabs my hand, but I stay firmly planted in the doorway.

"You don't have a girlfriend, do you? Because if we're about to do what I think we're about to do, it's not happening if you have one."

He raises his eyebrows at me, seemingly unprepared for that justified question. "No, no girlfriend. I haven't had one of those since college." He tugs me against his chest. "Any more questions before I ravage you?"

I shake my head slowly with a flirtatious smile.

"Good." He pulls me into the bathroom and locks the door behind us before he pushes me up against it. His hands grab my face as his lips softly brush against mine, tasting and teasing me. My bottom lip is pulled into his mouth and I moan, granting him full access as I part my lips and his tongue sweeps inside.

"Fuck, Dylan." He moves his tongue against mine, biting and licking my lips. *Holy hell, this guy can kiss.* His mouth expertly explores mine for what seems like hours, and I slowly feel a pull building in my core. This kiss actually makes me feel bad for all of the other kisses I may get from guys in the future. The bar is being set ridiculously high here, certainly unattainable by the majority of the male race. My hands rake through his hair, holding his head to mine as my body responds to his touch with moans and whimpers. There's no controlling myself here; I'm completely abandoning all my reservations and giving in to everything I'm feeling. I'm suddenly picked up, my legs wrapping around his waist as he carries me over to the vanity, our mouths still working each other's. He tastes like spearmint and liquor as I lick him off my lips while his mouth moves down my neck.

"You taste so sweet. I bet every part of you tastes like this."

I groan at his words as his lips brush against the swells of my breasts, which are poking out from my dress. My hands tangle in his mess of hair. His lips move along each collarbone and over each shoulder, tasting and nibbling every inch of exposed skin.

"Reese."

His hands hike up my dress and trail up the insides of my thighs. His fingers slide along the length of my panties and his eyes meet mine. They're the greenest eyes I've ever seen, no other color mixed in. It's almost hypnotizing staring into them. Deep pools of emerald. My panties are quickly slid down my legs; my eyes widen as he tucks them into his pants pocket. *Shit, that's hot.* My fingers work frantically at his suit jacket, prompting him to slip it off and place it next to us. I'm practically clawing at his dress shirt, fumbling with the buttons with my shaky hands. I need to see him bare in front of me. I want to see his muscles contract as he moves inside of me, and by the way his shirt stretches across his chest, I know without a doubt he'll be unbelievable to look at.

"This has to be quick, love. I don't think we have time to get completely naked before someone tries to come in here." He presses his forehead against mine and I growl as he brings his mouth back to mine. Two fingers slip inside of me and I cry out.

"Oh, God."

"You're so wet and really fucking tight." His lips move along my jaw. I'm panting against him, arching into his touch. "Does that feel good, love?"

"Yes. Please, I need you," I beg as his free hand pulls a condom out of his back pocket.

He hands it to me. "Hurry."

I hold the wrapper with my teeth as my frantic fingers work his button and zipper, my legs helping to slide his pants and boxers down to his mid-thigh. My eyes widen at his length, and I groan loudly as he works me with his fingers, his thumb circling my clit. "Am I distracting you?" His lips move against my neck and I can only nod and moan my response. I swallow against his lips and feel them curl up on my skin. I'm getting close already, but I want him in me; I need him in me. Going without sex for a year has been worth it if it leads to it happening with Reese.

Regaining my focus, I rip the wrapper with my teeth and slide the condom down his length while he stills in my hand. His heavy breathing mixed with mine fills the room. I stare, fascinated by how much it has to stretch to form around him, and trail my fingers underneath, hearing him inhale sharply. He's long and heavy, my fingertips barely touching as I grip him. The man is gifted. Crazy gifted. *Will he even fit in me?* My mind scrambles at the thought. *Well, wouldn't that be a nice fuck you from karma. Here, Dylan, feast your eyes on this magnificent penis that you can't even handle.*

Pulling out his fingers, he wipes a line of my arousal on the top of my breasts and immediately licks if off as I lift into him. "You taste fucking amazing." He leans back and locks eyes with me, licking his lips. "I need to be in you. I can't wait anymore." His hands wrap my thighs around his waist as he enters me in one deep push, a loud groan escaping both our mouths.

"Reese!" His thrusts are deep and quick as I hold onto his neck with one hand and the edge of the vanity with the other, my knuckles stark white. Our eyes are on each other's as he slows his movements, guiding his length almost completely out of me before he rams it back in.

"Dylan, holy shit." He continues the slow torture as a bead of sweat drips from his hairline down to his jaw. Darting his tongue out, he licks his bottom lip before pulling it into his mouth, biting on it as I stare, mesmerized.

Rocking my hips into his thrusts, I feel him deeper than I have ever felt anything in my life. His green eyes are burning into mine, full of intensity and desire. His words to me echo in my ears as he tries to control our quickly climbing orgasms. "So good. So fucking good, Dylan. Let me hear you. Scream for me." No guy has ever talked to me during sex, and it's probably the hottest thing I've ever heard. His fingers dig into my hips and I think he might bruise me, but at the moment, I don't care. The slight pain he's inflicting on me is actually fueling my need for him.

"I'm close. Come with me," I grunt, seeing his eyes light up. Sliding his hand between us and under my dress, his thumb presses against my clit and begins to move, bringing my climax to the surface. My nails dig into his neck as I throw my head back and erupt. "Reese. Oh, God."

His free hand grips my neck and pulls me into his thrusts, which are now so powerful I think I might split in two. "Fuck!" he cries out. I reach up and pull his hair as he comes. His eyes never leave mine and my name escapes his lips at his release. I thought most guys closed their

22   J. DANIELS

eyes when they climaxed, but not this one, and something about him watching me, letting me see him completely unravel, makes this even hotter somehow. He stills inside me and pulls my face toward him, bringing our lips together. His kisses are soft and sweet, going from one corner of my mouth to the other. My lips are swollen and chapped, and I couldn't care in the least. I'd kiss this guy until my lips actually fell off.

"What the fuck was that?" he asks, my eyes flickering open and searching his face. *Amazing. Mind blowing. Beyond anything I could have imagined.* I want to say these things, but don't, not really understanding why he would ask me that question or what the hell he means by it.

He shuts his eyes and pulls out of me, tossing the used condom before he pulls his pants up and tucks himself back in. Turning his body toward me, he picks up his suit jacket and slips it across his broad shoulders, his face completely impassive. *Ah. The awkward aftermath of sex with a stranger.* I avoid his eyes as I hop down and turn to fix my dress in the mirror, realizing he still has my panties in his pocket. *Fuck, is he going to give them back? Or does he expect me to ask him for them?* I meet his eyes briefly in the mirror, breaking the contact almost immediately at the sight of his tight jaw and creased brow. *Fuck that. I'm not asking him anything.*

The door rattles. "Shit." His voice is clipped and irritated as he glances at me before turning toward the door. "I'm really sorry," he says as his fingers slide the lock back and he opens it, allowing two men to enter as I stand at the sink.

"Well, well, well. What have we here?"

I shake my head and push past them, my shoulder brushing against Reese as I walk down the hallway and quickly up the stairs, leaving him in the restroom. *Jesus Christ, what was his problem? What the fuck was he sorry for? He came didn't he?* I'm fuming, my hands clenched tightly at my side as I storm through the crowd. I make my way to my table where my two friends sit, picking at the food on their plates. Their eyes both lock onto my face and Joey grins wide while Juls studies me questionably.

"I need to get out of here," I say, grabbing my clutch that I had left on the table, and trying my best to avoid their stares.

"And where the hell have you been?" Joey asks, pushing his plate away as Juls stands up and walks over toward me. "Please tell me you just got thoroughly fucked."

"Yes, Dylan, where were you? You missed the cake cutting."

Goddamn it. That's the only thing I really wanted to see.

"Don't ask." I glance to my right and spot Reese as he walks toward his table, his eyes meeting mine briefly before flicking away. He looks thoroughly fucked as well, his hair a sexy disheveled mess.

"Oh, Christ. Please tell me you didn't do what I think you did with him?"

I bend down and kiss Joey quickly on the cheek, ignoring Juls' questioning. "Are you coming with me?" I ask.

"Nah, I'm going to spend some more alone time with Billy." He pulls me closer to him. "I want every fucking detail tomorrow."

I roll my eyes at him before I turn and walk out of the reception area with Juls. I make it down the stairs and to the front door before she stops me and demands answers.

"Well?"

"Well what? I forgot your question." *I didn't.*

She crosses her arms over her chest and glares at me. "Did you fuck Reese? Dylan, please tell me you didn't."

"Technically, he fucked me and thoroughly freaked out afterwards. Can I go now please?"

Her mouth drops open. "Fucking motherfucker. Dylan, he's married."

I have to grip the wall to prevent myself from falling over. "What? But he said he didn't have a girlfriend." My mouth drops open. "Oh, that asshole. I bet he thought he was really clever, telling me he hasn't had a girlfriend since college. I suppose a wife isn't technically a girlfriend." The tight sensation in my gut from my previous orgasm is now instantly replaced with nausea and an intense urge to punch Reese in the nuts. "How do you know he's married?"

Juls runs her hands down her face. "Ian told me he was married when I met all of them briefly for drinks last week. Wow. What a scumbag." *Indeed. Scumbag doesn't even come close to describe him at the moment. I'm thinking douche-bag, tool, asshole, fucking prick.*

Pinching the top of my nose with my thumb and pointer finger, I quickly replay the hottest sex I've ever had over in my head. I drop my hand and clench my fist. *I could kill him.* "And no fucking wonder he couldn't get away from me quick enough afterward. How the hell was I supposed to know he was married? He wasn't wearing a ring."

"Dylan?" We both turn our attention to Justin who is standing at the bottom of the steps, eyes wide and full of shock as he looks at me. *Well, this night just keeps getting better.*

I snap my eyes back to my best friend, ignoring the cheating loser on the stairs. "I'm leaving before I get arrested for homicide. I'll call you tomorrow," I say to Juls and Juls alone.

I open the door and walk out to the valet attendants, reminding them I'm the owner of the delivery van as they laugh amongst themselves. I'm fuming and so not in the mood for this shit. "You're working a fucking wedding, so I know you're not riding around in a Lexus. Just go get my fucking van," I snap at them and they immediately shut up. One scurries away quickly toward the parking lot.

"Dylan, can I talk to you?" Justin's voice comes from behind me.

"No. Congratulations, Justin. The ceremony was lovely." I feel his hand on my shoulder and I turn quickly, stepping out of his grasp. "Don't touch me. Shouldn't you be upstairs with your wife?"

He snickers and steps closer, his gray eyes full of mischief. "Well, if I heard correctly, aren't married men your thing now?" *Oh, no, he did not just say that.* My hand comes hard and fast, slapping him across his face as he stumbles back, wide-eyed and smiling.

"Fuck you," I snap. Seeing Sam pull up to the curb, I walk quickly to the driver's side. I can't pull away fast enough; tires spinning as I quickly make my way down the long driveway and away from my complete fuckup of a night. I should have never come to this stupid thing. *Hooking up with a married man at the wedding of my ex-boyfriend. Jesus, Karma, you are one hateful bitch.*

Chapter
THREE

S UNDAY WAS A COMPLETE BLUR. I spent the entire day in bed, unless I had to use the bathroom or get something from the kitchen. After several missed calls and texts from Joey, I finally turned my phone off and kept it that way the rest of the day. Juls probably made him aware of Reese being married, but whereas she was into lecturing me about the topic, Joey would high-five me, insisting I tell him every juicy detail about the hook up, and I wasn't in the mood for either. I didn't want to think about the best orgasm I'd ever had. I didn't want to think about the way his lips felt against mine, against my skin, the taste of his mouth, his smell, the way his face looked when he came, the sound of my name on his lips, the way he looked at me as he fucked me against the sink, or how ridiculously huge he was; because he was married. He was fucking married and a complete tool for hooking up with me behind his wife's back. I can't even have a one-night stand without it blowing up in my face. Then there was my jerk of an ex-boyfriend. Following me outside and putting his hands on me like that when he should have been glued to his new wife's side. Talk about a scumbag. Of course, he did get cheated on at his own wedding, which could not delight me more. That bastard got everything he deserved and whatever else is coming to him. I hope he doesn't find out about his wife's indiscretions for a while and thinks he's in a loving marriage. When in reality, she is out fucking anything that moves.

꩜

MY ALARM ANNOYINGLY WAKES ME at five a.m. on Monday, as usual. I like to get a run in every morning before I open up the shop, mainly because of the large amount of sugar consumption that happens regularly between Joey and me during work hours. Dressing in my running gear, I grab my phone and keys off my nightstand and go downstairs into the large kitchen. I live in a small loft above the bakery and have since I opened the place three years ago. It's practical for me living at my job since some days I'm required to get up in the middle of the night to work on something for a client. My loft consists of one large room, which I separated into two with a decorative screen, giving my bedroom area some privacy from the living room and kitchen. It is small, quaint, and cheap. Renting the room above the bakery only costs me eight hundred and fifty dollars a month, which is relatively inexpensive for the downtown Chicago area. Below the loft, the stairs dump out into the large kitchen/work space, which I spend the majority of my time in, with a doorway that leads out to the main bakery. I make my way through the doorway and smile at Joey's face, which is pressing against the glass, peering inside. He never misses a run. I step outside and lock up behind me, seeing his angry expression glaring at me as I spin to greet him.

"Well, thank God you aren't dead. What the fuck? I called you a million times yesterday." He stretches his back by twisting from left to right. "I believe I told you I wanted details."

I bend down and reach for my toes and he does the same. "I'm sorry. I needed to mentally check out yesterday. The wedding was a bit much." *Understatement of the century.* Stretching my hamstrings, I stand up and press my hand against the window of the bakery to steady myself.

"And are you going to just stand there and *not* tell me what the fuck that means?"

"I'm sure you already know everything, you gossip queen. Hasn't Juls spilled the big surprise?"

We start jogging down the sidewalk together, our feet hitting the pavement at the same time. It's already hot as hell outside and that just ups my annoyance level.

"What big surprise? Juls spent the rest of the reception sucking Ian's face and God knows what else, and I ate my weight in cake after I saw Billy flirting with a waiter."

"Oh, shit. I'm sorry, Joey. That really sucks."

"Whatever. He ended up driving me home, and I did him in the back of his Denali as punishment."

I push his arm, but he doesn't budge. The man is a mountain of muscle. "Jesus. Well, I guess you showed him."

"Oh, I did. Now, what surprise?"

We make our usual trek down Fayette Street on the deserted sidewalk, Joey initiating the pace as he always does.

"Reese is married." *God, it still sucked today saying it out loud. And why did my heart physically ache at the sound of it. I couldn't be that affected by a wedding hook up, no matter how good the sex was.* I stop running and look back at Joey who is frozen on the pavement, his blond curls already sticking to his forehead with sweat.

"He's what?" He starts up again, momentarily stunned, and I move with him.

"You heard me. Fucking married. Of course, he didn't mention this before, during, or after our hot as hell sex in the men's bathroom. He just simply asked me 'What the fuck was that?' after he came, told me he was sorry, and went on about his business." I push my legs faster as we run up a small hill, feeling the burn in my thighs.

"What a dick. Are you sure though? I mean, I didn't see a ring and you know I hunt that out first thing."

"Yeah, so do I. Apparently, Ian told Juls that he was married. He probably didn't wear his ring so he could fuck me blind. Oh, and I almost forgot, to top the night off, Justin followed me outside and alluded to me fucking *him* since married men are my thing now." *Asshole.*

Joey snaps his head toward me, eyes wide. "Are you fucking serious right now? Where the fuck was I when all this was happening? Oh, that's right. I was eating my goddamned feelings." He picks up his pace as I struggle behind him.

"Slow down! Your legs are miles longer than mine."

"Crap, sorry." He returns to my side. "I'm sorry about Reese, cup-cake. I really am. But—"

"Don't fucking say it, Joey." I know exactly what his next words would be.

"I'm just saying—"

"Shut it, Holt," I grit out as he spins around to face me, effortlessly running backward.

"You could be the sexy mistress. If the sex was *that* good, why give it up?"

Now *I* start sprinting and hear a squeal from him as he catches up within seconds. "Are you mental? I am not going to be his fuck buddy on the side. I don't care how amazing the sex was or how hard he made me come. Fuck that shit." I wipe my forehead with the back of my hand, the sweat already starting to build on my skin.

"Ooohhh, how hard *did* he make you come? Was he huge? Please tell me it didn't have some weird hook to it like Billy's did." He shakes his head quickly. "I'm not quite sure how I feel about that yet."

"Jesus Christ. It is way too early to talk about dick sizes and which way they curve." I pause. "But for the record, he's massive and as straight as you pretended to be in high school."

"I fucking knew it. You lucky bitch."

We run in silence the rest of the way around the neighborhood, the only noises coming from us being our breathing and the sound of our shoes striking the pavement. I run fast and hard, desperately trying to push the memory of Reese and our hook up out of my mind and hoping to run away from it. But that isn't going to happen, at least not today, and it isn't happening for my running partner either. I can almost hear Joey's mind working as we run, most likely coming up with all the possible secret rendezvous scenarios between Reese and myself. Needless to say, the five-mile trek today is both mentally and physically exhausting.

I shower and dress for the day after saying goodbye to Joey, so he can do the same. He only lives a few blocks from the bakery and will be back before we open at seven a.m. He is my only employee at the moment, seeing as I haven't gotten around to hiring anybody to replace

Tiffany after I fired her. I'm not entirely sure I need anybody else to work for me; Joey and I seem to manage just fine on our own. I grew up with him, going to high school together, and then to college where we both studied business. He was more than supportive when I dreamed of opening my own bakery and insisted on becoming my assistant so we could stay close. Although, deep down, I think he just wanted to sample all my new creations. Thank God for our daily runs, otherwise, I'm certain we would both be as big as a house.

I tie my favorite apron on and begin pulling the pastries, muffins, cupcakes, and cookies from the back racks and bringing them up front to the display cases. The house specialty is my banana nut muffins, which I spent five years perfecting the recipe on. They're insanely delicious and it's a struggle not to eat every one myself straight out of the oven. I sell out of them every day by noon and nothing makes me prouder. At a few minutes before opening, Joey comes hustling through the door carrying two coffees and his award-winning smile.

"I'm dick talked out, so don't even," I say as I open the register and count the money.

"Cupcake, there's no such thing, trust me. I had them put in an extra shot of espresso for you this morning, figured you might need it," he says, walking around the counter. "Although, perhaps you'd prefer hard liquor with your coffee today?" He hands me my piping hot cup and I smile weakly. He is handsomely dressed in dark jeans and a bright blue polo shirt that brings out the color in his eyes.

"Thanks and, yes, liquor would be my preferred beverage this morning, but I don't think the sight of me stumbling around the shop wasted off my ass would be good for business." I take a sip and let the hot liquid run down my throat, instantly perking me up as the front door swings open. "Good morning. And how are my favorite regulars today?"

Mr. and Mrs. Crisp live around the corner and come into the shop every morning for two of my banana muffins. They are beyond adorable and always start my day off with a smile when I see them. "Well, besides the fact that this one kept me up all night, snoring, we are just fine, Dylan." Mrs. Crisp motions toward her husband who smiles sweetly at her.

"You love it, dear. I'm sure you told me once how my snoring helps you sleep." Mr. Crisp lovingly rubs his wife's back as she bats him away playfully.

"Oh, that's ridiculous, Harry," she huffs. I pull out their muffins as I smile and place them in a bag, grabbing the money that was placed on the counter. "And how was the wedding, dear? You stick it to that nasty, no good ex of yours?"

I roll my eyes after handing Mr. Crisp his change. "Not the way I would have liked to." I cross my arms over my chest and lean against the counter. "Whatever, I'm just glad it's over with. The cake looked amazing and was apparently delicious." I motion toward my assistant who is nibbling on a muffin. "This one ate an entire tier by himself."

He snorts loudly at my declaration. "It was not an entire tier. Well, actually, yeah it probably was." The four of us all laugh together as he devours his breakfast. The man can put away the sweets.

The front door swings open, getting our attention, and an older gentleman carrying a white box walks in and up to the counter. Mr. and Mrs. Crisp wave their goodbyes and slip out.

"Can I help you?" I ask, staring at the box questionably. It doesn't have any labels on it, giving no indication as to where it's from.

He places it in front of me with a smile. "Good morning. Delivery for a Ms. Dylan." My eyes widen as Joey steps next to me.

"What the hell did you order?" he asks as I sign the slip for the man.

"I didn't order anything, I don't think. Who sent this?" The man just shrugs and takes his clipboard, pushing the box toward me on the counter and walking quickly out of the bakery. We both stare at the box, glancing up and meeting each other's eyes.

"Well, aren't you going to open it?" he asks, arching his brows at me.

I study it suspiciously before replying. "I don't know; don't bombs come in unmarked packages?"

"Who the hell would try to bomb you?"

"Well, for starters, a certain wife of a certain someone who banged my back out Saturday night," I huff. He makes a face at me and pulls the white ribbon that is tied on the top, lifting the sides of the box to reveal a folded brown card on top of white tissue paper. I open the card and quickly scan the handwriting.

Dylan,

I fucked up. I'm so sorry. I would love to see you again.

X Reese

My mouth drops open. "You have *got* to be kidding me." I hand the card to Joey and hear him gasp after a fleeting moment.

"Holy shit. He would love to see you again? Dylan!"

Snatching the card back, I pull apart the tissue paper and cock my head to the side as I stare at the contents of the box. "What the hell?"

Joey leans in and gawks. *"Oh, my God.* This has to be the sweetest thing I've ever seen."

I pull out a pound of flour and drop it on the counter as he squeals next to me. "Why would he send me flour?" I am beyond confused right now while my assistant is bouncing around like a bunny. You would think by the way he's reacting that I'm currently staring at an engagement ring instead of baking supplies.

"Don't you get it? Instead of *flowers* he sent you *flour* since you're a baker. Shit, that's romantic."

I shove him and he doesn't budge. "Romantic? A married man just wrote me saying he wants to keep fucking me on the side. He's married, Joey. This is not romantic. It's sleazy and disgusting." Picking up my coffee and stepping away from the counter, I stare at the flour and take generous sips. *This is insane and my assistant is an idiot.*

"You're missing some key adjectives there. A *hot* married man wants to keep *rightly* fucking you on the side. You must have blown his mind, girl. Plus, he sends you presents? I want him as my secret boyfriend."

I shake my head. "What a pompous asshole. He must think I'm some two-bit whore to willingly submit to this joke of a request. Fucking douche-bag." I pick the card up and toss it in the trash as Joey lunges for it. "Leave it."

"No. At least keep it for a day. You might change your mind."

"You are high off your ass if you think I would actually consider this."

"I fucking wish I was high right now. That would be an excuse for my insane case of the munchies." He throws his hands up dramatically.

We both giggle at each other and the situation. Of course, this is my life. I couldn't have some hot guy, who gave me the best orgasm, be interested in me. No, that would be too normal. He has to be a hot *married* best orgasm giver with a mouth I would pay to have on me again. *Figures.*

✑

THE MORNING WENT BY QUICKLY with the steady flow of customers. Mondays are always busier in the bakery, mainly with walk-in specialty requests, which I enjoy immensely and Joey hates. He prefers that I'm not tied up in consultations all day so we can chitchat and gossip. It's close to noon when Juls walks in, looking as chic as ever in her tight pencil skirt, white blouse, and heels to die for. I really need to raid her closet someday. Besides the height difference between us, we're similarly built and could swap clothes easily. We're both slender yet toned, given how religious we both are about our exercise routines.

"Hello, lovies. And how is everyone's Monday going?"

I moan as Joey smiles big, showing off his lonely dimple. "You look hot, Juls. Got a meeting with an annoying couple?" I ask as I straighten out the remaining red velvet cupcakes in the display case.

"Actually, I was just about to head over to Ian's work to have lunch. You know I gotta look good for my baby."

I perk up. *Perfect. I could tell him off in person.* "Mind if I joined you?"

She tilts her head to the side as Joey gasps dramatically. "Are you going to confront him?" The excitement in his voice is almost palpable.

I nod firmly. "Hell yes, I am. If he thinks he can proposition me to be his dirty little secret, he is seriously mistaken."

"Excuse me? What the fuck have I missed?" Juls brings both hands to her hips and stares at me, waiting for an explanation. Of course, before I can speak, Joey opens his big gay mouth.

"Well," he rests his chin on his hand, "Reese sent our sexy friend here a note with some flour saying he was sorry about fucking up and would love to see her again." His grin cracks his face open. "Isn't that fantastic?"

She stares at us with a furrowed brow. "Are you serious? Oh, damn it, I meant to confront him at the wedding after you left, Dyl, but he actually disappeared pretty soon after you did. Besides," she straightens out her skirt, "I was a bit preoccupied. Wait, did you say he sent you flour? As in baking flour?" I nod and she raises her eyebrows, her mouth slowly forming an O. "Ah, instead of the traditional flowers. That's actually pretty clever."

I stomp my foot. "Oh, for fuck's sake. Why am I the only person who didn't get that? And it wasn't clever. It was stupid, because he's stupid."

"Wow, you're really gutting him with that insult," Joey states sarcastically as I pull my apron off. I throw it at his face.

"Well?" I ask, turning to Juls.

"Well what?"

"Can I come with you?"

"Oh, hell yes. I would love to see you chew him a new one. I can't stand cheaters." We both move toward the door as I nod in agreement.

"Hey! What about me?" Joey yells.

I turn my head. "You need to stay here and man the shop. What, did you think I was going to close down for this?"

"Goddamn it! This is why we need another employee, Dylan. I fucking miss everything."

"Don't worry; I'll give you all the details *after* I cut off his testicles." Juls and I walk out of the shop together and toward her car as I give myself a mental pep talk. *Yell first then remove balls or remove balls then yell? Hell, does it matter?*

❧

I'M SLOWLY BEGINNING TO LOSE my edge as we walk into the crisp sleek foyer of the Walker & Associates building. Juls' heels are clicking on the marble and I inwardly curse myself for not changing my outfit before I so bravely decided this was a good idea. I'm wearing a pale blue button up shirt, skinny jeans that are dusted in flour, and my favorite ballet flats. This would have been so badass if I was wearing something sexy and revealing, showing Reese what he will never touch again. *Damn it, Dylan. Think next time.* At least my hair and makeup are on point. We step off the elevators onto the twelfth floor and I follow closely behind her, unsure where to go.

"Nervous?" she asks as she walks up to a small reception area.

"Nope, but he better be." She throws her head back and laughs as

I wiggle my brows.

"Julianna Wicks for Ian Thomas, please," she says to the pretty receptionist who smiles and picks up the phone, talking softly into it. She ends the call quickly.

"Go right in, Ms. Wicks."

She shrugs playfully. "I fucking love this shit. My man is so important that I need to check-in with someone before I barge in." I giggle at her and follow her through a closed door after she knocks quietly.

"There's my girl. I've been waiting for you." Ian stands up and walks around his desk, pulling Juls into his arms and smothering her with quick kisses. *Christ, they are annoyingly adorable.* "I'm starving and not just for food," he whispers before his eyes flick to me. "Dylan. Are you joining us for lunch today?" he sweetly asks as he plays with the ends of Juls' hair. He sounds sincere, but I have a feeling he'd much rather spend his lunch alone with my best friend.

I clear my throat. *You can do this, Dylan.* "Actually, I was wondering if Reese was here. I need to speak with him." Juls is too busy frantically working at loosening Ian's tie to even remember I'm in the room. I'm sure she would have snuck in a bitchy remark had she been paying attention.

"Oh, of course." He smiles wide. "Just continue down the hallway until you see the redhead at the reception desk. She'll point you in his direction." I nod and turn on my feet, giving Juls one last glance as I step out, closing the door behind me.

He's married. He's married. He's married. Who cares how fucking insanely hot he is. He's married. My thoughts are so loud in my head; I'm sure the redhead, who I am now standing in front of, can hear them. I smile weakly at her.

"May I help you?" she asks in a rather snippy tone.

"Um, yes. I would like to see Reese, please."

She cocks her head and narrows her eyes. *Jesus. Retract the claws.* Picking up her phone, her eyes run slowly down my body. "You mean Mr. Carroll? And who may I say is asking for him?"

Mr. Carroll. Oh, how fucking formal. I glare down at her. "Dylan."

"Just Dylan?" Her tone is borderline bitchy and I am beyond over it at this point. *Sweetie, this is not the day to test my patience.*

"Yes, just Dylan," I snap back, hands fisting at my sides.

She rolls her eyes and speaks softly into the phone, slamming it down with more force than is probably necessary. *"Go on in, just Dylan."* She motions with a quick swipe of her hand toward a door that stands at the end of the hallway. *What the hell is her problem?*

"Thank you. Have a nice day," I reply extra cheerfully to pluck her last nerve. She scowls. *Mission Accomplished.*

Not bothering to knock, I open the office door and step inside, stumbling a bit at the sight of the man behind the massive desk. *Yup, that's what he looks like. Completely perfect.* His eyes slowly come up to mine from his computer screen and soften.

"Dylan, this is a pleasant surprise. I assume you received my package?"

I close the door behind me and cross my arms. "Yeah, cute pun. Do you have a minute?"

He smiles and I stumble a bit. "For you? I have several."

Standing up, he gracefully moves his body around the desk and sits on the edge, crossing his long legs in front of him at the ankles and bracing himself on his hands. I shake my head at his cockiness. *Damn it to hell.* If he wasn't so gloriously attractive, this would be so much easier. He stands before me in a light blue dress shirt, gray plaid tie, and khakis, his hair a perfect mess and his green eyes freezing me where I stand. He raises an eyebrow, waiting for me to speak. I could speak. I had a lot to say. But right now, I want to either throw him down and fuck him right on his desk or slap him so hard across his face that he will feel it next week. *Hmm, I could do both. Oh, Christ, Dylan. No. Slapping him. That sounds satisfying.* I move quickly, his eyes widening as I stop just in front of him and strike him across his face, a loud crack echoing throughout the room.

"Jesus Christ," he almost yells, his hand coming up and rubbing his now reddened cheek. "What the fuck?"

"You fucking prick. Who the hell do you think you are?"

He stands up, towering over me in my flats. *Fuck, he's as big as a tree.* "Okay, I probably deserved that." His tone is sharp, but he doesn't sound angry. He seems more concerned than anything. "Look," he pauses, rubbing his cheek, "I'm sorry I kind of shut down after the bathroom. I'm not used to sex getting to me like that, and I handled it like an asshole."

I see red. "Are you serious right now? *That's* why you're sorry? Because you freaked out afterward?"

"Yes, well, that and the fact those men saw you in there with me. I'm sure they knew exactly what we'd been doing." He steps closer to me. "Why the fuck else would I be sorry? I'm not sorry it happened. Are you?"

I push against his chest, but he doesn't move. *Damn it, I need to start lifting weights.* "Yes, I'm sorry it happened. I do not fuck married men, Reese!" I'm shouting now and my throat begins to ache, but not enough to make me stop. However, his current look of confusion is taking away some of my fire. *He's a smart guy. Why isn't he grasping this?*

"Okay, that's good to know," he says with a furrowed brow.

"Great. Now you know. So stay the fuck away from me." I go to leave, but I'm stopped by his grip on my arm, turning me around to face him.

"What the fuck are you talking about?"

I step out of his grasp and look down at his left hand, narrowing in on his bare finger. "You asshole. Why don't you wear your ring? Hoping to get your dick sucked behind that massive desk of yours by some girl who *doesn't* know you're married?"

His look stuns me. I expected him to get angry with me for slapping him, maybe a bit disappointed in me for not wanting to pursue this any further, but the amused look on his face is not what I expected. He runs his hands down his face and laughs, stopping only when he sees my hardened expression.

"Married? Who the fuck told you I was married?"

I step back. "Juls. Answer my question. Why don't you wear your ring?"

"Really? And where did Juls hear I was married?"

I throw my hands up in frustration. "What the fuck does that matter? From Ian. Who else?"

He grabs my hand and pulls me with him toward the door, swinging it open and storming down the hallway.

"Where are we going? Let go of me."

"Shut up, Dylan." My fighting is useless. He is clearly on a mission as he walks toward Ian's office door, dragging my infuriated self behind him. "We're settling this right now."

"Settling what?"

"Mr. Carroll, Mr. Thomas told me to hold his calls."

"It's fine, Jill," he grunts at the nice receptionist as he swings the office door open, pulling me into the room with him.

"Fuck. What the fuck, Reese?" Ian's voice causes me to shriek, and then I focus on what is happening in front of me. My eyes widen at the sight of Juls bent over Ian's desk, completely naked and getting fucked from behind. Ian quickly moves and covers her up as Reese and I spin around and shut the door to keep the curious eyes from the hallway from getting a show.

"Shit. Uh, sorry, man. This will only take a minute," Reese says as we both stare at the door.

"Jesus Christ, Dylan. I was so fucking close," Juls growls.

I hold my hands up. "This was not my idea. Blame the asshole next to me." His head flicks toward mine and I stare him down. *Yeah, that's right. I said it.*

"Well? What the fuck is it?" Ian asks, still out of breath.

"Why the hell did you tell Juls I am married?"

He laughs. "Uh, I didn't. You? Married? That's fucking hilarious. Babe, who told you Reese was married?"

"*You* did. Last week when we all went to The Tavern after work. Right?" She sounds nervous and suddenly unsure of herself.

"This is so fucking stupid. Can I go please?" I ask and Reese's arm shoots out and prevents me from grabbing the door handle. I try to push it away, but my efforts are useless.

"Babe, I think you've mistaken Reese for Trent. Trent is married."

My stomach drops.

"Oh. Oh, fuck, you're right. Dylan, I'm so sorry. Shit, I really thought it was Reese. Honest mistake though, right?" She giggles nervously and clears her throat.

I drop my head into my hands. "Jesus Christ," I groan, hearing a muffled laugh coming from my left, and suddenly I want to hurl myself out the nearest window. *Oh, God, this is awkward.*

"Well, now that there's no confusion, can you two love birds please get the fuck out so I can finish?" Ian utters through a laugh. "And lock the door behind you."

"Yup. Uh, meet you downstairs, Juls." I quickly open the door, beginning to make my way toward the elevators when a pair of hands grab my waist and spin me.

"Oh, no. I don't think so," Reese states, gripping my elbow and leading me back down the hallway and straight to his office. *Shit. He's not married. Now what?*

Chapter
FOUR

'M COMPLETELY UNPREPARED FOR THIS turn of events. Everything was executed perfectly on my side. I slapped him, called him out on his infidelity, and didn't allow his blinding good looks to deter me in any way. I felt powerful storming into his office and telling him off the way I did. But now, now I feel like a meek little church mouse as I cower in the corner of his office. He isn't married. That's not something I was expecting to discover, and definitely not something I was prepared to have to contemplate. I mean, what did we share together other than a hot fling at a wedding? There isn't anything deeper going on here, is there? No, surely not. No one develops relationships from slutty wedding sex encounters. That's not how those things work. If they did, Joey would be in a new relationship every other month. My eyes slowly trail up his long, lean body and stop on his eyes, which are curiously watching me. He's regained his perch on his desk and hasn't said a word as I fidget with my fingers, debating on where to start. *Fuck. I owed him a major apology.* I clear my throat and step closer to him, seeing him shift a bit on his desk.

"So, I was wondering if it was at all possible for you to completely forget that I came storming in here like a crazy person and assaulted you. If not, I'm not entirely above groveling."

He tilts his head and strokes his jaw with his hand. Pushing off the desk, he bridges the gap between us. "Well, you did think I was a married man who was fucking around behind his wife's back. I think that slap was justified from your point of view." His hand brushes my hair off my shoulder, the small gesture causing my stomach to knot up. "Besides, I would hate to *completely* forget how incredibly sexy you look all feisty and pissed off."

I laugh slightly. "You thought that was sexy?"

He nods and licks his lip as he stares at my mouth. I step into him, feeling his hands grip tightly onto my jeaned hips. "Well then, I could rip you a new one for acting like a total dipshit after you fucked me. It's your call." His chest heaves rapidly as I run my hands up his arms and stop on his biceps, squeezing once before flicking my eyes up to his. Hard muscles tense against my hands.

"Do your worst," he whispers.

My fingers trail up the length of his tie. Yelling at him to make him want me is tempting. Really tempting. But he has, technically, already apologized for his behavior, and right now, I don't want to yell. Not unless he's fucking it out of me.

Gripping his tie in my fist, I pull him back behind his desk and push him down into his chair. "I choose groveling," I declare as his eyes widen. Kneeling before him and steadying my fingers, I slip them into his belt, loosening it and unzipping his khakis.

"Dylan."

My hand grips his length and I pull him out. Flicking my tongue across the head, I glance up into his eyes, which are now glazed with lust. My tongue swirls around the head and down the shaft, licking every inch of him. I trail soft kisses along the seam as his eyes stay glued on my mouth, his lips parting and his breath coming out in quick bursts.

"That's so hot, love. Suck it hard."

I smile and wrap my lips around him, guiding him to the back of my throat as he lets out a hiss. I want to take him completely, but that isn't going to be possible. Not with what this man is working with. Wrapping my hand around the base, I stroke him with my mouth, sucking and licking as his hands find my hair.

"Jesus. Just like that. Don't stop."

His hands guide me at the pace he wants. Up and down, licking around the head before I take him in as far as I can. My hand strokes him tightly, gliding up and down his slick length as my mouth follows its path. His fingers brush down my temple, along my cheek and across my jaw. I keep my eyes on his face, seeing the muscles in his neck tense with each suck and his head fall back onto his chair when I lick the tip. He moans, thrusting his hips into my movements as his hands hold my head in place. I never was a huge fan of blow jobs, but the noises coming from Reese right now are making this insanely hot. I'm not just getting him off; I'm getting myself off. My thighs are pressed tightly together as I kneel in front of him and I know without a doubt that my panties are drenched. He pulses against my tongue. Sucking hard, I pull him deep and let him hit the back of my throat as I relax my muscles.

"Fuck. I'm gonna come."

I pump him with my hand and feel his hot release shoot into my mouth, swallowing and feeling even more powerful in this moment than I did when I stormed into this office. His legs tense under me and his throaty grunts cause me to suck harder, pulling every bit out of him. He loosens his grip on my hair and gently brushes it out of my face.

"Holy fucking shit."

I sit back on my heels and smile at my minor victory. He's still desperately hard and I want to do it again, and again. Making him come apart with my mouth has been one of the hottest things I've ever done. Plus, he tastes good. Really good. I glance up into his eyes as his breathing steadies, his chest pulling at the buttons on his dress shirt.

"I'm not sure what's sexier, you yelling at me *or* you groveling," he says through a grin that's as infectious as it is adorable. I smile and bite my lip as my phone beeps in my pocket. I quickly slip it out.

JULS: *I came. Did you? Time to go, sweets.*

"Thanks for lunch," I say playfully, his smile still on his face as he resituates himself and stands, offering me his hand. I place mine in his and stand on my wobbly legs. *Holy crap, I felt like I just came.*

"That was incredible." He presses his lips against mine softly, lingering for a moment as my phone beeps again.

"Shit. Sorry, I have a bakery to run. Later, handsome." I pull away from him and turn to see him shaking his head. "Oh, by the way, I'd like my panties back." I keep my hand on the doorknob while waiting for his response.

"Would you?" His voice is thick and causes me to clamp my thighs together. My urge to throw him back onto his desk and ride him is stronger than ever.

I nod and regain my composer. "Yes, I would. That pair happened to be a favorite of mine."

He runs a hand through his hair as he smoothes out his tie with the other. "Too bad, they're also a favorite of mine." He arches his brow and I grip the doorknob tighter. *Holy fuck.* "I suppose I could get you another pair. Although, I'm not accustomed to perusing lingerie shops, and I might get the wrong ones. Maybe you should go with me."

Oh, man. The thought of Reese buying me panties is unbelievably hot. I can picture him, walking around and studying each pair with his curious stare, his hands raking through his hair when he can't find the ones he's looking for. I smile at the image, but quickly shake it off. I shouldn't seem too affected by this guy. "I'm sorry, aren't I standing in the office of a CPA? You're a partner right?" He nods, crossing his arms over his chest as he watches me. "Then a smart guy like you, who I'm assuming didn't fuck his way to the top, shouldn't have a problem finding them on his own. Unless, you *did* fuck your way to the top?" I cock an eyebrow and grin as he shakes his head, trying desperately to hold back his smile. "You can send them by way of your flour delivery boy." His grin bursts through as I quickly exit his office, my cheeks burning from my flushed state.

"WELL?" JULS ASKS AS WE make our way back to the bakery.

"Well nothing. He's not married, apparently." I keep a straight face, but feel like I'm radiating from the inside out. Giving Reese a lunchtime blow job has made my week, and I can't get his reaction to it out of my head. His widened eyes as I pulled him out. His face when he came. The feel of his hands in my hair. I shake my head and snap out of my stupor.

She laughs. "I don't know who you think you're talking to here.

But I'm your best friend, Dylan, and I know that face. You like him."

"I'm sorry, did you get the sense fucked out of you back there? I do not like him. He was my wedding hook up."

"First of all, yes, I did get the sense fucked out of me as I always do with Ian. The man is an Adonis."

"TMI," I chuckle.

"And secondly, you *totally* like him; otherwise, you wouldn't have cared if he was married or not."

I shake my head. "Please. The only reason why I cared was because the idea of sleeping with a married man was eating away at me. Now, that feeling of shame is gone."

She pulls up in front of the shop and puts her Escalade in park. "And now that feeling of shame has been replaced with love?"

I bark out a laugh and open the door. "I'm afraid you're mistaken. We still on for drinks tomorrow night?"

"Hell, yes. Give JoJo kisses for me."

I wave to her before stepping into the shop, spotting Joey pacing behind the counter.

His hands are continually tugging at the ends of his hair and he looks thoroughly stressed and irritated. Turning toward the sound of me entering, he drops his hands dramatically. "For fuck's sake. I have been dying here while you two whores played castrate the adulterer. What happened?"

I walk behind the counter to join him and down my now completely cold coffee. "Calm down, you queen. We didn't castrate anybody."

He raises a brow suspiciously. "Well, why the hell not? Wasn't that the whole point of storming over there?"

I'm about to answer when the shop door opens. Joey straightens up and sharply turns toward the door. "We're closed," he barks at the customer as I fold over in laughter.

"Joey." I nudge him and he smiles. "He's just kidding, sir, how can I help you?"

The gray-haired man smiles and moves up to the counter. "Good afternoon. Do you have any tarts? I love tarts and haven't had one in years." He eyes up my display case and taps lightly on the glass with his hands.

"I'm a bit of a tart, sugar," Joey says in his overly flirtatious voice.

"Good Lord. No, sir, I'm sorry, I don't make tarts. Although, maybe I will. What kind do you like?"

He smiles sweetly as his eyes light up. "Oh, all kinds. Strawberry, blueberry, kiwi, they're all delicious."

I giggle at his enthusiasm and pull out a notepad, scribbling down a reminder. "I'll tell you what; I will personally make some tarts and have them in the shop ready for you by the end of the week. How does that sound?"

"That's perfect. Thanks, sugar. I'll stop in sometime on Friday." He winks at me before turning and leaving the shop, the door dinging closed behind him.

Joey shakes his head at me. "Do you have to be so accommodating all the time? We do enough special requests as it is."

I place my notepad on the counter and put my hand on my hip. "Hey, special requests are what make Dylan's Sweet Tooth different from all the other bakeries around here. You can't just walk into Crumbs Galore on Main Street and ask for something they don't make. I like being approachable and accommodating. It gives me an edge." He rolls his eyes but smiles at me, knowing I'm one hundred percent right. Word of mouth about how customers can pretty much request anything in my shop has gotten me a ton of business over the past three years. I shrug and continue, "Now, would you like to talk about how awesome we are compared to our competition, or would you like to talk about how Reese *isn't* married?"

His eyes widen and he stumbles. "Isn't? As in he's single? As in you can continue to fuck him?"

My eyes rake through the display case and I straighten up. "Hmmm, hold on. We need more black bottoms." I move toward the doorway that leads back to the kitchen when Joey grabs me by the shoulders.

"Fuck the fucking black bottoms. You owe me at least an hour of uninterrupted gossip." His face is red and his eyes are bugging out at me.

"And I'll tell you every juicy detail, after I grab a tray of black bottoms." He lets out a string of curse words and allows me to step in to the back.

I honor what I promised and spare no detail with Joey as I place the cupcakes into the display case. He stands back, completely enthralled by my rundown of my lunchtime office visit. I tell him about how I caught Juls being nailed by Ian on his desk, and about how she had mistaken Reese for Trent. I mention how Reese thought my angry tirade was sexy, and how I was going to yell at him again, but opted for a blow job instead to properly apologize for my face slap. And I wrap up with his words to me when he apologized for his freak out behavior at the wedding.

"He said he's not used to sex getting to him like that? What the hell does that even mean?" Joey asks as he wipes down the glass of the display case.

I shrug and nibble on a muffin. "I don't know. I was hoping you had some words of wisdom. It's not like I'm an expert on this shit or anything."

He silently thinks for a minute, his hand holding his rag still on the glass. "Maybe he means that *you* got to him. Like he was only going into it as just being what it was, slutty wedding sex, a one-time hook up, a sexy romp with a bridesmaid—"

"I wasn't a bridesmaid," I interject and his hand comes up to silence me.

"You know what I mean. He expected it to be a one and done deal, but what he wasn't expecting was *you*. Oh, my God, you're a game changer. He wants more than just slutty wedding sex."

Going through the motions of rolling my eyes, I stop. *Is that what Reese meant? Did I affect him to the point of freak out? Is that even a good thing? No. There's no way.* I shake my head.

"I think you and Juls are still drunk from the wedding. That guy is way too hot for me. Yes, I managed to somehow seduce him after he had *several* drinks I'm sure, but in normal daily life where alcohol isn't free flowing and I'm usually covered in pastry flour and icing, he is way the hell out of my league." I finish off my muffin and toss the wrapper in the trashcan. "Besides, he told me he hasn't had a girlfriend since college, which I'm sure is by choice. Look at him."

Joey walks around the counter, grabs my hand, and kisses the back of it. "Yeah, he does have that whole unattainable bachelor vibe going on. And I'm sure he gets a lot of ass, but right now, he wants *your* ass." He arches his brow playfully. "For the record, I happen to like you covered in pastry flour. And you are *just* as hot as he is."

I smile sweetly at him as he drops my hand and gets back to cleaning. My two closest friends are crazy, rightly out of their minds, and between the two of them, I'm sure my wedding to Reese will be planned within the next month.

‿

I SLEEP FOR SHIT THAT night. Images of Reese's orgasmic face keep entering my thoughts, while I try to focus on anything but him. It's a useless act. No matter what thoughts enter my mind, whether it's searching my brain for what exactly is in a tart, or the anniversary cake consultation I have Tuesday morning, his beautiful face pops in uninvited. Tossing in my bed and now completely drenched in sweat, I sit up and glance at my alarm clock. Three fifteen a.m. *Jesus, I have to be up in less than two hours for my run and haven't slept a wink.* I slam back on my pillow. *This can't happen. I cannot let some hook up affect me like this. I'm never going to get a good night's sleep. You can forget about my morning runs with Joey and functioning properly in the shop. I'll lose my business and everything I've worked so hard for. No. Fuck this.* Hopping out of bed, I throw myself into a freezing cold shower and jolt myself even more awake. Sleep is for the weak. There's no way I'm getting any tonight, so I might as well bake. After dressing, I grab my phone and descend the stairs two at a time.

I know exactly what I'm going to make. It's what I always make when I can't sleep or need a distraction. My mocha cupcakes with espresso butter cream frosting. The perfect combination of caffeine and chocolate, both of which I could consume in massive quantities right now. I open my tattered recipe book and thumb through it until I stop on the familiar handwriting. It's a recipe of my grandmother's that she used to make when I was a little girl, stumbling clumsily around her kitchen as she baked all day long. She made them weekly and always let me help her, my big brown eyes watching her with complete awe as she cracked her eggs with one hand and never needed a measuring spoon because "A real cook will always trust her taste buds over anything else." My mother hated when she would make this recipe with me because I would consume them in mass quantities and be on an insane sugar and caffeine high for hours. My crash would be swift and hard, usually resulting in me passing out in the middle of the living room floor. I always think of my grandmother when I make these. She passed away ten years ago and it makes me sad to think she will never get to see her influence on me now. After pulling together all of my ingredients and starting the coffee maker, I create a group text message with Juls and Joey.

ME: *Just so you are both aware, it's 3:30 a.m. and I am making my mocha cupcakes. Yes, you read that correctly and yes, it's because I haven't slept at all. Don't bother asking me to go for a run, Joey. That ship has sailed.*

Once the coffee is brewed, I mix in the espresso powder and set it aside to cool while I whip up the remaining ingredients. The smell alone perks me up a bit and I'm not feeling like a completely pathetic, sleep-deprived loser anymore. This is what I know. Baking. I'm good at it and I can practically do it in my sleep. Which I guess right now is ironic considering my current zombie-like state. My mind begins to drift as I whip the batter, watching the electric beaters mix the eggs and sugars. *I wonder if Reese likes mocha cupcakes? Or maybe he's a cookie guy. Shit.* I turn the mixer off and put my bowl onto the counter as I rub my eyes. *Focus, Dylan. You could lose a fucking finger.* I combine the egg mixture with my batter and whip it quickly before dividing the batter evenly into my cupcake liners. After I shove the trays into the oven, I get to work on the icing.

The icing is made of espresso powder, vanilla, butter, and powdered sugar. It's ridiculously sweet, and one of my favorites. I could live off this stuff if I had to. Because really, is there anything better than icing? *Sex with Reese, his lips, his hands touching me, his sounds...*

"UGH," I yell, slamming my hands down onto the cool counter. This is insane. What the fuck is wrong with me? I've never been this affected by a guy before. I was with Justin for two years and could go days without talking to or seeing him and not even miss the asshole. Which I guess in hindsight should have been a dead giveaway. I mean, shouldn't you want to see your significant other nonstop? But I didn't, and that was at least a relationship. This, whatever it is that Reese and I are doing, or were doing and I may be completely crazy to assume we will continue doing it. This is not serious. And I need to get my shit together and stop acting like it is. I pull the cupcakes out of the oven and lay them on the counter to cool while I test the icing.

"Mmmm. Perfect." I'm half tempted to say fuck the cupcakes and grab a spoon and retreat back upstairs with my bowl. But I yawn instead. And yawn again. Glancing at my phone, the blurred numbers read four twenty-seven a.m. as my eyelids refuse to stay open. With a third yawn, I pull up a stool and prop my head on my fist as I sit and wait for the cupcakes to cool. Then I can ice them and get ready for my day. Yup. That's exactly what I'm going to do. I don't need sleep. Because with sleep came dreams of Reese, and I don't need that. My eyelids fall shut and my breathing steadies. Nope, definitely don't need sleep. Or Reese.

Chapter
FIVE

"CUPCAKE, I THINK YOU NEED to wake up now."

My eyes slowly flutter open and the bright sunlight beaming through my window makes me close them tight again. "Shit." I roll over and cover my head with my pillow, hearing Joey's soft giggle.

"Seriously, Dylan, you're going to sleep the day away if you don't get up."

Sleep the day away? I push back onto my shins to look at the clock.

"It's three thirty? In the afternoon? Fuck." I shoot out of bed and run into the bathroom. "Joey, why the hell did you let me sleep this late? And how did I even get up here?" He follows me into the bathroom and leans against the door as I brush my teeth and unruly hair.

"First of all, I came in this morning to find you passed out face down on the workbench. So, being the nice guy that I am, I carried you up here and put you to bed."

I splash my face with cold water and dry it with a towel, turning to smile at him. "Oh, God. I bet I was a sight." He shrugs and steps aside as I walk into the bedroom and begin getting dressed.

"And secondly, I've been trying to wake you for the past four hours."

I roll my eyes at his statement. Of course, he's been trying to wake me up and I've slept through it. What the hell don't I sleep through besides my alarm? I slip on my jeans and a black tank top before I walk out from behind the partition. "Four hours? Jesus. Oh, shit." My stomach drops. "I missed my consultation."

He smiles sweetly at me and I want to punch him. *What is he, mental? That's money lost.* "Relax, I took care of it. Mrs. Frey was more than happy to meet with me since you were suffering from a stomach bug. You're welcome."

"I love you. You know that, right?"

He wraps me up into a big hug and kisses the top of my head. "You better. Come on, I have something to show you."

I follow him down the stairs and into the bakery. Everything is in perfect order, which I knew it would be. Joey is more than capable of handling shit while I sleep my life away. "God, I'm starving. I feel like I haven't eaten in days. Ooohhh, and you iced the mocha cupcakes." I pull a blueberry muffin out from the almost bare display case and begin nibbling on it while spacing out the remaining treats. Joey emerges from the back carrying a familiar looking white box. *Oh, God.*

"Of course I iced them. And they have been selling like crazy too, along with everything else today. We've been slammed." He places the box on the counter in front of me and I swallow loudly. "But who gives a shit about cupcakes or anything edible right now. You have no idea how hard it has been to not open this." He pushes it closer to me. "Now get to it."

My heart begins beating so hard in my chest I think for sure it will crack my sternum. "Maybe later." I push it away from me easily. *Hmm. Definitely not flour.*

"Fuck that noise. Since you aren't going to freely tell me why you couldn't get any sleep last night, which I'm just going to assume was because a certain someone was on your mind, you *will* open this right now." He pushes it back in front of me and pulls the ribbon.

"Same delivery guy?" I ask and he nods. Not that I really had any doubt. Placing my half-eaten muffin down, I open the box, grabbing the brown card that is lying on top of the tissue.

"Read it out loud," he squawks.

"No. What if he's confessing to a murder? I would hate for you to be an accessory." Joey mumbles something under his breath as I unfold the note and step back, giving myself the illusion of privacy.

Dylan,

Next time I go to Agent Provocateur to replace something of yours, you will be accompanying me.

X Reese

"Fuck me." I throw the card at Joey and riffle through the tissue paper, slowly pulling out the pair of purple lacy panties with the tiny ribbons on the sides.

He slams his hand down on the counter. "Jesus Fucking Christ. He bought you panties?"

"Yeah. I mean, he took the ones from the wedding and I jokingly told him he had to buy me a replacement pair." I stare at the panties, my face instantly heating up at the realization that Reese actually went lingerie shopping for me. *Christ, this is seriously hot.* "I was totally kidding though."

Joey re-reads the note several times before he turns to me, fanning his face with the card. "This has to be the hottest note I've ever read. Like, I could seriously have an orgasm from reading this." His mouth drops open and he steps closer to me, admiring the panties in my hand. "Wait a minute. What do you mean he kept your panties from the wedding? You went home without panties?"

I snatch the note back and slip it into my pocket. "Oh, hold off on the judgment please. Like you haven't gone without your delicates before." He looks toward the ceiling for a memory and smiles as I laugh at him. "Shit, Joey. How hot is this?"

"Wickedly hot. Sweet Lord, you need to fuck him again and fast before I drug him and drag him over to my side."

I laugh until my side hurts and am only interrupted when the shop phone rings.

"Dylan's Sweet Tooth." I giggle into the phone as Joey studies my panties like a weirdo. "Give those back, you perv," I whisper away from the phone.

"Dylan?"

My back straightens and I almost drop the phone. *I know that voice.* Clearing my throat and pretending I don't, I answer after a beat. "Yes, this is Dylan."

"It's Reese."

"Oh, hi." I swat at Joey to get his attention and mouth *it's him.* He drops my panties on the counter and quickly snatches the phone away from me. *What? No!*

"Reese. You *stud* you. My girl is dying for you to impregnate her."

"GIVE ME THE PHONE."

He grins and nods as I jump up and try to snatch it. *Damn it to hell, he's tall.* "Yup. She just opened your package. Speaking of packages, just how big *is* your dick? As memorable as she says?" *I am going to kill him. Slowly.*

Grabbing the phone out of his hand, I punch him as hard as I can in his shoulder as he laughs at me. "Asshole. Shit, my hand. You're fucking dead, Holt." I shake my hand in the air and bring the phone up to my ear. "Hello?" I say through a wince of pain. *Oh, God. Please tell me he didn't hear any of that.*

"Hi, love. What's this about you wanting to carry my children?" I can hear the smile in his voice, obviously enjoying himself immensely. I, on the other hand, want to hurl myself into traffic.

"Sorry. Joey drinks." *This is mortifying.* "Can I help you with something?"

"Is your hand okay?"

A customer walks through the door and Joey gets to work helping her. After flipping him off, I watch him giggle at me as I slip into the back for some much needed privacy. "Yes, it's fine, I think." Making a fist to stretch it out, I smile at my next move. *He sends me a naughty note; he's going to get naughty Dylan.* "How's *your* hand?"

"My hand? And why would something be wrong with my hand, sweet Dylan?"

I sigh. *Sweet Dylan. Lord, help me, this guy is smooth.* "Well, I just assumed you jerked off repeatedly at the image of me in each and every item in that store today. In fact, I'm counting on it." The sound of coughing comes through the phone and I chuckle. "So tell me, why exactly would I accompany you to Agent Provocateur? I'm there enough as it is."

After a brief moment of just his breathing in my ear, which is making the hair on my neck stand up, he speaks. "Do you own any garters?" His voice is low and taut. *Christ, he sounds seductive, even at work.*

I can feel my pulse hammering in my neck as I bite my bottom lip. "Maybe, why?"

"Wear one tonight."

Tonight? I'm going out for drinks with Joey and Juls tonight. Of course, where Juls goes, Ian goes. And Ian must have told Reese. I suddenly can't wait for drinks.

"You know those cost a pretty penny, don't you? I would hate to lose such an expensive item of clothing when you decide to steal it." Even though I wouldn't mind it entirely. He can confiscate every article of clothing I have for all I care.

"Who said anything about you taking it off?"

I grip the workbench and close my eyes, suddenly feeling like I could combust.

"Reese."

"Dylan."

I glance down at my shirt, my aroused nipples highly visible now. I moan softly into the phone before I answer in a whisper, "I'm so wet right now."

A loud crack rings through the receiver and I know he's dropped it. *Ah, sweet victory.*

"Are you serious?" he murmurs and I chuckle at his response. "Shit. You can't tell me that when I'm stuck at work."

I run my hand up and around my neck, feeling the clamminess of my skin. "Well, I am. That voice of yours does that to me."

Joey pops his head through the doorway and I immediately freeze. "Cupcake, we need more éclairs."

I nod quickly, eyes wide as Joey's grin gets bigger. "I guess I'll see you later then?" I ask, moving toward the pastry rack. I know my face is beet red, and I feel like I've just been caught masturbating. Shit, I practically was.

He breathes heavily into the phone. "I'm counting on it." The call ends, allowing me to grab the container of éclairs with both hands after

I place the phone down on the worktop.

Turning quickly, I see Joey watching me, arms crossed. "You look all hot and bothered," he says slyly through his smile.

"I am. And I'm not sure how I feel about it either."

Pushing past him, I walk to the display case and fill the tray of pastries. He leans against the doorframe. "What does that mean? He wants you, obviously; you want him, again, obviously, so what's the problem here?"

I close the case. "No problem. This is just sex. Really fucking good sex. So, no problem." I brush past him and shake my head, silently communicating this conversation is over. Because this *is* just sex. And even though I've always been a relationship kind of girl, I am more than capable of handling hot casual sex. *Right?*

⁓

JOEY AND I ARRIVED AT The Tavern at eight thirty p.m. after I spent over an hour debating what to wear. I've settled on my cream summer dress that hugs my curves in the most sinfully way possible. It bunches in the front, accentuating my cleavage, and falls just above my knees. Paired with my matching heels, and feeling my garter cling to my thighs, I feel secretly sexy. My hands shake as we step through the door, Joey leading the way through the packed bar. I have no idea why I'm so nervous. I've already had sex with the guy. And now I know for sure he enjoyed it as much as I did and doesn't regret it. But for some reason, my heart is pounding in my ears and my stomach is clenched tight. *Come on, Dylan. You can do this. He wants you and you sure as hell want him.*

I follow Joey to the bar where Juls is perched on a stool, messing with her phone. With no members of the Chicago man candy club in sight, I breathe a sigh of relief.

"Finally. Holy hell, Dylan. That dress. Shit, that might actually kill him." She grins wickedly and runs her eyes down my body.

I twirl quickly as Joey whistles. "You bitches annoy me with your hot little figures," he grumbles, motioning for the bartender.

"Joey is buying because he's a shithead who steals phones out of people's hands," I say as Juls hops down from her stool.

"Excellent. I love it when Joey is a shithead. White Zinfandel for me, JoJo."

He glares at her and then at me.

"Don't you dare look at me like that. Telling Reese I wanted to have his babies. You're lucky I'm only making you buy us drinks." I cock my head to the side and stare him down.

"Ha! Oh, my God. You would have the prettiest babies," Juls squeals.

"I know, right?" he echoes.

I roll my eyes. "You're both mental."

Juls grabs my hand and tugs me through the crowd, stopping at an empty tall table. My eyes scan the room as I settle on my stool. I quickly tap my fingers on the table and bite the inside of my cheek.

"You're nervous," she states as my eyes meet hers across the table.

"I don't know, maybe this is a bad idea."

She arches her brow at me.

"I feel like I'm trying too hard. I mean, I'm wearing a fucking garter under this for Christ's sake."

"So am I. High-five, sweets." I can't help but giggle at her naughty enthusiasm as I humor her and slap her hand. Of course, Juls is wearing a garter. Between the two of us, I'm sure we've accumulated one of every item in Agent Provocateur.

Joey returns moments later with our drinks. "Well, in case Billy is a no show, Ty the bartender is available for my licking."

I grab my drink and take a sip as Juls snickers. "What *is* going on with Billy? Have you spoken to him since the wedding?" I ask.

He takes a sip of his beer before answering. "He's texted me a few times. You know me though, always gotta have one waiting for me in the wings." He's being evasive. Joey is never evasive.

"I love how you think *that* answer is going to satisfy us. And since when are you tight lipped about your hook ups?" I say as Juls nods in agreement.

"Seriously, JoJo, who the hell do you think you're talking to here? I happen to know from a very well hung, reliable source that you and Billy saw each other last night. And pretty much every night since the wedding."

"Ian told you that? Christ, he is whipped. Your pussy must be like some fucking nirvana or some shit."

My mouth drops open as Juls smiles and shrugs playfully. "Oh, is that right? I thought you weren't sure how you felt about him and his curved penis?"

He looks quickly around the room and takes a sip of his beer. "It's growing on me."

"I bet it is, on you *and* in you," Juls barks and we fall into a fit of giggles as her phone lights up. "Ooohhh, they're here," she squeals excitedly.

My back goes rigid and my pulse begins to race. As if my body is somehow wired to his, I look up at the doorway just as he walks through behind Ian. I listen to my heavy breathing as he moves like liquid through the crowd of people. Eyes dark and hooded in the amber glow of the bar, hair perfectly messed up, making my fingers ache to touch. And that sexy as hell mouth that is glistening as if he just licked it. *Good God, he is glorious to look at.* Needing the liquid courage, I down my drink and earn myself a wide-eyed look from Joey as the men walk toward our table.

"Hey, babe," Juls says as Ian wraps his arms around her back. He smothers her in quick kisses as she moans softly against him.

"Dylan, Joey, it's nice to see you both," Ian says.

I raise my glass at him as Joey does the same, my eyes locking on to Reese. He walks around the table, his gaze never leaving mine as he comes and stands next to my stool.

"Hi." His voice is low and soft as his hand rests on my lower back, claiming me in front of everyone. *Yes, that's right. I'm with him. Move along, ladies.*

"Hi, yourself." I turn my body and cross one leg over the other, the hem of my dress rising up on my thigh and quickly catching his attention. I admire him while he admires my legs. He's looking as hot as ever in a dress shirt and tie, which is partially loosened, and regarding me sweetly, with soft eyes and parted lips.

"You look…" he runs a hand through his hair and I smile, his eyes slowly scanning my body. "…I like your dress. A lot."

"Thanks. Wait till you see what's under it."

Stepping closer to me so his leg is brushing against mine, he slowly trails his hand up my thigh under the table and stops at the metal clips of my garter. His neck pulses as he swallows and slides his hand back out, pulling down my dress.

"Per your request," I say as his lip curls up in the corner.

"So, Dylan, how's the bakery business going? That wedding cake you made was really fucking good, right, Joey? Didn't you have like six pieces?" Ian says as he steals Juls' stool before pulling her into his lap. She runs her fingers along his collar, blissfully oblivious to anyone but him.

"Whatever. I burned it off later with Billy."

"Well, I'm glad you guys got to enjoy the cake since I didn't. I was a bit preoccupied with my own drama." My eyes quickly flick to Reese who is watching me, studying me with a small smile. I give him a quick wink before I turn back to Ian. "But yeah, business is good. Busy as we usually are in the summer. I think I have a wedding every weekend to bake for until September."

"Yeah, we're crazy busy. And when she's not whipping up wedding cakes, she's floating on cloud nine all over that damn shop from the love notes and deliveries she's been receiving." Joey sighs dramatically as I tense in my seat. "It's all very romantic."

Reese's hand moves on my back, his thumb rubbing the material of my dress.

I quickly shove my chatty friend and spill some of his beer on the table. "Remind me why I hired you as my assistant?"

"Because I'm gorgeous and can sell anything to anyone," he replies playfully.

"Please, you say that like my treats don't sell themselves." I twirl my ice in my glass. "If anything, you're more of a liability to have around. Just how many sexual harassment suits are pending against you this month?" Not that he really has any, but it wouldn't surprise me with the way Joey flirts daily with customers. He rolls his eyes as Juls giggles against Ian.

"Jesus Christ. You two fight like you're married," Billy says as he approaches the table with three beers, passing two of them to Ian and Reese.

"We practically are, and before you ask, I'm the man in the relationship," I reply, sucking on an ice cube before dropping it back into my glass.

Reese laughs quietly next to me and I glance up at him, meeting his stare.

"Baby, do you hear what I have to put up with daily? Tell Dylan to be nice to me." Joey strokes Billy's arm, and I see my opportunity.

"Hey, Joey, would you like me to get you anything from the bar? Another beer, some food, your balls maybe?" Juls slams her hand down on the table and laughs as Billy's face lights up. Ian and Reese both chuckle as Joey glares at me.

"Bitch," he murmurs.

"Anyway," Billy stretches out before his eyes flash to Reese and then quickly to mine. "Reese tells me you thought he was married. That's probably the funniest thing I've heard all year."

"Fuck off," Reese mutters against his glass.

Billy chuckles and sweetly rubs Joey's arm. "Oh, come on. You? Tied down?" Billy's eyes shift from Reese to mine after I register Reese's slight head shake. "It was even funnier when we heard how you slapped the shit out of him for it."

"Shit yeah it was," Ian chimes in and kisses Juls quickly on the cheek. "I would've paid to see that." I shrug and glance up at Reese who seems to be thinking of something, his eyes staring off past the table.

"You should have seen how pissed she was in the shop. I actually thought she was going to return back to work with your balls in her purse," Joey directs toward Reese, and I shift in my chair, feeling his eyes on me as I slowly glance up and meet them.

"Well, I happen to be very fond of my testicles, so I'm glad that shit got cleared up." He looks around at everyone before dropping his eyes back to mine. Leaning in, he holds my neck with one hand and whispers into my hair, "Come home with me."

I shake my head slowly and smile, glancing quickly around the table. Joey and Billy are now in deep conversation as they both walk toward the bar together, and Juls is straddling Ian's lap. *Sweet Jesus, get a room is right.* My gaze goes back to Reese. His eyes narrow as he picks up my glass and slips an ice cube in his mouth, slowly sucking on it and making my skin tingle. I swallow loudly.

"Why not? I want to take you to bed, immediately."

I blink slowly, suddenly feeling drunk from his voice and the intensity behind it. "No beds," I say flatly, seeing his expression shift to curiosity. I explain myself. "Beds are intimate. And we're just having fun. Keeping it casual. Right?"

He studies me as he places my empty drink down. "Of course."

"Sex in beds leads to sleepovers, and I think it would be better for me if we didn't take it there." This has to be said. If I'm going to attempt to just have casual sex with Reese, I can't do anything that would lead to me getting attached. I'm already losing sleep over the man and we barely know each other.

"Are you telling me that I'm restricted to fucking you in public places only?"

"You say that like it's a bad thing."

"No, love, fucking you *anywhere* could never be a bad thing. I was just dead set on getting your hot little ass in my bed." His eyes burn into mine as his hand lightly trails down my shoulder.

I smooth his tie down as his fingers trickle down my arm. "I just think this is how it needs to be. Besides, I'm sure there are at least a handful of hard surfaces in here that you've already thought about throwing me up against."

His infectious laugh pulls me in and I join him. "Yes, you're right about that." His hand holds the side of my face and he leans in, brushing his lips softly against mine before pulling back an inch. "But I want to get you naked, and I'd prefer it if I did it without an audience. Are you opposed to fucking in vehicles?"

After swiping my tongue across my lip to taste him, I grab my purse and stand up. "Not at all. Lead the way, handsome."

We say our goodbyes to Juls and Ian who pay us little attention. They're practically having sex at the table now anyway and couldn't care less what we do. He grabs my hand and pulls me through the bar and out the door, leading me down the sidewalk and stopping in front of a vehicle that makes my jaw hit the pavement.

"Holy shit. You drive a Range Rover?" I ask as he pulls his keys out and hits the unlock button.

"Yes. Is that okay?"

"Don't these things cost like ninety grand?" My eyes rake over the car with amazement.

He laughs and opens the back door. "Something like that."

I squeal as I'm lifted off my feet and pushed into the back seat. Reese slides in behind me and closes the door. Pulling me into his lap, I straddle his waist as his hands slide down my sides and hold tightly on to my hips. His thumbs press against the front of my pelvis and I feel my core constrict.

"Are you sure I can't convince you to let me take you to my place? I want to slowly devour you, and I feel like this venue won't allow me to appreciate it as much."

I laugh against his mouth, slowly licking his bottom lip until he opens for me and tangles his tongue with mine. *Christ, I forgot how good he was at this. Just kissing.*

I somehow manage to break away for a second. "Mmm, devour me, huh?"

He nods, tilting my head up with his hand and kissing down my neck. My hem is hiked up with his other hand and his fingers graze my stockings where they meet my garter.

"Would you be able to devour me on a couch?"

He pulls back and I drop my head. "Couches aren't intimate?"

"No, not at all. And I want to be devoured on yours. Slowly." His forehead is resting against mine and we're both panting. I've given in easily to the idea of going home with him, really easily. But honestly, this man could convince me to do anything at this point. I'm fairly certain that if he asked me to commit a major felony with him, I would do it willingly and with the same fucking smile that I'm wearing now.

His eyes widen and he slides me off his lap. "Fuck yes. Let's go, love."

Chapter
SIX

STANDING IN AN ELEVATOR WITH Reese Carroll in a massive building full of luxurious condos is one of the most surreal moments of my life so far. I can't believe what I'm doing, or what I'm about to do with this man. Well, I mean, of course I knew going out tonight was going to lead to sex with him, but I had firmly decided on not leaving with him. I figured we would sneak off into the bathroom at The Tavern or into a dark and secluded corner to hump like rabbits. But here I am, riding the elevator of his building to the tenth floor with him watching me from across the small space. It's taking every ounce of self-control to not drop to my knees on this pristine marble floor and suck him off right here and now. I feel green eyes on me as I stare ahead at the numbers on the panel, loving the fact he hasn't stopped looking at me since we got out of his car.

"See something you like?" I ask playfully as he leans against the mirrored wall.

"Very. But why are you standing so far away from me? Afraid I might violate you before we even get to my couch?"

I swallow loudly. *Violate me? Yes, anytime.* The elevator pings and the doors open before I have a chance to answer.

We're barely in the door of his condo when it's kicked closed behind us and I'm being pinned against the wall. His mouth is hot and needy against mine, sucking and tasting every dip and corner as our tongues move together. I grip the back of his head and pull his tongue into my mouth and suck it slowly, drawing a long groan from his parted lips. His hands move over every inch of my back and down to the hem of my dress.

"Take it off," he orders as he grips my hips and moves backward, leading me out of the entryway and into a giant living room. My eyes widen at the sight of it.

"Whoa. Your place is really nice." I quickly glance all around me. We've stopped in front of a long black leather sofa that faces a fireplace, with a giant television mounted on the wall.

"Dylan, take the dress off."

I smile and look up at him from under my lashes, slowly turning around and gathering my hair over one shoulder. "Unzip me please." Startling a bit at the touch of his hands on my bare shoulders, he keeps one there while the other slowly pulls the metal zipper down my spine, stopping just above my backside.

"Thank you," I say softly as I stay facing away from him and pull my arms out of the sleeves, letting it drop to the floor and hearing a sharp inhale of breath from behind me. *And this is why garters were invented.* I smile without him knowing.

"Holy shit. Turn around." *Mmm, I like bossy Reese.*

Taking a little longer than he probably would have liked, I turn on my heels and step out of my dress, standing directly in front of him in my cream-colored lacy bra, matching panties and garter, and my sheer stockings. His chest is moving rapidly inside his shirt as he slowly trails down my body with his eyes, and even more slowly back up to my face. I see his Adam's apple roll in his throat.

"Be gentle," I whisper, and for a brief moment, something flashes in his eyes. Something I've been feeling and hope he can't see. *Is he nervous?*

"You're so fucking beautiful," he says. I melt on the spot. No man has ever called me beautiful before. Sexy, hot, and I even got "good enough to eat" one time. But never beautiful. *Shit, why did he have to say that?* He steps in to me and wraps his arm around my waist, pulling me against his chest as he slowly lowers me down onto the couch.

"Oh!" I yelp at the cold leather as it touches my bare skin.

Kneeling next to me on the floor, he grabs my one leg and hooks it over the back of the couch and brings the one closest to him up to rest over his shoulder. I begin to shake against him, knowing exactly what's coming. He trails light kisses up my inner thigh. "I've been dying to taste you again. It's all I've thought about." He moves to my other thigh and repeats the action, causing me to tremble. "You have me so fucking wound up here, Dylan. You *will* come in my mouth several times before I fuck you."

"Jesus, you keep talking like that and I'm gonna come before you touch me." My body arches toward his mouth as he laughs against my skin. I know he's right. I know he'll bring me multiple orgasms tonight because he's *that* good. His hot breath warms me against my panties and I moan, feeling his finger slide the thin, sheer material to the side ever so gently.

"Oh," I groan loudly.

His first lick is slow and lingering, ending with a sharp flick of my clit and causing an involuntary tremble of my body against his mouth. Throwing my hands over my head and digging into the arm rest, I look down my body and meet his eyes. His tongue licks in between every fold, and swirls around and inside of me.

"Oh, my God, you're so good at that." My chest is rising and falling rapidly as he works me. I've never had oral sex feel like this, not even close to this. A strong urge begins slowly building in my gut as he brushes hard against my clit and pulls it into his mouth, sucking relentlessly.

"Feel it, Dylan. Feel what I can do to you." Darting his tongue inside me and fucking me with it, my leg that is hooked over the couch begins to slip as I buck against him. His hand darts out and pushes it back over, leaving me wide open for him to expertly explore with his mouth.

"Oh, God," I cry out, tightening every muscle in my body.

Two fingers take the place of his tongue as he licks above his hand, giving extra attention to my swollen nub. He moves slowly, stretching me with his fingers as I begin rolling my hips against his face. My orgasm hits hard and fast, sending me spinning off into orbit as I scream his name and reach down to hold him right where I need him.

"Mmm," he moans against me and the vibration shoots up my body and hits every nerve. His fingers slow their torture as he continues licking me, bringing me down slowly, but not quite enough to ease the throbbing.

"Oh, God. Reese, please."

I know begging him to stop is of no use. Plus, do I really want him to stop? I've never had an orgasm from a guy's mouth on me before, and I know my next one isn't far behind. I moan loudly and bite my lip as he glides one hand up my body, massaging my breast as he licks between my legs.

"You taste amazing. I could do this for days, love."

I groan and arch away from the couch, his hands lifting my ass into the air. "Don't stop." My skin ignites and the fire that has been barely doused comes roaring back to life inside me. The only parts of my body touching the couch now are my shoulders and my head. Reese is supporting everything else as he moves his fingers quickly, slipping a third one inside and pushing with the perfect amount of pressure against my clit with his thumb. His mouth nibbles on the tender skin of my thigh and I cry out.

"Reese. Oh, my God."

"Give it to me, Dylan," he growls.

I come again and it's even deeper than my last one. The leg that was hung over the couch is now resting on his other shoulder and I grip my thighs tight against his head. He sucks on my clit and rides out my orgasm with me, finally allowing me to touch back down after my trembling stops. Slipping my legs off his shoulders, he places them gently on the couch, and this time, the cold leather feels welcoming on my now glistening skin.

"That was… that right there… was…" I have no words. No words have been invented to describe that. My breathing is so strained I can barely speak, even if I *did* have the words. I open my eyes and see him standing next to the couch, slowly pulling at his tie with his amused expression.

"Epic?"

I quickly swing my legs over the side and stand up, stumbling into his arms. "Jesus, you've rendered me crippled."

"Lie back down. I'm nowhere near done with you, love."

I slowly raise my eyes to his and lick my lips. "I figured, but I want to undress you."

He arches an eyebrow and licks my arousal off his lips as he holds his arms out to me. I step out of my heels and drop down a few inches, the top of my head now falling just below his nose. Reaching up slowly, I pull at his tie and slide it off from around his collar, dropping it at my feet.

"I've been dying to see you naked. It's all *I've* thought about," I say as my fingers begin working at the buttons on his dress shirt. "You're wearing way too many clothes for me." I'm fumbling nervously, the anticipation of getting his clothes off causing me to fidget a bit, but I don't care. I focus in on my task.

"Yeah, I know the feeling. You look incredible, but I can't wait to get you *out* of that."

I glance up at him from under my lashes and part my lips, seeing his eyes on my chest. I haven't thought about the fact that he hasn't seen me naked yet. I'm still wearing everything I had put on earlier underneath my dress. Bringing one hand behind my back, I quickly unhook my bra while the other stays firmly planted on his chest. I slowly slide it down my arms and let it drop to the floor, hearing a soft moan escape him. My heavy breasts bob freely and tingle in the anticipation of his body on them. He brings his hands up and rakes them through his hair. "Problem?" I ask, continuing the unbuttoning of his shirt.

He shakes his head, his eyes lingering on my chest. "No, no problem. Those could never be a problem."

I smile and push his shirt over his shoulders and down his arms, reaching quickly for the bottom of his T-shirt and pulling it over his head. *Holy shit.* My breathing picks up as I run my hands over the sharp outline of his chest and down to his abs, tracing the lines of his six-pack. *Or eight pack? Jesus.* Never have I ever seen or touched a body like this. He's hard and defined, but his skin is smooth and it tenses as I graze over every inch of it.

"You're so beautiful," I say softly, licking my lips as I begin tugging at his belt. A soft laugh causes me to look up.

"Can I please be something a little more manly? Beautiful should only be reserved for you." He brushes the back of his hands up my stomach and trails the underside of my breasts.

"Handsome then? Superbly handsome?" I smile up at him and he nods, the corner of his lips curling up.

His thumbs run over my erect nipples. *Fuck the slow touching. I need him now.* My fingers spring to life and I unbutton and unzip him quickly, pushing his pants and boxers down, and stagger back at the sight of his erection. *Yup, just as massive as I remember.* A crazy thought enters my mind as he pulls his shoes and socks off, stepping out of his pants. Not crazy, fucking insane. But before I can think where the hell this thought came from, my mouth opens.

"I'm not sleeping with anybody else," I say quickly, my eyes running over his naked body. His waist is narrow, the prominent V staring me right in the face. Long muscular legs run on for miles. Even his feet are perfect. *Jesus, his body is deadly.* I glance up at him and see his expression. He's watching me, studying me. "I just, I know this is just sex and nothing else, but I'm not going to be sleeping with anyone but you." I'm talking so fast, I'm unsure if he's catching any of what I'm saying. *Where the fuck is this coming from?* "I want to be monogamously casual, or casually monogamous. Fuck, is that even a saying? I don't know. We don't have to be. I mean, if you want to sleep with other women, then that's fine. But if you don't—"

"Dylan."

"I'm sorry." I cover my face and feel completely mortified, but I don't stop. It's like word vomit at this point. "It's just, I want to feel you. Just you. I've never done it without a condom before and I'm clean. I've only been with one other guy, and we always used protection. And I've been on birth control for years." *Fucking hell, I'm an idiot.* "Christ, never mind. Forget I said anything. I'll go grab a condom out of my purse." I drop my hands and turn to walk toward the entryway where I dropped my purse in the heat of passion. His hand grips my wrist and stops me.

"Why are you so nervous all of a sudden? We've already had sex and you've had two orgasms tonight already. You should be completely relaxed with me."

I look anywhere but his face. Yearning to touch his chest, his broad shoulders, and his cut arms. I feel his hand on my chin as he lifts it to meet his eyes. "I don't know, you're naked." I motion to the wonder that stands before me. His tight body is definitely making my brain scramble. "I'm having trouble thinking straight."

He muffles his laugh. "Relax. I *was* sleeping with someone else up until the wedding, but I ended it. It wasn't serious anyway. I don't usually do serious." *Okay, that made sense.* "I think monogamously casual is a saying, and if that's what you want to be, then that's what we'll be." He pauses and I step closer to him, granting him access to my body. He snakes his arms around my waist and holds me against him, skin to skin. The sensation warms me instantly. "And I've always used condoms. Always. If this is what you want and you're sure—"

I brush my lips lightly against his, cutting him off mid-sentence. "It can't just be what I want. If you don't—"

"Dylan, of course I want it too. Do you think I haven't thought about it?" His hand comes up and strokes my cheek as I trace the outline of his chest. His face is completely serious, and I'm suddenly grateful for my extreme case of verbal diarrhea.

"Okay." I step back out of his arms and hook my fingers into my panties. I watch him watch me slowly pull them down my legs and step out of them, leaving me standing in only my garter and stockings. If it's even possible, he gets harder. My eyes bulge in my head as he sits down on the couch, pulling me toward him. *Oh, God, he wants me on top?* I slowly, almost hesitantly straddle his waist as he watches me, his eyes never leaving mine. I brace myself on my knees. "Umm, I'm not used to doing it this way. I don't really know if I'll be good at it like this."

The corner of his mouth twitches. "You can't be bad at it, love." His big hands cup my breasts and begin to slowly knead them, my nipples scratching against his rough palms. Moving closer and relaxing down a bit, I gasp when he brushes up against me, rubbing me in the most perfect way imaginable. He moans softly. "See, whatever feels good for you will sure as hell feel good for me."

"Oh. Oh, wow," I groan as I move against him, up and down in my wetness as his hands slide down my sides and grip my hips. He controls my movements, not allowing me to speed up when I want to or hover

over him to allow him to penetrate me. I grip his head between my hands and lock eyes with him as my body responds to his.

"Reese, I need you."

"Mmmm, I love it when you say that." He closes his eyes tightly, a low growl emanating from his throat before he opens them again. "Fuck, you feel incredible against me. Can you come this way?" He slowly trails kisses along my jaw.

I know I can. This feels almost as amazing as his mouth on me. He is unbelievably hard and I'm completely drenched. Plus, at this angle, our faces are inches apart and I can see just how much he's enjoying this. Soft deep groans escape his slightly parted lips and his forehead is glistening with sweat.

I groan before I answer. "Yes, but I want you in me. Please, please let me fuck you."

He moves in and pulls my bottom lip into his mouth, urgently swiping his tongue against mine. He tastes like me, like my orgasm, and it's surprisingly hot. I moan and put everything I have into this kiss. I can't get enough. His mouth can please every inch of my body, and I want to surrender to him completely. *Shit, at this rate, I should just sign the rights to my body over to him now and be done with it.* No other man will ever make me feel like this. My thighs shake against his and I move quicker, gliding up and down against his length, which is now soaked from me. My hands grip his head, tangling in his hair as my body begins to pulse against his.

"Please, I need you."

As his one hand holds my hip tightly, his fingers digging into my skin, he positions himself under me and drives his hips up and into mine. We cry out together. He's so deep in me this way, deeper than anything I have ever felt. "Reese." I go to rock forward on him when his grip on me tightens.

"Shit, don't move." He closes his eyes and drops his head back onto the couch. I stare wide-eyed as his Adam's apple rolls in his neck, the veins along the sides pulsing against his skin.

Oh, crap. What happened? "Is it okay? I mean, does it feel okay?" I'm suddenly wondering if I'm completely screwing this up and way the hell out of my element. But it's a justified question. I really have no idea what I'm doing here.

He tilts his head up and looks at me curiously, brushing my hair behind my ear. "Is it okay? I'm struggling to not blow my load in you right now and you're not even moving." My eyes widen and I can't contain my smile. *I'm making him lose it. Yes!* "Just give me a minute."

"Okay, take your time." I'm completely giddy as he resumes his position, closing his eyes and leaning his head back. I stay perfectly still on top of him, my hands slowly trailing down his neck to his shoulders. Molding my hands against him, I take this opportunity to feel his every muscle. I run my palms down his arms and back up again, softly massaging his biceps and triceps. Skating down his chest, I trace the lines of his abdominals, which are clenched tight and seem to firm up even more from my touch.

"That feels really good," he says as he lifts his head and watches me.

"What? You in me or my hands on you?" I keep my eyes on him as I rub him, wanting to feel every inch of his skin underneath my hands. It feels amazing, touching him like this, feeling his body react to mine and seeing him relax from my contact.

His hand comes up to my face and he strokes along my jaw. "Both," he replies, his green eyes burning into mine.

I wink at him as my fingers trail up his sides and back to his chest. "What does it feel like?"

"Being in you like this?" I nod and he continues. "Warm and really soft." His eyes drop down between us and he stares at me. There. I swallow loudly. "It feels like I fit in you perfectly. Nothing has ever felt like this, for me anyway. Have you ever felt like this before?"

I stare at him, unable to blink as he studies my face. *What did he mean by that? Was he just referring to the sex? Or did he mean just being with me? The two of us together? Shit.* His question is fucking with my head. *I've sure as hell never felt anything like this, in both ways. I'm drawn to this man. The undeniable tangible pull between us is electric. But I'm sure it's one-sided. He's just referring to the sex.*

"Never. Can I move now, please? I'm dying here." I've never been on top during sex and suddenly have a strong overpowering desire to do it and do it well.

"Please," he answers as he keeps one hand on my hip, digging into my skin.

Gripping onto his shoulders, I rock my hips forward against him, moaning loudly as he slides out of my wetness. I push back and continue riding him, back and forth, up and down, bringing him almost completely out of me before taking him back in.

"Holy shit. Just like that, love." He clenches his teeth and rocks into me as I drive against him, pushing himself deeper and deeper with each move. One hand teases and massages my breast while the other holds my side. "Jesus, you feel incredible. So fucking good, Dylan." He keeps his eyes on me as he leans in and pulls my nipple into his mouth. I throw my head back and scream his name as the fever begins to spread throughout my body. He sucks and bites me as I still my movements, arching my back to give him full access to my breasts. I look down and meet his eyes as his mouth stays latched around me, pulling my nipple into his mouth and flicking it with his tongue.

"I love your mouth."

A small smile pulls at his lips as he moves to the side of my breast and sucks hard, leaving a very prominent red mark on my pale skin. His eyes study mine for approval.

"Do that again."

He licks over to my other breast that is now being teased with his fingers. Sucking on the skin just above my nipple, he pulls back after a few seconds and admires his work. I'm marked by him, where only his mouth has pleased me and it's the hottest thing I've ever seen. He's claiming my body and I'm willingly letting him have it. His hands move to my ass and he grips me tightly, picking up my pace.

"Yes. Oh, God. Oh, God." My stomach clenches and twists as my pussy aches. He slides one hand around my waist and down my stomach until his thumb is working my clit. My fingernails dig into the leather as he rubs me in the way that only he knows how. I'm pulsing, shaking against him. My climax is already on the brink before I crash down on top of him. The feel of him inside me with no barrier and now working me the way he's doing, pushes me quickly over the edge. I throw my head back and give in to the release. "Reese, I'm coming." His hand grabs my face and tilts it down, forcing me to look at him. His eyes burn into mine, capturing me as he grunts loudly.

"Dylan, oh, FUCK." I feel his orgasm burst inside me, warm and lingering, and I never want anything more than I want him in this moment. This is amazing. Everything about him is amazing. He pumps once, twice, three times and stills, his eyes staying on mine and giving me the satisfaction of watching him come undone. And then I collapse on top of him, my head hitting his chest as his hand comes up and holds me there. I've never felt anything like this. Not even close. He has officially ruined all other men for me and I am perfectly fine with that.

Chapter
SEVEN

I AM WRECKED, RUINED, AND completely okay with it. I stay in Reese's arms for what seems like hours after we both climax. He holds me, never asking me to move or shift in any way. I can feel him slowly getting hard again inside me, but he doesn't push for us to do it again. He seems as content as I am, just softly stroking my back as my head nuzzles into his neck. I relish in his scent, the smell of him after sex. He still smells like citrus, but it's mixed with sweat and I know right then that nothing will ever smell this good. Or feel this good. Which I hate myself for thinking. His air is the only air I want to breathe now, and it does me no good to think like this. But I can't help it. I'm officially screwed and I know it.

We spend an hour on the couch together, laughing and talking as he holds me against him. I feel terribly embarrassed for not knowing minor details about the man who brought me the most pleasure I've ever experienced. Like the fact that he is thirty-one years old. He grew up in South Side and graduated from the University of Chicago when he was twenty-six with a Bachelor of Science Degree in Accounting and a Master's in Business Administration. He made partner when he was twenty-eight which sounds like a major feat for someone so young. The man is as smart as he is attractive, and I feel completely relaxed listening to him talk about college and his family. He has a younger sister who lives in Detroit who is married with two kids, and his parents are still married after thirty-eight years and live in Maywood. I tell him about my parents and how they encouraged me to open my bakery. Being an only child, they are immensely proud of me and speak of me like I've invented a cure for cancer and not a fabulous white chocolate truffle recipe. We talk about how close I am with Juls and Joey, and how Juls and Ian are practically living together now. Inseparable and mad for each other. I tell him about my morning runs and how most days I wish I had an iPod to drown out Joey's bitchy rants, but other days I enjoy them.

It is an amazing night, and not just because of the sex. I've never enjoyed just talking with someone the way I do with Reese. I don't want to move at all. I could stay in his arms all night, but I know I shouldn't. No sleepovers. After a few hours, I ask him to drive me home, and the look on his face when we pull up in front of the bakery is priceless. He had no idea I live here. *Of course, he wouldn't know that; you aren't dating, Dylan.* I kiss him briefly goodnight, wanting more than anything to invite him inside to see my place, but I don't. I manage to be strong in this one moment. This is just sex, and if I want to keep doing this with Reese, I need to remember that.

I haven't seen or talked to him since our amazing fuck fest on Tuesday, which is making things easier and harder at the same time. Easier because I'm realizing he sees this for what it is and it's making me keep myself in check. And harder because a part of me doesn't want him to see it this way anymore. I spend all day Wednesday staring at my cell phone, waiting for a text or a call from him, until I stupidly realize he never actually got my number from me. The one time he had called me, he'd called the shop directly.

Thursday, Joey and I are slammed with four consultations, two weddings, an anniversary cake, and a birthday cake request. The wedding consultations both take forever because the brides have decided to include the grooms' inputs and no one can decide on anything. Luckily for me, Joey is great at getting people to compromise, a trait that I love more and more about him with each passing wedding consultation. After I've finished up with my meetings, I spend the rest of the evening in the kitchen throwing together the tarts I'd promised the gentleman on Monday. They're relatively easy to make after I fuck up the first one royally. I end up using strawberries, kiwi, and mangos, and then top the tarts with an apricot jam. After managing to only eat one of them, I pass out in my bed and dream the same recurring Reese sex dreams, which keep getting better. I've stopped fighting it. It is useless really. Besides, the sleep I'm now getting is some of the best I've ever gotten. Especially when I wake up from an orgasm.

☙

STANDING BEHIND THE COUNTER AT eleven thirty a.m. on Friday, I let my mind wander to what Reese is doing at this exact moment. I can picture him strikingly sitting behind his desk, working on some audit or whatever and doing it in a way that only he can make sexy. His hair is a right sexy mess, his green eyes are narrowed in on his task, and his massive erection is waiting for me. The shop door opens and I shake my head to clear it.

"Something or someone on your mind, cupcake? I know that look." Joey strolls in, returning from our favorite little sandwich shop down the street and placing the bag of the best chicken salad sandwiches in Chicago in front of me. My mouth begins to water at the smell and I suddenly realize that all I've eaten the past few days has been predominately sugar. *I'm going to develop diabetes if I don't watch myself.*

"No, nothing on my mind except for this sandwich that I'm about to destroy." The bell on the front door dings and I glance up, my heart thumping hard against my bones at the sight of the delivery man.

Joey hurriedly scurries to my side. "Ooohhh, goody. Today has sucked ass and I need something romantic from my favorite numbers guy." The delivery man smiles and places a small brown envelope onto the counter, handing me a slip to sign on his clipboard.

"*Your* favorite numbers guy? And what about Billy?" I ask, handing the man back his paperwork and staring at him suspiciously when he doesn't exit the shop.

"He's not a numbers guy. He's a lawyer. A hot ass lawyer who is taking me someplace uber fancy tonight."

"Awesome. Did you need something else?" I ask the man who stands patiently waiting.

"I've been instructed to wait until *after* you've read the letter to leave," he states nonchalantly.

"Oh, okay." I turn to Joey who looks at me like he has no idea what is going on either as I open the envelope and pull out a small card. My heart begins hammering in my chest and I automatically reach up and place my free hand over it.

Dylan,

It's come to my attention that the only number I have for you is the bakery number. Now how am I supposed to send you text messages saying I want you to sit on my face? Or I can't stop thinking about the way it felt to be inside you? OR I want to see you sometime this weekend if you're free. Please be free.

X Reese

P.S. If you would like these sorts of messages, please give your number to Fred.

Oh, man. I sigh loudly as Joey snatches the note out of my hand. Finding my notepad under the counter, I bite my cheek to stop from smiling so much as I scribble down my cell number and hand it directly to Fred, the delivery man.

"Thanks, Ms. Dylan. Have a great day," he says, turning quickly and walking out of the shop.

"He wants you to sit on his face? Well, that's it, Billy needs to take lessons from Reese on explicit letter writing." He hands me back the note and I place it back in its small envelope, putting it under the counter where I'm now storing them in a small tin. "You know you're practically swooning over there, right?" he says to me as I pull my hair up into a high messy bun.

"Swooning? Who the fuck says swooning? What are you, ninety?" I pull a few stray pieces out and tuck them behind my ears.

He pulls his sandwich out and hands me mine and we start digging in. "So, what did he mean by 'the way it felt to be inside you'? I mean, you've already had sex with him, so why would he... oh... oh, my God. Did you fuck him without a condom?" He spits bits of chicken salad at me as he shouts hysterically.

"Jesus. Close your mouth. I'd prefer to not be covered in your sandwich." *Crap. I really didn't want Joey to know about this, but I manage to forget how fucking insightful he is sometimes.* I grunt loudly before I answer. "Even though it's none of your business, yes, I did." I make a face and wipe a hunk of mayo off my apron that had managed to hit me in the middle of my shop logo.

Slamming his hand on the counter for dramatic effect, like he needed it, he finally speaks after chewing and swallowing his bite. "That's fucking huge and really fucking serious. *I've* never even done that. Shit, how was it? Good enough to swear off condoms permanently?" He smiles wickedly at me as I nod slowly.

"With him? Yes, absolutely. It was perfect."

"So you two are officially a couple now? Fuck yes. That's what I'm talking about, bitch." He holds his hand up for me to high-five him. I shake my head as I chew up my bite. *Damn it. Thanks for the reminder.*

"No, we're not a couple. We're monogamously casual." I take another bite of my to-die-for sandwich.

"What the fuck does that mean?"

I swallow my bite and stare at my sandwich, avoiding his judging stare. "It means we're not serious, but we're only sleeping with each other. So it's still casual and only about sex." I feel a sharp pain in my chest. "Now that we both have established that we'll only be with each other in that way, we don't have to use condoms. Besides, he was my first and I was his." *And that part right there eases that pain.* I glance up at him and see his unconvinced expression.

"Umm, okay. Honestly, I think you're both delusional if you think it's casual for either one of you. *You* light up when you talk about this guy and *he* writes you love letters. Fuck the casual bullshit." He crumbles up his wrapper and shoots it into the trashcan. "On another note, I think it's really sweet that you were each other's first times without it. I'm sure it meant just as much to him as it meant to you."

I grumble loudly, "Shut up, it's just sex. And he doesn't write me love letters. He sends me flour and panties with tiny notes."

"Yeah, you keep telling yourself that. Want something to drink?" he asks, moving toward the kitchen as my phone beeps in my pocket.

"Please," I reply, pulling it out and seeing an unknown number.

UNKNOWN: *There you are. Now I don't have to worry so much about Fred intercepting my letters to you.*

I smile and type frantically.

ME: *Here I am. And I happen to like your letters so I hope you don't mind the risk of Fred intercepting them.*

REESE: *The risk is worth it, love. Can I see you this weekend?*

ME: *I think I can squeeze you in somewhere. I have a wedding cake to work on tonight, but I'm free tomorrow night.*

Joey returns with two sodas and places one in front of me on the counter.

"Thanks. So, where are you and your hot ass lawyer going tonight?" I force myself to keep my eyes on Joey and not the phone that is in my hand.

He notices the struggle instantly. "Some ritzy Italian joint. And you don't have to hide your enthusiasm about Reese texting you. I'm done trying to convince you it's more than you're both letting on." He takes a sip of his soda and pulls his phone out, pointing to the clock on the wall and smiling wide.

"Sweet. Dance party time," I squeal, setting my phone down on the counter as he docks his phone onto the speaker station and flips to a song.

Every Friday at noon, Joey and I dance and sing along to one song in the shop. It doesn't matter if customers come in and it doesn't matter how busy we are. We always make time for one song on Friday. A few months ago, I had an entire wedding party in here dancing along to "Locked out of Heaven" by Bruno Mars. It was awesome. Justin Timberlake's "Love Stoned" blares through the speakers as I spin around and begin dancing and singing along to the lyrics with Joey.

I'm on a serious roll when he cuts the music and stands, staring at the shop door, the familiar *hot guy in the building* look on his face. Spinning around to see what the fuss is about, I see a very amused face staring at me. Smiling in a suit and tie, the attractive blond steps forward and tilts his head.

"Well, thank Christ I decided to stop in here during my lunch break. Otherwise, I might have missed that hot little show." He steps closer to the counter and presses his hands on the top, causing me to stumble back a bit.

"Sweet Mother. You're like a sexy man-magnet lately," Joey mutters to me softly.

I clear my throat and smile. "Sorry about that. Can I help you?"

"I hope so, Dylan." His eyes drop to my nametag and then flick back to my face. *Good, but didn't have the same effect as my name coming out of Reese's mouth.* He's tall and blond, hair cut short and spiky with chiseled cheekbones and thin lips. "My father came in the other day and requested something. He's not feeling well, so he sent me to come pick it up." He glances down at the display case and then back up at my face. "Do you have any idea what I'm referring to because he wasn't specific?"

I think for a minute before it dawns on me. "Oh, the tarts." I shuffle quickly to the kitchen and bring out the container of treats. "I'm sorry to hear he isn't feeling well."

The man smirks. "Yeah, well, I can't say I share your sympathy. His illness did bring me in here to see you." He smiles wide, showing perfect teeth and winks at me. I shudder a bit.

"Jesus," Joey utters as he steps behind the register. I ignore him and the comment from the man.

"Umm, well, the tarts are three seventy-five apiece. How many would he like?"

"I don't know, three I guess? Can I get your number?"

I freeze midair as I'm reaching into the container to pick out the tarts. *Jesus, Joey was right. I don't think I've ever been this popular with men before.* Quickly shaking off his question, I pull four tarts out of the container and place them into a pastry box as Joey rings him up.

"I'm seeing someone. Here you go, the fourth one's free." I push the box across the counter and meet his eyes. They're the strangest color, a mix between mustard yellow and pale blue. It's a bit unsettling and I quickly glance away.

"Well, that's too bad. If he fucks up and you stop seeing him, give me a call." He smiles and pulls a card out of his pocket, sliding it across the table. I glance down at it briefly before flicking my stare back up to him. There's something about this guy that I find to be a major turn off, but I can't quite put my finger on it. "Thanks for the tarts," he says, turning and exiting the shop as I pick up his card.

"Bryce Roberts. Well, he was disturbingly forward." Spinning around, I toss his card into the trashcan and dust my hands off, brushing the creepiness off my skin.

"Excuse you. Why are you throwing out a hot guy's number? I thought you and Reese weren't serious?" Joey pries as my phone beeps.

I reach excitingly for it and hear his quiet laugh. "I have the *hottest* guy's phone number. I'm set."

REESE: *I'll come to you. 8:00p.m.?*

ME: *Sounds perfect.*

⸙

I WORK ON THE CAKE for the Smith/Cords wedding all night, finally passing out a little after two a.m. It's one of the prettiest cakes I've made yet. The bride has requested edible cherry blossoms along the base of each tier, and I've surprised myself at just how realistic they've turned out. I snap a close-up picture of one before sending it to Reese, since he seems to appreciate my work. His response is nothing short of swoonworthy. Yes, now that word is being thrown around in my vocabulary as well.

Joey texts me early on Saturday and tells me he isn't feeling well, thinking he had some bad food at the restaurant with Billy and is being taken care of in bed all day. I'm sure that means not just in a *bring you chicken soup and popsicles* kind of way. This means I'll be making the cake delivery on my own today. I'm a bit nervous. I haven't done this in years, the last time being when Joey spent a weekend with a very hot Greek guy he met at a club. They fucked and fought while I busted my ass trying to carry a six-tiered cake up a huge flight of stairs. He paid for that one for weeks.

I stare out at Sam through my shop window. The van is pulled up in front of the shop, back door wide open and ready for me to slide the cake inside. It's almost noon and I need to leave now if I am going to make it to the reception hall to drop off the cake in time. Traffic is always a nightmare on Saturdays, and I know it's going to take me longer than I would like to get there. I'm stalling, not really wanting to attempt to carry the cake by myself and possibly have a major mishap. "Damn it, Joey." I grab my phone out of my pocket and scroll to my favorite wedding planner's contact info.

"Hello, sweets," she sings with her chipper *I'm going to keep everybody in this goddamned wedding party calm* voice. I chuckle into the phone.

"Hey. I'm just now leaving to drop the cake off, so I might be a bit late."

"We're running late as it is, so no worries. This fucking bride is driving me insane." She sighs dramatically. "I seriously feel bad for her groom. Pretty sure he's in for a lifetime of annoyance." I hear commotion in the background and can only imagine what Juls is dealing with. She's had some doozy brides.

I sigh in relief. "Thank God. I'm flying solo today since Joey is playing house with Billy. I really hate doing deliveries alone."

I hear her gasp dramatically. "What are you doing? Go find the preacher. He's been MIA for twenty minutes. Sorry, I gotta go, Dyl. This wedding isn't going to start at all without me. Hey, are we still on for a much needed girls' day tomorrow?"

I jump in excitement, almost having completely forgotten about the massages and facials we booked weeks ago after declaring how little we see of each other. "Yes. I'm so ready for the spa and my Juls time. Good luck with your nightmare bride."

"Thanks, I'll need it. Bye, sweets."

I click end and turn around, staring the cake down as it sits on my side table that I do consultations at. "All right, it's just you and me. Don't fucking piss me off and I won't eat you. Got it?"

I prop the front door open and drop down, carefully and oh, so slowly picking up the cake and carrying it out to Sam's back door. Setting it down on the ledge, I ease it inside while holding my breath and saying every prayer I can think of silently. After successfully putting it where I want it, I close my eyes tightly and force the air out of my lungs. *Okay, half the battle's over.* Moving the holder in place that keeps the cakes from sliding all around the back of the van, I secure everything tightly and close the back doors. Spinning around to walk to the driver's side, I'm halted immediately as I run straight into a brick wall of a chest. *Oh, terrific.*

"Jesus Christ, Justin, you scared the shit out of me." I push away from him as he lets out a small annoying laugh.

"Sorry, Dyl pickle."

Ugh. I hate when he calls me that. I haven't been able to eat a dill pickle in two years.

"What do you want? I'm running late and really don't have time to chat." Nor do I want to. I move to step around him when his arm shoots out and grips my waist. "What the hell? What are you doing?"

"Oh, come on, baby. I saw the way you looked at me at the wedding." He pins me against the van, grinding his erection into my hip. I'm struggling against him, but his grip is firm. Really firm. "You still want this. I can tell."

"Are you insane? Get the fuck off me!" I yell, whipping my head from side to side at the dead street around us. Figures, any other time of day people are bustling up and down the sidewalks. "What the hell is wrong with you?"

"I know you prefer married men now. Give it up, baby. It's all good. Sara apparently likes to fuck around behind my back, so I can do the same to her." His breath reeks of alcohol and my shoulders begin to burn where he's squeezing me, pressing my body into the side of my van. He runs his tongue over my ear and I buck against him. "Still sweet."

I continue pushing against his chest, trying to back him off a bit. "You're disgusting. I'm not interested. I'll never be interested again. Fuck, you're hurting me, Justin. Let go!" His fingers are digging into my skin and I want to cry, but I somehow manage to hold it in. I've cried enough over this asshole.

He pulls me toward him and then slams me once more against the van, this time knocking the air out of my lungs and dropping me to my knees. I fall over onto my side, gasping for air as he bends down and leans his face into mine. "Your loss," he whispers and storms away as I finally take in enough air to calm my screaming lungs. I cough and wheeze, clutching at my chest as I struggle to pull myself up onto my feet. *What the fuck? What just happened?* Justin turned psychotic; that's what happened. My entire body is in pain and I want to go back inside and nurse my wounds, but I can't.

"Fucking hell," I whimper as I climb into Sam and start him up. I pull the visor down and quickly try to recover my appearance so I don't look like I just got molested in the street. My hair is a mess, completely unraveled from my bun and my face is streaked with makeup. I wipe under my eyes, removing my mascara, and clean up the rest of my face. Peeling my top down to reveal my shoulder, I wince at the bright red fingertip-sized marks that are highly visible. "Jesus Christ. That fucking prick." I pull my shirt back up and cover them up quickly, resting my head back and taking in several slow deep breaths. *That bastard. I'm going to dismember him the next time I see him.* I shake my head and fix my hair. I can't deal with this right now; I have a job to do and I need to fucking do it. I push the events that just transpired out of my mind and pull away from the curb and to a wedding where, hopefully, the only dick the bride will be sucking will be her husband's.

Chapter
EIGHT

VERYTHING INVOLVING THE CAKE DELIVERY went smoothly. Everything except for what happened before the actual cake delivery. Soaking my sore muscles in my tub, I run through the events that transpired several hours ago in my head. Justin was never aggressive with me when we were together. He never put his hands on me like that before. So I can only chalk up his fucked up behavior to him discovering his wife's wedding indiscretions and dealing with it like a lunatic. I find it rather perfect that he's getting what he deserves, as long as he doesn't deal with it at my expense. One thing is for sure, if he touches me again, he won't have a dick to cheat on his wife with. I'll cut that shit off and make him eat it.

My phone beeps and I sit up in the tub, pulling it off the sink and reading the message.

REESE: *We still on for 8:00p.m., love?*

I sigh heavily and stare at his message. I'm beyond excited to spend the evening with Reese, but I don't want him to see the hideous marks that grace the skin of my shoulders and my upper back now. And spending time with him and not fucking is going to be a challenge. Of course, I could convince him to do clothes *on* fucking like we did at the wedding. That was still insanely hot. I nod at my decision as I type.

ME: *We better be. I'm in the tub right now getting ready for you.*

REESE: *Prove it.*

So many options here. I slump down so the tops of my knees are sexily poking out of the water and press them against each other. I take a quick picture and send it to him.

REESE: *I love those legs. Especially when they're wrapped around my head.*

ME: *I especially love that too. Now stop distracting me. I have an incredibly hot CPA coming over in less than an hour.*

REESE: *Lucky bastard.*

I dress in my favorite pair of skinny jeans, which make my ass look higher and tighter, a tight black T-shirt that has a wickedly plunging neckline, and my black pumps. For casual wear, I have to say I am looking pretty doable. My wavy blonde hair falls smoothly past my shoulders and I stick with minimal makeup tonight, just some tinted moisturizer, mascara, and some lip-gloss. A soft tapping on the glass door downstairs sends me carefully hurrying down the stairs and through the kitchen, stopping in the doorway at the sight of my date in the window. *Shit, not a date. Not a date, Dylan.*

I walk through the dark bakery up to the front door, waving sweetly at him as his smile grows. Reaching up to unlock it, I see his eyes roam down my body, taking in every inch of me before they finally return to my face. I hold my hand on the lock as he studies me.

"Hi, handsome," I say, still not turning the lock to allow him entry. His green eyes are soft and warm and I'm dying to let him in. But I'm going to wait.

"Hi, love. Are you going to open the door or are you expecting someone else? Another incredibly hot CPA maybe?" He places his hands on either side of the door and tilts his head to the side, arching his brow at me. *Oh, how I love playful Reese.*

"No, just you. How well can you see me from out there?" The sight of him in jeans and a fitted gunmetal grey T-shirt, hugging his body perfectly the way I want to, is making me feel scandalous all of a sudden.

"Uh, pretty well." He narrows his eyes at me. "What are you getting at?"

I step back a few feet and stand still. It's dark outside already, but a street lamp that is on the nearest corner is illuminating Reese. His tall frame is the only thing I can see through the glass. I smile widely at him. "If I'm right here, can you see me okay?"

He nods. "Not as well as I'd like to, but yeah. What's up?"

I pull my bottom lip into my mouth as I hold up a finger, indicating for him to wait a moment as I disappear into the kitchen. Carrying out a wooden chair, I sit it down in the middle of the room where I had just been standing and turn my eyes toward him. He's studying me curiously, his eyes indicating he has no idea what's coming. Or who is coming for that matter, because someone will definitely be coming.

"Is the sidewalk busy tonight?" I ask, moving gracefully into the chair and facing him, legs crossing in front of me and my heeled foot drawing circles in the air.

He scratches his head and glances to his left, then to his right before turning back to me. "No, I think I'm the only guy out here waiting for you. You are going to let me in, right?"

And that is the only confirmation I need to get the show started.

"Yes, in a minute." I uncross my legs and spread them, my feet firmly planted on the tiled floor as I lean back against the hard wood. I keep my eyes on him as I slowly trail my hand down the front of me, gliding over my breasts and stopping at the top of my jeans.

"Dylan, what the fuck are you doing?"

Taking both of my hands, I pop the button of my jeans and slide my dominant hand into my panties, letting out a loud moan as I begin moving two fingers against my drenched clit. Reese braces himself against the glass with wide eyes and an open mouth.

"Dylan. Holy fucking shit. Love, let me in." His one hand grips his hair while the other pulls at the door handle repeatedly, the glass shaking slightly.

Tilting my head back, I bring my free hand up to my breast and squeeze, pulling at my erect nipple through my sheer bra and thin shirt. My fingers dip lower, spreading my wetness around and up to my enlarged hot spot as my breathing becomes loud and jagged. He begins pacing outside the window, never letting his eyes leave me or what I am doing.

"Reese, oh, God. I'm pretending it's you touching me." This is absolutely true. I can't touch myself anymore and not imagine it isn't him.

"Fuck. Let me in and I *will* be touching you."

Closing my eyes, I move my fingers in quick circles. I think of the first time he touched me at the wedding, the way his hands slid up my thighs. The way he gripped my hips and pulled me against him, meeting his thrusts with such force that I thought he would break me. His eyes, his lips, the way he filled me completely on Tuesday and the feel of his skin against my skin. How he kept his eyes on me when he was devouring me between my legs. I'm moaning loudly, working myself up, and then I feel it. The pull. The heat. Slow and steady pouring over me and flushing my entire body. I pulse against my hand, coming long and hard all by myself.

"Reese." Bucking against the chair, I hold my fingers still but apply enough pressure to give me what I need. My eyes are closed and my head is thrown back, but through my moans I hear several bouts of pounding on the glass going on and know he's dying out there. I don't know why, he'll definitely be getting his in a minute.

Lifting my head slowly, I push myself out of the chair and calmly button my jeans before I move to stand directly in front of the door. I smile slyly at his appearance. I feel amazing and he looks completely frazzled, hair sticking out all over the place, eyes wide, jaw tightly clenched. I bite my cheek and giggle.

"You're going to kill me. You know this, right?" he says as I slowly slip my fingers into my mouth and suck on them. He runs his hand through his hair while the other one grips the door handle. "Dylan, if you don't let me in right now, I'll be replacing your door tomorrow."

I snicker and pull my fingers out of my mouth, quickly reaching up and unlocking the door as he barges through and pulls me against him. Picking me up and wrapping my legs around his waist, he turns and locks the door behind us with his free hand before he brings his mouth to mine, his other hand holding me up.

"So fucking sexy, love. But don't do that again," he says between kisses, and I pull back, seeing his serious expression.

"You didn't like my show? It was just for you." He carries me over to the counter and sits me down on top of it, settling his body between my thighs. His hands run up my arms, brushing lightly over my shoulders and up my neck as he slowly traces my throat with his fingers.

"I loved your show. But I don't like not being able to get to you. I was dying out there." I smile and press my forehead against his as he trails his fingertips down my neck and over the top of my breasts. "You look beautiful by the way," he says softly before pressing his lips firmly against mine. I open for him, allowing his tongue to dip softly into my mouth. His kisses aren't urgent this time. They're slow and lasting, as if he's savoring this moment with me. Swallowing my moans, his breath comes out in hot spurts and fills me with my favorite minty flavor. I press my chest against his as his hands wrap around my waist and slowly stroke my back, my hands clamped behind his neck. We both break away at the same time, our foreheads reclaiming their spot against each other's and our uneven breathing surrounding us.

"Missed your face," I say, regretting it instantly because he didn't need to know that. *Crap. I have an orgasm and drop my guard like an amateur.*

"Just my face?" he asks playfully. He brushes my hair behind my ear and runs his fingers through the waves.

I shake my head and begin slowly scratching the back of his neck. His eyes close and a tiny sound of pleasure escapes him, making me smile. "I missed your face too," he replies as he reopens his eyes and traces down the sides of my temples, across my cheekbones, and down to my lips where I kiss the tips of his fingers.

His words warm me the way they shouldn't and I know I need to break this moment before I say something I really don't want him to know. I'm not only weak when it comes to sex around this man. He is slowly infiltrating every part of my soul. "Want a tour?" His lips pull up in the corner and he steps back, holding out his hand to help me off the counter. I quickly drop my hand out of his before I become too familiar with the sensation and walk through the doorway that leads to the kitchen. Flipping on the lights, I walk around the large workbench, feeling him watch me from where he stands.

"Okay, so this is where I spend my time whipping up my fabulous creations and trying desperately not to eat them, which I usually fail at miserably." I motion around the room and hear a soft laugh from his direction. "Storage, fridge, freezer, and oh, shit." I spot a vat of icing that I'd made earlier this morning when I was testing out a new recipe. Grabbing the bowl I'd placed on the shelf, I stick my pinky finger into the hot pink frosting and slip it into my mouth.

"Mmm, yummy," I say as I flick my eyes up to Reese who is perched against the wall. His arms are crossed over his chest and he's watching me with concentrated interest, which I'm beginning to notice is a pattern of his. "Oh, I found this recipe for chocolate peppermint frosting and had some extra time this morning to play around with it. Until I realized I *didn't* have extra time, and I stupidly left it out." I lick my lips and his eyes widen. "Wanna taste?"

"Sure," he answers, moving toward the workstation. I hop up on top of it and wait patiently for him to stand in front of me, as his hands rest lightly on my thighs.

I dip my finger into the frosting. "Open," I command, holding my finger in front of his now slightly swollen lips. They curl up into a small smile before he opens his mouth, his tongue wrapping around my finger and pulling every last bit off. *Jesus, he could probably get me ready for sex just by licking an envelope in front of me.*

"Good?"

"Very, especially coming off you."

"I love mint chocolate. I think it's the perfect union of flavors." I dip another finger into the frosting and pop it in my mouth as he licks his lips.

"I think you're the perfect union of flavors," he responds, causing me to grin even wider.

"Want some more?" I go to reach my finger into the bowl when he grabs it, taking the bowl out of my hands, and placing it next to me on the workstation. Dipping his own finger into the bowl, he runs his tongue along his bottom lip as he swipes the hot pink frosting down the side of my neck to my cleavage. I whimper as his tongue licks off the line of frosting he's drawn, paying extra attention to the dollop that is now dripping between my breasts.

"Lift your arms," he whispers, grabbing the hem of my shirt and tugging it over my head after I obey him. His eyes enlarge and flick from my face to my shoulders, his face hardening instantly. *Oh, fuck.*

"What the hell? What happened to you?" His fingers trail the small fingertip-sized bruises that graze over my shoulders and I wince at him. Moving my hair out of the way, he leans around me and I hear a soft grunt as he discovers the bruises on my upper back. *Shit. I meant to keep my clothes on. This conversation could have been easily avoided. Damn him and his ability to cloud my judgment.*

"Why the hell are you covered in bruises?" He moves back in front of me and eases in between my legs again, commanding my attention.

"Uh..." *Do I tell him? What would he do? Would he go after Justin? Is that something your casual sex partner would do or is that strictly a boyfriend move? Did I want him to care?*

"Dylan."

My case of word vomit suddenly rears her ugly head again. "Justin came by when I was loading Sam today to go deliver a wedding cake and he came on to me. He'd been drinking and he wouldn't let go of me even though I was screaming at him, and then he threw me up against Sam." I watch his expression shift right in front of me to anger. His teeth clench tight, causing the muscles in his jaw to quiver and his nostrils flare. I move back a bit. *Damn. Angry Reese is intimidating and sexy as hell.*

"That asshole put his hands on you?"

"Yes, but—"

"And who the fuck is Sam? Did he bring another guy with him?" He slams his hand down on the worktop next to my thigh and I jump. "They're both fucking dead," he says, turning away from me. I grab his shoulders and prevent his escape.

"Don't, just wait a minute." His eyes meet mine and he raises his brows. "Sam is my delivery van. Yes, I named it. It's stupid, I know. And yes, Justin did this, but he's never put his hands on me before. I don't think he would've actually forced himself on me. He was probably just upset that his wife cheated on him." *What the fuck? Now I'm making excuses for that asshole?* I run my fingers down his arms and pull his hands into my lap, squeezing them gently.

"Are you fucking serious?" His voice booms throughout the kitchen. "I don't give a shit if he was drunk, upset, or whatever the fuck. He touched you; he's dead."

"Reese, please, what would you do? You can't hurt him. He could press charges against you. I mean, it's not like it's self-defense or something. Please, just let it go. It really looks worse than it feels." That is a complete lie. It hurts like hell. But I am absolutely terrified Reese will end up getting into trouble over this, and that will hurt a hell of a lot worse than the bruises.

He runs his hands down his face before he reaches out and holds mine, his expression softening. "You should have called me. Why didn't you?" His thumbs stroke my cheeks as he studies me.

I shrug. "I had to go deliver the wedding cake and I was already running late. Besides, I wouldn't want you to do something that could get you into trouble. He isn't worth it." I reach up and hold his hand to my face. "Promise me you won't do anything."

He steps closer to me, bringing our bodies only inches apart and allowing me to wrap my legs around him. "I'm sorry, I can't do that."

"Reese."

"No, love." He kisses me quickly, shutting me up before he continues. "I can't and I won't let anybody hurt you. He'll never touch you again. *That* I can promise you."

I nod slightly. The truth of the matter is, I like that he cares about me enough to want to protect me. And Reese is smart. He won't do anything that could fuck with the career that he's worked so hard for. I shouldn't worry about this.

"Okay, but can we go back to the frosting now?" I ask, seeing his eyes light up at the memory of it.

He nods slowly, the desire sparking back into the green pools that glare at me.

Oh, this is going to be fun.

Chapter
NINE

'M LYING COMPLETELY NAKED ON my workbench, my thighs clamped tightly together in anticipation as Reese continues to remove his clothing. I've never realized until now just how sexy it is to watch a man undress. But I'm quickly realizing that whatever this man does, he does it in a very sexy way. I bite the inside of my cheek as I watch him pull his T-shirt off with one hand, revealing his brilliantly sculpted upper body. I moan softly at the sight of him and catch his attention, seeing his lips curl up in the corner. His boxers come down with his jeans and he steps out of them, grabbing the bowl of frosting that he had placed on a nearby stool before he moves toward me. His free hand grips my thigh, spreading me open, and giving himself room to settle between my legs. I feel the tip of him push against my clit and I whimper.

"Now, where should I begin?" His eyes run down my body and he smiles wickedly.

"You can begin with sticking that big dick in me," I answer, wiggling against him to give me some relief. *Christ Almighty, he feels amazing.*

He chuckles and bends forward. "Somebody's greedy. Did you not get yourself off well enough?" He drops his head and kisses between my breasts. "You should have let me in when I told you. I would have made you come so hard you wouldn't be begging for my cock just yet."

He holds out his hand to lift me so I'm now sitting up, my eyes doing a quick rundown of his body and seeing him notice it.

"Yes, you caught me, I was looking, but I can't help it." I lean back onto my hands and stick my chest out. "Now, get busy."

"Are you always so bossy?" he asks as he dips his finger into the frosting and spreads a generous amount onto each erect nipple. I try to keep still as best I can but am quickly getting worked up. *But let's be honest here, I've been worked up from this man since I fell into his lap.* He looks so focused, so meticulous with his pattern he's drawing on me that it makes me vibrate with silent laughter against his hands. "Stop squirming." He scoops another glob out of the bowl and trails it down the center of my stomach, swirling the pink sugariness onto my clit. I bite my lip to keep from jerking, watching him set the bowl onto the wood next to me and step back, admiring his creation.

"You like?" I ask, my eyes glued to his massive erection, which I am aching to jump on.

His hand strokes his jaw as he studies me. "Fuck, yes." His eyes flick up to mine and I clutch the edge of the workbench with my hands. *Shit, his sex stare could melt me like a candle.* Moving quickly to bridge the space between us, his hand grips my head and crashes my mouth against his. He's rough, swiping into my mouth with his tongue, his breath hot and minty on my face. We're all lips, tongues, and bursts of air as he sucks and bites my lip, the tiny pain of it fueling my desire for him. Breaking away to ease me back onto the wood, his tongue darts out and licks the icing off my left breast.

"Oh, yes." I tangle my hands into his hair as he strokes my nipple with his tongue, pulling it into his mouth and sucking hard before releasing it.

"Mmmm, you taste almost *too* good." His mouth moves to my right breast where he licks it clean before flicking my nipple. He sits up and stares down at me. "Now what?" he asks, and I know the look on my face is one of pure delight. *Am I in control of this?*

"Lick me."

"Be specific, love."

I sit up quickly and wrap my hand around his cock, hearing a sharp gasp from him as he grabs my neck. He shakes his head and removes my hand gently, causing me to frown.

"Not yet." He guides me back down onto my back and I playfully try to reach him as he bats my hands away. "You were telling me to lick you, and I want to know where."

I smirk. "You know exactly where."

He shrugs and slowly begins tracing my belly button, moving the icing around and causing my stomach to clench. "Where, Dylan?" *Good Lord, the man is persistent. I wish I found that to be anything but a major turn on.*

Okay, I can do this. I clamp my eyes shut. "Reese, please lick my pussy until I come in your mouth, and then fuck me until I can't walk." Slowly peeking one eye open, I find a very amused man staring down at me with the biggest grin I've ever seen on his face. I can't help but laugh. "You're a pervert."

"So are you." Dropping in front of me, he latches onto my clit and sucks hard. I groan loudly and arch my back, feeling his hands grip my ankles and plant my feet flat down on the wood. I'm completely open to him and go to drop my feet off the sides when he holds them in place.

"Move and I stop."

I stare down my body and look into his bright green eyes. "Seriously?" I shake my head quickly. *Crap. I feel so exposed like this. He can see everything.*

He keeps his eyes on me as he trails sweet kisses on my inner thighs. "Do you have any idea how beautiful you are, Dylan? Every single part of you. Especially here." His hand brushes between my legs and I whimper. "I want to see you like this." *Well, in that case.* I drop my head back and firmly plant my feet, letting go of my anxiety and opening up to him and his extremely talented mouth.

"Oh, yes." I move my hips against him as he slowly strokes up my length and around my clit, licking off every bit of icing. I want him to pull me into his mouth and suck hard, knowing full well that when he does, I will surely lose my mind. But he doesn't. He keeps up the rhythm of deep caresses, swiping just over or just under my clit and driving me insane. He only dips his tongue into me just enough to make me grip his head with my thighs and then he slowly removes it.

"You're so close, love."

"I know that. Why aren't you letting me come?" My climax is there, right there, and he's toying with it. My body is shaking on the hard wood, the slight chill of it cooling down my heated skin.

"I can feel you pulsing against my tongue. I want you to come, Dylan. I really do." He gives me slow even laps with his tongue, swirling and dipping. Brushing just over my clit, I bring my hips up to make him go where I want him, where I need him, but his hand quickly clamps down on my stomach and presses me to the table.

"Please. I need... please just... little lower. No higher. Please. What the fuck?"

"Are you not enjoying this?" *Lick.* "Because I sure as hell am. In fact," *Lick,* "I think I'll do this for the rest of the night."

Oh, God, he's trying to kill me. Fuck that. If he won't get me off, then I'll fucking do it. Quickly dropping my hand to my sex, I go to rub my two favorite fingers on my spot when he grabs my hand, forcing it back down to the wood and holding it there firmly. Letting out a string of colorful curse words, I finally let myself go limp on the table and give up.

"Why are you doing this?" I whimper as he continues his torment.

His breath warms me between my legs. "Because you wouldn't let me touch you. Do you have any idea how close I was to breaking through your window?" He licks my clit quickly and I pant. "I want to be the only one to give you pleasure, Dylan. Your orgasms belong to me." *Holy shit. I am completely fine with that. Yes. Absolutely.*

"So I can't touch myself anymore?"

"No, you can, but only if I am there to help you. You'll never come as hard as when I do it anyway." Another lick and I shake. "You know that, don't you?"

"Yes," I agree, knowing he is indisputably right. The orgasms I give myself are bland compared to his. Even this anguish he is currently inflicting on me is better somehow. I moan loudly. "Please, you're the only guy who's ever made me come."

He stops, completely frozen between my legs. I feel his hot breath against my skin, but nothing else. *Shit, was that not something he should know? Awesome. No Reese style orgasms for me tonight. Good job, Dylan.*

Brilliant.

"Really?" His question hits me after several long seconds of silence.

I nod and cover my face with my hands. "Really. It's just you." Oh, those words rip through me in a way I don't need them to. I'm going to fuck this up, and it'll be entirely my fault. I open my mouth to say something, anything, when he wraps his lips around my clit and pulls it into his mouth. "Oh, God," I cry out. Sucking hard, then harder, he growls against me and I go off like a missile.

"YES." Mid-orgasm, he stands up, and before I can protest the sudden change of direction, he charges straight into me. "Reese."

"Dylan. Holy fuck, you feel incredible." His words are barely audible over my cries as the first orgasm rips through me and another comes up close behind. His hands mold to my breasts as I grip the edge of the workbench and hold on for dear life.

"Tell me again. Tell me I'm the only man who's ever made you come." He pants as his powerful hips crash against my legs. My eyes are glued to his broad shoulders, which are flexing with each drive.

I release my lip that I've been biting and look up at him. "You're the only man. And you're so fucking good at it." My eyes are locked onto his face, his chest, his neck as it pulses with each thrust. His gaze drops to between my legs and I know he's watching himself enter me over and over, stroking me hard and deep. "So sexy, love. Christ, I'm close." Pulling his bottom lip into his mouth, his hands dig into my hips and pull me against his pelvis. I fall, giving him another orgasm as I arch my back off the workbench and clench around him. He groans loudly and pulses inside me, giving me his release with my name on his lips.

"Holy shit," I pant between quick breaths as he splays his body on top of mine.

"Yeah, holy shit," he says into my neck. I wrap my arms around his back and hold him to me. I've missed this. The feel of his chest against mine, the way my skin warms instantly against his. Having him killing me slowly between my legs with his mouth is worth it if it allows me to be this close to him. At the movement of his head, I glance down to see his eyes turn up to mine.

"Handsome," I say, smiling as if I'd just won the lottery. He winks at me and quickly kisses my breasts before he stands up and glances down at our hot pink covered bodies.

"Love, I think we need a shower." He arches his brow at me and I quickly sit up, nodding frantically. *Shower with Reese? Hell fucking yes.*

"This way." I hop down and grab my clothes off the stool as he retrieves his, trailing behind me as I start up the stairs.

"Ah!" After a quick slap on my backside from him, we make it to the top and I turn around to face him, backing farther into my living space. "This is me," I say, watching him take it in. It doesn't take him long. There isn't much to look at. He peers around the partition and wiggles his brows at me when he spots my bed. *No way, buddy. Not happening.*

"I like it. It's tiny though," he states with a smile as he follows me into my bathroom.

Turning on the shower, I place my clothes on the sink top and catch a glimpse of myself in the mirror. I am flushed and covered in sticky frosting, and I love it. Coming up behind me, he places his clothes next to mine and wraps his arms around my waist, pulling me back against him. Rolling my head back to rest on his chest, our eyes meet and he smiles at me. I will never, not ever, get tired of his smile and the little lines it brings out next to his eyes.

"Are you mad at me for what I did?" he asks, causing me to narrow my stare a bit but cracking when his eyes bulge. The bathroom begins to fill with steam and I turn in his arms, lightly pressing a kiss to his jaw.

"No, however, if you would have kept my orgasm from me, you would be purchasing a new ninety thousand dollar vehicle because I would have keyed the shit out of the one you have."

He chuckles, "Noted. Now, let's get wet."

I grin deviously and open my mouth to say something dirty, *of course*, when he stops me with his finger to my lips.

"Pervert."

৩ৎ

I'VE NEVER SHOWERED WITH A man before, and I must say, I'm pretty sure that's the best way to go. I am completely pampered. He laughs at my fifty thousand shampoo, conditioner, and body wash choices, which are stacked against the wall, and studies several before choosing the ones he says smell like me. He picks the scents I use most often and I beam inside at the idea of him knowing what I smell like. He insists on washing my hair, taking his time and giving me an amazing head massage as he lathers me up. Washing my body, his face hardens as he carefully rubs my shoulders and my back, but gets back to playful when he washes between my legs. *That* he spends a little extra time on. After I rinse clean, he drops his head and freshens up his marks on my breasts as I moan softly against his mouth. He seems just as happy about them being there as I am.

When it's my turn, I skip the loofah and squeeze the body wash directly onto my hand, wanting to feel every inch of him as I wash him. His muscles relax against my touch and I rub his arms the way I did on Tuesday, seeing his eyes close and his head fall forward. The only muscle that doesn't relax, and seems to not be able to at all during our entire shower together, is my favorite muscle of his. I stroke him long and hard, the lather building as he holds onto my waist and buries his face in my hair. He kisses me deeply, almost lovingly when he comes in my hand. The feel of his hot liquid against my skin is exhilarating and I want to fuck him again, but don't. More than that, I want to get out of the shower and nuzzle against his chest, breathing my favorite air. But Reese has other plans. He wants something besides frosting in his stomach.

I perch myself up on the counter and watch as he raids my fridge, his hair wet and fuckably messy. "Where is all your food? The only thing in here is milk, some weird cheese, and jelly." He closes the door and glowers at me. I'm busy pulling my damp hair up into a messy knot on top of my head when his question finally hits me.

"Oh, I eat out a lot. And what weird cheese?" I hop down and stick my head in the fridge, following his finger to the second shelf. I quickly close the door. "That is not cheese. Maybe it was at one point, but now, I'm not sure what it is."

He laughs and pulls his phone out of his pocket, kissing the top of my head. "All right, well, I need to eat something besides you. What do you want? Chinese?"

I shrug. "I don't care. I'm not really hungry."

Pressing the buttons on his phone, I study him as he licks the slit running down his lip and brings his cell up to his ear. I reclaim my spot on the counter as he moves between my legs. This is becoming a regular position for us. My fingers slip under his shirt and I trace the hard lines of his stomach.

"Yeah, I want to place an order for delivery. Dylan's Sweet Tooth on Fayette. Yes, one order of General Tso chicken and one order of shrimp lo mein. Nope that's it." He moves the phone away from his mouth. "What's your last name?"

My jaw drops open. "You don't know the girl's full name who you are currently fucking? That's just awful. I know yours, Carroll." I cross my arms over my chest and push my boobs up, seeing his eyes flick down and linger for a long second.

"Dylan."

I shake my head in disapproval. "It's Sparks," I huff.

He chuckles in amusement. "Wow. That's ridiculously fitting." Before I can ask him what the hell that meant, he looks away from me and pays attention to the call. "All right, thanks." Placing the phone back in his pocket, he kisses me quickly on my nose and I groan in protest.

"Why is Sparks fitting?"

His lip twitches. "Because, you're like this little firecracker." I laugh as he plants a kiss on my forehead, running his hands up and down my arms. "Dinner will be here in twenty. Oh, before I forget, we're having this big meeting with some clients on Tuesday, and I was wondering if you would like to provide some of your treats for it."

I run my fingers through his damp hair, causing it to curl a bit at the ends. "I'd love to. What kind of treats?"

"I don't know. It's at ten a.m. so I guess breakfast treats?" His forehead creases as he looks past me and thinks it over. *Lord, he is adorable.*

I smile and play with his T-shirt, bunching it up in my hands. "Well, I happen to make some mean breakfast treats. How many people am I providing for?"

"Twelve."

I nod. "Okay. I'll make sure to have enough for everyone to have three, that way if they don't get eaten, which is absurd, then you can have the extra."

"Great. I'll pay you in orgasms." *Well, that is way too tempting.* His smirk lingers as I carefully think about his offer, looking up at the ceiling for my answer.

"Eh," I finally reply and he wraps me up, kissing me once and then once more, longer and softer as I melt.

We sit in comfortable silence as we eat our dinner on the floor in my living room. Reese makes sure to point out that I am indeed hungry, watching me with amusement as I tear into both of his orders. And I make sure to point out that he is the one who ate *most* of the frosting. I exhale heavily and lean against the partition, resting my hand on my belly as he sticks the leftovers in my fridge and returns to sit across from me.

"Full?" he asks.

"Very. That was crazy good though. I haven't had Chinese since Joey and I ordered it on Easter weekend and we puked it up in my bathroom after a night of binge drinking." He motions with his hands for me to elaborate. "He got dumped by this guy through a singing telegram."

"Jesus, that's really shitty. I didn't realize those things were still around."

I nod and laugh slightly. "Me either; it was awful. The telegram came to the shop and he sang in front of all these customers. Joey was so embarrassed." I brush the tendril that is tickling my cheek out of my face. "So in typical *you just got dumped and your best friends are going to cheer you up* fashion, Juls and I bought all this alcohol and we played drinking games all night. It was really fun until we all got sick." I shake my head at the memory. "And *that* is why Tequila and I are no longer on speaking terms."

He laughs, resting back on his hands, his long legs stretching in front of him brushing against mine. "I can't imagine you drunk. Do you get even feistier or are you an angry fireball? Because, honestly, I can kind of see both."

I giggle and rub my bare foot against his leg. "Neither actually. I get really loud and start giving people nicknames, and then I usually get emotional which is always fun for everybody." I laugh and he smiles at me. "What about you? Do you get extra flirty or do you start hitting people? Cause I can kind of see both." He moves closer and pulls my foot into his lap, rubbing it and causing me to moan softly.

"I don't get drunk. Well, at least I haven't since I was seventeen. I don't usually have more than a few drinks at a time." He pauses briefly and narrows his eyes at me. "How old are you?" His weird line of questioning causes me to give him a strange look. He notices it and continues, "I just realized I have no idea."

"Jeez, good thing I'm legal." He smirks at me and I shake my head disapprovingly. "I'm twenty-six. So, why don't you get drunk?"

He seems to mull over my answer with a smile. "I don't want to, so I don't. I think drinking specifically for the purposes of getting drunk is bullshit."

"Well, *you* haven't had someone break up with you through a musical number." I pull my foot out of his grasp when he starts tickling it, quickly tucking it under my other knee. I try to stifle my yawn but give in to it, rubbing my eyes with the heels of my hands. I am thoroughly exhausted from all my orgasms, and my full belly is making me sleepy. Reese stands up and holds his hand out to me and I allow him to help me to my feet. This gesture will also never get old.

"I should probably go," he says, running his hands up my arms and holding me at my elbows. I yawn again. *Damn it, I really don't want him to leave, but he can't stay. No fucking way. No sleepovers.* "What are you doing tomorrow?"

I lick my dry lips and place my hands on his chest. "Juls and I are having a girls' day. We're going to the spa to get massages and facials and talk about boys." He smirks at me and I give it right back to him. "I feel like I haven't had her all to myself since she met Ian, which I totally get. She's crazy about him."

His hands grip my hips. "I'm sure the feeling's mutual. He talks about her constantly and I give him all kinds of shit for it." I smile at his admission. *Definitely telling Juls that tomorrow.* After a brief moment, his face scrunches and he runs his hand through his hair quickly, looking a bit unsure of himself. "Uh, when you get massages, is it a girl who does it?"

I roll my eyes. "And you call *me* the pervert?"

"What? Oh, no that's not what I meant. Pervert." He snorts and I shrug. *Yup, that's me.* "I mean, is a guy going to be giving it to you, because I don't think I'm okay with that."

Wait, what? I answer honestly. "Actually, I have no idea. Juls booked them weeks ago. But, why does it matter? It's a massage; it's not sexual."

"It just does. If you want a guy to massage you, I'll give you a massage. I'd prefer it if it was a girl and not for the perverted reasons your mind is thinking."

I step back and stare at him. *Seriously?* "Okay, well, I just don't understand why this bothers you." *If this is just casual, then it shouldn't. Right?*

He throws his hands up and looks exasperated. "You're right. Never mind, it doesn't bother me. I should go." He leans in quickly and kisses me on my temple before turning for the stairs.

"Reese." He looks over at me, stopping on the stairs. My head is full with things I want to say to him. I want to ask him to be honest with me, to tell me exactly why it bothers him to have a man massage me. I want to ask him if this is becoming more for him than how it started out. But I don't. I don't ask him anything. "Goodnight."

He smiles slightly and continues walking away. "Goodnight, love." I watch him disappear down the stairs and hear the door close shut behind him as I'm left to ponder what just happened.

Chapter
TEN

I WAKE UP FEELING JUST as confused as I did before I passed out last night. Plus, on top of that fun emotion, I'm also completely exhausted after the shitty night's sleep I got. His words played on repeat in my mind, seeping into my dreams and leaving me full of questions. Questions I want desperately to have answered by him, but don't have the guts to ask. I don't get it. Why would me having a massage from a man bother him? Massages aren't sexual at all in that setting. I'm sure they could be if Reese was to give me one, and the thought of that gives me chills, but at the spa I'm currently driving to with Juls? No fucking way.

I've had men give me massages before and I enjoy them a bit more than from women because they are stronger and their hands are bigger. I like my muscles to be worked deeply, and not with little dainty woman hands. But never, not ever have I once felt anything during a massage from a man other than pure relaxation. Christ, most of the time I pass out and have to be woken up, drool sticking to my face and looking like a hot mess.

I grunt as I look out the window. I'm tense and anxious and I need to fucking relax.

"You're awfully quiet, sweets. Not looking forward to our day of beauty?" Juls asks after giving me my alone time to contemplate what the hell happened last night. Not that it helped any.

I sigh heavily. "Something strange happened last night with Reese and I'm not really sure what to make of it." I turn my attention to her. "Do you know if my massage is booked with a man or a woman?"

She laughs a bit. "Uh oh. Did someone voice his opinion of not wanting another man touching you?"

"Sort of? I don't know. He said he'd prefer if it was a woman and when I asked him why it mattered so much because it wasn't like I was getting a happy ending out of it, he said it *didn't* matter and then he left." I rest my head back and rack my brain. "I just don't get why he cares if this is just sex between us."

She makes a sound of amusement before answering. "You, my lovely best friend, are an idiot."

"What? Why?" The car slows as she pulls into the parking lot of Tranquility Day Spa and my stomach tightens. *Fuck. Do I really want to go through with this if it's booked with a guy and I can't switch it? Do I even want a massage anymore?*

She pulls into a parking spot, shuts the car off, and turns toward me in her seat. "Dylan, seriously? What if Reese was the one getting a massage and some fucking hot chick was rubbing her hands all over his body and giving him pleasure. Would *you* be okay with that?"

Well, shit, I didn't think about it like that. "No, I definitely wouldn't be okay with that." I cover my face quickly and rub it. "Damn it. I'm such an asshole."

She laughs and pulls my hands down. "No, you're not. You're expecting him to not care about you because what you two are doing is what you keep foolishly referring to as *casual*. But you're very hard not to care about." Her thumb softly strokes my hand and I smile weakly at her. "Even if you guys are just having fun, he's allowed to want to keep you to himself and so are you." *God, I miss these talks with Juls. She always makes perfect sense out of any situation.* She stops lovingly caressing me and slaps my hand, causing me to shriek. "Now buck up and put your girl talk game face on. You are mine today."

ॐ

THE MASSAGE IS, OF COURSE, booked with a man, but I quickly protest and am able to switch to an available woman who had a client cancel on her. I relax immediately after that is taken care of and enjoy my facial first, laughing with Juls as we lie next to each other on a double-wide table and get pampered together. I hadn't realized she has made it so we will be attached at the hip all day, but am instantly grateful. As we are left alone to let our masks dry, I take her silence as my opportunity to spill my juice.

"So, Reese told me last night that Ian talks about you constantly. Just thought you should know." I crack a smile and hear her react next to me, a soft gasp coming from her lips.

"Oh, man, I think I love him, Dylan. Like totally head over heels, I want to spend the rest of my life with him kind of love. Is that crazy? I mean, we've only known each other a few months and I've already picked out my fucking wedding colors."

I let out a hearty laugh and grab her hand, squeezing it tightly. "And what color will I be wearing? If you say something pastel, I'm pushing you off this table."

"Oh, fuck no. You know I've always dreamed of a fall wedding." She grunts in annoyance. "Jesus, why are we even talking about this? It's not like Ian is anywhere close to proposing to me. He hasn't said he loves me, if he even does, which he probably doesn't. And I am not going to be the fool who says it first and stands there like an idiot waiting for his response. No fucking way."

"Maybe he's just waiting for the perfect moment. You said he's romantic as hell. Maybe he wants to make sure you're ready to hear everything he has to say."

The door opens and our two estheticians return as I scrunch my face up and feel the mask crack. Juls sighs. "I don't know, maybe. Whatever, I refuse to say it first, that's all I'm saying."

"Me, too," I respond without any thought at all and hear a loud gasp from my right. *No. No way. I am not in love with Reese. Nope.*

"Oh, my…" she starts, but I squeeze her hand tightly and hear a yelp instead of the rest of her sentence.

I stammer, "That's not what I meant. I didn't… I mean, I don't.

Shit." I turn my head and see her wide eyes, a smile cracking open her face. "You mention a word of this conversation to Joey and I will tell Ian myself that you've picked out the names of your children." She begins to silently giggle and I slowly join her. *Jesus Christ. Note to self, don't go to spa days with Juls anymore because you lose your fucking mind.*

ஒஃ

WE SETTLE IN FOR OUR massages and once again, I completely forget about the state of my upper body after I strip and sprawl out on my stomach, waiting for my masseuse. "The fuck is that?" My best friend screeches as she settles in next to me. I grunt into the open headrest I'm staring at the floor through. *Well, I might as well spill it since her reaction can't be any worse than Reese's.*

I exhale loudly before I explain. "Justin stopped by the shop yesterday, drunk out of his mind, and came on to me. I wasn't very receptive and he didn't handle it well." I can feel her body tense next to me as I keep my head down. *Here it comes.* If you haven't had the pleasure of being introduced to hurricane Juls, consider yourself lucky.

"WHAT THE FUCK, DYLAN! That sorry ass motherfucker will *wish* he was dead when I'm done with him!" Her voice is so loud; I'm certain every person at the spa is getting a taste of this.

"You sound like Reese."

"Fuck that. Reese can have him *after* I get my hands on him first. No guy should ever put his hands on a girl." She pauses and I hear her tense breathing. "He hasn't… Dylan, please tell me he's never done this before."

I push up and rest on my elbows. "Are you serious? He has *never* touched me before, ever. I would have killed him and you know it. Now can we drop this please? I want to relax and you freaking out next to me isn't helping."

"I'm going to cut his balls off and mail them to his mother." Juls scowls at me as the door opens and two older ladies come in. She settles down on her stomach and curses under her breath.

"Oh, my. Honey, those bruises." The one masseuse states and I grunt, resting my head back down.

"Yeah, yeah. Just work my lower back and my legs please," I say flatly and in a way to let everyone in this fucking room know I am done talking about this. Because I am. If Justin ever touches me again, I won't have to worry about Reese getting into trouble for retaliating or Juls ripping his heart out of his chest, because I will end him myself.

☙

"I WANTED TO MAKE A quick stop before we went to lunch. That okay with you?" she asks after pulling onto the highway. My eyes are heavy and I feel completely relaxed after our day together, which is nice considering how stressed out I was when the day started.

"Yeah, I don't care. Hey, have you heard from Joey at all? I know he's spending the weekend with Billy, but when the hell have you ever known him to not call one of us immediately after he gets nailed?"

She laughs, "I think Joey does the nailing, right? Isn't he the man in his relationships or whatever the fuck?"

"I don't know. Do they switch it up?" I glance out my window at the passing cars. "I mean, do they take turns doing the nailing?"

"I don't think so. Wouldn't it be like you switching with Reese or me switching with Ian?" She pulls off the highway and down a familiar street, turning into a large parking lot that overlooks a view of athletic fields and basketball courts. Pulling behind a tree, she puts the car in park and turns to me, smiling wide.

"Yeah, I guess you're right. Umm, what are we doing here exactly?" I gaze out the front window and see the crowds of people in front of us. There is a large playground filled with kids and their parents, a soccer game going on in the middle of the large field, and a group of men playing basketball. My eyes widen and I grip the seat. *Oh, my.*

"I thought we'd stop and enjoy this beautiful day for a second before we stuff our faces. See anything you like?"

I spot him right away, almost instantly. Shirtless in loose fitting black running shorts, Reese dribbles the ball between his legs while Ian guards him, stepping back slightly before gracefully pushing the ball into the air and whooshing it through the net. *Fuck me, he looks edible.* I hear my breathing quicken as my eyes take in his gleaming muscles, drenched in sweat and practically calling out to me. *Touch me, Dylan. You know you want to.*

"Holy hell." I slam my head back and hear her giggle. "I can avoid lunch entirely if you'd like. Who the hell needs food anyway?" My voice is thick and it takes me a minute to swallow the lump in my throat.

"Seriously, what the hell *is* food?" she says through a laugh and I feel my body temperature rise as Reese steals the ball from another guy and goes up to dunk it. "Wanna get a closer look?"

My eyes widen. "I don't know; he's so pretty from right here. I think if I get any closer I might pass out." *That and the fact it will probably take an army to pry me off his body.*

"Yeah, I know what you mean. Christ, look at Ian. If he keeps moving his hips like that, I might come right here next to you." She unbuttons the top of her blouse and sighs heavily. "How's the sex with Reese anyway? Amazing?"

"Amazing doesn't even touch the surface with him." I moan softly as he goes up and blocks another man's shot. "It's like his body is specifically wired to bring me to orgasm, and I mean *every part of his body.*" My eyes go straight to his lips as he bites on his bottom one. "His mouth is insane."

Juls covers her mouth and giggles. "Fuck, I know what you mean. Ian is obsessed with eating me out. He has to do it every time he sees me or it's like he can't function properly. And, Christ Almighty, is he good at it."

I glance over at her. "Who would have thought a bunch of accountants could write a book on oral sex." My eyes flick back to Reese as he dunks the ball again. "Jesus Christ, he's good looking. It really is unfair to the rest of the male population."

"Ooohhh. Send him a text message. That way we can see his face when he reads it. I fucking love that. Seeing a guy's reaction to you when he doesn't know you're looking. So fucking hot."

I smile and pull my phone out of my purse, thinking for a moment before my thumbs begin to move.

ME: *Hi, handsome. Just so you know, I had a wonderful massage from a very strong woman named Betsy today. However, I would like another one from you if you're still offering. Does yours come with an orgasm?*

I press send and watch as Reese, after a moment, turns toward a pile of clothes that are tucked against the chain link fence. Holding up a finger, he jogs over to it and searches around before he lifts out his phone. His chest is rapidly rising and falling and his hair is drenched, sticking out all over the place. I can only see his profile and bite my lip as his turns up slightly.

"Ah. Look at that. So worth it," Juls says and I completely agree.

Dropping his phone on his clothes, he jogs back over to the game with his beautiful grin. My phone beeps and I hold it up for us both to read.

REESE: *Hi, love. I'm glad you enjoyed your girls' day, and yes, the massage from me that you will get very soon definitely comes with an orgasm. Pervert.*

I giggle and turn to see the strangest look on my best friend's face. "What?" I ask, seeing her eyes beginning to water. *Oh, Christ.*

"He calls you love? Ah, hell, Dylan, I don't know who's more romantic." She wipes under her eyes and I feel mine well up. "You better hold on tight to that one, sweets."

"Yeah, tell me about it," I say and blink rapidly, trying to dry mine up.

Juls backs out of the parking space and drives through the lot, slowing down and staring past me through my window. "Hey, isn't that one of the desk girls from their work? She looks really familiar."

My eyes follow hers and I recognize the girl immediately, the hair a dead giveaway. She's sitting on a bench partially obstructed by a tree and staring in the direction of the basketball game. "That's Reese's receptionist. Fucking bitch. She was so rude to me when I went to kill him on Monday, acting all possessive and catty. Why the fuck is *she* here?" Part of me wants to hop out of the car and run straight into his arms, declaring in front of her and whoever else wants to watch, that he is mine. But I don't. Instead, I just glare at her profile.

"I don't know, but she's staring at them like a creep. Redheads freak me the fuck out."

"Me, too. Come on, let's go eat."

Now that I seem to have not completely blown it with Reese, my appetite is back with a vengeance. Although, it is still a bit unsettling seeing his receptionist eye the lot of them up like she wants to eat them. *Maybe she's dating one of the other three guys?* I make a mental note to ask Reese about it next time we see each other, which I decide will not be until Tuesday. I can't see him every day. I'm already struggling with keeping my feelings and emotions out of this thing between us enough as it is.

❧

MONDAY MORNING COMES QUICKER THAN I would have liked. I pass out early on Sunday and sleep soundly, not hearing my phone ring when Joey calls in the middle of the night. Noticing the missed call when my alarm goes off, I dial him quickly, putting it on speaker phone as I get into my running gear.

"I have news, cupcake. I'm on my way though, so meet me out front."

"Okay." I end the call and slip on my sports bra, tank top, and running shorts before popping into my Nikes. Grabbing my phone and my keys, I run downstairs and out the front door, locking up behind me as I begin to stretch.

It's already humid out and my top begins to stick to me in the most uncomfortable way possible. Summers in Chicago can be brutal, and when you start sweating immediately after stepping outside in the early morning hours, you know you're in for a hot one. This is one of the reasons why I don't understand the appeal for a summer wedding, at least not here anyway. Maybe somewhere with no humidity that doesn't turn your hair into a frizz fest after spending hours on making it look nothing less than perfect. I attended an outdoor wedding a few summers ago where I appallingly watched my beautiful three-tiered white chocolate creation melt in front of everyone at the reception. It was awful. Luckily, the bride thought it was hilarious and didn't care one way or the other because she was so deliriously happy to be married to her husband. Juls worked that wedding with me and told me the couple had only been dating nine weeks before he proposed to her, and at the time, I remember thinking there was no way in hell that marriage was going to last. How could anyone know without a doubt that they wanted to be with each other forever after only being together a few months? Juls agreed with me, saying the bride had mentioned how strongly her family was against the marriage, but she didn't care. She told my best friend she didn't want to wait any longer to start her life with him and that when it's right, it's just right. The past three summers on their anniversary, I've gotten a thank you card from the bride for helping make their day so special. And now look at Juls. She's only known Ian a few months and is crazy in love with him. *And look at you, Dylan. No, don't look at me. Nothing to see here.*

My eyes flick toward the pavement as Joey's tall frame comes jogging in my direction. Stopping in front of me and pulling his knee to his chest, he looks giddy beyond his usual giddy self.

"Are you going to make me ask?" I question, stretching my arms over my head.

He smiles and switches legs. "Billy asked me to move in with him."

Whoa. "What? Are you serious? That's crazy. What did you say?"

"Yes. Obviously." He jumps up and down on his feet and motions to me that he is ready to start running.

"Obviously? Joey, do you even really know this guy? He could cut out your organs and sell them on eBay. He could have a weird fetish."

He shakes his head. "I know him as well as you know Reese and you're in love with him."

Fucking Juls. Jesus Christ, I need some new friends. "I *cannot* believe she told you that. I will cut a bitch next time her skinny ass walks into my shop." Realizing Joey has stopped running, I glance back and see his expression. *Motherfucker. He is one sneaky bitch.*

"I fucking *knew* it. You love him, Dylan. Oh, my God, this is fantastic." Running up to me, he grabs my shoulders and pulls me against his already drenched shirt.

"Gross, you're all sweaty. And I am not in love with him. Juls told me she was in love with Ian and I said something about maybe, possibly, doubtfully one day being in love with Reese. That's it. End of discussion."

Stepping back and holding me at arm's length, he studies me for a moment before he speaks. "Okay, whatever. But I think I'm in love, so can we focus on that fucking weirdness for a second?"

We hit our stride and I let Joey tell me all about how he's seen Billy practically every night since they met at the wedding and how he's never felt anything even close to this before, which I knew already. Joey is never shy about his feelings toward his hook ups and always shares more information than I would care to know. He tells me how they were hanging out at Billy's last night, lounging and watching television together when he just came out and asked Joey to move in and without hesitation, Joey said yes. He says he didn't have to think about it; he knows he wants to be with Billy every free second he has and he has never been this happy before with just one person. I'm speechless. I am literally without speech. This is Joey Holt we're talking about here. The man who went through other men like he was going for some kind of record. He once hooked up with three guys in one night at a club and did it without them knowing about each other. His longest running relationship was five minutes. And now, after a little over a week of knowing somebody, he's wifing up? I'm not sure whose wedding I'll be getting fitted for first, Juls' or Joey's.

I call Mrs. Frey that afternoon, confirming the details of her anniversary cake she wants me to create for her since I missed our meeting on Tuesday. She sweetly asks me how I am feeling and tells me how excited she is to be celebrating fifty years of marriage with her husband. Fifty years. I can't even imagine. She's a bit undecided about her cake flavors, knowing only her husband wants a chocolate cake, but not having any other preferences. I smile to myself when I ask her if the two of them like mint chocolate and she squeals into the phone. Suggesting my newly discovered chocolate peppermint frosting and telling her how absolutely decadent it is, she settles on her cake and I reassure her it will be ready for pickup on Friday.

After ending her call, I slip my phone out of my pocket and scroll to the contact info of a certain icing lover.

ME: *Guess what kind of cake I get to make for someone's anniversary? I'll give you a hint. It's a flavor you seem to be quite fond of.*

I walk into the back as Joey helps a customer, and begin pulling out ingredients. I have a good amount of baking to do tonight to prepare for the meeting I'm supplying tomorrow and want to start on it as soon as possible. I decide to make an assortment of muffins, blueberry, poppy seed, and my banana nut ones, some apple turnovers, and a variety of fruit and cheese danishes. The excitement of seeing Reese is almost palpable at this point and I need to stay busy. Placing my mixer on the worktop, my phone beeps and I run over to where I've laid it down on the other side of the table.

REESE: *Could it be a cake with a certain hot pink frosting that I licked off you?*

Mᴇ: *That's the one. I don't think I'll look at that frosting the same again. Or my worktop for that matter.*

Rᴇᴇsᴇ: *Well, I'll definitely never look at my couch the same. How's your day going?*

I giggle and pull the baking flour, sugar, and salt off the shelf.

Mᴇ: *Good. Busy like every Monday. I'm going to be slammed all night making the breakfast treats for tomorrow. How's your day?*

Rᴇᴇsᴇ: *Full of meetings that I'm having trouble focusing on. My mind is elsewhere.*

Mᴇ: *Oh, is that right? And where is that dirty mind of yours right now?*

I grab several mixing bowls and baking sheets and spread them out in front of me as I let my own mind wander elsewhere.

Rᴇᴇsᴇ: *Well, it's imagining you spread out in front of me wearing a dress with nothing underneath it, your legs open and my face buried between them. But earlier, I was fucking you on my desk, against my window, and in my chair. I've had a very unproductive day.*

"Shit." Note to self, never read a dirty text from Reese while opening a bag of flour, which I am now currently covered in. "Nice one, Dylan."

"You all right, cupcake?" Joey yells from up front as I quickly dust myself off.

"Yeah. Reese is also really good at the explicit text messaging. Like *really* good."

"Goddamn it, Billy."

I laugh under my breath at Joey's comment as I sweep up the flour I've just spilled everywhere. Wiping my hands off on my apron, I grab my phone and quickly reply.

Mᴇ: *Well, I think we should be able to make at least one of those things happen tomorrow. That big dick better be ready for me.*

Rᴇᴇsᴇ: *My dick and I can't wait. See you tomorrow, love.*

Chapter
ELEVEN

JOEY AND I LOAD UP Sam on Tuesday at nine thirty a.m. with the breakfast treats, leaving me with just enough time to run back inside to give myself a quick once over before it's time to go. I've picked out a pale pink summer dress and paired it with some strappy sandals, pulling my hair up into a bun before I run downstairs and lock up the shop. Joey is perched against the van and messing with his phone when I finally emerge.

"Okay, how do I look? Professional with a hint of playful? Do you think the dress is too much? Maybe I should wear my apron. Should I wear my apron?" *Christ, why the hell am I nervous? I've supplied tons of business meetings with treats before. Of course, I wasn't banging any of the men I supplied for until now.*

He smiles and slips his phone away. "The only way I would suggest for you to wear your apron would be if you were to *only* wear your apron. You look great, cupcake."

"Thanks. I think Reese likes me in dresses." I walk around to the driver's side and hop in as Joey gets in on his side.

"Hmmm, I wonder why?" He laughs as my phone beeps. I quickly slip it out of my purse.

REESE: *Counting the minutes. (19 to be exact)*

I giggle.

Me: *Oh, come on, Mr. CPA, I'm sure you can do better than that.*

Reese: *1140 seconds. Also, I met you roughly 823,447 seconds ago. Now get your sweet ass here safely so I can kiss you.*

I hear a muffled laugh from my right. "Are we going to be driving to the Walker & Associates building or are they coming to us for the meeting?" Joey asks as I put my phone in the cup holder, grinning like an idiot.

"Smart ass. Does Billy know you can get testy in the morning?"

He laughs as I pull away from the shop. "Oh, he knows, cupcake. He knows. By the way, this Saturday we're having our coming out as an official couple party or whatever the fuck, Billy's idea. Seven p.m. at his place, I mean, our place. Ooohhh, I love the sound of that."

"You're adorable. What should I bring? Booze?" I ask, weaving in and out of traffic.

"Obviously, bitch, and a housewarming gift for yours truly." He sneaks in that last part under his breath and I laugh. I'm giddily excited to go to this particular party, and not just because I get to see Billy and Joey together and the home they will be sharing, which I'm sure is insanely chic. Joey has impeccable taste, and even though I've only seen Billy a few times, the man can dress. But I'm also excited because a certain numbers guy that I'm crushing on will most likely be attending with me. And the thought of that makes me drive a little bit faster toward our destination.

ॐ

I MAKE JOEY CARRY THE bulk of the load as we walk into the foyer, across the marble floor, and to the back of the lobby to the row of elevators. Riding up to the twelfth floor, I shift anxiously on my feet as I hold my two boxes of muffins in my hands, glancing over at the top of Joey's head that sticks up behind his seven boxes. Trying to muffle my giggles, I hear him grunt and make tiny noises of protest as the elevator stops on our floor and I walk behind him, placing my hand on his back.

"If I drop this, cupcake, it'll be your fault. This is once again a perfect reason why we need another fucking employee."

"Stop bitching, we're almost there." I walk down the long hallway, guiding Joey along with me, and stop at Ian's reception desk. The young blonde looks up and smiles warmly.

"Ms. Sparks?" she asks and I nod.

"That's me. Where should we take these?"

Joey turns his body so he can see the girl. "Seriously, where, honey, cause I'm about to drop all of these, and those sexy businessmen can eat them off the floor for all I care."

She laughs a bit. "First door on your right. Go on in. Mr. Thomas and Mr. Carroll are expecting you." I smile at her and walk with Joey to the tall door, opening it with my free hand and allowing him to walk ahead of me.

We step into a large conference room, which has a killer view, tall floor to ceiling windows that overlook the bustling city, and a long rectangular table. A few men, all in nice suits, glance up from their seats as they flip through files while another group of men stand in the corner by the window, conversing together. My eyes find Reese like a homing missile. Standing in a dark gray suit with a two-button jacket and a light and dark gray patterned tie, he stops mid-sentence as his eyes fall on me. I feel it, that familiar pull in my gut that makes me want to drop my boxes and spring up into his arms. The man rocks a suit better than anyone. But instead of acting on impulse, I settle for a smile.

"Hi," I say softly as he moves toward me, his long legs bringing him to me quickly. I hear a laugh coming from the corner and think I recognize it as Ian's, but can't be positive. Right now, the only other person in the room with me is Reese.

"Hi, yourself. Here, let me take that." He grabs my boxes and places them on the table while Joey mutters something under his breath.

"I can't wait to dig into these, Dylan. My girl talks about your creations nonstop and I'm starving," Ian says as he walks up to the table and opens a muffin box.

"Well, I hope you enjoy them. The banana ones are my favorite. Oh, nobody has allergies, right?" I ask and hear a round of muffled "Noes."

"Will someone take these from me already? For Christ's sake, Reese," Joey says and I cover up my mouth quickly to hide my laugh.

Reese takes his gaze off me and grabs several boxes off the top, revealing a very red-faced Joey. "Sorry, man," he apologizes and spreads the boxes out at the end of the table. Joey shakes his head in frustration, placing the remaining boxes on the table in front of the businessmen and opening them.

"Gentlemen, please help yourselves to the treats provided by Dylan's Sweet Tooth. We'll get started in five," Ian announces. Shuffling of papers and footsteps fill the room and I watch as Reese turns away from the table and walks toward me. Joey steps aside and pulls out his phone, smiling at something and giving me the indication that the something he is smiling at is Billy related.

"Handsome," I say softly as Reese stops just in front of me, his hands rubbing softly up my arms.

"Love, you look so pretty. I love you in dresses." My chest constricts as he leans in and plants three gentle kisses on my lips.

"And I love you in suits. I'm about to say fuck your meeting and take you right here on this table in front of everyone."

He laughs and looks at me wickedly. "I wouldn't object. This meeting is going to bore the hell out of me. Maybe I'll make you stay to keep me company."

I play with the buttons on his jacket, pulling him closer to me. "If you think for one second that I could stay in this room with you looking like that and not wrap my lips around you, you're crazy."

His hand grabs my face and he leans into my hair, brushing his lips against my ear. "Pervert. I love that dirty mouth of yours." He glances down briefly at his watch before grabbing my hand. "Come with me."

I look over at Joey who sees me getting pulled toward the door. Before I can speak, he grins and winks at me. "Meet you downstairs, cupcake." I blush instantly as I nod at him.

"Don't you have a meeting to run?" I ask as Reese pulls me down the hallway toward his office. My stomach is doing flips in anticipation of getting him alone.

"The meeting can wait. I need you." My heart squeezes at his words as we walk into his reception area. *Stop interpreting things the way you shouldn't, Dylan.* Scanning the small area as we walk toward his door, I lock onto the redhead behind the desk who glares in my direction, her eyes going to my hand that is in Reese's and her jaw clenching before she looks back up at my face. "Uh, Mr. Carroll, you have that meeting."

"Not now, Heather."

Her face hardens as he pulls me into his office and closes the door behind us, locking it before he presses me against it.

"Fucking hell, I need more than five minutes, Dylan. I don't like rushing with you." His lips find mine and I part for him, stroking my tongue against his as he reaches down and wraps my legs around his waist. I moan into him as his erection digs right where I want it, rubbing me right where I need it. My hands grip his head and hold it to mine as his one hand slips in between us. He undoes his belt, unzipping and unbuttoning his slacks and pulls himself free.

"This is going to be hard and quick, love."

"Please hurry, I need you." My panties are moved to the side and the touch of his finger between my legs makes me gasp. A low grunt escapes his lips as he buries his face into my neck and pushes inside me. He growls loudly, his one fist coming up and banging the door above my head.

"You're so wet. I love how ready you are for me," he says between muffled sounds as he pounds into me. I hold on tightly around his neck, groaning as he strokes inside me with the perfect amount of pressure. I won't last long and I know it. I've been primed for him all morning. My legs tremble around his waist as his hands hold my ass and pull me toward him to meet his thrusts.

"Reese, oh, God." I throw my head back and bite my lip to quiet my sounds. I want everyone to hear us and I don't at the same time. Part of me doesn't care that I am being fucked hard against his door with his secretary just outside, but the other part of me wants it to be just us in this moment. He licks up my neck to my ear and bites down lightly, pulling the tip into his mouth as his one hand comes around me and holds my face. His lunges become harder and I dig my nails into his neck and pull him closer, needing him as close to me as I can get him.

"Dylan."

My name on his lips pushes me to the top. The burning sensation shoots through my body and I lose control willingly. "I'm coming." I strain and arch into him, giving him the angle we both need to get him deeper. He growls and I feel him twitch inside me as I erupt around him at the same time. Warm release fills me and I pull his head back to allow me to watch him. "Look at me."

His eyes fixate on mine, wide and dilated as he stills and exhales sharply. Blinking heavily, he drops his head. "Jesus Christ," he says. His forehead is beaded with sweat and his hair is a right hot mess, which makes me smile. No one can pull off the *I just got fucked* hair like Reese. I am placed down on my feet and have to keep my arms around him to steady myself.

"Wow. You might have to carry me out of here," I say through a laugh. He grins and studies me as he tucks himself away, watching me pull my dress down.

"I could do that." He moves quickly to his desk and grabs a few tissues, dropping down in front of me and wiping between my legs. He discards them in the trashcan and returns in front of me, brushing the strand of hair that fell from my bun away from my face.

I'm certain I look thoroughly fucked, but don't care in the least. This man owns my body and I will let him use it wherever and whenever, and the thought suddenly frightens me. I swallow loudly and back up a bit. "I think your meeting may have started without you." I make sure my dress is covering everything, glancing behind me quickly. His hand stills on the door handle, getting ready to turn it when he looks over at me.

"I want to see you tonight." His voice is low, his eyes hooded as if he's bracing himself for my reaction.

I study him for a second before I respond. "But you just saw me." I want to see him too. I want to see him every second of every day, but I can't. I'm not strong enough for that.

He moves closer to me. "I know. Is there a rule that says I can't see you twice in one day?"

"Shouldn't there be?" My question hangs in the air between us for a moment before he nods in agreement. And then I see it, the shift in his expression that makes my stomach tense. He looks nervous and uneasy. *Is he struggling with this as much as I am? Isn't this what he wants?* I don't ask, but I hate seeing him like this, so I step in closer and slide my arms around his waist, planting a kiss on his jaw as he holds me against him.

"I just… I don't want to get too attached." *Because I'm falling in love with you and it will kill me when you're done with me.*

He clamps his lips together and nods before planting a kiss on my forehead. "I know. Come on, pretty girl. I have a meeting to run." I stand on my toes and plant quick kisses on his lips as he laughs against my mouth. *Serious conversation over, playful Reese back.*

Swinging his office door open, he places his hand on my lower back and ushers me out into the reception area and down the hallway. My eyes briefly fall on little Miss Uppity, her expression cold as usual, but I don't linger. I laugh under my breath and Reese looks down at me. "Something funny?" He stops in front of the conference room door and turns to me.

"Your receptionist is kind of a bitch."

He chuckles. "Ignore her." Pulling me in for a lasting kiss, the door opens, but I don't register it until after he has broken our contact. I wobble. This man can make me weak in the knees if I even cared about *having* knees anymore. The sound of a throat clearing causes us both to look into the room at the table full of men, Ian standing at the door and wearing his biggest smile. "Caught ya. Come on, man, we need to get started." I feel my face flush as Reese straightens his tie quickly and grabs the back of my head, pulling me into him for a quick kiss in my hair.

"Bye, love," he whispers.

"Bye, handsome. Go crunch some numbers or audit something or whatever the fuck it is you do." He shakes against me with laughter and pulls back, winking before he walks into the room. My eyes quickly scan the table for my empty bakery boxes when I stop on a familiar smirk that is plastered on the face of the man who had picked up the tarts for his father last week. His eyes rake over my body, slow and sleazy like, and I suddenly feel dirty as Ian clears his throat, earning my attention.

"Bye, Dylan," he says and I wave awkwardly, turning on my heels and hearing the sound of the doors close behind me.

What the fuck is that guy doing here? And why the hell did he stare at me like that? I ride the elevators down and march purposely through the lobby as my mind races. I find Joey outside in the van talking on his phone as I hop in the driver's seat and start it up.

"Okay, baby. I love you, too. Bye." He ends his call and lays his head back dramatically onto the seat. "I'm in deep, cupcake."

"I can tell," I reply playfully. "You are *not* going to believe who I just saw sitting in the meeting." After waiting a minute for effect, Joey motions with his hands for me to hurry the fuck up with my information as I drive down the street. "That guy who gave me his card the other day in the shop. The cocky one who picked up the tarts."

I hear his sharp breath intake. "Are you serious? What the hell was he doing there? Does he work there? Holy shit, are him and Reese co-workers?"

These are the same questions that are running through my mind. "I don't know; I didn't get to ask. I really hope not though. Asshole stared at me like he wanted to eat me." I feel a chill run through me at the memory of it.

"That's probably because he does. He wasn't shy about wanting you last week, and I'm sure seeing you again with Reese's dick in your mouth didn't help."

I scowl at him. "Christ Almighty, Joey, he just saw me kiss him." *In fact, everyone saw me kiss him.* "Okay, so you're kind of an expert at the whole casual sex stuff, right? Have you ever seen a guy who you are just fucking more than once in the same day? I mean, do you space out the times you spend together or do you just say fuck it and see him whenever you both feel like it?"

Joey chuckles before he answers. "Honestly, when I've done the *just sex* stuff before, we saw each other often because we wanted to fuck often. I think as long as you both can keep yourselves from getting too wrapped up in it, there shouldn't be that many rules." He slips his phone out of his pocket and begins messing with it, ending our discussion.

I contemplate Joey's explanation to me as we drive to the shop. There shouldn't be too many rules? I feel like rules are extremely necessary, at least for me to be able to do this successfully. There are certain things that just can't happen between Reese and me. Like sleepovers and meeting each other's families and doing anything too romantic or intimate. Keeping myself from getting too wrapped up in him is the biggest struggle of my life, but immensely worth it. I want to do this with him more than anything because I love being with him. The alternative, ending this because it's too hard for me, sends a pain through my body at the very idea of it. If anyone is going to fuck this up between us, it's going to be me. He isn't going to interpret things the way they aren't meant to be interpreted, and he isn't going to get too attached, so neither should I. He's used to not doing serious, and even though I'm not, I can keep up. I'm determined to make this work and I will. I just need to stop acting like a stupid girl about it.

I close up the shop on Tuesday night at six p.m., saying goodnight to Joey after he helps me put any uneaten goodies away. My mind has been on Reese all afternoon, and I'm aching to be with him, and not just for sex. I want to talk to him and play with him. I just want to see him. And he wants to see me. I had originally planned on spending my night watching television or taking a long bath, but neither one of those options sound appealing anymore. I stop fighting it and quickly make up my mind. Slipping off my apron and grabbing my purse and keys, I lock up the shop behind me and stroll toward Sam.

Driving to Reese's building is an easy route from the bakery. He lives in Printer's Row, which is just south of downtown Chicago, a mere five minutes away. I'm very familiar with the area, having catered to several businesses in the trendy upscale neighborhood. I like this part of the city, and tell myself I really should come down here more often as I park Sam down the street a bit and lock him up, beginning the short walk to the front of the condos.

I practically sprint off the elevator and down the hallway, stopping sharply in front of Reese's door and looking down at my flustered state. You would think by the way my skin is tingling that it has been days since I last saw him. Slipping my phone out of my pocket, I smile and quickly type a message.

ME: *I really want to see you tonight. Is there any way you could stop whatever it is you're doing and come to my place?*

I wait patiently and then a thought hits me that makes me feel like a complete jerk off. *What if he isn't home? What if he's at his office or out somewhere and is going to leave to go to the bakery and I'm not there? Shit.* But just as my blood pressure starts elevating to a crazy height, his door swings open and I smile at the sight of him typing on his phone with one hand, his keys in the other. My phone beeps and he quickly glances up, his lips parting and a sharp breath escaping at the sight of me. I'm still in my pink dress from earlier, but now my hair is down and it frames my face in soft waves. As his eyes take me in, it hits me. Reese had stopped whatever it was that he was doing to come to me, and I know I would have done the same if he had asked. And I am done trying to convince myself otherwise.

Chapter
TWELVE

"DYLAN, HI. I DIDN'T... I thought—"

I lift up my hand to stop him. "Hold on, I just got a text from this crazy hot guy. It might be important." He leans against the door and beams at me as I swipe across my screen and fail miserably at holding back my ridiculous smile.

REESE: *I'll always stop whatever it is I'm doing to come to you.*

Oh, man. I tilt my head and step toward him, kissing him briefly on the lips before I turn away from him. "Got my fix. See ya," I say and yelp as his hands grip me around my waist and lift me up, pulling me back against him as he carries me through his doorway. "Put me down, you barbarian." I laugh and he shifts me so I am now hanging over his shoulder, my face in his perfect ass. I smack it loudly and feel his hand pinch mine as he walks me through his condo, which I am now getting my first real look at; of course, it's all upside down at the moment. Stopping finally, he slides me down his body and places my feet on the floor.

"You're here," he states as I give him a quick once over. He's wearing sweatpants and a T-shirt and looks entirely too snuggly. I reach up and run my fingers through his hair as he smiles down at me, the little lines popping out next to his eyes.

"I am, and, thank God, so are you. I panicked that maybe you were out on a hot date or something."

He looks at me curiously and runs his fingers along my jaw. "No hot date tonight, I'm afraid. And what exactly are *you* doing here? I thought we shouldn't see each other more than once in the same day?"

I shrug and step back from him, glancing around the massive living area that we are standing in. This has to be the nicest condo I've ever been in. "I was feeling rebellious. What were you doing before I got here?" My eyes fall on the couch that I am very fond of as his hands wrap around my waist, pulling me back against him.

"Watching TV on my favorite couch." He reaches around and plants a kiss on my ear. "Would you like to join me?"

"I thought maybe we'd play a game. Do you have any cards?"

He releases me and disappears down the hallway and into a room while I turn and sit on the armrest of the couch. Re-emerging moments later, he tosses me the deck and I stand up and walk to his round dining table, pulling out a chair and sitting in it. He sits across from me and I blow him a kiss.

"Handsome." I pull the cards out and begin shuffling them.

"Love, what game are we playing?" He leans back in his chair, his shirt tightening across his broad chest. *Who the hell looks this good in sweats?*

I think for a moment before I reply. "I actually don't think it has a name, so I'll just explain it to you." I stand up and walk around the table, pulling my chair so that it is now next to his, and sit down. He turns his body toward me and begins lightly running his fingertips over my bare knee. I place the stacked deck face down on the table in front of us.

"So, we take turns drawing cards, each suit representing something different. Hearts are kissing, diamonds are oral, clubs are stimulation using your hands, and spades are massages." His eyebrows raise and he licks his grinning lips. "The numbers on the cards represent how many seconds you get to do that activity, for example." I pull the top card and turn it in my hand, showing the five of hearts. Leaning in, I press my mouth against his and swipe my tongue across his lips as he moves with me. I savor his minty taste for five, well worth it, seconds and then break away, placing my card down on the table. "Oh, and I've kept the jokers in. You pick one of those and you get to fuck me."

He rubs his hands together eagerly. "No time limit on the fucking?" Dropping his hand on top of the deck, he waits anxiously for my response with a raised brow.

"No, but I would like to play a little before we get completely lost in each other, so I'm hoping neither one of us draws one for at least a couple turns."

He looks like he is about to respond, but quickly shakes his head as he picks up a card. I dance in my seat as he shows it to me. "Diamonds are what again?"

"Oral." I lean back in my chair and spread my legs as he amusingly kneels down in front of me. He looks just as enthusiastic about this as I am.

"Count it out," he says, slipping off my panties and tucking them into his pants pocket.

"I will be getting those back before I leave," I state, praying he'll actually refuse me.

"Good luck with that." Burying his head between my legs, I wait to start the count until I feel the first lick.

"Oh, wow. One, two, threeeee." He sits up and licks his lips as I reach the end of my count. "Stupid. I should have removed all cards with numerical values less than ten."

"You should have. Three seconds between your legs is not nearly enough time for me."

Picking my card, I stand up and walk behind him as I drop it into his lap. "Count please," I say as I begin massaging his upper back and shoulders.

"Mmmm. One, two, three, four, five…" His numbers trail off as I rub down his arms, digging into his muscles and offering the perfect amount of pressure. I will never get tired of touching him. He's extremely responsive to every little movement of my hands. I move around front and take my seat, pulling his hands into mine and kneading his palms with my thumbs. "Ten." Slowly opening his eyes, he looks at me, completely relaxed and borderline sleepy. "I love it when you do that."

I kiss each palm before I drop them. "I know you do, and I love doing it. You look so freaking cute when you're relaxed like that."

He picks his card and quickly sticks it back into the middle of the deck.

"Hey. What was that?" I ask through a laugh, trying to grab the deck as he brushes my hands away.

"Something I'm not ready for yet. Back off, Sparks." Drawing another card, he flicks it at me and it lands on my dress face up. "Hands?"

I nod through a closed lipped grin. Reaching out and pulling me into his lap in one quick motion, my back against his chest, his fingers run up the inside of my thigh and between my legs. "Reese." I let my head roll back against his.

"Count, love." He slips two fingers inside me and begins rubbing my spot with his thumb in his perfect rhythm.

I swallow loudly. "One, two, Jesus Christ, three, six, Reese." He laughs into my ear and slowly pulls out as I groan in protest. "I fucking hate this game. We should have just played strip poker." I cross my arms over my chest after reclaiming my seat.

He quickly sucks on his fingers before he picks another card and hands it to me. "I like it."

I snatch the card away from him and glance at it quickly, smiling at myself. "Not for long. You're about to hate this game as much as I do, Carroll." Turning the card in my hand, I reveal the four of diamonds. "Pull it out; I don't have all night."

His eyes widen as he reaches into his pants and pulls out his cock, holding it at the base. He's impossibly hard already as I kneel between his legs. Leaning in and planting a kiss on the head, I hear his breathing quicken at the anticipation.

"Count please," I say before taking him in as far as I can. I moan against his skin and feel the muscles of his lower body tense.

"FUCK, one, two, Dylan, oh, God, please don't stop at—"

"Four," I say as I give one last kiss to the head and sit back into my chair.

"Fuck this game," he grunts and pulls me onto my feet, turning me around so I'm facing the table, his chest to my back. "I want this dress off."

Reaching down with shaking hands, I grab the bottom of my dress and pull it over my head in one quick motion, leaving me standing completely naked. His hands reach around and cup my bare breasts, pulling at my nipples as I arch into his grip.

"I need you."

"God, Dylan. Do you have any fucking clue what you're doing to me?" His voice is strained and his breath is hot against my hair. One hand leaves my breast and grips my hip. I feel him between my legs, positioning himself at my entrance. I'm completely soaked and ready for him, but he doesn't enter me. Placing my palms flat on the table, I lean forward and feel his mouth on my back, his tongue and lips caressing the skin on my spine. My elbows are shaking and I can barely hold myself still.

"Reese, please." I need him in me, and wiggle against him, feeling his hitched breath against my back. His hand that is holding my breast runs down my taut stomach and rests between my legs.

"You're all I think about," he whispers so softly that I barely hear it over my panting. But I definitely hear it. His thumb begins moving against my clit as he rubs against my entrance with his erection. "Dylan."

"You're all I think about, too." I drop my head down, somehow feeling even more exposed than just being naked in front of him. His hand grips the back of my neck and rolls me forward, giving him the angle he needs to push into me. We cry out together at that first drive, and he starts moving, harder and harder, faster against me with such force I think I might snap in half. Both hands move to my hips and pull me against him, allowing himself deeper entry and hitting every nerve in my body.

"Reese. OH, GOD." I shake against him, pushing against his every thrust. One arm wraps around my waist and pulls me back to him. He's still wearing his shirt and it slides against my skin, rising up with each movement so more and more of his bare chest is felt against my back. His tight muscles flex against me, the arm holding my waist contracting against my stomach. I reach above me and wrap my one hand around his neck, the other gripping tightly onto the arm around my waist. He's so powerful, every part of him, and not just the way he moves during sex. He's in complete control of every part of me and everything we do together. Fuck feminism. I need Reese more than I need my next breath. His words ring out around me, telling me how good I feel, how nothing has ever felt like this, how he can't get enough of me. Everything he says gets me closer.

"Come for me, love."

"Oh, God, YES." My core ignites and strikes every nerve inside of me as we release together, his name on my lips as I fall forward and sprawl out naked onto his table. He stays in me, his head resting on the middle of my back as his breath warms my already heated skin. We remain just like this for minutes, neither one of us pulling or pushing away from the other. The only sounds filling the condo is our breathing. I finally begin to wiggle against him and he kisses me quickly on my back before pulling out, allowing me to stand and stretch my muscles.

"I was getting the worst cramp. Would have been totally worth it though just for the record," I say as he picks my dress up off the floor and smiles down at me. Studying it quickly in the most adorable Reese way, he holds it over my head and allows me to slip back into it, kissing me quickly on my lips as my head pops through the top.

"Stay here," he orders before turning and walking down the hallway and through a doorway. He walks back out and steps into another room, but now with something in his hand. The sound of running water peaks my curiosity and I'm about to follow him when he re-emerges, carrying a wash cloth in one hand and something else folded up in the other. Dropping to his knees in front of me, I yelp at the chilled cotton as he wipes between my legs, cleaning off what he gave me. "Here, step in." I glance down as he holds open a pair of his boxers.

"Well, this could have been avoided if someone didn't have a panty fetish." He shimmies the cotton blend up my thighs and winks at me. Gripping the waist band, I roll them until they become very short and look like tiny boy briefs. *Mmm, please let me keep these.*

"Yes, but if I wouldn't have taken them, I wouldn't be standing here looking at your hot little ass in my boxers." He reaches around and smacks me. "Hungry?" he asks just as my stomach growls.

I embarrassingly push against it and he smirks. "Yeah, well, I didn't put much thought into dinner since I rushed over here; so technically, it's your fault I didn't eat." I walk over to the couch and plop down sideways so my bare feet are resting on the cold leather.

"Oh, is that right?" he says as I hear movement in the kitchen. I decide not to look and let him surprise me as I grab the TV remote and begin flipping through the channels. I stop on a cooking show and watch with interest as the host begins flattening out pastry dough. "Do you like spaghetti?"

"Yes, I love it. Are you actually going to cook me dinner?" I rest the side of my head on the leather and play with the hem of my dress.

"I'm going to heat it up. Oh, by the way, the guys at the meeting today loved your treats." The microwave dings and I smile. "Those apple things were insane. I ate like four of them."

I radiate from where I sit, and then the thought of the meeting brings back the smirk I'd received before I left. "Hey, there was this guy in your meeting today who came into my shop last week." I close my eyes and try to picture his business card. "Umm, weird first name. Cocky. Thinks he's way hotter than he is."

Reese rounds the couch with two bowls and hands me one before he sits down next to my feet. "Bryce?"

I nod as I take in a mouthful of spaghetti, moaning softly around my fork.

"What about him? 'Thinks he's hotter than he is,' that's funny."

I roll my eyes and chew up my bite. "This is really good. Did you make this?" He smiles and nods as he takes a massive forkful. "Anyway, he doesn't work with you, does he? I mean, if I were to come and see you at work, would he be there?"

He chews up his bite and shakes his head. "No. He's an investor, and I have to deal with his stupid ass occasionally, but he doesn't work in my building. Why, did he do something? If he fucking touched you, Dylan—"

Slurping in my noodles, I hold up my hand to stop him. "No, he didn't touch me. Jesus, Hulk, relax." I earn myself a stern look and quickly swallow my bite. "He just came into the shop last week and asked me for my number, which I didn't give him, and I didn't like how he looked at me today."

His eyes narrow and his fork stills in his bowl. "Did he look at you the way *I* look at you?"

I swallow my bite. "No. You don't make me feel like I'm being mentally taken advantage of. But he doesn't work with you, so don't worry about it."

His eyes quickly flick to mine. "If he comes into your shop again, I want to know about it."

My eyes widen. *Oh, for fuck's sake.* "Don't you think that's a little extreme?" I place my bowl into my lap. *Is he seriously going to injure every man who looks at me twice? Is he always this possessive with his flings?*

"No." He puts his bowl back down. Turning his body toward me, he pulls my feet into his lap, and his green stare burns into mine. "I have a huge fucking problem with guys putting their hands on you or making you feel uncomfortable. Don't ask me not to react to that."

I lean forward and grab his bowl, seeing one side of his mouth curve up as I get a fork full and hold it out to him.

"You're not going to fight me on this?" he asks suspiciously before taking the bite off the fork.

"No, I get it. I would slap a bitch if she put her hands on you or made you uncomfortable." His mouthful muffles his laugh as he grabs his bowl from me. "But just so you know, I can handle assholes like Bryce. I just didn't want to have to run into him when I come see you at work. *If* I come see you at work." I grab my bowl and pull another bite into my mouth, wiggling my feet in his lap.

"If? No, I don't think so. I like *when* better."

"You only say that because both times I've been there, you've gotten off. It must be nice to have orgasms during your work hours." I move my foot and rub it against him, feeling him twitch under me.

He arches his brow. "You know damn well that if I could escape my office to make you come behind that bakery counter of yours, I'd do it. And I don't just like you coming to my work to blow me or get fucked against my door." I loudly slurp a noodle into my mouth, making him laugh. My ringtone sounds through the condo and I hop up, grabbing it off the kitchen table and exhaling noisily at the name on the screen. *Oh, great.*

"Hey, Mom." I plop back down on the couch and squeeze the top of my nose. I have an awful feeling that I'm going to regret answering this call right now.

"Sweetheart. How are you? I've been meaning to talk to you since the wedding, but your father—"

"Her father what, Helen? Her father what?" *Oh, Lord, help me.* My parents are notorious for both staying on the line during our conversations. "You know damn well what, Bill. Anyways, dear, are you home because we're only five minutes away."

"Mom, I'm fine. The wedding was fine, but no, I'm not home right now." It has been a few weeks since I've seen my parents, and I do want to catch up with them, but now is not the time. Not while I sit next to Reese.

"Just fine?" he asks beside me, earning himself a right shove. "I'm sure when you were screaming my name it was more than just fine in that moment."

"I'm going to murder you," I mumble through clenched teeth as he eyes me up with his wicked grin. I can feel my heart beating rapidly and curse myself for not letting this shit go straight to voicemail.

"Well, where are you? We're in the neighborhood and want to see our only child. Are you at Juls' house? We know where that is," Mom says and I hear the sound of traffic through the phone.

"No, Mom, I'm not at Juls' house. I'm at…" My eyes flick to Reese who is anxiously waiting for my explanation, devouring his spaghetti with a playful grin.

"Would you like *me* to tell your mother where you are?" he asks, reaching for the phone.

I quickly turn away from him and get out of his reach. *Well, this is just perfect.* "I'm at a guy's house. Can I call you later?"

"A guy? What guy? Oh, honey, did you meet someone? What's his name? Can we meet him? Is it serious? What does he do, Dyl? Oh, I'm so glad you found a new boyfriend."

"He's not a democrat is he?" my dad adds. I want to crawl into a hole and die. My mother has been trying to marry me off since I was nineteen. She wants grandbabies and she wanted them yesterday.

"Oh, my God, can I please call you back?" Before I can comprehend what's happening, Reese grabs the phone out of my hand and stands up, placing it to his ear. *Oh, God, no.* My eyes widen and my jaw hits the couch as I slowly watch my world implode.

"Mrs. Sparks? This is Reese Carroll, your daughter's boyfriend." I run at him and knock him off his feet, sprawling him out on his back as he holds me at arm's length. *Does the man have a death wish?* He seems completely unaffected by my move and just gives me a sly grin. "Oh, and, Mr. Sparks. It's so nice to talk to you both."

"Give me the phone, Reese." I grunt and try to move around the arm that is holding me away from him. *Jesus Christ. Why does every male in my life think it's okay to take the phone away from me?* "Give it." My efforts are useless, only making me out of breath while he beams up at me like the gorgeous god that he is.

"Yes, she is very special, isn't she?"

"You are never getting laid again."

"That sounds wonderful." He laughs into the phone. I glare at him and he winks at me. *Jerk.* "I'll tell Dylan to set it up. I look forward to meeting you, too. Okay, here she is." He smiles in his minor victory over me and holds out the phone. "Here you go, love."

Snatching it away from him with one hand, I give him the finger with the other, as I stand up and begin to pace. He stays on the floor, tucking his hands behind his head and follows me with his eyes.

"Hello?" I ask and brace myself for my mother's rant. I sit down on the arm of the couch and rub my temple with my free hand.

"Oh, my. He sounds lovely, sweetheart. And so polite."

I shake my head. "Well, I wouldn't get too attached if I were you. I'm plotting his slow death as we speak." Reese stands up and moves toward me, brushing his hand over my chest before he walks down the hallway. I shudder at the contact.

"Oh, hush. Anyways, darling, since you're busy with your *boyfriend* we'll have to see you another time. Love you lots."

"Love you, sweetheart," Dad says.

"Bye, love you, too." I press end and slip my feet back into my sandals, walking myself over to the table to retrieve my keys. *Great. My parents think Reese is my boyfriend. They'll want to meet him now. Just fucking great.* My head is spinning and it's officially time to go home before he decides to go through *all* my contacts and explain our situation to each and every one of them.

"Please tell me I didn't piss you off to the point of you leaving?"

His voice washes over me as I turn and see him walking slowly toward me. His sweats hang loosely on his hips and the tiniest amount of skin is now on display under his T-shirt. *Damn him and his body.*

"Why the hell would you tell my parents you're my boyfriend? Are you insane? Do you have any idea the amount of phone calls I'm probably going to get now? Since Justin, I've been able to limit my mother to once a week check-ins. But *now,* she'll never leave me alone."

Stopping in front of me, he pushes my hair back and grips my head between his hands. My face is stuck in scrunched up hate Reese mode, but it is quickly fading due to his softness, and his hotness, and his overall Reeseness. *Stay strong, Dylan.*

"What should I have said? That I'm casually fucking their daughter and not in a relationship with her? That sounds terrible."

"I don't understand why you had to say anything, but fine. Every time she calls me, I'm just going to give her your number and *you* can deal with her." Crossing my arms over my chest, I stare him down as he backs up and shrugs.

"That's fine with me. I can dig for some Dylan dirt." *How is he completely calm and collected over this? Why the hell would he want my parents to think I'm seeing him in that sort of way?*

Flipping my keys in my finger, I turn toward the door. "Everyone has gone crazy. It's decided. I'm the only sane person left in Chicago."

His footsteps follow behind me and I feel his hand grab a hold of mine. "Hold on, I'll walk you out." He turns toward the pair of tennis shoes that are by the couch and slips them on quickly.

Stopping in front of Sam, I glance over at Reese who is staring peculiarly at my vehicle, no doubt hurting my precious Sam's feelings in the process. *Good Lord, we can't all drive Range Rovers.* "Why the hell did you drive your delivery van over here?" His finger traces the cupcake design on the side as he studies it in his usual Reese way.

"Um, because it's my only car." I open the driver's side door and hop in as he moves to stand by me.

"You don't own a regular vehicle?"

I shake my head. "No, Mr. Money bags. I used to drive an old Corolla, but it broke down and I never really had the money to get a new

car, so I just take Sam everywhere. It pisses Joey off, but I don't mind."
Reese runs his hand through his hair and I sigh. "Don't you dare hate
on Sam. He's been the only man in my life that has never let me down
besides my father."

He squints at me and leans in, brushing his lips against mine. "And
me, I hope."

"Humph. The jury's still out on you, handsome." I feel him pull
back to allow me to leave when I grip his T-shirt and pull him close to
me again, nuzzling my head into my favorite spot on his neck. "Just
give me a minute." I hear a tiny laugh as his hand comes up to hold me
against his body. Even though I'm a little irritated and a lot confused,
everything seems to melt away when I'm close to him like this. I inhale
deeply, allowing his smell to run through me and, hopefully, rub off
enough to take some of him home.

"You can stay with me and do this all night if you want," he says
softly. I close my eyes and shake my head against him. "Fine, but just so
you know, I'm not a fan of this bullshit 'no sleepover' rule."

I pull away from him and rest my forehead against his, seeing his
serious expression. "I should go," I whisper and he grabs my face and
plants kisses all over it as I try to contain my euphoria. Playful Reese is
hard to let go of, but I somehow manage. Closing my door, he walks
to the curb and watches me as I pull away, his incredible build slowly
getting smaller in my rear view.

My mind is racing as I drive home. So many things happened tonight
that I wasn't anticipating and don't quite know how the hell to react to.
Between him dropping everything to come to me, telling me I'm all he
thinks about, and declaring himself my boyfriend, I feel completely unprepared for what to expect out of him next. Fuck my rules. Reese has his
own set that he is playing by and I'm completely oblivious to all of them.

Chapter
THIRTEEN

IT POURS DOWN RAIN ALL day on Wednesday, preventing our usual steady flow of walk-in customers from making the trek down Fayette Street. I stay busy in the kitchen all day, which I tend to do most rainy days, while Joey rifles through my planner to make sure we're prepared for all upcoming orders. I have one wedding this weekend and the Frey's anniversary cake to make, which I've decided to get started on after lunch on Thursday. In between mixing the ingredients, I scroll over the last several text messages between Reese and myself that had transpired yesterday. He really is an expert at the flirty text messages thing. I've just managed to slip the cake into my double oven when Joey's voice comes ringing through the shop.

"Cupcake, you have a delivery," he sings and I move quickly past the worktop and through the doorway. Fred is standing in front of the counter and smiles at me, his gap-toothed grin spreading across his face.

"Hi, Fred. How are you today?" I ask as he steps up to the counter. Fred is the only other man who makes my heart flutter at his appearance, and it's only because he always comes with something from Reese.

"I'm great, Ms. Dylan. Here you go." Sliding a brown envelope across to me and holding out his clipboard, I sign for it and hold up my finger to him. I grab a bakery box and fill it with some apple turnovers, slipping one into a separate small bag and handing them out to him.

"Would you please give this box to Mr. Carroll for me? The one in the bag is for you," I say and his smile manages to grow.

"Sure. Thanks, Ms. Dylan. See ya, Joey," he responds excitedly, turning on his feet and walking out the door.

"Bye, Freddy," Joey replies in his flirty voice, earning himself an eye roll from me.

"Seriously? He's like sixty."

"Age is just a number, cupcake."

I open the envelope and pull out the tiny brown card, my heart beating so loud I'm sure Joey will give me shit about it.

> Dylan,
>
> Have you heard the song "Do I Wanna Know?" by the Arctic Monkeys? I can't listen to it anymore without thinking of you, not that I'm complaining or anything. Miss your face.
>
> X Reese

Oh, I miss his face terribly. Handing over the card to Joey, I watch his expression get all weepy while he digs his phone out of his pocket.

"I don't think I know that song," I say as he docks his phone and hits a few buttons. Music begins playing through the speakers, music that instantly reminds me of sex. *Holy shit.* I can actually picture Reese thrusting into me at the tempo.

"Jesus, is this it?" I ask and Joey nods through a grin.

"Yup. I fucking love this song. You should listen carefully to the lyrics, cupcake. I think he's trying to tell you something," he replies as he hands me back the card and starts organizing the display case. I lean against the counter, listening to the song as the front door swings open and Juls comes barreling through.

"Hello, my lovies. Ooohhh, I fucking love this song. Reminds me of sex." She echoes my thoughts as I nod in agreement.

"Reese said it reminds him of Dylan. What you think about that?" Joey asks, and her eyes widen.

"Damn. I think he wants to fuck you sideways, Dyl."

I giggle and smooth out my apron. "Well, naturally." I glance over at my best friend who is standing in the middle of the shop, rubbing her eyes and looking positively glowing. *On a Thursday?* "What's up with you?" I ask.

"Nothing, I just have something in my eye," she replies, as she keeps wiping below her lashes with both hands. She's really going at it and I look over at Joey whose mouth has dropped open.

"JULS!" he yells and startles me so bad I have to grip the counter.

"Jesus Christ, Joey. What?" I ask, my eyes falling on Juls who is now only holding up her left hand. My eyes flick between my two best friends, back and forth, still feeling completely lost until something sparkles and catches my attention. My jaw drops as I finally focus on what Joey has seen. Her delicate hand is now adorned with a shockingly large diamond and I scream. Joey screams. Juls screams. There is a lot of fucking screaming going on.

"You're engaged?" I shriek and she nods frantically, her hands coming up to cover her face as Joey and I round the counter and charge at her. "Oh, my God." The ring is beautiful and totally her. Massive and sparkly, the princess cut diamond is surrounded by smaller delicate diamonds and gleams brilliantly. Tiny diamonds run along both sides down the band as well. "Holy shit, it's gorgeous. When did this happen? How did it happen?" I ask as Joey studies the ring closely.

"Seriously the most beautiful ring I've ever fucking seen. Damn," he chimes in as he holds her petite hand in his.

She wipes the tear that has streamed down her face and shuffles excitedly on her feet. "Last night. Ian took me to Grant Park for a stroll after the rain had let up and he dropped down in front of that massive fountain. I died, right there on the spot." More tears come down and she quickly rubs them away. "He told me he's loved me for so long and he'll love me forever. God, it was so fucking romantic."

My waterworks are now free flowing and turning toward Joey. I see he is as much of an emotional wreck as I am. "You're going to be the most beautiful bride," I manage through sniffles. "I'm assuming we're looking at next September or October for the big day?"

"Fuck that noise. I am not waiting a year to marry that man. We've decided on September seventeenth." Joey gasps and I'm pretty sure I do also. I'm stunned, completely shocked. *Is she crazy?*

"That's like three months away," I say as the shop phone rings.

"Oh, please. Have you forgotten who you're talking to here? I could plan a fabulous wedding in a month if I had to." I dash behind the counter and grab the phone on the fifth ring. She is right though. If anyone could pull off a spectacular wedding in three months, it's Juls. Besides, I'm fairly certain she's already planned most of the details without Ian's knowledge of it.

"Dylan's Sweet Tooth," I chirp into the phone as Joey and Juls excitingly talk about the wedding.

"Hi, sweetheart." My mom's voice instantly sends my back rigid and I squeeze my eyes shut. *Oh, great. It's starting*

"Hi, Mom. What's up?" I ask casually. Please, Lord, let her be calling to tell me someone died or something else non-romance related. *Maybe she's forgotten all about Reese.*

I hear muffled noises in the background, most likely the sounds of my father getting shushed. "Oh, nothing much. So how exactly did you meet Reese? I'm dying to know all about him and Google only tells you so much."

"You Googled him?" I didn't even think my mother knew how to use the internet. Now she's googling the man I'm sleeping with? *Hmmm, maybe I should do that.*

"Yes. Good grief, he's handsome. Now tell me, how did you two meet?" *Oh, you know, he nailed me up against a bathroom sink at my ex's wedding. Crap.* I need a distraction and the sight of my bouncing best friends gives me inspiration.

"Mom, Juls is engaged. Isn't that great? And she's getting married this September." Nothing like wedding news to get my mother sidetracked. She's a sucker for hard gossip, especially when it involves my friends.

She gasps dramatically. "That's wonderful. Oh my, that's so soon." I hear her hands clapping together through the phone. "How lovely. Juls will make such a beautiful bride. You know who *else* would make a beautiful bride?"

What? Shit! I scramble around the counter and grab Joey by the hair, a loud scream emanating from him followed by a string of curse words directed at me. "Oh, shit. Gotta go, Mom. Joey's having a gay emergency. You know him. Love you." I end the call quickly before she can throw out any questions. *Whew. Crisis Averted.*

"What the fuck, Dylan? That hurt. And why does it have to be a *gay* emergency?" Joey rubs his scalp, his face scrunched up in pain as he glares at me.

"Ha! Like there's any another type of emergency involving you," Juls laughs.

"Sorry. Really, *really* sorry about that. My mom knows about Reese and I'm trying to avoid her at all costs." I exhale forcefully. "You know how she is." I decide to keep the 'Reese telling my parents that he's my boyfriend' news to myself. I would never hear the end of it.

"Oh, yikes," he states. "Actually, that reminds me." He quickly combs through his hair. "You remember how Billy thought it was hilarious that you thought Reese was married?" I nod as Juls moves next to me and faces Joey, her arms crossing over her chest. "Well, I thought that was weird. I mean, why is that so fucking funny? He's gorgeous. He could have been married."

"Joey, is there a point to this?" I ask

He huffs in annoyance. "Yes. I asked Billy about it and he said Reese is completely against getting serious with a girl. He won't do it." My stomach rolls. "When they start getting clingy, he moves on to the next one."

"Joey, that's enough," Juls says.

I blow my breath out. "It's fine. I figured as much." But I wasn't expecting it to hurt this bad to hear it out loud. *Shit.* I feel like my heart has been shoved into a vice.

He moves closer to me and grabs my hand, stroking the back of it with his thumb. "Dylan, I'm sorry. I just, I don't want to see you to get hurt." He squeezes me gently. "I like Reese, I really do, and I like him for you, but I don't know if he'll ever want you for more than just sex."

Juls steps in between us and grabs my shoulders. "Don't listen to him, Dylan. *I've* seen the way he looks at you. I don't care how many girls are lining up for him. He only sees you." She speaks softly, her hands applying light pressure to my tense shoulders. He is *currently* only seeing me; I want to correct her. But I don't. I manage to paint on my most convincing *I'm not affected by this* face and smile.

"It's fine. I'm fine. I wasn't expecting this to become a fucking relationship or anything more than what it is so, whatever; I'm fine." Juls studies me closely as Joey manages half a smile. "Anyway, where are we headed tonight to celebrate?" My change of topic catches on and they both start rattling off names of bars. "You two discuss it. I have some work to do."

My stomach churns as I walk past my friends and into the kitchen. Images of hundreds of women walking into Reese's office, closing the door behind them, and then re-emerging moments later looking rightly fucked pour through my head. *How many girls have blown him in that office? How many has he fucked against that door?* The thought of Reese screwing anybody besides me makes me instantly queasy. "God, what the fuck am I doing with this guy?" I say to myself as I check on the cake.

Juls pops her head through the doorway. "Six p.m. at The Tavern, sweets. Love you." She waves with her blinged out hand and I giggle.

"Love you," I reply with genuine enthusiasm just as my phone begins to ring. Reese's name flashes across my screen and I hit decline. I can't talk to him right now. I have work to do and staying busy is my best defense at keeping my mind off him. Walking over to the shelf, I grab the ingredients I need for the chocolate peppermint frosting and place them on the worktop. I reach for my mixer next as my phone rings through the kitchen. Leaning across the worktop, I see his name again and huff loudly as I press decline. "No," I state firmly. Perching myself up on a stool, I begin rifling through my recipes. I really need to organize these better. And rewrite some of them. My grandmother's chicken scratch handwriting is beginning to rub off and most are borderline illegible. Hearing the text message alert on my phone, I wipe my hands on the front of my apron and reach for it.

REESE: *Are you ignoring me?*

No, Mr. Persistent, I'm just putting some distance between you and my heart. The sound of the song, which Joey has apparently put on repeat, seeps into the kitchen and I soften. A song reminds him of me. A song that I need to remember to look up the lyrics to. My thumbs get to work.

Me: *No, just really busy. Juls stopped in and showed off her massive engagement ring and now I'm behind on some baking. What's up?*

I press send, pleased with myself for not berating him with questions about previous lovers and office sex romps. I'm about to place my phone down when his name flashes on my screen with an incoming call. *Damn it. I can't just ignore him again; he knows I'm not too busy to text.* I swipe the screen.

"Not feeling the text messaging today?" I ask through a smile that I inwardly curse myself for having. He hasn't even spoken yet and I'm glowing.

"Not when I can hear your voice instead. How are you today, love? Any new favorite songs?" The sound of crunching comes through the phone and I suspect he's received my special delivery just for him.

"Maybe. And I'm okay. I'm just still in shock over the engagement news." I swallow the lump in my throat. *Christ, cheer the fuck up, Dylan. This hot man has chosen you over all other women in line to play with. He chose you.* "So, are you coming out to celebrate with us tonight? I have a few nicknames I'd like to throw at you once I get all kinds of tipsy." The timer on the oven sounds and I walk over to it, clamping my phone between my ear and my shoulder to retrieve the cake.

He laughs softly and I can picture my favorite smile lines next to his eyes. "Yeah, but probably not till late. I have some stuff I need to take care of first." He pauses and the sound of crunching fills the receiver again. "Should I be concerned you're going to get shitfaced without me there? Because a part of me is concerned. Actually, isn't there some rule that says you can't get drunk without me?"

I laugh and poke the center of the cake with a knife, pulling it out clean. The idea of seeing him in a few short hours has blanketed all of my stupid girl concerns and I'm now my usual drunk on Reese self. I wouldn't even need alcohol tonight. "First of all, I'm not going to get drunk. If I did, I would completely blow my chances of riding you later on because I would pass out." I turn the oven off and grab a mixing bowl for the frosting. "And secondly, my friends know how to handle me and know when to cut me off. I think you forget that I'm twenty-six and not twenty-one. I've been doing this for a few years you know."

He grunts and I automatically roll my eyes into the phone. "None of what you just said gives me any comfort. I'll just make sure to get my shit done quickly so I can cut you off myself."

My hand not holding the phone goes to my hip. "If you storm into that bar and throw me over your shoulder like some caveman, Carroll, we will be having words when I sober up."

"Hmm, thanks for the idea, Sparks."

"Reese." The sound of the dial tone blares in my ear and I stuff my phone back into my pocket. *Oh, for Christ's sake.* He would do something embarrassing like that. I can just see myself getting hauled out of there tonight with my face stuck in his ass again. Well, two can play at that game. If he's going to manhandle me in front of my friends, then I'll just have to make sure I'm wearing something to make him lose his shit. That's my only defense really, causing him to stumble at the sight of me and giving me, hopefully, enough time to run away from him. But do I even have an outfit that could pull that off?

"Joey, we're closing up early so we can go shopping." I begin throwing the ingredients for the icing together into a bowl. I register his elated response and focus on my task at hand. Finish making the frosting, ice the cake, and blow Reese's fucking mind. I grin mischievously at myself. He has no idea who he's messing with.

෴

AFTER PERUSING THE RACKS AT La Bella for over an hour, I finally settle on a sleeveless coral dress with a deep v neck and exposed back. It isn't too clingy, allowing me for movement and hiding the lines of my white garter with matching bra and panties. But it is short, really fucking short. I had decided on the garter immediately after our phone call ended; that and the fact I would be picking out some sort of dress for the evening. Reese looks at me differently when I wear dresses. He still has that raw animalistic stare that could melt the panties right off me, but there is also this sweetness behind it, a gentleness that I see when I wear them around him. He looks at me like I'm delicate, and I like that.

Joey has gotten his car back from the shop and drives us to meet

Juls at The Tavern, not failing to remind me that we both look better in his ride than in mine. *All this Sam hate.* I'm already two rum and cokes in when Ian and Billy show up, my heart pounding at the anticipation of Reese's arrival.

"I would just like to say, Ian, that you did an amaaazziinngg job on the ring. Like fucking brilliant, dude. You're like the lord of the rings now. Ooohhh, you're Frodo." *Yup. I am definitely in the nickname giving stage of my night.* I bop around on my stool, tapping my hands lightly on the bar in rhythm with the song playing overhead.

"Wow, how many drinks have you had?" he asks as Juls wiggles in his lap. She can't stop looking at her ring and it's absolutely adorable. I'm certain she's shown it to me fifty times since we've arrived, as if I haven't seen it already.

"Psst, like none," I reply. "So have you two thought of a honeymoon spot?"

"Fiji!" Juls yells and Ian barks a laugh.

"I don't really care, just as long as I get my sexy wife in a bikini, and then quickly out of it," he says and I feel my face flush. "I can't *fucking wait* to marry you." He speaks so low, I almost don't hear him. But I do. Tears fill my eyes and I meet Juls' rapidly blinking teary-eyed stare.

"Ladies room?" I ask and she nods.

"Babe, will you get me another drink please?" she shouts back at Ian who gives her a quick wink. We walk arm in arm to the bathrooms and slip inside, the sound of the bar crowd dying down as the door closes behind us. Stepping in front of the mirror, I smooth my dress out and fluff up my hair as Juls reapplies her lipstick.

"By the way, this Saturday I'm holding you hostage after your cake delivery," she says as she hands me the tube she's just used. I take it and shake my head, slowing applying the nude color onto my lips and then quickly wiping it off.

I grunt in annoyance. "I can't pull off lipstick. It makes me look like a hooker. And why am I being held hostage on Saturday?" I hand her back the tube and she sticks it into her purse.

"Excuse you. Maid of honor duties." I screech and jump on my heels. "We've got some dress shopping to do." She wraps me up in a hug as we giggle against each other.

"I'm going to lose it when I see you in a wedding dress. Fair warning," I say as we let go of each other.

She grabs both of my hands and beams, taking in a deep breath before she slowly lets it out. "I'm so happy, sweets. I can't believe he chose me." She pulls her bottom lip into her mouth and bites it to stop it from quivering.

I squeeze her hands with both of mine. "Who wouldn't choose you?" I drop her hands and turn back toward the mirror, wiping under my eyes. "Is, uh, Reese in the wedding party?" *Please say yes.* The sight of him in a tux is something I would pay to see.

"Of course, he's the best man, which means you two will be paired up. You're welcome." She giggles at me and I watch in the mirror as my cheeks burn up.

We exit the bathroom together, Juls walking ahead of me and blocking my view, but it doesn't matter. I could have been blindfolded and I'd have known he was here. I always feel his presence before I see him. As she steps through the crowd, my eyes lock onto Reese who is standing at the bar talking to Ian. My stomach tightens and I clench my fists as I walk slowly, studying him and waiting for him to notice me. He's in his work attire, dress shirt and tie with khakis, his hair sticking out all over the place, and I decide that walking slowly is for morons. Pushing my way through the crowd, his eyes turn to mine and he smiles sweetly before his mouth drops at my appearance. I pick up my pace and run straight at him, jumping up into his arms and hearing Juls and Ian's collective laughs as I cling to him like a vine. His smell hits me and I softly moan.

"Handsome," I whisper into his ear as I squeeze him tightly, no intention of letting go any time soon. "I thought you'd never get here."

"I came as soon as I could, love." He inhales me deeply, holding my body against his as I keep a solid grip around his neck. Shifting me against his body, he turns and lowers himself onto a stool, pulling me into his lap. I lean back and study him. Green eyes blazing, parted full lips, and smile lines. *Man, he is lethal.* He opens his mouth to speak when his eyes trail down my body and stop on my thighs.

"Fuck, Dylan." I glance down quickly at what's possibly caused his outburst and curse loudly at the sight of my exposed garter. *Shit. This dress is not meant to be sat down in.* "What are you wearing?" I'm quickly placed on my feet in front of him as he begins tugging at the material, frantically attempting to bring it down to a more appropriate length. The giggling from me comes naturally at his flustered state.

"Are you trying to give me a heart attack? What the hell is with the dress?" he asks through clenched teeth as I quickly scan the red faces of Ian and Juls who are watching in amusement. Joey squeals on the dance floor as Billy dips him and kisses him deeply in front of everyone. The relentless tugging of my dress brings my eyes back down in front of me.

"You don't like it? I thought you liked me in dresses," I tease.

"This shouldn't be allowed in public. Seriously, what the fuck? You've been here for how long in this shit?" He glowers at me and runs his hands down his face, bringing my attention to his right hand that looks like he's spent the night dragging it against bricks. His knuckles are cut up and slightly swollen and dried blood stains his skin.

"Jesus Christ. What the hell happened to your hand?" I reach for it to examine it more closely when he quickly pulls away from me.

"Don't worry about it. The dress, Dylan. Why are you wearing that?"

Oh, no fucking way is he going to react like this and not give me any answers. I grab my clutch off the table and make to turn away from him. "Fuck you. I wore this for you, you stupid asshole." His hand grabs my elbow, but I somehow manage to snatch it out of his grip. "Let go of me. How dare you come in here with your hand looking like you beat the shit out of somebody and give me a hard time about my outfit. You have no fucking right to act like that." *What the hell? This is not the reaction I was hoping to get out of him for wearing this.* I push through the crowd of people and see the exit, but feel his hands on my waist before I can get very far. *Figures. Engage barbarian mode.* I am turned sharply and pulled against his chest, his mouth pressing firmly to my temple.

"I have *every* fucking right to act like this," he growls.

"No, you don't. What the fuck happened to your hand?" I push away from him and take a step back, sternly staring him down for an explanation.

He steps closer to me, eliminating the gap I just created. "Your ex is what happened to my hand. I told you I'd make sure he never touched you again, and I fucking did. Now explain to me why the fuck you're wearing that? You knew I wouldn't be here until later, so don't fucking say it was for me."

I move quickly, there is no thought behind it, just pure shock, and slap him hard across his face. The sound of the crack echoes through the bar, but no one seems to pay us any mind, except for Juls and Ian. Apparently, lovers' quarrels are common in establishments like this.

"Are you *actually* trying to insinuate that I'm wearing this for somebody else? Fuck you. You drive me fucking crazy." I bring my hand back again, but Reese reaches out and stops it, bringing it down to my side and pulling me against him. His chest is heaving rapidly and when I press my lower body against his, I feel his need for me digging into my hip. *Fuck, he's turned on by this?*

"You drive *me* fucking crazy. Now, say your goodbyes so I can take you home and fuck some sense into you." I catch my breath at his words, but know right then, even before he said it, that I want it just as much as he does. He knows how and when to push my buttons and he does it better than anyone.

"Juls, I'm leaving. Love you," I yell, but keep my eyes on Reese.

"Holy hell. That was crazy hot. Bye, sweets," she yells back, and before I can object, I'm being dragged out of the bar by a very hot and bothered CPA. *But who am I kidding here? Like I'd ever object.*

Chapter
FOURTEEN

"I HOPE YOU REALIZE JUST how pissed off I am at you right now,"
I say as I sit in the passenger seat of his Range Rover, watching him
weave easily in and out of traffic. We've been driving in silence
for eight long-ass minutes and my annoyance level is through the roof.

He turns the radio down and clears his throat before glancing over
at me. "Why, because I don't want other men looking at you? Tough
shit. That dress should be illegal." His hand grips the center console and
I stare at his red cut up knuckles.

Crossing my legs and letting my dress ride up on purpose, I cross
my arms over my chest and stare him down. "What happened? You
didn't kill him, did you? I'd prefer it if I didn't have to visit you in prison."
*Although, a conjugal visit with Reese might be worth Justin's demise. Mmmm,
he could rock the hell out of some jail attire.*

Stopping at a red light, he flexes his injured hand before he reaches
over and slips his finger under my garter, snapping it against my skin
and making me yelp. "No, I didn't kill him, but he probably wishes he
was dead right now. He won't bother you again." I bat his hand away
to keep him from pulling at it as the red light turns to green. "Did you
have fun tonight?"

Forcing out a laugh, I turn to him and see a hint of teasing in his set profile, his lip twitching slightly. "Oh, yeah, I was having a blast until this crazy man showed up and freaked out over my wardrobe selection, which, by the way, *was* for your eyes only. You owe me multiple orgasms for that little tirade."

He lets out a laugh as he pulls into the parking garage of his building. "Oh, I think I'm the one who is in need of multiple orgasms. It is *my* birthday after all." *Wait, what?*

"It's your birthday? Today?" He nods with a smile and parks the car, stepping out as I stay frozen in my seat. My door is opened for me and his hand grabs mine, pulling me quickly out of the vehicle. "Is it really?" The man could be lying just to get his multiple orgasms.

He reaches in his back pocket, pulls out his wallet and hands it to me. I flip it open and stare at his license, which of course contains a picture of him looking annoyingly good. *Who the hell takes a good driver's license photo?* Focusing on his birthday, I confirm what he has just revealed to me.

"Why didn't you tell me?" I ask, handing him back his wallet as we walk into his building. His hand rests on my lower back as he walks me toward the elevators, nodding politely at the people we pass.

"I just did," he replies, pulling me into the elevators and pressing the tenth floor button. I wrap my arms around his neck and press my body against his as we ride up to his floor. His scent fills my lungs and I swoon.

"But you should have told me sooner. I would have made you a cake. It's what I do, you know."

His hands grip my waist as he presses quick kisses into my hair. "Well, you can make me a cake now." The doors open and he quickly pulls me with him down the hallway and into his condo. *Jeez, is he in a rush?*

Flipping on the lights, I follow behind him as he sets his keys down on the counter and walks into the kitchen. I slip out of my heels, set my purse down, and begin rummaging through his cabinets, praying for ingredients.

"Do you have any flour?" I ask as he closes the fridge and hops up onto the counter. Unscrewing the cap, he takes a sip of his water and looks to be in deep thought, his eyes staring at the cabinets. "You're in my spot," I say as I watch him with amusement.

"Umm, no. I don't think I have any flour. And yes, I am in your spot.

But it's my birthday, so I'll do whatever the fuck I want." He smirks at me and I give it right back to him, turning and glancing up on a high shelf.

"Can you reach me the Bisquick please?" I ask as I open the fridge and pull out the eggs. He hands it to me with a kiss and hops back up.

"Are you making me birthday pancakes?"

I pull out a bowl and grab a fork. "Nope, I'm making you my four ingredient banana cake that I used to whip up in college. Juls and I roomed together and I would create desserts out of whatever crap we had lying around. Bisquick was always on hand because she's a breakfast junkie." I grab the sugar bowl and set the oven temperature. "You've given me little choice here. I'd be set if I wanted to make you a cake made out of ramen noodles and chunky soup." He watches me intently as I mash up the banana and begin mixing the ingredients together in the bowl, occasionally glancing up and seeing him studying me. He always seems so fascinated by whatever it is I'm doing, and I wonder if he looks at every girl like this. *Ugh.* The thought makes me whip the eggs viciously.

"So you're thirty-two today," I state, sucking the batter that has splashed up onto my knuckle off with a soft moan.

"I am." My eyes go to his and he winks. "I'm six years older than you now. Does that bother you?"

His question baffles me, so I decide to really give it some thought. Our age difference doesn't bother me at all. If he was ten years older than me, I wouldn't care. Scrunching up my face and thinking hard, I see his grin widen as he waits for me, a soft breathy laugh escaping him. I shake my head. "Nah, but that's mainly because you act half your age." His eyebrow arches. "Besides, I have a thing for older men." Tipping the bowl, I pour the cake batter into his one and only baking dish and shuffle it to even out the distribution.

He hops down and comes up behind me, his hands spreading across my stomach. "Do you? I had no idea," he says as he pulls my hair over one shoulder and kisses down my neck. I close my eyes and grip the baking dish tightly. *Lord, this man knows how to wind me up in no time.*

"Well, I have a thing for you," he growls into my ear, his hands sliding up the front of my dress and molding to my breasts. My head falls back against his shoulder and I groan. "I need to put this in the oven."

He grumbles in protest but finally steps back, allowing me to place the dish into the oven and set the timer.

"Okay, birthday boy, you've got twelve minutes to play with me until it's ready." I turn to see his wicked grin and he wastes little time, grabbing my hand and pulling me into the living room. Stopping in front of the couch, he pulls me into his arms and runs his hands up my spine as his face drops to bring our lips together. He opens my mouth with his and snakes his tongue around mine, coaxing me to move with him and I obey. My hands fumble with his tie, loosening it and dropping it to the floor as his mouth assaults mine, teasing and tasting every inch of me. I feel his arm muscles flex around me and then the sound of a loud rip comes from behind me as the fabric of my dress is torn from my body.

"Did you just... I can't believe you just did that." I spin around quickly and step back and out of his arms, seeing the handful of material clutched between both fists before he drops it at his feet. *Are you fucking serious?* "Dick. Do you have any idea how much that dress cost me?" I step into him and deliver a sharp poke to his chest with my finger. *Yeah. That'll show him.*

He cocks his head to the side and narrows his eyes at me. "If you say more than five dollars, you got ripped off. That thing was the size of a handkerchief." His arms wrap me up and he tosses me onto the couch like I'm some sort of rag doll. I yelp in protest as the cold leather hits my skin, but am only momentarily chilled before his body is pressing against mine, warming me instantly.

"You are ridiculous. What the hell am I supposed to wear now when I leave?" I grumble between kisses. His mouth meets mine the moment he relaxes down on me. I moan as his tongue dips into my mouth, delivering long strokes against mine and filling me with his minty flavor. "Fuck, I'm so mad at you." I grunt as he laughs against me, moving his lips down my neck and licking a trail to the top of my breasts. *Stay mad, Dylan. Don't give in. Don't lose it. That was a two hundred and fifty dollar dress.*

"I love it when you're mad at me. You're so fucking sexy; I can barely contain myself here." He molds his hands over my breasts and pulls my bra down, slipping a nipple into his mouth as I grab his head. "Mmmm, these are always on my mind. So fucking beautiful." He licks and sucks me, drawing loud moans from my mouth. Brushing his nose against the mark next to my left nipple, which is slightly faded, he sucks on the small patch of skin. My hands grip his hair and hold him against me. I hate that his marks are fading on me and am more than happy to let him bring them back out. Moving to my other breast, he freshens the mark there and then plants a soft kiss to it before he glances up at me. His smirk makes me grunt.

"You're an asshole," I groan as he moves lower, licking and nibbling at my stomach. Wrapping my legs tightly around his waist, I push him up and grip his dress shirt with both hands tightly before I rip it apart, tiny buttons flying out in every direction. My hands push it off his big shoulders and down his arms, pulling his T-shirt quickly over his head.

"Impatient much? We have all night, love," he says as he works his belt, sitting back between my legs.

"You started it." *All night?* My hands stretch out and rub his ripped chest, brushing down his stomach along the tight muscles. *God, I love touching this man.* My index finger plays in the patch of hair that runs below his belly button. "What do you want for your birthday?"

He reaches into his pants, pulls himself out and leans forward, rubbing himself along the length of my wet panties. I groan and dig my nails into his back. *Wasn't I mad about something?* "You in my bed," he says against my mouth. Our lips are close, our heavy breathing mixing together and I tremble against him, his words bringing out my fears. "Nothing has to change. This is still just sex. I just need to have you in there."

Seconds, minutes go by and he stills against me, waiting for my response. I don't know what to do. I want to do this for him, for me, more than anything. Being in his bed, surrounded by his smell and imagining what it would be like to stay there with him is a thought that is constantly running through my mind. But can I do this? He said nothing has to change, but can I keep it from changing for me? I think long and hard and make my decision. Yes, I can. Because this is worth it. He is worth it. I close my eyes tightly and nod, hearing a small sound escape him and I'm quickly lifted to my feet. We round the couch together when the oven alarms, causing me to dash in and pull the cake out.

"Jesus, you should only be allowed to wear *that* in my kitchen," he says as I insert a knife quickly into the top and pull it out clean. Glancing down at my attire, I smile at him as I meet him in the dining room where he stands waiting for me. My hand is placed in his as he leads me down the hallway and opens the last door on the left. Stepping aside for me, I walk ahead of him and take in my surroundings.

His bedroom is big and spacious, containing a large four-poster bed with one nightstand on each side, a tall dresser and a chair in the corner next to a small bookshelf. I scurry over to it and glance at his reading material, all educational and way the hell out of my depth. "Wow, you're a bigger nerd than I thought." Pulling out a massive textbook with the words *Corporate Accounting* on the front, I sit in the chair and flip through it, feeling his eyes on me as he moves into the room. The sound of his clothing removal catches my attention and I glance up at him from under my lashes. He is now standing completely naked and staring at me, holding out his hand and arching his brow.

"I'm reading," I mutter through a grin and am quickly yanked from my chair, book crashing to the floor in the process as he lifts me up and tosses me on the bed. The smell of him hits me like a truck and I whimper. *Crap, this is going to wreck me.* Wrapping his hand around the back of me, I am moved up the bed so my head is resting on his pillow, his body settling between my legs. I watch intently as he slides my panties down and tosses them, leaving my garter on and tracing the clips with his fingers.

"So fucking sexy," he says against my thigh, kissing the skin along my garter. "You're so soft, love, and you always shake when I'm right here." His lips brush against the skin of my inner thigh and I gasp, trembling on cue. "I love how I do that to you."

I quickly remove my bra and reach out for him. "Come here. I need you." I grip his shoulders and pull him up as he shifts above me, pushing straight into me in one quick motion.

"I've dreamed of this. You, in my bed. Fuck, Dylan." His words ring through my ears as he strokes me with long slow movements. Pulling almost all the way out before he glides back in. My legs tighten around him and I pull his mouth to mine, needing his kiss, needing his breath on me and in me.

"Me, too. Oh, God."

He groans loudly and I pull his lip into my mouth, dragging my teeth along his skin. My hands are brought over my head and held above me with one of his. His eyes burn into mine with such raw emotion that it rips through me, crippling me. I turn my head to break the contact.

"Look at me," he grunts, his hips thrusting hard and fast, slamming against mine and pushing me up into the headboard. His grip around my wrist tightens and I arch off the bed, pushing my chest against his. "Dylan, I need to see you." I turn back to him, giving him what he wants and letting myself feel it. Heat spreads across my skin, radiating from deep within me as his free hand holds the side of my face. "Don't pull away from me," he pleads, but even if he hadn't said the words, his eyes are telling me the same thing. They show every emotion, every unspoken thought. I am completely lost in his green stare, completely lost in him. Everything about him holds on to me, keeping me right with him in this moment and there isn't a single part of me that wants to pull away, that will ever want to pull away. I can do this. I'm strong enough for this.

My body is quickly on the brink, undeniably responsive to his and I want him there with me. I pull my lip into my mouth and clench around him, seeing his eyes widen and halting his thrusts.

"Holy fuck." His eyes clamp shut and I do it again, contracting my muscles and feeling him react with a jerk. "Jesus Christ. Love, if you keep doing that..." And I do. I do it again, this time holding it, and his eyes open and lock onto mine.

I clench around him once more and he grunts loudly before he starts to move. I moan and bring my hips up to meet his charges, giving him deeper entry and pulling a low groan straight out of him.

"Come with me, love." His mouth comes down and devours mine, pulling my tongue into his and sucking hard and deep. I come fast, my body shaking and pulsing, my screams swallowed by his mouth as he gives me his release. Warmth runs through me, clinging to me, to us. Our bodies fit perfectly together and I pray he'll never get tired of me, of this. Because I never will.

Our breathing steadies as he stays on top of me, pressing my body into his mattress. He's heavy, but not uncomfortable and I find the weight to be the perfect amount of pressure against my body. My fingers trail lightly along his back as his hot breath bursts across my neck. My touch deepens and I rub his hard muscles, working up to his neck and firmly digging in. I giggle at his tiny moans of pleasure. He loves it when I touch him, and right now, that's what I want to do. I wiggle underneath him and his gorgeous face turns up to gaze at me.

"Let me up. I want to give you a birthday massage."

He quickly and with great enthusiasm pushes himself back onto his knees and allows me to move around him. Grabbing a few tissues off his nightstand, I'm wiped clean of his release and the trash is quickly discarded. As he settles back down on his stomach, I straddle his waist and admire the view. He has the sexiest back I've ever seen, broad and built, but not overly muscular. I hate big bulky guys, and Reese has the perfect muscle to leanness ratio. After giving one quick smack to his perfectly sculpted ass, I begin rubbing up and down his back, gauging his reaction to find the amount of pressure he wants. A few soft moans indicate I'm pressing him just how he likes, and I move to his shoulders and start working him.

"Tell me something I don't know about you," I say, wanting to find out every little detail I can. Reese seems really open after sex and I'm going to use that to my advantage.

He moans, "Mmmm, I hate cats." His muffled answer makes me belt out a laugh.

"That does not even count. Come on, Carroll, you can do better than that. I totally hate cats too, though. They're so smug." My hands work his upper arms, pushing and pulling his muscles until they loosen. His breathing is peaceful and steady underneath me.

"I don't know; it's hard to think when you're touching me like this. Why don't you just ask me a question?" He turns his head and rests on his cheek, eyes closed with his long lashes brushing his cheekbone. *Jesus, I would kill for lashes like that. Why do guys get the best lashes?* "Dylan."

"I'm thinking." I have questions, so many questions. But am I brave enough to ask them? I bite my lip and decide to start slow. "Do you hook up with a lot of girls at weddings?" That isn't too bad. It's not like I asked him how many girls he's slept with, which I *am* very curious about. His eyes open for a moment and then he closes them again.

"I'm not sure what classifies as a lot, but yes, I've hooked up with women at weddings before." He moans as I press my thumbs deeply into his upper back. "I'm sure I wasn't your first either."

"Yes, you were," I blurt out, seeing his eyes pop open again. He blinks rapidly before he flips under me, holding me still so I'm now straddling his stomach. His hands run up my thighs and play with my garter as I begin rubbing his chest. "Well, you were my first slutty wedding sex. I've had a few drunken make out sessions at weddings before." I haven't, that's a total lie. I've actually never done anything with a stranger at a wedding besides dance with them. But the way Reese is staring up at me right now, eyes full of wonder, I feel the need to not sound like such an angelic virgin hovering over this experienced player. I clear my throat and massage down his arms, seeing his eyes close again and giving me the opportunity to stare while he isn't watching me. "Have you called other girls 'love'?"

A small smile forms on his lips as his eyes remain closed. "No, just you."

I feel my heart swell. *Hmm, I like that.* "Were there a lot of girls before me?" I speak without thought and clamp my eyes shut, bracing myself for his answer. The same image runs through my mind of the hundreds of girls in his office and I pray for a low number. A really low number.

"Dylan, do you really want to go there? Can't you just ask me what my favorite movie is or some shit?"

I slowly open my eyes and see him staring at me, green eyes blazing. *Jesus, is it that big of a number that he doesn't want to tell me? I think I have the right to know.* "You know my number; it's only fair. Just tell me if it's in the triple digits or not." My hands rest on his abdomen and I get a shocked expression.

"Jesus Christ. Triple digits?" He scrubs down his face with both hands. "I don't know, close to twenty probably. Does it really fucking matter?" His hands return to my thighs and I glare at him.

"Yes, it really fucking matters, otherwise I wouldn't have asked." Sliding off his body, I kneel next to him on the bed and grab a pillow to cover myself with. He quickly takes it away. "Give me that."

"No. It's my birthday and I want to look at you." He tucks the pillow behind his head. "Now, tell me why it matters?" I shake my head and get off the bed, walking toward the doorway. "Where are you going?"

"To get some cake. It's not like I can leave or anything. You destroyed my dress and I don't have a car," I call out behind me as I walk down the hallway. My mind is racing. *Close to twenty? I've been with one guy besides him. One.* I walk around the couch and pick up his dress shirt, slipping it on and letting it hang open since all the buttons had been ripped off. I bring the collar around my face and inhale deeply. *Oh, man. Please let me keep this.* I slice two pieces of cake and place them on plates, grabbing some forks and heading back down the hallway. Reese is now sitting up, his back against the headboard and the covers pulled up around his waist

"Wow." I stop at the end of the bed and stare at him after he speaks, his eyes fixated on my attire. "You look beautiful in my shirt. Keep it."

I smile and climb up on the bed, handing him his plate. "Here, happy birthday, handsome." I lean in and give him a quick kiss with his cake, lingering for a few seconds as he moans against my lips.

He smiles at me and takes it, grabbing a huge bite with his fork. "Mmmm, this is really good." Watching his perfect mouth work the bite, I see his Adam's apple move as it slides down his throat. "You can make this for me every year."

My fork hovers in the air as I'm about to take a bite myself. His eyes fix on mine and I quickly look down and pull the bite in. *Every year?* I moan softly around my bite and relish in the delicious banana flavor. This cake is too easy to taste this good. I watch in amusement as he devours his cake quickly, leaning over and placing his empty plate on the nightstand. The muffled sound of a ringtone rings through the bedroom.

"Shit," he says as he hangs over the side of the bed and pulls his phone out of his pants. He shakes his head quickly before he answers it, exhaling and leaning back against the headboard.

"Hi, Mom. Thanks. Yeah, I'm good, how are you? How's Dad?"

Now usually, I would just sit back and enjoy my dessert and not think of anything devious to do in this situation. However, the memory of Reese stealing my cell phone and giving my mother unwarranted information creeps into my mind, along with a brilliant idea. I sit up and lean across him, feeling his eyes on me as I place my plate on the nightstand next to his.

"Oh, yeah? That sounds like him. When's he trading it in?" Grabbing the sheets with both hands, I yank them down and quickly crawl between his legs, my mouth enveloping his partially erect cock and feeling it come to life immediately. "Shit. Uh, nothing." I smile around him and grip the base, holding him tightly as I lick up his length. His thighs clench and his free hand fists the sheets. "Mom, can I call you back?" I pull him into my mouth and slide up and down his length, hearing small throaty grunts from above me. "No, I'm just in the middle of something. *Oh, fuck.*" My hand glides along the wetness and meets my mouth. He pulses against me as I suck him hard, then harder. "I'll call you back." The phone is chucked off the bed quickly and his hands grip my hair.

"God, yes. Just like that."

I groan against him, my free hand reaching under and holding his sac. "Tell me how good it feels," I say as I lick the tip. My hand pumps him, long even strokes as I glance up at his expression. Eyes dark and powerful, brow creased and jaw clenched.

"So fucking good. Your mouth is incredible." He jerks and I slip him back into my mouth. His hands grip my head, pulling me up and down at the rhythm he wants, and I let him. It is his birthday after all. His hips thrust up and he fucks my mouth as I tame my gag reflex. He's so deep in me, hitting the back of my throat and making my eyes water. His soft praises keeps me going even though my jaw is beginning to ache. "Dylan, so good, oh, God, I love your mouth." I feel a pulse and know he's close. Increasing the pressure, I suck as hard as I can and cup his balls, feeling them tighten in my hand. He groans loudly and twitches. I squeeze every last drop out of him and swallow, savoring his taste. My eyes flick up as I lick him and see him watching me, always watching me. I've missed the look on his face at his release, but the look he's giving me right now makes up for that loss. He's in complete wonderment. He brings his hands up and runs both through his hair.

"Damn, that was unreal. Come up here."

I wipe my lips with the back of my hand and move up his body until I am straddling his waist. "Do you like it when I do that?" My hands rest on his arms and I squeeze them gently.

His laugh warms my face. "Are you kidding? Did I not just come in this pretty little mouth?" His finger runs along my bottom lip and I kiss it lightly. "Do you like doing it?"

I nod quickly and we both laugh. "I love it. I used to hate it, but with you, I love it." He smiles sweetly and runs his hands down my arms. "Have you always liked eating pussy?"

My question causes him to stumble back a bit and he shakes his head at me, giving me a strange look. "Uh, I'll always like eating *your* pussy. Let's leave it at that." He narrows his eyes at me, seeing my unsatisfied expression. "Dylan, really?"

"What? I'm just curious. Why do you like mine so much?" I glance up at him from under my lashes and see his eyes trail down to the topic of discussion. "Don't all women taste the same?"

He licks his lips and smiles, causing me to bite the inside of my cheek to hold in my grin. I have no idea why I'm so curious about this, but I am. His eyes meet mine and he shakes his head. He trails his finger down my stomach and dips into me. "Yours is the sweetest pussy and the only one I want. I'm a bit obsessed with it." I moan softly as he moves around before slipping out of me.

"Good," I state as he pops his finger into his mouth and smiles around it. *Good Lord, that's hot.* He engulfs my face in his hands and moves in slowly, planting the sweetest, most gentle kiss he's ever given me. Pulling back ever so slightly, we study each other. There are no words, just the sound of our breathing as my eyes examine every inch of his face. He looks completely relaxed right now. No furrowed brow, no tension in his jaw. Just slightly parted lips and soft green eyes. My finger runs down the prominent slit in his bottom lip to his chin, feeling soft stubble along his jaw. I sigh. The sight of Reese with a five o'clock shadow would surely cripple me. Trailing his fingers along my skin, he brushes over my eyebrows, down my temples and across my cheekbones.

"What are you thinking right now?" he whispers and I lean in, pressing our foreheads together and closing my eyes. *God, what wasn't I thinking?* That I love being with him like this in his bed, that I am so wrapped up in him, and at certain moments, I think it might break me.

That I'm scared, terrified, of my feelings for him and his possible lack of feelings for me in the same way. I need to give him an answer so I do.

I open my eyes and connect with his. "That I'm scared I'm going to fuck this up," I reply, so soft, so low that I think maybe he misses it, until his eyes widen. I swallow and continue. "I don't really know what I'm doing. I mean, I've never done this before." His hand brushes my hair back. "You make this look so easy, and I just… I feel like I'm struggling." My voice breaks at the end. I sound weak. Pathetic even. His silence eats away at me so I shift down a bit to lay my head against his chest in my favorite spot, nuzzling his neck. I need his scent right now. I am anything but relaxed after that admission and I know it will soothe me.

"I think you're amazing," he pronounces into my hair, his hands wrapping around my waist and holding my body against his. *Amazing? At this? Really?* I exhale slowly and feel all the tension leave my body. That is all I needed to hear. If he thinks I'm amazing at this, then I must be doing something right. Closing my eyes, I concentrate on his breathing and let his smell wash over me. His hands dip under his dress shirt and stroke my back lovingly, just like he did last week on his couch after our long talk. And once again, there is silence between us. But this kind of silence, the kind where no words are welcome because just being together, holding each other, is better than anything that could possibly be said. This kind of silence is perfect. And then I pass out from my favorite form of intoxication. Reese Carroll.

Chapter
FIFTEEN

'VE ALWAYS SLEPT SOUNDLY IN my bed, wrapped up in my nine hundred thread count sheets and down comforter. My feather top mattress gives the illusion of sleeping on a cloud and once I lay down on it, I'm out for the count. Dead to the world. I can usually sleep through anything except my daily five a.m. alarm. I once slept through the commotion of two fire engines and several ambulances when a building across the street caught on fire. I had no idea. When I eventually woke up mid-morning on that Saturday, I was shocked at how loud the sirens were that I had slept through. So most mornings, even when I have to wake up at five a.m., I feel extremely well rested and ready for the day. A good night's sleep is very important for your body to properly function and I usually achieved one nightly. But this morning, as I slowly shift my head from side to side, eyes still closed and the feel of something heavy on top of me, I feel like I've been sleeping for days. I've never felt this revitalized. Slowly fluttering my eyes open, I spot a wild mess of dark brown hair spread across my chest. Hot breath blows across my breast, tickling my nipple, and it takes me a minute to process what's in front of me, or really, what's on top of me. My eyes shoot open and I turn to the alarm on the table next to me. Seven twelve in the morning it flashes. *Seven twelve? Fuck!*

"Reese. Get up." I wiggle underneath him, but he's not budging. He's not even shifting his weight at all. He's clinging to me like Saran Wrap, his head nuzzling between my breasts and our legs tangling together in the sheets. I almost don't want to move because being under and wrapped up in him this way feels amazing. But it's morning, and I fucking slept over. "REESE." Gripping his shoulders and snapping back into my sanity, I push with everything I have and he grumbles, rolling over onto his back and slowly opening one eye. That one eye scans my body and he smiles.

"Morning, love." *Whoa.* I'm momentarily stunned by his deep groggy bedroom voice. Low and throaty, it sends a chill through me. I glance down quickly, noting that I'm still wearing his dress shirt, which is completely open, and my garter and stockings. Darting his arm out, he pulls me close to his body and wraps around me again.

"You look wildly sexy right now, in my shirt and in my bed." His hand runs down my stomach and brushes between my legs. I involuntarily moan, knowing full well that I do not have time for this. But my body belongs to this man and I can't help how it reacts. "You're so wet. Were you dreaming about me doing this?" One finger dips in, then two, and I throw my head back and arch my body off the bed.

"Oh, yes, right there." My head falls to the side and my eyes meet the clock again as his fingers move in perfect rhythm. It's after seven. The bakery opened at seven a.m. "Fuck. I'm so late." I bat his hand away and try to sit up when he slams me back down, moving on top of me and pressing me into the mattress. "Reese, seriously, I don't have time for this. Joey is probably freaking out right now." He rolls his hips against my pelvis and I moan at the sensation. *Bakery? What bakery? Who the fuck is Joey?*

He kisses me hard, darting his tongue into my mouth and I taste toothpaste. *Toothpaste?* I shake him off me. "Hey, why do you taste like you've brushed your teeth? Have you been up already?" If he says no, then the man even has perfect morning breath, which would not surprise me. My eyes widen as his smell hits me. It's his usual decadent scent, but it's stronger. Fresher. His wicked grin beams down at me and I grit my teeth and grunt. "Reese, did you already take a shower this morning?"

"You're not the only one who gets up at five and works out. And

Joey is not freaking out." He plants a quick kiss on my lips. "I called him and explained the situation." Another hip roll catches my breath. *Focus, Dylan. It's just a penis. The best penis, but still, just a penis.*

I glare up at his giant grin. "Are you telling me that you got up at five and didn't wake me? Do you *not* realize I have a business to run? And what time do *you* have to go to work or are you *that* important that you can come and go as you please?" I groan as he rolls again. "And stop doing that." My hands frantically push against his body to remove him off me but nothing happens. *Shocker.* He leans off a bit and grabs my arms, bracing them on either side of my head. Dropping his head, he rests his forehead against mine.

"So feisty. You make me want to keep you here all day just to see how mad I can make you." I open my mouth to protest and his tongue slips in, capturing mine and slowly sucking on it. *Oh, Lord, help me. I have no will power when it comes to him.* He releases me all too soon. "But I won't because I do have to make it into work sometime today. And just for the record, I did try to wake you up to go for a run with me, but you were in a coma." I grunt loudly and make a face at him. *That I can definitely believe.* I wiggle underneath him and he arches his brow, moving his hips up to rub his length against my clit.

"Oh, God," I whimper, clamping my eyes shut.

"Now, you have three options here. You get to pick how I make you come before I take you to work." He wiggles his brows at me and I giggle. Playful Reese is impossible to say no to.

"I don't have time for this," I plead weakly. His eyes narrow at me and I issue him a smirk.

"Who are you trying to fool here, Dylan?" Hip swivel and I groan. "I could make you come in two minutes if I had to." *Yeah right. He's good, but not that good.* "Hands, mouth, or me."

Holy hell. I'm trying desperately not to allow my smile to crack my face in half, but I'm failing miserably and hardly caring. I jerk my hips up against him and see his eyes widen. "You." He licks his lips and releases my arms, reaching down and wrapping my legs around his waist. He enters me in a quick thrust and I cry out, my head rolling back and my arms reaching above me to grasp the headboard. "Yes, oh, yes." My hands grip the posts and I push down with my arms, meeting his movements and forcing him deeper inside me. "Reese."

Gripping my thighs, he brings my legs to his front and rests them on his shoulders as he pummels into me. His groans are loud and throaty. "Feel it, love. Feel what only I can do to you." He arches back and holds my legs as he drives into me. "Nobody will make you feel this good, Dylan, just me." My eyes are glued to his and I can't look away. I want to tell him he's right, that I know no other guy will ever make me feel like this and I never want to give one the chance. But I don't. Instead, I just feel him. Every stroke, every push, I feel and take everything he gives me.

Deeper, deeper, harder and he's relentless. I'm close, so close that I can't believe I actually doubted what he does to me. Clearly my insanely good night's sleep has rendered me stupid. His hand trails down my leg as he thrusts and his thumb finds my spot. With the slightest twitch, I'm done.

"I'm coming. Oh, fuck." I close my eyes and scream so loud my voice breaks. I hear his loud cry and flick them back open to see him glued to me. Green and piercing, he captures me and I watch him fall apart. He pulls his bottom lip into his mouth and bites down as he pumps into me, giving me his release. Turning his head, he presses his mouth to my leg and pants, his jagged breath bursting across my shin. He stills inside me as we slowly come down together.

"Jesus Christ." I feel and see his lips curl up around my skin. My legs are dropped from his shoulders and he moves off the bed, lifting me up into his arms. He carries me down the hallway and straight into the bathroom. I'm placed on my feet in front of the vanity and glance at myself in the mirror. "Oh, shit." My hair looks rightly fucked, but not in the unbelievable Reese hair sort of way, my lips are swollen, cheeks flushed, and my breasts are beautifully tainted with his marks. My fingers frantically comb through my hair as he smiles behind me. "I need something to wear out of here. Any suggestions, or would you like me to just wear what I have on?" I arch my brow and crack a smile as his fades. *Oh, Mr. Possessive is back.*

His hands come up and rake through my hair, messing up what I've just tamed. "You're hilarious. Would you like to take a shower with me?"

he asks as he walks over and turns it on. His bathroom is far nicer than mine, massive even with a shower that could probably fit ten people. *Nine women and Reese possibly? Ugh. Don't go there.* I shake the thought out of my head.

"Yes, but it has to be quick. No funny business." I bend and begin unhooking my garter, sliding my stockings off my legs. He disappears after I catch him watching me for several long seconds. Always watching. He reappears moments later as I slip into the shower, a pile of clothes in his hands. "You don't have conditioner?" I ask as the warm water cascades down my body. The only thing in his shower is shampoo and his body wash, which I grab quickly and take a sniff of. I close my eyes and let the citrus scent run through me, opening them to find Reese standing in the shower with me and smiling.

"You use that and you'll smell like me." He smiles, pulling it out of my hands and squirting some into his palm. "I think you like how I smell."

"I *love* how you smell," I reply as his hands work into a rich lather and he begins rubbing them over my body. "And now I won't even have to see you again today to get my Reese fix." He laughs softly and I watch his concentration as he washes me, starting at my neck and moving down each arm. He covers every inch of skin in suds and I giggle as his hands work my breasts, meticulously washing them for several minutes. "I think they're clean."

"I'll be the judge of that." His hands move down my stomach and around my waist, dropping to my ass and working the lather there as I squirm against him. "So, since you've survived a sleepover with me, that means we can have them all the time now, right?" he asks playfully, his eyes twinkling with mischief.

"Absolutely not. I never intended on sleeping over, in fact, I think you let me fall asleep on you on purpose and tricked me into it." He kneels in front of me and washes between my legs, lingering with a grin before he moves down. He massages my thighs and my shins, bringing each foot up and washing them thoroughly as I grip the shower wall. I'm terribly ticklish and he knows it. I think about what he just asked me. Sleepovers all the time? There's no way I can do the sleepover thing again, let alone all the time. Even though I did get the best sleep of my life, and the sight of him wrapped around me this morning is a memory I'd like to hold onto forever. "That was a special birthday treat." I hold on to his head to keep my balance.

He stands and grabs his shampoo, squeezing some into my hand and doing the same to his. "Honestly, I had every intention of taking you home last night. But I think we must have fallen asleep at the same time. The last thing I remember before passing out is you lying on my chest." We begin washing each other's hair together, my eyes closing as I enjoy the scalp massage. He really is good at this. "And then when I woke up at five and couldn't get you awake without a fog horn, I called Joey and told him you accidently fell asleep and you'd be a little late today. He didn't seem surprised." Our hands drop and I back up into the water, rinsing my hair and smiling at the scent that is now going to be on me all day. I've honestly never smelt anything better, and I live in a fucking bakery.

"Do you always want your flings to spend the night?" I move out of the water and switch spots with him, allowing him to rinse his shampoo out. I grab his body wash and squirt some into my palm. *Shit. Do I really want to know the answer to that? No, I don't.* "Never mind. I don't want to know that." My hands begin to wash his body as his eyes study me. "It doesn't matter. I just don't think we should make a habit out of it." He moans softly as I move over his shoulders with pressure, down his arms, his chest, and his stomach. I get nice and close to reach around and wash his back, inhaling him deeply while I do it.

I kneel down and wash his legs, his erection staring me right in the face. "Dylan, we're casual and everything, but I think you're more than a fling at this point. I don't usually fuck my flings repeatedly." I stand and look up into his eyes as he rinses the soap off himself. His jaw is tight and his brows are furrowed. "Okay?"

I swallow and nod slowly. *Okay. So I'm above his fling status, but still casual, nowhere near the girlfriend zone. And according to Billy, he doesn't do girlfriends, so with Reese, there isn't a girlfriend zone. I guess he does care about me more than his other hook ups.*

"I'm all clean, feel like getting a little dirty?" I ask and his eyes widen instantly. He reaches for me just as I slip quickly out of the shower. "Sorry. No time for that this morning." I wrap a towel around myself and quickly grab the clothes he placed on the sink, making a break for it toward his bedroom. I hear his laughs behind me as I drop the clothes on the bed and examine what he's picked out for me. Sweatpants, a T-shirt, and a pair of his boxers. *Wait, where are my panties?* I glance around the room, looking all around the bed when Reese walks in with a towel wrapped around his waist. I look up at him and my eyes widen. *Sweet Lord.* I've seen the man naked several times already, but the sight of him in just a towel makes me clench my thighs shut.

"Like what you see?" he asks, winking at me as he walks into his closest, momentarily stunning me.

I drop to my knees and glance under the bed. "Panties?"

He's not long and re-emerges with a dress shirt, khakis, and tie, shrugging at me and barely holding in his smile.

I stand and grip my towel. "You have them, don't you? What, are you starting some weird collection of my lingerie?"

He drops his towel and begins dressing, causing me to look away quickly before I jump on him. "I have no idea what you're talking about, but I believe I provided you with some boxers to put your sexy ass into, so I'm not sure what the problem is." He slips on his boxers and pulls his white T-shirt over his head.

"Humph, pervert," I reply and his smile spreads across his face as I drop my towel. I feel his eyes on me as I step into his boxers, rolling them as I did before to make them fit me better. Next, I get into the sweatpants, which I also have to roll several times at the waist. Slipping on my bra, I pull the T-shirt over my head. It's an old University of Chicago shirt and has apparently been worn repeatedly. *Did he give me one of his favorite shirts?* I glance at him as he stands in front of the mirror hanging on his wall, putting on his tie. He looks devastatingly handsome and oh, so yummy in the morning, freshly fucked and showered. He eyes me quickly and I smile before I walk out of the bedroom, needing to leave his presence before I rip his clothes off. Grabbing my purse off the dining room table, I slip into my heels and shake my head at how ridiculous I look in them with his sweats.

"Ready?" He walks down the hallway toward me and stops when I turn to him. I let out a heavy sigh at his appearance as his eyes fall onto my feet. "You look beautiful," he states as if it's obvious, and I run at him, meeting him in the hallway and wrapping my legs around his waist. "Whoa. Hi, love."

"*You* look beautiful. I look rightly silly. Now come on, I'm late enough as it is and you're making me want to throw you back into your bed." He turns me around and starts back toward his bedroom as I giggle into his neck. "No. We can't."

He grunts in protest as he carries me toward the door and we finally leave with me still in his arms.

ع

AFTER STOPPING TO GET A couple coffees, we drive down Fayette Street and pull up in front of the bakery. I glance out the window and see Joey standing behind the counter. "Did you have a good birthday?" I ask as I unbuckle my seat belt and turn to see his eyes on me.

He smiles sweetly and reaches out, pulling my hand into his and lifting it to his lips for a quick kiss. "I had the best birthday." *Oh my.* He drops my hand and I lean in, pressing my lips against his and lingering there for a moment. I suddenly don't want to get out of his car. Not after last night, not after this morning, and definitely not after what he's just admitted. He's minty and delicious, he smells heavenly, and he's dressed way too good right now.

I lean back a bit and his eyes open. "Make out with me," I say in my best flirtatious voice.

He licks his lips. "Isn't that what we were just doing?"

I shake my head, wrapping his tie up in my hand. "No, that was a goodbye kiss. I want you to devour me."

His hands reach around me and he pulls me toward him, sliding me sideways into his lap. "You mean, like this?" he asks and brings his mouth firmly to mine. His tongue twists in my mouth, moving with mine, stroking, licking, and tasting every inch of me. I'm panting so heavily that I'm certain the windows will start fogging up any second.

"I fucking love kissing you," I say as I manage to break away briefly and kiss down his neck to his collar, relishing in his scent.

"See, we could do this every morning if you'd sleep over more."

I move back up and latch back onto his mouth, silencing his ridiculousness. The man is crazy. After several long, totally worth it, minutes of sucking face, I somehow manage to pull away and lick his taste off my lips. "Have a great day, handsome." I open the door and hop out, turning back after nearly stumbling from the make-out session.

"You too, love," he replies. I glance down and notice his erection, reaching in quickly and rubbing against it. His hand clamps down on mine and he moans, pulling his bottom lip into his mouth and shaking his head at me. "Go, before I throw you back in here and take you to work with me to finish what you've started." I shriek and hear his laugh as I shut the door and wave. I'm floating, completely high off him as I make my way into the shop, ready to start my work day.

Chapter
SIXTEEN

"**M**ORNING," I SING AS I walk into the shop and get a massive smile from Joey. I quickly rush upstairs and change into more appropriate work attire, smiling as I fold up Reese's clothes and stick them into my dresser. *I will definitely be wearing these again, and often.* I slip on jeans and a blue blouse and pair them with my favorite pair of strappy black sandals. After throwing my still damp hair up into a messy bun and applying some makeup, I re-emerge into the bakery and see Joey tapping a familiar white box on the counter.

"You have so much to tell me about *after* you open this," he says with a grin. I think he looks forward to my deliveries from Reese as much as I do.

"Did that just get here?" My eyes rake over the box as I pull it close to me. *How in the hell did he have time to send this to me already? He's probably just now settling in at his office.*

"Actually, it was waiting out front this morning. I guess he wanted you to have it as soon as you got here." He sighs. "So fucking romantic. Goddamn it, Billy."

"Oh, leave poor Billy alone, not all men can be as perfect as Reese Carroll." *Jesus, did I just say that out loud? Is Reese perfect?* I think silently for a moment as I stare off into space and decide yes, he is perfect. Catching

Joey's *hurry the fuck up* stare, I excitedly pull the white ribbon and open the box, my eyes widening as I hover over it and glance at the contents. "Holy fuck." I pull out several pictures of an orgasmic Reese. Literally, I know this face, the face he makes when he climaxes. "Oh, my God." I rifle through the box and see pictures of him from the waist up, someone obviously having taken them as they were riding him until he came, waiting for that exact moment to capture it.

"Jesus Christ. Is he... is that... he sent you these?" Joey squeals and grabs a few of the pictures. I allow it only because there's none containing anything from the waist down. *I can't believe this. There's at least a dozen in here. He sent me pictures of him fucking someone else? Or to be more specific, someone else fucking him?* My heart drops as I stare at his face. He's looking at the camera, looking into the eyes of the person taking the picture as she brings him to orgasm. His jaw is clenched, crease in his brow, piercing green eyes. *I'm going to be sick.* "FUCK." I snatch the pictures out of Joey's hand and shove them all back into the box. "I can't believe him. Why the fuck would he send me these? WHAT THE FUCK, JOEY?" My scream causes him to stumble back and he holds up his hands.

"Christ, I don't know. I mean, these are pictures of him having sex with someone, right?"

"Yes. Did you not see his face?" My eyes fill with tears and his face softens. "Why would he send me these?" I drop to the floor. "Oh, God." My hands cover my face and I sob as Joey moves around me. I'm expecting him to drop to the floor with me, but he doesn't. And his voice tells me why.

"Yeah, Reese Carroll please," he says and I glance up to see him holding the shop phone to his ear. *Oh, fuck.* "I don't give a flying fuck if he's in a fucking meeting. Put his ass on the phone now."

"Joey." I stand and try to grab the phone out of his hand, which I realize is useless. We've been down this road. His eyes widen and I see his jaw twitch.

"You stupid fucking prick. What the fuck is wrong with you?"

I can't move and my tears are still falling down my face. I should stop Joey. I can handle my own battles. But right now, I can't form a single thought in my head.

"Don't play dumb, Reese. Dylan got your fucking delivery, you fucking asshole." I stare at the box that's practically screaming at me on my counter and grab it, dropping it into the trashcan. I feel dirty all of a sudden and have a strong urge to go jump in a bath of hand sanitizer. "What delivery? You fucking know what. Why the fuck would she want to see something like that? Fuck you. Don't fucking come near her again." He slams the phone down, his breathing erratic as he turns to me and pulls me into his arms. I cry against him into his chest, letting go and convulsing in violent shakes. My phone begins to ring in my pocket but I ignore it. I know exactly who it is. "Jesus, I'm so sorry." The shop door swings open and we both turn to see Mrs. Frey walk in. I quickly push away from Joey and wipe away my tears.

"Mrs. Frey. Hi, how are you?" I ask as her eyes search my face.

"Dylan? Oh, sweetie, are you all right? Is this a bad time?" She moves toward the counter and I frantically shake my head.

"No, no, not at all. Umm, boy drama." She nods in appreciation and smiles at me as I force a friendly expression. "Let me grab your cake." I walk in the back and pull her cake out of the fridge, placing it on the worktop to give it a final once over. My phone rings again in my pocket and I once again ignore it. *Fuck him.* I open the cake top and glance at my creation. The chocolate peppermint frosting messes with me and the tears come again. "Pull your shit together. You're at work," I say to myself quietly. I can't let this affect my job. I was warned about Reese, multiple times actually. I shouldn't be surprised. It's my own fucking fault for reacting this way. I quickly close the cake box, plastering on a smile as I walk back up front.

"Here you go. One double chocolate peppermint cake. Happy Anniversary."

Mrs. Frey beams at me. "Oh, Dylan, it looks lovely. You even scrolled our names on it. Bless you, dear." She leans in and gives me a quick hug before she waves at Joey and turns to leave.

As soon as the shop door closes, my fake expression drops and I crumble. "Joey, I need a minute." I quickly run into the back, up the stairs, and hurl myself into my bed.

I'm immediately reminded of waking up with Reese as I wrap

myself around my comforter that doesn't smell like him. However, I do. *I fucking smell like him.* I used to love this comforter, but right now, I hate it. I used to love everything about this bed, but not anymore. Not after last night. Last night was obviously some sort of a fucking joke to him since he decided to remind me ever so sweetly this morning of all his other hook ups. *What were his words? Close to twenty probably? What a whore.* My phone beeps a text message alert in my pocket and I pull it out and chuck it across the room, sending it crashing against my wall. I close my eyes and think back to last night when I hear commotion coming from below me. Familiar commotion. *Shit.*

"Reese! Do not fucking go up there!" Joey's voice screeches and I panic, flinging myself out of my bed and running toward my bathroom as I see his head quickly emerging up my stairs.

"Dylan!" he yells, panicky, but I make it to the bathroom and slam the door, locking it quickly. The door shakes as he pounds on it. "Dylan, what the fuck is going on?"

I back away from the door and sit on the edge of the tub. "Go away, Reese." The tears sting my cheeks as they stream down at a faster pace. My eyes are locked on the door as it shakes furiously. "Go the fuck away!" I hunch over and cover my ears the best I can. *Where the fuck is Joey?*

"Dylan, what happened?" The banging stops. "Please talk to me. I don't know what delivery you got, but I didn't send you anything today. I fucking swear to God I didn't." *He didn't send me anything? But it was in the same box. The white box.*

I stand. "You didn't send me anything?" My broken voice stings my throat.

"No, love, please open the door. I need to see you." I hear the sound of a light thud and picture Reese dropping his head against the door. My mind scrambles. *If he didn't send me anything, then who did?* "Dylan?" I quickly wipe under my eyes and turn the lock, opening the door and looking up at him. He immediately grabs me and pulls me into him and I don't protest. I let him hold me until I remember the pictures, which only takes me a few seconds.

"Let go of me!" I yell and push past him, feeling his hands on my waist and spinning me around.

"Love."

"No. You may not have sent me those pictures, but someone sure as hell did. I can't fucking believe this." The images are burned into my mind and I'm fuming.

"What pictures? What are you talking about?" I go to walk downstairs, hearing Joey's voice and someone else's, but Reese holds on to me.

"Let go of me and I'll fucking show you."

He does, but not before I hear him mutter something under his breath that sounds an awful lot like *drives me crazy.*

I march into the bakery and see Ian pinning a very red-faced Joey against the wall. "Jesus Christ. Let him go, Ian." He does and Joey shoves him hard before turning toward me.

"Are you all right?" he asks, flicking a glare toward Reese who has followed close behind me.

"Yes. No. I don't know." I reach into the trash and pull out the box, thrusting it into Reese's chest. "So glad I got to see these. Really made my fucking day." I walk over to Joey and make sure he's okay.

Ian walks up to us both. "Sorry, man. I just needed to give my boy a chance to talk to his girl and knew you wouldn't let him."

Joey smoothes out his shirt. "You're lucky you're marrying one of my best friends; otherwise, I would have hurled you through that window. Asshole."

"Fuck," Reese says and we all turn to him and see him fishing through the box. "That fucking bitch. Dylan, I'm so sorry you saw these." He moves closer to me and I step back, putting my hand up to stop him.

"Who sent them?" I ask sternly. His eyes flick to Ian and I move in closer. "Reese, who the fuck sent these to me?"

He swallows loudly. "The girl I was last…"

"Fucking?" Joey fills in.

Reese nods.

"Classy," Joey adds.

Ian's eyes widen. "Shit, man. I knew she was pissed that you fired her, but I guess she was way past pissed. And clearly unstable. Fuck." *Fired her? Oh, please don't tell me.*

I shake my head and feel all three pairs of eyes on me. I rub my temples. "Let me guess, bitchy redheaded receptionist?" Reese and Ian's eyes both react the same way. I run my hands down my face. "Wow, nice, Reese. Have you fucked every girl in your office or do you just have a thing for the ones who give your current hook up access to you?" He doesn't answer that and it's probably for the best. I can feel my blood pressure boiling and I want to hit something. I need to hit something. "One of you better fucking volunteer or I'm slapping all three of you."

Joey immediately backs up. "Fuck that. What the fuck did I do?"

Ian looks at Reese who quickly steps forward, holding his hands out to me. I step in and slap him hard, harder than I've slapped him before and yelp as my hand begins to sting. "Shit." I shake my hand and feel Reese grab it, looking at it as his reddened cheek glares at me. *That looks like it hurts. Good.*

"Jesus," Ian says and Joey muffles a laugh. The redhead pops into my mind and so does the image of her sitting on the park bench last weekend. "Oh, my God. I knew that bitch was psychotic." I yank my hand out of Reese's as he begins to rub it.

"What are you talking about?" he asks.

"Juls and I saw that whore staring at you guys while you played basketball on Sunday. It was really fucking weird." My eyes flick from Ian to Reese and I see a small smile pull at Reese's lips. "What the hell are you smiling at? You *do* realize I have another hand to slap the shit out of you with, right?"

"You were watching our game?"

Oh, damn it. "No," I snarl and his smile widens. I hear a muffled laugh from Ian. "Maybe. That's not the point. She was staring at you guys and it was really fucking creepy." I grit my teeth. "That stupid bitch. She better pray I never see her face again, otherwise I'm going to break it." I know my face is blood red and see all three men smiling at me in amusement. "Shut up," I snap and turn at the sound of the shop door opening. I freeze as Justin steps into the bakery and possibly also into the room he will die in.

"Fuck," Joey and I say in unison as Reese moves quickly, grabbing me with one arm and pulling me behind him.

"What the *fuck* are you doing here?" he blasts as my eyes stay glued on Justin. He looks fucked up, seriously fucked up. Eyes are swollen, his nose is jacked up, and he has a massive cut in the corner of his mouth. I briefly feel sorry for him until I remember his hands on me last week. His mouth is hanging open and his eyes widen at the sight of Reese. Clearly, he wasn't expecting him to be here.

"I told you to stay the fuck away from her!" Reese shouts, loud enough that I think the glass window rattles.

Ian moves to stand between the two men. "Justin, this isn't the best time, man," he says as he keeps his hand on Reese's heaving chest.

This is not what I need right now and I'm angry enough to deal with this asshole myself. I move quickly out from behind Reese and step in front of Justin, feeling Ian's body tense. "I suggest you leave now before I cut your dick off and feed it to you." His eyes widen as he backs up slightly. I step closer and close the gap. "I'd say I'd make you choke on it, but let's be serious, that thing never once satisfied me." My eyes flick quickly to his crotch before I smirk back in his face.

"HA!" Joey laughs behind me and I want to turn around and high-five him, but I don't. I just watch my ex shrink a few inches in front of me.

"Jesus Christ. I just wanted to apologize for what I did, Dylan. I'm sorry, okay?" His eyes flick to Reese. "Really fucking sorry."

My body relaxes a bit and I nod once before flicking my eyes to the door. "Good, now get the fuck out."

"Whatever." He turns sharply and leaves the shop and I force all the air out of my lungs. *Fuck, I feel like I need a drink.*

"Shit, Dylan. Remind me never to cross you. You're a bit terrifying." Ian laughs behind me as I spin to see two very amused expressions and one that isn't so amused.

Reese looks a right mix of angry and apprehensive. "I need to get back to work, but we need to talk about this."

I cross my arms over my chest. "Talk about what? That one of your twenty hook ups sent me pictures of her making you come? Nah, I'm good." I push past him and feel his hand on my arm, spinning me back around.

"We *will* fucking talk about this," he growls and puts the box under his arm before he pulls me in and kisses me forcefully on the lips.

I hear a soft moan in my throat and try to swallow it down. *Damn it, stupid body. Stay angry with me.* He pulls away and turns toward the door. "Let's go, Ian."

Joey and I stand in the middle of the shop and watch as the two hot CPAs walk out the door and pile into the white Range Rover parked out front.

҈

THE REST OF THE DAY goes by without a hitch. No more obscene deliveries and no more mangled ex-boyfriends coming in with overdue apologies. This day started out so great and turned awful within a matter of minutes. I'm miserable and bitchy and Joey is paying for it because he's the only person I can yell at right now. I'd never call Reese at work and cuss him out, no matter how pissed off I am at him. I'm much more of a show up and barge into his office type of girl. But I won't do that today either because I really don't want to see him. The man is hard to stay mad at in person, and right now, I need to stay mad. Juls is wrapping up with a bride all day, dealing with last minute wedding preparations, so she's off limits too. So my poor assistant has been dealing with my mood swings, and they have been a doozy.

Mainly because the memory of the amazing night and morning I had with Reese keeps filtering into the memory of the photos I received. And I get it; it's not his fault the photos were sent to me. He obviously didn't send them. But he allowed them to be taken and had to have known they could possibly be leaked or shown to somebody. I've never let anyone take pictures of me like that or taken ones of myself and sent them to anybody. So why did he let her do it? Did she mean something to him? Was she special in some way or did he allow all of his hook ups to take pictures of him like that? That thought makes me want to drink myself into tomorrow. And then there's the quantity that I received. There had to be at least twelve different shots of him having an orgasm. Twelve separate times they fucked and she made him come. Were there more than that? Did she only send me the best images? His words from our shower together run through me. *I don't usually fuck my flings repeatedly.* So she obviously wasn't a fling. She was more than that to him. Just like me. Maybe she got too clingy and that's why he ended things with her. She was the girl he wasn't really serious with before the wedding. And he's not really serious with me. How am I any different than her?

"Cupcake, you all right?" Joey asks as I put the finishing touches on the cake for the Brown/Tucker wedding. Even though my mind has been elsewhere, I'm still able to put together a beautiful, four-tiered, white chocolate creation with sugared Gerber daisies cascading down the side. "Dylan?"

I step back and admire my work. "I'm fine. Come look at this, will you?" Joey shuffles back into the kitchen and I hear his reaction, causing me to smile. I turn and see his adoring expression. "Looks pretty good, right?"

He moves next to me and puts his arm around my shoulder, pulling me against him. "Gorgeous. You never cease to amaze me, cupcake." He plants a quick kiss into my hair as my phone beeps. Somehow, even though I had hurled it with all my strength against my wall earlier, it managed to survive the assault. I reach quickly into my pocket after wiping my hands off on my apron.

REESE: *I need to see you tonight.*

I show it to Joey. "Well, you knew that was coming; the boy is persistent." He leans in and checks out the flowers. "What are you going to do?"

I stare at his message before I answer. "I don't know. I think I need a night with my two best friends and no boys. Can that happen?" He smiles and pulls his phone out, quickly messing with it. I'll deal with Reese tomorrow when we both attend Billy and Joey's party.

His phone beeps and he turns toward me. "Juls is in, cupcake. No boys." I nod and smile weakly as I reply to Reese.

ME: *I can't tonight. I need some time to think.*

Joey walks back up front while I await his response. It doesn't take long.

REESE: *Don't pull away from me.*

He guts me with his words, the same words from last night. Is he *that* worried I'll end this? Or he is just worried I won't give him the opportunity to explain the situation. I type quickly.

Me: *I'm not. I just think I need some space. You have no idea what this feels like for me.*

I go to press send, but don't, my thumb hovering over the button. *Shit. Do I really want space from him?* Hitting the back button, I shorten the message before I send it.

Me: *I'm not.*

⁂

JOEY DRIVES US TO JULS' house after we close up shop and make a quick liquor store run. There is no way in hell I'm not drinking tonight. I'm actually surprised I didn't dive into the vodka bottle that's been in my freezer for months at some point today. But I'd never drink at work, no matter how hurt or pissed off I was. Reese hasn't sent me any more messages or tried to call, which I'm grateful for. But it also surprises me. He is so damned persistent about everything that I half expected him to barge into the shop before closing, throw me over his shoulder, and take me home with him so we could fuck, talk, and fuck some more. And I hate that a chunk of me wishes he would have. But tonight isn't about boys. It's about spending time with my two best friends, laughing and hanging out like we did before the three of us fell fast and hard for members of the Chicago man candy club.

Joey parks outside Juls' building and we walk inside together. She lives in Hyde Park, which is about fifteen minutes from the bakery, in a two bedroom apartment. She's lived here since graduation, and it occurs to me as we walk up the flight of stairs to the second floor that she will only be living here for a few more months. She will surely move in with Ian after the wedding, and the thought of her not living in this place that holds so many of our memories saddens me. I sigh and catch Joey's attention as we step out onto the floor.

"Come on, cupcake, we're here to have fun, not sulk." I follow him to Juls' door and he opens it without knocking, in true Joey form. Once he's been to your house, he feels like he lives there along with you.

"I'm not sulking. I'll just miss this place once Juls moves in with Ian." We spot her in the kitchen opening a bottle of wine and she beams at us. "Do you remember that time we threw that eighties party here and you dressed up like Vanilla Ice?" He blushes at my memory as we plop down in front of the television on the floor.

Juls walks over with three wine glasses and hands them out. "That was fucking hilarious. You knew the entire rap from Teenage Mutant Ninja Turtles," she says. I giggle into my glass and take a few large sips.

"Christ, I will never live that shit down. Thank God no one took any video of that mess."

"That party was insane," Juls says behind her glass. "Dyl, remember how pissed off you got at Justin because he was the only person here *not* dressed up?"

I nod and picture the memory, rolling my eyes at it and taking a sip. "What an asshole. He spent the entire party bitching about the music selections. It was a fucking *eighties* party. What did he expect?"

Joey laughs around his glass. "I think he expected you to just leave with him and not have an amazing time. But you have never been that girl, cupcake, and he should have known that. What a waste he was." Juls and I mumble in agreement.

"A waste that ended up getting *exactly* what he deserved. Prick," she adds, tossing us each a pillow so we can sprawl out on the floor. "Are we going to talk about the pictures, sweets?"

"No," I quickly reply.

Joey rolls onto his side. "You can't be mad about girls he's fucked before you. That's not fair. He didn't even know you when those pictures were taken."

"That's not why I'm mad." I sit up, glaring at both of them. "Well, okay, yes it bothers me that he's been with other women. And I know it shouldn't because I wasn't a virgin when we started this thing between us, but I've only been with Justin." I put my glass down. "Reese gave me a ballpark figure of close to twenty girls and that's a fucking lot. Which is fine, whatever. I can deal with that as long as it's not thrown in my face. But it was." I close my eyes and picture one of the images from the box. Grabbing my glass off the small table, I down it quickly before I continue. "I'm not even mad at him about this. Not even in the slightest, which is what's making this so fucking confusing. The only thing he did wrong was allow for the pictures to be taken of him and not confiscate them after he ended it with her. He didn't send them to me. He doesn't talk about other girls he's been with. He tells me I'm amazing and I'm all he thinks about." I sigh heavily and throw myself back down onto my pillow. "But now I have to deal with psychotic ex-hook ups and I'm not sure I'd do well in prison. I'm too hostile." This is true. I'd probably end up permanently in solitary confinement after getting into too many fights or disobeying orders.

I glance over and see the bursting smiles on my two best friends' faces, desperately trying to hold in their hysteria. I motion for them to let it out and the three of us fall into a fit of giggles.

"All right, so I have a question," Joey says and I shake my head, preparing for the worst here. "How the hell did you wind up spending the night with him last night? I thought you were against sex in beds and sleepovers and anything too intimate."

"You slept over at his house?" Juls asks.

"It was an accident. He wanted to fuck me in his bed for his birthday, so I let him, and then we passed out together. I'm not letting it happen again." I glance over and see Joey's mischievous grin and Juls' teary eyes. "What?"

"You were his birthday present? Oh my," she says and blinks rapidly. *Good Lord, she's emotional lately.*

I glare at Joey. "And what's up with you?"

Crossing his hands behind his head, he continues after a dramatic pause. "I just think it's cute that you *think* it was an accident. I mean, he could have woken you up and driven you home, but he called me instead and told me you would be late today. It was no accident, cupcake. He wanted you there."

My eyes widen and I sit up. "He called you this morning, right?"

He shakes his head and grins wide at me. "Nope. He called me last night after you passed out."

I shuffle over and sit on top of him, hearing him squeal underneath me. "What the hell do you mean he called you last night? Are you serious?" His grin answers for him and I glance over at Juls who is laughing hysterically. "I can't believe this. He lied to me."

"Oh, relax, sweets. I think it's romantic that he wanted you to spend the night with him. How was it anyway?"

The memory of last night runs through me quickly and I feel my lip curl up into a smile. I shrug and play it off. "It was okay." *Wow. I don't even sound convincing to myself.* I roll off Joey and lay back down on my pillow. "I sure hope he enjoyed himself because that shit is never happening again."

"Hmm mmm," my two best friends say in unison. I bite my lip to contain my laugh but crack, letting it out as they fall apart next to me. This is how the rest of the evening plays out. Laughing and joking on the living room floor in Juls' apartment as we polish off two bottles of wine. There's Juls and Ian's wedding talk, Joey and Billy's moving in together talk, and mine and Reese's crazy fight hard, fuck harder, non-relationship talk. It's a much needed gab fest among three friends who used to only rely on each other. After several hours of gossiping and alcohol consumption, I pass out in the middle of her living room and slip into my Reese coma.

Chapter
SEVENTEEN

AFTER A FAST BREAKFAST WITH Juls, Joey and I return to the bakery and put the finishing touches on the wedding cake before loading it up into Sam. The reception hall is thirty minutes away and traffic is a nightmare, but we make it on time and drop the beautiful, white chocolate, Gerber daisy cake off without any issues. I shower and dress after saying my goodbyes to Joey and lock the shop up, deciding to sit outside on the bench, which is a store down from mine, while I wait for Juls. Today is dress-shopping day and I'm not sure who is more excited about it, her or me. I've never been in a wedding party before and am delighted to be a part of Ian and Juls' special day. Plus, I *would* have the hottest date on the planet. Of course, that's if we are still doing this thing between us in three months. The thought unsettles me and I scroll through my phone while I sit on the bench, pulling up his last text message.

REESE: *Don't pull away from me.*

What the hell does that even mean? I'm sure it doesn't mean the way I'm interpreting it, which is in the most gigantic scheme of things way possible. I'm sure he's only referring to my justified freak out over the pictures I received yesterday. *Shit.* The thought of them makes me queasy. His face, the face I had hoped was only reserved for me, clearly isn't because it's been captured by another woman. I sigh forcefully and jam my phone into my jeans pocket. How stupid of me to think he only looks at me like that. That I'm the only woman he watches intently as he's coming. I close my eyes tightly and the sound of a car approaching causes me to peek them open. Juls' black Escalade pulls up to the curb and the passenger window rolls down as I stand up.

"Let's go, sweets."

I smile, pushing all of the Reese drama to the very back of my mind. I can't think about this shit right now. Today is about Juls, and I'm going to keep my mind occupied with all things maid of honor like.

℮୬

WE'VE ARRIVED AT CHRISTIAN'S BRIDAL Shop, and after a few moments of quick hysteria over the fact that we are *actually* shopping for Juls' wedding dress, we walk around the store and peruse the selections. Juls' sister Brooke, who will be the other bridesmaid next to Joey, met us here shortly after we arrived. I haven't seen her in a while and she's been talking my ear off nonstop about the lack of men in her life and probing for information on mine.

"Oh, come on, Dylan. Tell me all about this guy who works with Ian. I'm dying for some hardcore gossip and Juls won't tell me shit," she says from the dressing room next to me. We've been handed a few dress choices and I'm currently slipping myself into a chocolate brown strapless number that feels and looks incredible. *Damn. Would it be weird to buy this if Juls doesn't pick this for her big day?* I zip up the back and open the curtain.

"There's nothing to tell. He's just a guy I'm having fun with." I step out and hop up onto the pedestal in front of a massive mirror, seeing Juls' reflection as she stands behind me.

"Holy shit. I love that one. What do you think though? Is it comfortable? Do you think we should go for something more cheery, like maybe a burnt orange color?"

I spin around to face her. "Burnt orange? How the hell is that more cheery? And are you trying to make us look like pumpkins?"

She bites her bottom lip and eyes up my dress as Brooke walks out in the exact same one. "I love this one. Juls, pick this because the other three are fucking hideous and make me look like I'm six months pregnant."

Juls moves to stand by her sister and runs her hand over the material. "Yup, this is it. You both look amazing in it and I love the color." She smiles and bobs her head. "Well, that was way too fucking easy. Now it's time for the real fun." She wiggles her brows and walks to her dressing room while Brooke and I stand and gaze at our reflections.

"And what do you mean you're just having fun with this guy? Are you telling me it's strictly a sex thing between you two, because if you are, I think that's bullshit. Guys can make that shit work, but I don't think girls can. We're too emotional." *Jesus. Did she hit the nail on the head or what?* Leave it to Brooke to be exceedingly insightful when she hasn't even met the guy I'm just having fun with yet.

"I'm keeping my emotions out of it." *Or, at least, I'm desperately trying to.*

"Ha! Yeah, okay, good luck with that. How's the sex?" I glance over at her and issue my wicked grin. "Damn. I need to start checking out office buildings for smart men. You and my sister are making bank."

My phone beeps in my dressing room and I hop down quickly, racing in to pull it out of my discarded jeans. My heart sinks a bit at the message sender.

JOEY: *Party is postponed. My baby has the stomach bug that's going around. How's the dress shopping going?*

ME: *Oh no! Tell Billy I hope he feels better. We just picked out our dresses and Juls is trying hers on now. I'll send you a pic.*

Well, shit. I guess I won't be seeing Reese tonight at the party after all. My disappointment quickly gets blanketed by the realization that it might be a good thing to go a few days without seeing him. Between the accidental, but not really accidental, sleepover to the photos I received, I have a lot of shit to think about. I hear a gasp from Brooke and I quickly slip out of my dressing room and let my eyes fall on Juls who has just emerged from hers. *Holy shit.*

"Holy shit. Juls… oh my, that's… oh, wow." There are no words to describe the woman I'm staring at right now. She's beautiful, exquisite even, in a strapless tight laced bodice and ruffled skirt, her tiny waist accented with a deep brown sash that falls down her back and onto her train.

"Wow. You look amazing," Brooke states as her sister takes her place on her pedestal and begins to twirl slowly.

"It's beautiful, right?" She shakes her hands out by her side and I can tell she's nervous.

"What is it?"

"I don't know. Is it weird that I have no desire to try on any other dresses? I mean, this is the first one I put on and I feel like this is it. I can see myself marrying Ian in this. Maybe I should try on more."

"Fuck that. Who cares if it's the first one you try on. You look amazing in it. Like crazy amazing. I can *totally* see you marrying Ian in this dress," I reply and see the tension leave her shoulders. Leave it to Juls to worry about the standards of bridal gown shopping. Her smile widens in the mirror and I can tell she's on to something. "What?" She quickly hops down and slips back into her dressing room.

"Damn it. I wanna get married. There better at least be some hot groomsmen for me to fool around with at this thing," Brooke grunts.

"The best man is off limits, just so you know," I reply and she squints at me.

Juls re-emerges with another gown in her hands and walks over to me, thrusting it into my arms. "Here, try this on."

"What? Are you crazy?" *She must be if she thinks I'm slipping into a wedding gown.* "I am *not* trying on a wedding dress."

"Why not? This would look amazing on you, right, Brooke?" *Oh, for Christ's sake.*

Brooke steps up and admires the gown. "She's right, Dylan. It's a halter and you always look amazing in halter dresses with those boobs of yours. Remember prom? God, I fucking hate you both."

I back up. "You are both nuts. There's no way I'm putting that thing on or any other wedding dress for that matter. I'm pretty sure I'd seal my fate as being perpetually single if I did." This is an honest fear. Karma has been increasingly hostile toward me lately and I can see her crossing her arms and stomping her foot at me now, daring me to push my luck.

"Oh, come on, Dyl. Brooke will try some on too, right, Brooke?" We both look at her sister who is sulking on her pedestal.

"Whatever. I fucking hate weddings."

I shake my head and turn back to Juls who is staring me down. "No."
She stomps her foot and grits her teeth. "Excuse you, but as maid of honor you're supposed to do everything I ask."

"And that includes trying on wedding gowns? Are you mental?"
She frowns big time at me and I melt. *Damn it.* "Fine, give me the stupid thing." I rip it from her hands and march with fury to my dressing room as she squeals in delight. *This is insane and completely ridiculous.* After stripping out of my maid of honor dress, annoyed, I step into the wedding gown and slowly zip it up, my eyes widening as I gaze down at myself. "Oh, shit," I whisper, obviously not low enough because Juls rips open the curtain.

"Wow. You look incredible." She pulls me from my room and pushes me up onto the pedestal as Brooke walks up behind me.

"Damn, Dylan. Would it be weird to put that shit on hold indefinitely?"

I smile subtly at her comment and gaze at my reflection. My chest tightens at the sight of myself. Me, in a wedding gown, and I look amazing. *Crap.* I'm covered in lace from my detailed halter down to my train. I was never a fan of lace, but right now, standing in this dress, I'm a *huge* fan. A clicking sound comes from behind me and I turn to see Juls taking a picture of me with her phone. "What the hell?"

"Oh, relax. I won't send it to any sexy CPAs or anything. It's just for us." I can't imagine what would happen if Reese got a hold of that picture. He'd probably freak the fuck out and end things for sure. *Talk about being clingy.* "Seriously, Dylan, look at us." Juls hops up onto my pedestal and grabs my hand, linking it with hers. Besides the fact that we are both standing in wedding gowns, humorously, we're complete opposites in appearance. Juls with her dark brown, straight hair and me with my uber blonde, naturally wavy mess, her piercing blue eyes contrast with my wide brown ones that seem to take up the majority of my face, and she's a good three inches taller than me as I stand up on my toes to bring me up to her five foot nine height. "Goof. I'm getting married, Dyl."

"You are and I'm not, so I'm getting the *fuck* out of this thing." She giggles as I hop down and slip back into my dressing room. But before

I take it off, I admire myself alone for a brief moment. I've never given much thought to getting married. Having only been in one serious relationship, Justin never appealed to me as the marrying kind, which now seems ironic since he *is* married. Just not happily, or faithfully. But standing in this dress right now, for the first time in my life, I can picture myself walking down the aisle toward the one person I want to spend my life with. And before I can put a face to that one person, I slip out of the dress and back into reality.

After saying goodbye to Juls and her sister, I spend the rest of the day keeping myself busy with a massive amount of baking. Seven dozen muffins, six batches of cookies, and an assortment of pastries later, I finally slip upstairs and crash, passing out immediately.

I WAKE UP CRANKY AND miserable on Sunday morning, having experienced one of the shittiest nights of sleep I've ever had. I tossed and turned all night, my usual dreams of Reese and I together replaced with him and a string of women with red hair who he's fucking relentlessly. I wake up constantly, drenched in sweat and when I pass back out, another redhead replaces the previous one. I chalk it up to the fact that I haven't seen or heard from him since Friday afternoon and I'm in desperate need of my fix. But he hasn't called me or texted and I have no fucking clue how to interpret that. Coming from a man who pursued the shit out of me, sending me sweet notes and packages, and texting me daily. And now, nothing. Panic runs through me that I've actually royally fucked this up by telling him I needed time to think. But time to think doesn't mean leave me alone. It just means what it means. That I've been thinking, which I have, and I'm done.

I've decided I'm done being pissy over the photos I received Friday because it's not doing me any good. It wasn't his fault and knowing him, I'm sure he's dealt with that spiteful bitch to prevent any future deliveries from her. I have no right to be mad or jealous about his previous hook ups, especially since we're not serious. And I've also decided I'm okay with that. This is what Reese wants, the only thing he does, and I'm having fun doing it with him. I refuse to let my emotions screw this up because this, what we're doing, is the best thing I've ever done with a man. He's sweet and fun and hot as hell. And he chose me. Of all the girls lining up, he chose me. What we're doing is enough for him and it can be enough for me. I don't need to be in a serious relationship to be happy; I've never been this happy before in my life. The sound of my phone ringing sends me sprinting up the stairs where I plugged it in before I decided to organize my pantry. Disappointment runs through me as Juls' names flashes across my screen.

"Hey, what's up?"

"Can you meet me, like right now, sweets? I really need to talk to someone and I want it to be you." She sounds upset. Juls never sounds upset.

"Yeah, of course. Where?"

"The coffee shop on West Elm okay? I'm only five minutes away."

"Okay, I'm leaving now."

I hang up and dress quickly, grabbing my keys and locking up behind me as I dash around the corner where I keep Sam parked. Juls' voice is really worrying me and I want to get to her as fast as I can. She's never upset. Her two favorite emotions are elated happiness, which is frequent lately after Ian came into her life, and pissed off hurricane Juls mode. The drive to Brocks Coffee Shop is a short distant from the bakery and I park behind her black Escalade, hopping out quickly and dashing into the building. I spot her at a table in the corner, her dainty hands wrapped around a coffee cup.

"Hey. Sorry if you've been waiting long. Fucking traffic."

"No, I just sat down. Do you want something to drink?" Typical Juls, always concerned about other people and not what's bothering her. God, love her for it.

"No, I'm fine. What's wrong? You sounded upset on the phone."

She glances down into her mug. "I don't know what's wrong with me. Ian and I went out yesterday after I dropped you off and checked out some wedding venues and reception halls, and I just didn't care. Like at all. I mean, what the fuck? I've been dreaming about my wedding day since I was six." Her eyes fill up with tears as she turns them up to me. I reach over and cover her hand with mine. "I love weddings, everything about them. That's why I became a wedding planner. But when it comes to my own wedding, it's like I have zero opinion about anything. I don't care whether or not we get married in a church or if it's an outdoor ceremony. I don't care what music I walk down the aisle to or what favors the guests will receive or what my cake looks like, no offense."

My lips curl up into a smile. "None taken."

"I don't even care who the hell is invited. All I care about is marrying him. As long as Ian's there, that's *all* I care about." She blinks and her tears fall down her cheek. "Dylan, honestly, do you think there's something wrong with me?"

I laugh softly and shake my head. "No, not at all. I think you're focusing on the *only* thing that matters. Who cares about everything else?" My hand squeezes hers and she smiles. "I kind of love how marrying Ian is the only thing that matters to you, because it's the only thing that *should* matter. You're going to spend the rest of your life with this man who clearly worships the ground your pretty little feet walk on, so who gives a shit what the fucking centerpieces look like or what the dinner options are for the guests. Fuck the guests." She bursts out laughing and shakes her head at me and most likely herself for thinking this way. Although, I am a little shocked she doesn't have a few things she's dead set on.

"I love you, Dylan. You really are the only person who understands me."

Leaning back, I cross my legs under the table. "Well, and Ian, I'm sure. So what does he say about all this?"

She takes a quick sip of her coffee. "He keeps saying 'whatever you want, babe,' which would be perfect if I had any opinions at all. I kind of wish he would just take over and make all the decisions, because if he leaves it up to me, nothing's going to get done. Except my dress choice, of course."

"Of course, and what a dress. Does that thing even need to be altered, because it fit you perfectly?"

"Hmmm, so did yours, both of them." She pulls out her phone and swipes the screen a few times before handing it over.

I glance down at the picture of me staring at my reflection in the lace halter dress. *Jesus, it looks good.* "I should make you delete this in front of me." I hand her back her phone.

"Not a chance in hell." She slips it back away, quickly so I don't grab it and delete it myself, I'm sure. "What's new with Reese? You heard from him since the picture incident?"

My stomach knots up and I sigh loudly, rubbing my hands down my face. "No, not a peep. But I guess the distance is good right now. We really shouldn't be attached at the hip."

"Dylan."

I glance up at her serious face. "Julianna." I never call her by her full name and can barely say it without smiling.

She rolls her eyes. "Are you in love with him?"

I lean my elbows onto the table and cover my face with my hands. After a slow exhale, I reply honestly, "I don't know. I feel like I'm putting a lot of energy into *not* falling in love with him, but it's the hardest thing I've ever done." I glance over at her. "For a guy who normally doesn't do the relationship thing, I think he'd be damn good at it. But how stupid would I be to fall in love with someone who doesn't do anything serious? I'd just be setting myself up for a major heartbreak, right?" I begin to rub my temples as she fights a smile. "I've never loved any man before. Definitely not Justin. But with Reese? Fuck, I don't know."

She leans forward and rubs my arm. "Just because he's never done relationships before or anything besides casual fucking, doesn't mean he isn't capable of doing it. Dylan, for Christ's sake. The man is crazy about you. Everyone can see that."

"He's crazy about fucking me." I glance around quickly to make sure my heightened voice didn't draw any unwanted attention. "That's all this is."

"You're really fucking stupid if you think that's true. Just grow a pair and tell him how you feel already."

I shake my head at her and purse my lips as she sips her coffee. Of course Juls doesn't understand where I'm coming from here. She and Ian have been more than serious since they started dating. A thought that's been running through my mind since Friday comes streaming back. Why *did* Reese end it with that red headed pyscho? Was it because she wanted more, that she was in love with him and he didn't or couldn't feel the same way? I can't help but think the same fate is lined up for me if I were to let myself fall, so I won't. I'm going to keep those unwanted feelings buried deep inside me for now, until maybe he eventually decides he wants more. *Please, God, let him want more.*

☙

I CRAWL INTO BED SUNDAY night after getting a bite to eat with Juls. We both wanted more than just coffee in our system and ate at a local Thai place that we frequent often. I wrap myself up in my comforter and the University of Chicago T-shirt that Reese lent me and stare at my alarm clock. It's only a little after eight p.m., and I know I won't pass out anytime soon, but I'm at least going to try. Closing my eyes, I picture his face, the face I catch him having when he's watching me, studying me. Crease in his brow, jaw set, eyes narrowed in on whatever it is I'm doing. Always so studious.

A loud, deafening crash sends them flying back open. *What the hell was that?* I shoot out of bed and dash down the stairs, skidding to a stop behind my worktop when I see a hooded figure standing outside my now shattered glass store front through the doorway. "Oh, shit." Panic, sheer panic runs through me and I dash back upstairs, grab my phone off my nightstand, and begin dialing the only person I can think of.

"Pick up, pick up, pick up." I dart into my bathroom and close and lock the door behind me. *Jesus Christ! Someone's broken into my bakery! Who the fuck breaks into a bakery?* After three long rings, I hear his voice.

"Dylan?"

"Reese! Someone's in my shop! I heard a loud crash and ran downstairs and—"

"Where are you? Are you safe?" His voice is filled with worry and I can tell he's on the move. *Oh, God, please be at your place and not far from me.*

"I'm in my bathroom. They broke the window and I saw someone." I hear commotion, a lot of commotion through the phone as I crawl into my bathtub and close the shower curtain. *Like that's going to do any good if they decide to break into the bathroom. This is so horror movie cliché; I almost roll my eyes at myself.* "Please, I need you," I cry, dropping my head between my knees and letting myself sob.

"Stay in there. Don't come out no matter what you hear. GOD-DAMN IT. SHIT." Echoes of footsteps ring through the phone and he's out of breath, but his curse words keep flying. "I'm on my way. Call the police."

"NO. Please don't make me hang up." I'm crying, shaking with fear and my words are broken and strained. I hear the sound of a car starting.

"Fuck. Move the fuck out of the way!" Car horns and another string of cuss words come through the phone as I clutch it tightly. "Love, you have to call the police. I'm almost there. I won't let anything happen to you, I promise. Just hang up and call them and then call me back, okay?"

"Okay, okay. Please hurry."

"I am."

I quickly hang up and dial 911, rapidly telling them the situation and giving them my location. They tell me the police are on their way and to stay where I am. That's not going to be a problem. I have zero intention of moving from this spot until I hear Reese on the other side of the door, even though I haven't heard a noise coming from below me since the sound of the window breaking. I hang up and dial him again.

"I'm here. Don't open the door until I get up there, okay?"

"Okay, but stay on the phone with me." I hear his heavy breathing and the sound of glass crunching and cracking. *God, please don't let that person still be here.* If I hear Reese getting into a struggle with someone, there's no way in hell I'm staying in this bathroom. I don't care what the consequences are. I will claw the fucker's eyes out if he puts his hands on Reese. I hear footsteps outside the door and hold my breath.

"Dylan?"

I drop my phone and crawl out of the tub, scrambling for the lock and swinging the door open. I don't even register his appearance before I jump into his arms and cling to him. "Oh, my God, I was so scared." I'm holding onto him like I haven't seen him in years, my body completely glued to his. "Is he still here?"

His arms wrap me up and he breathes into my hair, his chest heaving against mine. "Dylan." I moan softly at the sound of my name. "It's okay; I've got you. I didn't see anyone, but your front window is completely smashed to shit." He carries me away from the bathroom and into my bedroom area.

I'm shaking against his body and tighten my grip. "Jesus Christ. Why would someone break into my bakery? Do you think they wanted treats?" I hear a small muffled laugh escape his lips, which are pressed into my hair. My tears are streaming down my face as he places me on my feet in front of my dresser. I look him over and take in his appearance. Hair a right mess, no doubt from the rough treatment of his hands as he drove over here, clenched jaw, and prominent crease in his brow. His green eyes are burning into mine, and even though they're filled with worry, they still carry the same intensity as always.

"Here, you need to put on pants before the police get here. They're going to want to ask you questions." He starts rifling through my drawers and I see him taking out several pairs of pants, tops, and panties.

"Umm, do I need to put on layers?" I wipe underneath my eyes and finally stop my tears. Now that Reese is here, I'm no longer scared, and the only emotion running through me right now is elated joy from the sheer sight of him.

"No, but you're not staying here tonight, so you need to pack some clothes. I'm taking you home with me." He glances over at me as he closes my drawers.

"Okay," I reply, picking up a pair of jeans and sliding them up my legs.

"Really? You're not going to try and tell me you could just stay at Juls' house, or how you're not breaking the 'no sleepover' rule again? You're just going to say okay?" He looks utterly shocked and I almost laugh. *Jesus, am I that defiant?*

"Yes, I'm not always so argumentative." The sound of police sirens flow up the stairs and I quickly grab a bra and put it on, keeping his T-shirt on in the process.

He notices it and smiles a bit as he places my things in a nearby duffle bag. "Do you need anything else?"

I take a quick look around the room. "Umm, I guess just my bathroom stuff." I scurry in there and grab my toothbrush, hairbrush, face wash, moisturizer, phone off the shower floor, and conditioner because I'm more than happy to use his shampoo and body wash. Spinning, I see him standing in the doorway. He's studying me, eyes narrowed in on the collection in my hands. "What? I'm a girl and I can't take another shower at your place without conditioner. We can't all have gorgeous, no-product-necessary hair like you." His lips curl up as I drop the goodies into my duffle and follow him down the stairs.

After talking to the police and giving them my very vague description of the hooded figure standing outside my shop, they ask me if I know of anyone who might possibly want to hurt my business or me personally. My eyes quickly flick to Reese who clenches his jaw before giving them his ex-receptionist name and information. He tells them about the package I received and claims she became unstable after he stopped seeing her. I had assumed the figure I saw standing outside was a man because of the dark hoodie covering their face, but I guess it could have just as easily been a woman. I'm assured my insurance will cover the damage, which luckily is only to one of my windows. No damage was done to the inside of the shop, which I am extremely grateful for. The police found a brick that was used to break the glass, which had slid underneath my consultation table, and are going to dust it for prints. I will only have to remain closed for one day for the window to get repaired, so that isn't too bad. It could have been a lot worse. Way worse.

As we drive in silence to his building, the night I just endured is the last thing on my mind. Right now, with my duffle bag packed full of clothes sitting behind me in the back seat, the *only* thing on my mind is how I'll be having another sleepover with Reese. And I can't help but tense in my seat at the anticipation of it.

Chapter
EIGHTEEN

H E'S QUIET, TOO QUIET AS he walks into his condo and places my bag on the floor next to the couch. He hasn't said two words to me since we left the bakery and it's making my skin crawl. I plop down onto the couch and kick my shoes off, bringing my feet underneath my body as I hear him banging around in the kitchen.

"Here." He hands me a bottled water and I take it, seeing him walk around the couch and sit on the far end, way the hell away from me. He begins flipping through the channels and stops on some basketball game that I couldn't care less about. *What the fuck is this? He comes to my rescue, and I know damn well I heard him call me love, which means he can't hate me, asks me, no, tells me I'm coming to spend the night with him, and now he's barely acknowledging that I'm even here.* I turn my head and stare at him and his perfect profile as it remains impassive but interested in the game he's watching. He's in running shorts and a navy blue T-shirt that has some emblem on the front that I can't make out. Several long minutes go by as his eyes remain on the television, not once flicking toward me. *Jesus, is this how it's going to be all night? Fine then. If I'm sleeping over, I'm at least going to get comfortable.* I stand up and quickly shimmy out of my jeans, tossing them on top of my duffle and reach up and slip my T-shirt off. Turning around so I know he can see me, I drop it on the couch and remove my bra. I make quick eye contact with him as I slip my bra down my arms, his eyes lingering briefly, really fucking briefly on my chest before flicking back toward the game. I grunt and grab his T-shirt and slip it back on before I snatch the remote out of his hands and turn the television off.

"What the fuck?"

"What the fuck is right. What's wrong with you? You're acting weird."

He reaches forward and plucks the remote out of my hand, turning the game back on. "How am I supposed to be acting?" His eyes go back to the game and I no longer want to be here. Picking up my duffle, I quickly put my pants back on and throw my bra inside as I slip on my shoes and turn toward the door. "Where the hell are you going?"

"Like you give a shit. Thanks for making sure I didn't get murdered." I'm almost out the door when his arms grab my waist and pull me back inside, locking the door behind us.

"You're not going anywhere." I'm picked up, carried in his usual caveman style manner and taken back over toward the couch. My duffle is dropped by the edge and I'm dropped on the cushion.

"You don't want me here, obviously, so why should I stay?" I yell up into his stare. His hands come around me, bracing himself on the cushion behind me and bringing his face inches from mine.

"What the fuck makes you think I don't want you here? I always want you here."

"You haven't called or texted me since Friday afternoon, I get topless in front of you and you barely react, and you're not looking at me the way *you* look at me. You don't even want me anymore. You just want your stupid game." Tears fill my eyes and I'm not sure if it's from the night I've endured or the Reese style rejection that's knocking the wind out of me. His hand drops and grabs mine, forcing it against the massive bulge in his pants that I hadn't noticed. *Oh, wow.*

His face inches closer. "I *always* want you." And then it happens. His mouth, his hands, his everything is on me in seconds, ripping my remaining clothes off as I frantically try and keep up with the removal of his.

"Tell me *you* still want me," he grunts as he flips me onto my hands and knees and positions himself behind me. Before I can answer the obvious response, he rams into me and I cry out at the force.

"REESE." I grip the leather with my fingers, scratching into it with my nails as he pounds hard, then harder, into me.

"Answer me, Dylan," he grunts and I yell out between cries.

"Yes. Yes, I'll always want you." He's fucking me harder than he ever has and I know it's because I challenged him and he's proving himself to me. That or he's making damn sure I don't question it again. Either way, I'm letting him handle it. His hands grip my hips, pulling me back to meet him, and if I wasn't so turned on, so hot for him all the time, I might not be able to handle his power. I'm moaning, crying out with each thrust and he's right there with me. "Oh, God. Harder."

"Shit. You want harder?" His thighs crash against mine and my elbows give out. "This hard enough for you, love?"

"Yes!" I scream, needing him to give me this right now. I push back against him and feel his one hand grip my shoulder while the other digs into my hip the way I like.

He groans loudly, his sounds filling the condo. "You drive me fucking crazy. Fuck, Dylan."

"Touch me." His hand wraps around my stomach and drops between my legs. I whimper as his fingers rub my clit while his other hand grips harder on my shoulder. He's so forceful that he's knocking the air out of my lungs. "I'm gonna come." I manage to get out through a faint breath.

"Not yet. Wait for me."

I reach down to remove his fingers but he tightens against me, moving them in his perfect rhythm. "I can't. Please."

He rams into me harder and I cry out, hearing his loud throaty growl. "Now, love." And I let it go, all of it. The pain of the past several days without him, the anger from the pictures, the terror of the hooded figure. I let it go and feel him, just him. I'm panting, barely able to take in a full breath as my upper body collapses down onto my forearms and I feel his head drop to my back.

Hot breath warms my spine and I loosen my grip on the leather. "Hold on." He pulls out of me and I wince a bit in pain, which has never happened with him before. Of course, I've never been fucked like that before, so hard that my teeth chatter with each push. I roll onto my side, facing the cushions and curl into a ball. That was intense, really intense and I'm actually a bit sore after that Reese style fucking. He returns moments later holding a washcloth. "Lie on your back." I obey and keep my eyes on him as he wipes me clean, gently after he notices my scrunched up face. "I hurt you."

"I'm okay, it doesn't hurt that much." He bends down, planting a gentle kiss between my legs before he scoops me up into his arms. I quickly bury my face in his neck and nuzzle the shit out of him. "Mmm, this is my favorite spot, right here." I inhale deeply and let out a soft moan.

"I know; you seek it out often." He carries me into his bedroom and places me gently on the bed. I pull the covers around me and scoot over to allow him some space.

"Now that I've fucked some sense into you, let me be perfectly clear about something." I've already settled on his chest, my leg draped over his and my hand wrapped around his waist as my eyes slowly glance up at him. "I haven't called or texted you since Friday because *you* told me you needed time to think. And I don't know what the fuck that means because no woman has ever told me that before, but I assumed it meant you didn't want to hear from me." His fingers gently stroke my back, trailing across my skin and I moan softly.

"Okay."

"And just because I don't jump on your breasts the moment you whip them out doesn't fucking mean I don't want to. I didn't know where we stood, so I wasn't going to push my luck." I bite my lip to hold in my smile. He looks rightly irritated with having to explain himself, but the explanation is needed. "Dylan, I'm really sorry about those photos."

"I don't want to talk about it. I'm done talking and thinking about it. Between Friday night with Joey and Juls and all day yesterday and to-day, I'm done." My arm wraps tighter around him. "Nothing's changed between us. It didn't change anything."

He lifts my chin up to meet his face and I see the tension in his jaw. He looks unsure and that look sends a panic through me. *Nothing's changed for me, but has it for him?* I sit up quickly and move to lie next to him when his hands grab my waist and pull me back down, only this time

I'm flipped around, straddling him. The movement's so quick I barely have time to register it. "Don't," he states.

I take a second to study his features in my new position, given the fact that we're now eye to eye. Crazy mess of hair that I'm noticing makes him look younger than he is, green eyes that are narrowed in on mine, and stubble? A lot of stubble. I reach out, brush my hand along his chin, and can't contain my smile. *Oh, man. Reese with a day or two worth of facial hair is sexy beyond belief.* "Why did you just try to move away from me?"

I shake my head quickly.

"Dylan." *Oh, Mr. Persistent.*

"Nothing's changed for me, but has it changed for you?" I ask quickly, getting out the question I fear the answer to before I can think myself out of it.

"No," he answers firmly.

"So you still want this?"

He drops his head and it hits the headboard with a loud thump. "Yes, whatever the fuck this is, I still want it. You're in control here, Dylan. You have all the fucking control." His eyes are burning into mine with the same intensity they've always shown for me. *I'm in control? Of what? Of us?* I decide not to probe because I'm not sure I want to know the answer. He lets out a forceful breath that warms my face. "If something would have happened to you tonight…" His eyes close tight and the crease in his brow appears. *Oh, Reese.* The man's mood swings are enough to give me permanent whiplash.

"Nothing happened. I'm okay. I called you and you came for me." I reach out and stroke his face as his eyes pop back open, green and blazing. His tenseness softens a bit.

"I tried locating Heather and sorting this shit out with her, but I didn't find her. All fucking weekend I've been looking." He grits his teeth. "She wasn't at her house and she's not answering my calls." I swallow loudly and he shakes his head. "I'm fucking dealing with it. I just want you to be prepared. Fred didn't deliver that package, so just don't open any that aren't from him. Okay?" I nod. *Jesus. I really don't want to have to deal with this again.* But if Reese is dealing with it, then I'm sure it will be dealt with, in a very Reese like manner no less. "But after tonight,

Dylan, I don't want you there by yourself." His hands grip my waist and pull me closer to him, our foreheads falling together.

"I don't want to be there by myself either, but I want to keep an eye on my shop. It's important to me. It's mine and I've worked hard for it." His hand reaches up and pulls my bun loose, letting my hair fall down my back. "I'm going to have a door installed at the top of the stairs. I'll call about getting it done along with the window repair and a security system tomorrow. I can't believe I never thought about having some type of system in place already." He nods at me, but I know that isn't what he wants to hear. I lean in and kiss him gently. "I'll be fine. I've lived there on my own for three years. Plus, I have you and you're only five minutes away if something happens."

His hands brush lightly down my back, playing with the ends of my hair. "It will never take me five minutes to get to you. I think I made it there in two tonight." I giggle slightly and see his lips curl up. "I might be getting a few red light camera notifications in the mail."

"Worth it?" I ask, running my hands through his hair.

"Worth it. You hungry?"

I nod frantically and he laughs, the infectious sound pulling me in with him. "Sit tight." I'm slid off as he hops out of bed, disappearing down the hallway as I watch his glorious backside stride away. Laughing quietly at the realization that he *always* asks me if I'm hungry after sex, I grab one of his pillows and press it to my face, inhaling deeply as his voice comes down the hallway.

"Do you like your pizza cold or heated up?"

"Cold." *Yum. Cold pizza and a sleepover with Reese? Yes please.* Glancing around the room, I spot his iPad on his dresser. I scramble out of bed and grab it, flipping it open and turning it on. I have some googling of a certain CPA to do. The screen comes to life. *Oh. Oh my.* The wallpaper is a picture of me, in this bed. I'm sleeping, curled up on my side with the sheets covering me up to show only a tiny bit of cleavage. My hair is a mess of blonde waves that are spilling down my right shoulder and my lips are parted. The camera is mainly focused on my face and I look to be in a deep sleep. I look up and see Reese staring at me, stopped in the doorway carrying our food.

"Umm, you found my iPad I see." He moves toward the bed and puts the plates down on his nightstand, his eyes only momentarily leaving mine. "Nobody sees that. I would never show that to anybody."

Placing it down on the bed, I get up on my knees and crawl to the edge where he's standing, pulling him toward me and wrapping my arms around his neck. After a moment's hesitation, he wraps his arms around me and relaxes against my body. "You're not mad? I can take it off."

I reach around and place my hand over his mouth, silencing him. "I'm not mad. It can stay on there." Dropping my hands, I scoot back over and reach out for my plate playfully as his smile returns.

"Cold pizza, huh? I thought I was the only other person who still preferred it cold to heated."

I take a bite and shake my head. "I hate heated leftover pizza. The cheese gets all rubbery and gross." He drops a chilled bottled water in my lap and I yelp. "So, why did you take that picture of me?"

He stops chewing briefly, looking over at the iPad on the bed. "I don't know. I think I just wanted a reminder of you in my bed, just in case you refused to get back in it." I laugh and he winks at me. "I watched you for hours before I took it. Do you know you make little noises while you sleep?"

I swallow my bite and arch my brow at him. "Little noises? Like what?"

"Like moans. Tiny little whimpers."

"What? No, I don't." I unscrew my bottle and take a big sip while he nods at me. "I do not make any noises when I sleep."

He turns and places his empty plate on his nightstand. *Jesus, the man devours his food in a matter of seconds.* "Yes, you do. You even said my name a few times." My mouth drops open.

I place my plate down on the nightstand before I trample him. "No, I did not. Take that back, Carroll." I'm poking him everywhere, trying to find a weak ticklish spot on his body and he's only laughing at me in amusement.

"Reese. Oh, Reese. Right there."

I feel my face redden. "You're evil," I scoff before I roll off him and lie back on my pillow, pulling the covers up over my head. *Good Lord, I hope he's joking because if he isn't, how embarrassing is this?*

His laugh shakes the bed and I feel the covers slowly slide down to reveal his face hovering over mine. "Love."

"What?" I try to pull the covers back up, but he holds them down. I've never been told I talk in my sleep before or make any weird noises, and I've had plenty of sleepovers with Juls and Joey. Of course, I doubt *they* watch me for hours after I pass out. *Humph.* He climbs under the covers with me and pulls me close to him so we're nose to nose.

"So, I hear we're going to be paired up at the wedding." His hand trails down my shoulder to my waist and holds me there as I try to keep my smile at bay. "You okay with that? It will be like a date you know. Rather intimate." His lip curls up and I give in to it.

"I'm okay with that. I *have* been on a few dates before. Have you?"

"No, well, not in a really long time." *A really long time? What classifies a really long time? Why is he so against dating now?* I push these questions out of my head and focus on another.

"Have you always been monogamously casual with girls?" This has definitely been on my mind recently. I had initially pegged him as a total player with multiple women at all times, but had never dared to ask.

His eyes flick to mine quickly before he drops them. "No." I reach up and run my hand down his arm, rubbing his shoulder the way he likes and seeing his eyes close slowly. "I've never really wanted to be before you." I stop breathing at his admission. *Holy shit. Was Joey right? Am I a game changer?* My hand stills on his bicep and his eyes shoot open, locking onto mine. "You make me want different things, things I've never wanted before."

"Why?" I force out and continue rubbing his arm. I need to know the answer to this. I want to know if his reasons are the same as mine. I've experienced more before, but not in the way I want with Reese. I want everything with him.

He keeps his eyes on me and sighs softly. "I don't know, but I can't stand the idea of *not* being monogamously casual with you. I have no desire to be with anyone else and the thought of you with another man," his hand comes flying up through his hair, stopping my massage, "it fucking *infuriates* me."

Well, that settles that. Like there's any other man on the planet I want to ever be with now that I've experienced this one. I scoot in closer and continue working his arm, reaching around toward his back. "I know the feeling," I reply as his eyes close shut again, his lips quivering into a smile. Silence falls between us and I let my mind wander while I work his back and shoulder. I feel like I'm making progress with Reese, progress out of the casual zone and toward something more serious, which I am dying to sprint to. But I know I can't rush him and he'll have to do this at his own pace if he even wants to. If I've learned anything from the past few weeks with him, it's that he does *everything* at his own pace. He likes to be in control, even though he told me I have it all, which completely threw me for a loop. I'm chalking that up to him just worrying about my safety. He was obviously scared for me, and when you're scared, you say crazy shit. He likes to show how much power he has and his authority over situations, as he clearly displayed when he destroyed my dress. So I'll let him control this, control us, because I like the pace he's taking. As long as he takes me with him.

Chapter
NINETEEN

AFTER GIVING HIM A DECENT one handed massage and enjoying all of his tiny little moans of pleasure, Reese flips on his back and pulls me on top of him. He scoots up so his back is against the headboard and we're chest to chest. All the tension in his face is gone and the only thing bothering *me* anymore is my now stiff hand from his drawn out rub down. His hands wrap around my waist, tightening their grip and I feel him, his desire for me growing against my backside.

"Missed your face," I whisper and see his lip curl up in the corner.

"Just my face?"

"Never." I move in slowly and capture his mouth with mine, licking along the seam of his lips until he opens up for me, which only takes half a second. I relish his minty flavor and moan into his mouth. His tongue strokes mine in a way that sets my skin on fire, and I'm desperate for him. Tangling my hands in his hair, I pull him closer to me and rub my chest against his. His hands run up my back, tickling along my spine and grazing around toward my front. I'm not sure what he's better at, touching or kissing. Both send me into a frenzy where I feel like I'm going to combust at any moment. His callused hands expertly squeeze my breasts. "Mmm, right there." I kiss him along his stubbled jaw and toward his ear. "I need you."

His mouth runs down my body between my breasts, kissing and licking every inch of me. "Dylan, I want to do something."

My lips pull at his ear and I release it enough to reply, "Anything." Because I would do anything with this man. It's obvious to everyone at this point. I feel his hot breath on my chest and he hesitates, causing me to lean back. He lifts his face up to mine. "Anything," I repeat.

His Adam's apple rolls in his neck and his lips part. "I want to make love to you."

I gasp, completely shocked and unprepared for this request. I was honestly expecting something along the lines of anal play, which I'm totally up for with him, even though I've never done it before. The thought of anal sex terrified me once, but this, this request that he's just thrown out between us? I'm not sure there's anything *more* terrifying. But I want to, and I can at least try, right? For him, for Reese Carroll, for the look he's giving me right now, yes. I can at least try.

My heart constricts so much that I reach up and place my hand on it, making sure it didn't just beat for the last time. He wants to make love to me. Love. Not fucking. My mind is scrambling for words. He's studying me, waiting for my response. I know I've been silent for at least several minutes and I'm sure it's killing him inside, but he's not showing it. His face is soft and pleading, eyes searching mine and conveying that we can do this. That I can do this.

"Okay," I say finally, and I think we're both shocked that I actually spoke. "I just need to use the bathroom first." He grins wide, my favorite lines appearing, and kisses me quickly on the lips as he lifts me off him. Without a glance back, I scurry into the bathroom and close the door behind me.

Shit. I'm about to make love to a man who I'm struggling to not fall in love with? What am I insane? I stare at myself in the bathroom mirror and quickly comb my fingers through my hair. My cheeks are flushed, my nipples are hard, and I'm beyond ready for him between my legs. Everything about me is ready for this right now, everything except for what's burning inside my chest cavity. I can't even begin to imagine what making love to him consists of. Fucking him is intense and borderline intimate as it is. And that's definitely all we've done so far. If I didn't know it before, his request just confirmed it. So what exactly am I in for? Have I ever even made love before? I think long and hard about that as I quickly use the toilet. No, no way. Not with Justin. I'm not even sure he's capable of making love to anyone. He was always so distant when we were having sex that he barely kept eye contact with me. And making love consists of eye contact I'm sure. I hurriedly wash my hands and try to mentally prepare myself for what's about to happen as I exit the bathroom and return to his bedroom. I'm halted in my tracks. *Oh, God.*

I'm stopped in the doorway by the sight of candles lit and covering both nightstands, providing an amber glow throughout the room. Reese is messing with his phone as he places it on the docking station on his dresser when he turns to me, seeing my expression and straightening instantly. "Too much?"

I bite my lip and shake my head. *It's perfect; he's perfect.* "No, I like it." I settle on the bed, kneeling and resting back on my heels as I watch him continue playing with his phone. He's looking for a song and I'm almost one hundred percent sure I know what song he's looking for. *Damn it, I need to look up those lyrics.* But that's not what starts playing as he walks over toward me. "Look After You" by The Fray pours through the speakers. I'm familiar with this song and its lyrics, which will surely rip my heart out if he's not trying to tell me something with this selection. "This isn't cliché is it? Candles and music?" he asks as he runs his hands through his hair and down his face.

I smile playfully at his nervousness. "No, there's nothing about you that's cliché." This is completely true. I've never met a man like him before and I doubt I ever will. Reaching out to him, he slips his hand in mine and allows me to pull him toward me. "Make love to me, handsome."

I see it, the layer of anxiety drop in front of me as he crawls onto the bed and pushes me onto my back. Settling between my legs, he begins kissing me in the gentlest way possible. There's tongue, because with him there's always at least *some* tongue, but it's different. I'm used to the rough, quick strokes of his against mine, against my lips, but these strokes are much more unhurried and tender. Groaning softly into his mouth, I'm quickly melting around him and I'm suddenly not sure what kind of Reese kissing I prefer. His hard *I want you now* kisses are insanely hot, but this, the *let me make love to you* kisses are radiating through my body, sparking something untouched. He slowly works his way down, kissing every part of me with the same gentle mouth I just personally got very acquainted with. The song begins to play again. *He's put it on repeat?* I feel his hot breath between my legs and arch up into him.

"Yes, God, yes." The first long lick causes me to fist the sheets tightly between my fingers. I pull my bottom lip into my mouth and bite it hard as he works me.

"Look at me," he pleads and I immediately drop my gaze, meeting his green eyes. He's watching me, capturing my every response to his movements and I'm not holding anything back. His tongue laps in and out, around and between every fold and dip. He's even somehow making *this* more intimate with his unrelenting stare. His strokes are soft but carry the perfect amount of pressure. I don't want to come yet so I concentrate on the lyrics of the song to give me a distraction. *Like that's possible. The man's mouth is a machine.*

Damn these lyrics. I'm not sure about him, but they are definitely pushing every emotional button in my body. He moans against me and my eyes roll back into my head, the sensation moving through me like a current. His lips pull my clit into his mouth and I cry out, unable to hold back any longer. "Reese." I'm panting and moving my hips against his mouth as I come, long and hard. His tongue laps up every ounce of my arousal, slowly and tentatively, keeping me on the brink of another orgasm. Gradually releasing me, he places sweet kisses on the insides of my thighs as I stare down at him.

"Come up here."

He crawls up my body and settles between my legs, gazing down at me as he positions himself at my entrance. I feel him right there, and know the slightest movement will plunge him into me. But he doesn't move. His hands hold my face and I stare up at him, hearing the beginning of the song and smiling.

"I like this song."

"Me, too," he whispers, bending and trailing kisses to my ear. With a slow push, he's in me and I grip his back tightly, gasping and clinging myself to him. "Fuck," he says into my ear before he leans up and holds himself above me. Keeping my gaze, he begins moving slowly, his hips thrusting gently into mine. I stare at his chest as it tightens with each push, the muscles in his abdomen rippling with his movements. He's never been this unhurried with me. This is different, way different from what we've done before. The intimacy is pouring straight out of him into me and I feel him everywhere. His eyes are soft and warm, penetrating mine and conveying unspoken words that I pray I'm not misreading. I want to tell him so many things in this moment as he lovingly strokes me, in and out, but I don't. I wrap my legs around him and let myself feel it.

"Tell me you've never done this before," I whisper, seeing his eyes dilate above me. "That you've never made love to anyone but me."

There's no hesitation in his reply. "Never. It's only you, Dylan. Just you." I grab his face and bring his lips to mine. Our moans are silenced by each other's mouths and the music that is playing all around us. His panting increases and my hands are gripped as he brings them on either side of my face and laces his fingers through them. I love it when he does that to my hands. It's such a boyfriend move. My breathing quickens as his tongue works against mine. Slow and steady thrusts, I'm pulsing around him and trying not to end this too soon. Making love to this man has gone way above any expectation I could have conjured. He increases his pace, thrusting deeper and harder, and I'm close, so close, but I want him to unravel with me. I need it like a drug.

"Come with me," I beg and he drops his forehead to mine and grunts loudly. I'm there instantly with the look he gives me and fall out around him, trembling against him and feeling his warmth run through me.

"Dylan," he whispers my name instead of his usual climatic scream, pumps into me and stills, collapsing down on top of me as I soak him and what we just did in. Our breathing is uneven and loud, his blowing across the skin of my neck and mine pushing out above us. I don't care that his is making me hot, I don't care that his hip is digging into mine and causing a shooting pain across my pelvis. I don't want to move. Ever.

"That was..." I start to say but can't finish because there are no words.

"Yeah, that was." He kisses my lips quickly before sliding off the bed and muting the music. "Are you sore?" I flick my eyes up to meet his stare, his serious expression also containing a bit of hesitation.

"No, I'm perfect. That was perfect." *It was beyond perfect.* I reach up and stretch above my head, as he crawls back over top of me, settling on his side and pulling me close to him.

"Hi," I whisper.

"Hi, yourself." His sweet smile pulls at his lips.

"So, tell me all about how you called Joey *after* I fell asleep Thursday night and not Friday morning."

His eyes widen and his grin spreads. "I was wondering how long he'd keep that from you. Did he even make it twenty-four hours?" His hand reaches up and brushes my hair out of my face, tucking it softly behind my ear.

"No way. Once the wine started flowing Friday night, he blabbed everything." I reach out and run my hand along his jaw. "I like this, a lot. You should go all scruffy more often."

"So should you." His hand brushes between my legs and my eyes widen.

"What? Seriously?" I reply through a shocked grin.

"No, I like you like this. I can see every part of you without anything in my way." I wiggle my brows at him and his infectious laugh pulls me in. "You know how much I hate anything getting in my way when it comes to you."

"Is *that* why you steal my panties? To prevent me from putting a barrier in between us?"

He shrugs playfully, his lips curling up into a smile. "You wax it, right?" I nod. "Doesn't that hurt?"

Yes. "Nah, Will is really gentle." *Oh, I'm devious.*

"Excuse me?"

My smile cracks through and his face releases some of its tension, but not much. *He's too easy.* "He is. He's been doing me for years."

I'm quickly being pressed into the mattress by his tall frame. "I hope you're fucking joking. I am *not* okay with a guy waxing you there." My arms are pinned to my side by his knees and I'm now face-to-face with his erection. *Whoa. He's hard again, already?*

"What if I told you he was gay?"

"Doesn't fucking matter." He inches forward and brushes the tip against my mouth.

"Oh, please, are you going to discipline me by making me suck you off? That's hardly a punishment." I dart my tongue out and lick the tip, seeing him shudder a bit as he stares down at me.

"It will be once I withhold *your* orgasm, which you know damn well I'm good at doing." *Oh, shit.* The memory of my worktop flashes through my mind. *That was horrible.*

"All right! No, it's not a guy named Will. It's a girl named Lacey."

"Really, Lacey, huh?" I roll my eyes at his sexual tone. *Men.*

"You're perverted."

"I am and so are you. Now, open that pretty mouth of yours and make me come."

"Say please." Another quick flick of my tongue pulls a groan out of his throat.

"Fuck that. Not after what you just put me through. Open." *Yum. Hello, dominant Reese.* I smile and open my mouth as he inches forward, granting me full access to his member.

"Fuck yes," he grunts through gritted teeth as he fucks my face. Bringing one hand down, he holds the back of my head and plummets deeply into me, his quick thrusts causing my eyes to water. I glance up and see his other hand gripping the headboard until his knuckles are white. "So fucking good."

I moan around him, my lips vibrating against his skin as he shifts his knee and pulls my right arm out. "Wrap around me." I grip the base with my hand and begin sliding up and down his length as he stills, keeping just the tip of him in my mouth. I'm gliding easily, the saliva from my mouth completely drenching him. Working him hard and fast, my tongue flicks against him and my lips tease his head. He pulses inside me and I see the tension in his jaw. I love doing this to him and get just as much pleasure out of it as he does. Dropping his head back, his Adam's apple slides and his veins protrude in his neck as he moans deeply. His body is vibrating with his sounds, moving against my tongue. I keep my eyes on him, watching his chest heave with each thrust and his stomach clench as I work him. Sucking and teasing him, my hand grips harder and I see his shoulders hunch forward. "I'm close, love. Don't stop."

"Do you want to come in my mouth?" I ask, as I lick the tip.

His eyes widen. "Yes, unless I have options?" His voice is strained and I know he's on the brink.

"You could come on me if you want. I think I'd like that."

He swallows and quickly backs down my body, angling himself at my breasts. "Here?" he asks and I nod, pumping him hard and seeing his lip pull into his mouth. We both stare at the spectacle of him coming on my breasts, the white warmth rolling between my mounds and a few drops landing close to my neck. "Holy shit. That's so fucking hot."

I nod in agreement and stare down at myself, letting go of his cock and seeing him shiver a bit. "You marked me again." I swirl a bit of it on the softened red mark on my left breast and see him watch me, studying me.

"I think you like it when I mark you."

I dip my finger into my mouth. "I love it when you mark me." He climbs off the bed and disappears into the hallway as I gaze down at my sticky mess. It really is hot, seeing what I've pulled out of him. Having him label me with it. *I wonder if he's done that before. Nope, stop it, Dylan.* He comes back in moments later with a small hand towel and begins wiping me off.

"That was amazing, you know," he says through a smile.

"I know. I want to mark you now."

His eyebrow arches as he tosses the towel onto the floor, planting quick kisses to both my nipples. "Do you? With what?" My eyes search around the room and land on a notebook that's sitting on his dresser with a pen marking a page in it. I quickly hop off and grab it, scurrying back over to the bed and pushing him down onto his back. "Are you going to draw on me?"

"No, not draw. I'm going to write on you, but where?" My eyes rake all over his beautiful body as I suck on the pen cap. "I mean really, your body is almost too pretty for tattoos. Would you ever get one?"

He shrugs. "I don't know. I'm not opposed to it entirely. What are you going to write?"

"Patience, professor." He muffles his laugh under me as I drop his arm open and begin writing on the inside of his bicep. The ink is dark, a deep blue as I scroll in overly girly handwriting and smile at myself.

"You seem to be enjoying yourself. Why are you putting it there?"

"Because I love your arms and it's hidden. I like thinking that I'm the only one who knows it's there. Just for me."

"You say that like it's permanent."

I shrug. "I can rewrite it daily if I have to." I retrace the letters to darken them and feel his eyes on me. "Do you study everything the way you study me?"

"No. Unfortunately, not everything in my life is as fascinating as you are."

"I'm a twenty-six-year-old baker who's lived in South Side her entire life. How is that fascinating?"

"I don't know, just is. And you study me just as much, so I should ask you the same question."

I recap my pen. "Well, that answer should be obvious. I'm looking for a new tax guy." Leaning down, I blow gently across his arm and dry the ink. "There, all done."

His head raises and he glances at his arm, the words DO I WANNA KNOW? printed on him in my script. He studies it for a moment, pulling his bottom lip into his mouth and I watch his long lashes flutter before his eyes flick to mine.

"I like your mark."

"Me, too." I chuck the pen onto the dresser and settle in next to him, pulling the covers up around us. He wraps his arm around my waist and closes his eyes, his breathing slowing down to a soft rhythm as I observe him. It doesn't take long before I know he's sleeping. Chest rising and falling slowly, eyes fluttering as if he's mid-dream, and lips slightly parted to allow for his breath to escape. I study him for minutes and then minutes become hours. I'm so ridiculously happy in this moment that when I begin to silently cry next to him, I don't know what to think besides what I'm now willing to admit to myself. I'm crazy in love with this man. I love everything about him. From the tiniest detail like the little lines next to his eyes and the slit that runs down his bottom lip, to the way I can only seem to be able to take a full breath when he's near me. I love the words he says to me and the look he reserves only for me;

even if that look is one that's a preamble to a Reese style flip out. I love the way I can sense his presence and the way my heart beats in my chest when I finally lock eyes with him. I love him. Just him. And the tears I let myself cry are both of worry that he's not going to reciprocate these feelings, and because I'm finally willing to let myself feel them. So I'll let my tears fall, because I've been denying my feelings for him since the moment I fell into his lap, and because I'm a silly girl who is going to turn into a brave woman tomorrow and finally tell him how I feel. Fuck being casual. I'm so over that bullshit.

Chapter
TWENTY

I WAKE UP MONDAY MORNING, my eyes fluttering open slowly to adjust to the sunlight pouring through the window, and I notice immediately that I'm alone and not in my bed. Glancing over at the clock, I note the time is nine forty-two a.m. and realize he's probably gone to work after trying to wake me countless times. I really need to figure out a way to be woken up out of my slumber. What if we eventually have kids and they try to wake me up to make them breakfast or some shit and I'm dead to the world? *Jesus, did I just say if we eventually have kids?* When have I ever thought about having children before? *Never.* I've *never* thought about having children. I picture a miniature Reese meandering around the house, trying to keep his siblings in line and raking his hands through his wild hair when they don't listen. I giggle silently at the thought and quickly push it out of my mind. *Crazy, Dylan. Utter craziness.*

I crawl out of bed and duck into the bathroom briefly before finding my clothes scattered all around the couch. The memory of their quick removal sends a shiver through me. *That was fun. I should challenge his desire for me more often.* Slipping on my panties and his University of Chicago T-shirt, I find my phone and quickly dial Joey, feeling like a complete idiot and shitty friend for not having called him last night after the break in.

"Cupcake. What the fuck, girlie? Can you believe that psycho broke our window out?"

I plop down onto a dining room chair and begin rubbing my head. "Well, at least we think it was probably her. I'm so sorry I didn't call you last night, my mind was all over the place." I sigh heavily as the image of the hooded figure creeps into my mind.

"No worries, your casual fuck buddy called me when he was on his way over to rescue you. I'm sure he figured you had other things on your mind than reminding your assistant *not* to show up to work today." I grunt at the casual fuck buddy reference and spot a piece of paper hanging off the edge of the kitchen counter. I reach over and grab it, noticing my favorite handwriting.

Dylan,

I have no fucking clue how I ever survived not waking up to you. And before you say anything, yes, I did try to wake you up to go for a run with me. You were adorably out cold, as usual. Enjoy your day off.

X Reese

P.S. Here's a spare key if you go out today. Keep it

Swoon.

"Hey, so listen, I have some phone calls to make to the insurance company and to find someone to put in a security system and a door above the stairs, but when I'm done, any chance you could pick me up and take me to Reese's office?"

"Yeah, sure. I'm pretty bored myself over here since Billy's gone to work. What's going on at the office?"

I smile. "Oh, you know, the usual. Just me going to finally tell our favorite numbers guy that I'm madly in love with him." I hear the phone drop and Joey's insanely high pitched screams.

"DYLAN. Oh, my fucking God. Yes, girl, yes. Hurry up and make those stupid phone calls and then text me when you're ready. Ooohhh, I'm bursting over here."

"And don't say anything to Juls. I'd hate for her to leak it to Ian who would most likely blab. I feel like those men talk just as much as we do sometimes."

"Mmmm mmm. Don't you worry; my lips are sealed on this one. Take care of your shit, and then let's get to the important matters at hand."

❧

I CALL THE INSURANCE COMPANY and make sure I won't be responsible for any of the damage from the break in. They assure me the window is in fact being repaired during our phone call, and I will be up and running by tomorrow. Grabbing Reese's iPad off the bed, I look up the number to a security system company and get an estimate on a top of the line alarm system to install. Using the commission from Justin's stupid wedding, I go ahead and arrange for the men to come today and set it up. That way, it will also be ready by tomorrow. I'm not sure who the hell to call about getting a door put in, so I dial my parents and hold my breath knowing I'm about to get a huge ear full for not having called them last night.

"Oh, for Christ's sake, Dylan. Something horrible could have happened to you. You could have been raped, murdered, Jesus Christ. I can't believe you're just now calling us." My mother's tirade goes on for a good ten minutes before I'm able to get a word in.

"I know, I know. I'm sorry I didn't call. But I'm fine. Nothing happened and we're pretty sure we know who it was and the police are looking for her." *Stupid red headed bitch.*

"Her? It was a woman? What kind of a woman throws a brick through a store window? Good grief, what is the world coming to?"

"Just some ex-girlfriend of Reese's, Mom. Look, everything is fine. The window is being repaired right now and a security system is being installed today as well. I just need to talk to Dad about putting a door in to separate my living space from the bakery." Which, really, I should have done years ago. I just didn't feel the need to do so until now. That or I could get a guard dog. No, that has to be unsanitary around all those baked goods.

"Ex-girlfriend? Humph, a woman scorned no less. Well, at least you're safe and this finally makes you put in a well overdue alarm system." She exhales forcefully. "Here's your father. Bill, go easy on her, she's fine."

"Dylan, sweetheart, you're all right then?" My dad's voice is incredibly calm compared to my mother's, but that's always been his personality. I definitely get my short fuse from the women in my family.

"Yes, Dad, I'm fine. But I need to get a door installed at the top of the stairs leading from the kitchen. How do I go about doing that?" He immediately goes into daddy-mode and tells me not to worry about it, he will head to a local hardware store today and purchase a door for me. When I tell him I can handle it, he shuts me up quickly and I let him. I don't think there is anything my father enjoys more than doing something for me that keeps me safe. After I am reassured it will be taken care of today, I hang up, text Joey to head on over, and hop in the shower.

I relish in Reese's shampoo and body wash, letting the steam create a cloud of his yumminess all around me as I clean up. I'm surprisingly not nervous at all about telling him I love him. After last night, the love making, him telling me I make him want things he's never wanted before, I feel empowered to do this. I quickly slip into a pair of jeans and a cute top as a knock on the door sends me dashing through the condo. I fling it open and beam at my assistant.

"AH! I'm soooo excited. *Please* let me be there when you tell him."

"What? No way. This is a private moment. You may wait outside." I slip into my shoes and grab my cell and the spare key Reese left for me, slipping it onto my key ring and locking up behind us. "Okay, let's do this shit before I lose my nerve."

$\backsim$

WE STOP BY THE BAKERY on the way to his office. The men who are in charge of replacing the window are just finishing up and have me sign a few pieces of paper before they give it a final wipe down and leave. Joey and I both watch the security guys go over how to arm and disarm the system, giving us both the code and a few forms to sign as well before they too hit the road. My mom sent me a text informing me that my father has purchased a door with an insane amount of locks and he will be stopping by later on today to install it. I won't have to stick around, because other than Joey and myself, my parents also have a key to the bakery. So, after piling back into the Civic, we finish the short drive to the Walker & Associates building.

"How nervous *are* you right now?" he asks me as I sit in the car, and trying to find out where the fuck all my bravery has disappeared to. We've been parked outside the building for at least ten minutes and I haven't budged.

"Uh, a lot. Maybe this is a bad idea?"

"Fuck that." My seatbelt is unbuckled for me as he reaches across my body and opens my door, giving me a quick, but gentle, shove out of the car. "Go do it, Dylan. That man in there loves you fiercely. It's written all over his beautiful face. But I'm afraid you might be the one to have to say it first. Damn it, I had my money on Reese being the one to crack before you did, but oh, well." I quickly run my fingers through my hair and give him a weak smile. I'm certain he means what he says, no doubt a small wager having gone on between him and Juls. She'll never let him hear the end of losing to this one.

"Okay, thanks, Joey." He winks at me as I close the door and walk into the building and toward the back of the lobby where the elevators are lined up. My hands are clenched into fists and I'm shaking a bit, but I'm here and I'm fucking doing this.

Stepping off the elevators and onto the twelfth floor, I walk straight past the first reception area and toward Reese's office. I haven't even thought about the fact that I'll be seeing a new face sitting behind his reception desk until I see it. And it is a lot manlier.

"Good afternoon. How may I help you?" The young man, dressed sharply in a dark suit greets me with a crooked smile. His dark brown hair is slicked to the side with some sort of product. *Hmm. I like him already.*

"Hello. I was wondering if Mr. Carroll is available."

"Oh, actually he is in Mr. Thomas' office right now with a few more associates having lunch. Would you like me to call him?" He reaches for his phone but I shoot my hand up to halt him.

"Oh, no, that's okay. I know where Mr. Thomas' office is."

He gives me a warm smile and places the phone back down. "Wonderful. Well, go right on and knock since his receptionist is out at lunch.

Have a nice day."

"Thanks, you too."

Man, he is cheery. I can't help but giggle at the fact that Reese hired a man to be his receptionist instead of a woman. I walk quickly toward Ian's office, seeing the door already a few inches open, and go to knock when my favorite voice halts me.

"She's fucking psychotic. I've never had a girl go that nuts on me after I tell her I'm done fucking her," he says through a partially full mouth. *The man does love to talk with his mouth full.* I smile slightly and shake my head.

"Yeah, well, I'm pretty sure most women you stop fucking usually flip out on you in some way or another. But that's really fucked up that she targeted Dylan like that." I recognize Ian's voice and cross my arms over my chest, leaning against the wall as I listen in. "She obviously hasn't had the pleasure of seeing Dylan's pissed off side. Pretty dumb move on her part."

A third voice chimes in that I'm not familiar with. "Who is this Dylan chick anyway? She hot?" *Ahhh, yes, so glad I arrived here at this exact moment. Nothing like a little ego boost to brighten a Monday.*

I hear chip bags ruffle. "Hot doesn't even begin to describe her. She's fucking beautiful," Reese answers and I bite my lip.

"He met her at Mr. Walter's daughter's wedding a few weekends ago. She's Juls' best friend and one hell of a baker. She owns Dylan's Sweet Tooth on Fayette. That's the store that got the brick thrown through the window," Ian says through a mouthful.

"Shit. So, you like this girl or is she just another one of the many women that Reese Carroll destroys in his path?" The third voice asks and I brace myself. *Jesus Christ, that sounds horrible. Although, I can totally see how it applies. He is a force of nature.*

Silence fills the room, several long seconds of silence. I hear a few throats clear and then his voice.

"It's not serious if that's what you're asking me. You know I don't do that shit. I like fucking her, so I do." My mouth and my heart drop at the same time as I hear Ian's voice say something in response to his description of our situation, but I don't register it. Instead, I run quickly for the elevators and slip in the first one that opens.

"Oh, God. Oh, God. Oh, shit." I'm gripping the wall in the empty elevator as it takes me down to the first floor, my head spinning and my heart no longer with me, having left it on the floor outside of Ian's office. *I can't believe he said that. After everything. After last night and after his birthday. I'm still just someone he likes to fuck. That's it?* The doors open and I run through the lobby and toward the red Civic that is still parked on the curb. Joey is leaning against the passenger door with his phone up to his ear. My appearance makes him end his call.

"What happened?"

"Take me to his place, now. I need to get my shit." My face is covered in tears and he moves quickly, not asking any more questions as we both pile into his car.

The drive doesn't take long and Joey remains silent as I burst into the condo and grab my duffle, aimlessly throwing my belongings into it and triple checking that I don't leave anything behind. Because I'm never coming back here to get it. I grab my items out of the bathroom and break down when I spot his body wash, wanting to take a final whiff of it, but managing to pull myself away from the shower before I can let that happen. I run to his bedroom and grab the notebook that I got the pen out of last night and bring it out to the dining room, opening up to a blank page and grabbing the pen. I feel Joey's hand on my back as he comes to stand next to me.

"Dylan, what happened?"

My hands are shaking as I hover the pen above the paper, not sure what exactly I want to write for him to see. There's so much I want to say. I want to tell him how badly he's fucked up, how much I love him, and how angry I am at him for *making* me fall in love with him. Because that's exactly what he did. He pulled that love that I had buried down deep inside me right up to the surface, and now I'm drowning in it. I wipe under my eyes and look up at Joey.

"He doesn't love me. He's just fucking me. He doesn't do serious." I take in a deep shaky breath. "I'm done." My hand begins to move as he brings his over my shoulder and holds me while I write. It's a sloppy mess, but it's legible. I leave it open on the table for him to read.

Reese,

I can't do this anymore. I'm sure you'll have no trouble finding someone who can give you what you want, but it's not me. Please let me go.

Dylan

Turning, I drop my head against Joey's chest and cry harder than I've ever cried before. His arms envelope me and he whispers reassuring words into my ear as I sob, drenching his navy blue polo shirt.

"Sweetie, did he really say that?"

I nod. "Yes. He said he doesn't do serious and he's just fucking me because he likes to."

"Shit, Dylan, I've seen him with you. He's not going to let you go without a fight and you know it."

I shake against him and grip him closer to me. "Joey, I can't do this with him. Please make sure he understands that I can't see him. I fucking can't."

I back away from him and see him nod weakly, most likely fearing the Reese tirade that he will certainly be up against as I grab my keys and remove the spare one he gave me, placing it on the note I just scribbled. I look up at him. "I really hate to ask this, but would you and Billy mind if—"

"Fuck no. I already decided that you're moving in with us until this shit blows over. Reese will break through that new window of yours if he knows you're upstairs in your loft." I give him half a smile and pick up my duffle, swinging it over my shoulder as the tears begin to fall again.

"Come on, cupcake. You'll be okay." And with one final look, I lock up behind us and let Joey move my body down the hallway and toward the elevators, because I have no control of it myself anymore.

᧐

AFTER A QUICK STOP AT the bakery to pick up some things, Joey takes us back to Billy's condo and quickly pours us two massive glasses of wine. He offers me the guest room, which I place my stuff down in before zoning out on the couch, staring down at my glass. I'm still crying, but not as heavily, only a few tears streaming down my face in between blinks. I've rubbed and cried off all my makeup and haven't dared to look at myself in a mirror for fear as to what I might see. My heart physically aches, like it's slowly being pulled apart by some unseen force and it's taken its ever loving time doing it, too. I just wish it would speed up the process and rip it to shreds already. After several minutes alone with my thoughts, Joey joins me on the couch with a heavy sigh.

"I'm so fucking confused right now. Dylan, I really thought, shit we *all* thought Reese wanted more than just some casual bullshit." He grabs my hand as I keep my head turned down toward my glass. "I'm so sorry, cupcake. Do you want to call Juls?"

I take a massive sip, hoping to dull some of the pain because alcohol is the poster child for broken heart syndrome. "I will, although I probably don't have to. Once my note is discovered and he can't find or talk to me, he'll be calling Ian who will in turn inform Juls." I swallow another gulp. "I feel so stupid. Everyone warned me about him, you especially. Telling me what Billy said about how he doesn't and will never do a relationship." I shake with my cries and have to put my glass down, covering my face as it all comes back again. "I hate him." Joey wraps me up and hushes me as I convulse with intense sobs against his body.

This is it. This is what being broken feels like. And a man that I wasn't even in a relationship with did it to me. *Fucking hell.*

Chapter
TWENTY-ONE

Two days before the wedding

"**O**H, FOR CHRIST'S SAKE, JULS. You need to decide on a cake flavor now or you're not getting a fucking cake." *Good Lord.* I get that the girl only cares about her sweet husband-to-be, but shit. I'm in charge of providing something decadent and she's only given me the type of flowers she wants on it. Juls just laughs at me as she flips through my design book in my kitchen bakery.

It's been close to three months since I ended things with Reese. After he came home and found my note, my phone didn't stop ringing for a week straight. I ignored all of his calls and texts, and I also ignored everything Juls would try to tell me about him. I didn't want to know how upset he was or how bad he wanted to talk to me about things. I moved back into my loft after only spending a few days at Billy and Joey's condo. They were very sweet to me and overly hands on with my healing process, but I knew if I was going to move the fuck on, I needed to do it in my own place. The texts and calls from Reese stopped after a month, and a part of me wishes I hadn't deleted every text without reading it or every voicemail without listening to it. I miss his voice, and I hate myself for it. I miss his words even more, and that makes me want to punch someone. But he got the hint, and I haven't seen my phone light up with his name in exactly fifty-four days. Juls got the hint also and stopped bringing him up, but I think that is mainly because her wedding is quickly approaching and she's had a lot of shit to take care of. And Ian knows better than to talk about him around me. He's been a witness to some of my verbal attacks on men.

I've seen her and Ian a lot in the past two months, helping them plan the wedding that my best friend basically put into her husband-to-be's hands. He's been amazing, like really amazing, at handling everything except for the goddamned cake selection. *That* he decided to leave up to Juls, and I'm about to hit her upside her pretty little head with my design book if she doesn't pick something out already. The fact that I have her cake to make isn't the only thing stressing me out. Tomorrow night is the rehearsal dinner, and I will be stuck in the same room with the man who broke me eighty-three days ago. I've been reassured that we won't be sitting anywhere near each other, but that doesn't help much. I still have to rehearse the ceremony with him, which means I'll be standing directly across from him up on that stupid altar and my arm will be looped through his when we walk down the aisle. *God, I hate weddings.*

"All right, here's the deal," Juls says after thirty minutes of me tapping my fingers on my worktop at her. "I want a three-tiered, almond lemon cake with lemon filling and a cream cheese frosting. There, that wasn't so hard, now was it?" *Oh, she's gone mad.* She slams the book shut and pushes it toward me, her glowing bride-to-be smile chipping away at my remaining patience. "Now, onto more pressing matters, the bachelorette party. I want to go dancing."

I roll my eyes and laugh as I write down her wedding cake selection. *About damned time too.* "Sounds good to me. As long as the booze is flowing, I'm all in. I plan on staying highly intoxicated for the next two days anyways." I begin pulling the ingredients I need off the shelves to start her cake.

"Well, you better not be drunk at the wedding. You are in charge of making sure everything runs smoothly, and how the hell are you going to do that if your head is stuck in a toilet?"

"Oh, relax, of course I won't be plastered at the wedding. Just tipsy enough to tolerate the situation." I pull out my mixer and set it aside. "Where do you want to go tonight anyway? I'm going to have to meet you there since I have a shit load of baking to do." I glare at her at the end of my sentence and she gives me her goofy grin.

"I was thinking Clancy's since we haven't been there in forever. Oh, shit. Remember the last time you, me, and Joey went there? Didn't he end up hooking up with three different guys in one night?"

"Of course, in true Joey fashion. *That* definitely won't be happening tonight considering he's practically engaged as it is." My face drops at the fact that I'm the only single friend in our circle. I shake my head at myself. *No sulking. You don't need a man. Men are dickheads.*

"Dylan." She reaches over and grabs my hand that's on my mixer, pulling me close to her and gripping both of my shoulders. I brace myself for what's coming. "I know the next two days are going to be hard for you, but you're the strongest woman I know, and have bigger balls than *any* man I know." I let out a weak laugh. "If anyone can get through this, it's you." She pulls me in for a hug and I let her. At least she didn't mention he-who-shall-not-be-named. "He's just as miserable as you are." *Damn it. So close.*

"Juls, don't."

"Well, at least he was. I haven't heard anything for a while. Apparently, he's slammed at work."

"I don't give a shit!" I push away from her and begin ripping open my bags of flour. "He's miserable? Doubt it. I'm sure he's sticking his dick into every whore in the South Side zip code as we speak." My voice breaks at the end and I struggle to hold back my tears, but they've been on reserve lately and are never far away. Her arms wrap around my back and she sighs heavily.

"I'm sorry, sweets. I'm gonna head out, but will see you tonight at Clancy's, right?" I nod and sniff loudly as she plants a quick kiss on my back before she exits the shop.

I take a minute to dry my tears before I start mixing up the ingredients for the almond lemon cake. God, I can't wait to start drinking tonight. If I don't show up hung-over to the rehearsal tomorrow, it will surely be a wedding miracle.

CLANCY'S IS PACKED, BUT I manage to spot Joey, Juls, and Brooke propped up at a round table by the bar. I shimmy my way through the crowd and receive very alcohol induced greetings from all three of them.

"Dylan. Fuck yes! I'm heading to the bar. What do you want?" Brooke asks as she stumbles off her stool. "I'm good, I'm good. Good," she turns and says to whoever is watching her. *Well, drunken Brooke didn't take long to come out and play.*

I try to muffle my laugh. "Whatever you're having sounds good."

"No," Joey and Juls say together quickly.

"Oh. Uh, okay, glass of Pinot then?"

Brooke spins toward the bar as I eye up the other two. "Why don't I want to drink what she's having?"

"Because I'm pretty sure she's drinking straight jet fuel," Joey barks around his beer. "She's completely out of control and *I'm* in charge of babysitting her for some stupid reason." He narrows his eyes at Juls. "I'm letting it slide this one time since you're getting married in two days."

"Love you," she replies as she blows him a kiss. "After you get your drink, Dyl, we're hitting the dance floor." I nod and glance down at her phone, which is lighting up on the table.

"Hey, husband-to-be. Oh, just drinking and dancing. What are you boys doing? If you say strip club I'm finding myself another groom while I'm here." She takes a sip of her drink and smiles around her straw as Brooke returns, miraculously without spilling anything.

"Here you go, Dylan. By the way, the bartender asked for your number." I glance around her as Joey whips his head in the same direction. The big, bald bartender sends a wink my way.

"Uh, no thanks." I take a generous sip of my wine.

"Seriously, like he'd ever stand a chance with you. He's more your type isn't he, Brooke?"

"Fuck you, Joey. You've been on my ass all night. What's your problem? Billy holding out on you?"

"Please. I get laid *way* more than you do. Tell me, has your virginity grown back yet?"

"Jesus Christ, Joey," I bark and try not to crack up laughing at poor Brooke's expense. She isn't the only person at this table not getting laid.

He merely shrugs and glances toward the dance floor.

"So, Dylan, isn't tomorrow going to be insanely awkward for you?" I glare directly at her and suddenly wish I wouldn't have just come to her defense. Brooke Wicks and alcohol do *not* mix well. She talks a lot of shit and then ends up passing out or throwing up all over the place. Not a good look for anybody.

I brush my hair off my shoulders. "No, Brooke, I'm not expecting it to be awkward at all. In fact, I can't fucking wait to have a reunion with my ex-fling. It's not like things ended badly between us or anything." My voice is thick with sarcasm, but given her current state, she probably won't pick it up. *How much has she had to drink?*

"Christ, Brooke. Don't be so fucking rude," Joey says as Juls turns her back away from the table and continues her phone call. She's in blissful bride mode and I don't blame her for avoiding this conversation.

"What? I'm just saying, I would feel awkward if I had to play nice with my ex. You should just hook up with someone else in the wedding party."

"Jesus Christ, like that's the answer to all the world's problems. Just hook up with someone in the wedding party. For your information, the only two other men *in* the wedding party are gay or married, and even if they weren't, no. I'm not hooking up with anyone at the rehearsal dinner and definitely *not* at the wedding. That's how this whole fucked up situation got started in the first place." I glance over at Joey who is staring at me, wide-mouthed and stunned. "You remember right, Joey? 'Go ahead, Dylan. You know you want to slip off into some dark corner and do something else in that lap of his.' This is all your fault."

His eyebrows raise and he leans across the table toward me. "*My* fault? How is this my fault? I didn't push you into his lap. I didn't make you run off to the bathroom with him and tell him to fuck you. And I sure as hell didn't put a gun to your head to continue being his casual fuck buddy." His finger darts across the table and points directly at me. "That was all you, cupcake."

Juls spins around and glares at both of us, phone still up to her ear. "Jesus Christ, you two. Keep it down before we get thrown out of here."

I reach over and grab his finger, bending it a bit as he screeches and pulls it away from me. "All me? Are you fucking serious? *You* were the one who said to be his sexy little mistress when we thought he was married. And *you* were the one who kept trying to convince me that it was more than just casual sex. 'Oh, Dylan, the man sends you love letters and he's so romantic.' Remember *that* bullshit?" I point right back at him and he jerks back in his stool. "Don't you *dare* tell me you didn't have a part in this. I had you yapping in my ear all day about how what we were doing meant more to both of us when *clearly*, it only meant more to me." I slam my hand down on the table and grab my drink, downing it quickly. My sparring partner's face softens and he shakes his head.

"Fuck, Dylan. You're right." He throws his hands up in the air dramatically. "You're right. I'm sorry. I really hate fighting with you. You scare the shit out of me." We both burst out laughing and I feel a pair of eyes on me as I turn quickly to Brooke who looks confused.

"You two are fucking weird. And I don't care if the other two groomsmen are gay, married, or pre-female to male transformation; I'm getting laid by someone."

"Bitch, you better stay the hell away from Billy," Joey says sternly. Juls quickly spins around and all arguments come to a halt at the sight of her beaming face. We all regain our composure and she's none the wiser.

"Okay, baby, I love you, too. Have fun." She hangs up her phone and hops off her stool. "All right, bitches, I believe it's time for me to show your sorry asses up on the dance floor." She does a quick spin and her black dress fans out around her knees.

"Ha!" I yell playfully as I get down and run over to her, putting her hand in mine. A clumsy Brooke follows while Joey quickly downs his beer.

"Let's do this!" he yells.

We dance all night into the early morning hours, finally leaving Clancy's at two a.m. and all piling into the same cab. None of us drove, which was a good thing because we are all rightly smashed and in zero condition to do anything but go to bed. We're giggling like idiots in the backseat of the cab, throwing out our addresses and confusing the hell out of the driver.

"Christ, already. Who am I taking home first? I can't understand four directions at once," the driver yells back as we all fall into a fit of tearful chuckles.

"Brooke, oh, my fucking God. That guy you were dancing with looked like Mr. T." I laugh and she searches her brain for the image. "He even had all the gold chains."

"But he could move. Whew."

"Yeah, he could. I'm pretty sure he had better moves than me, which says a whole fucking lot," Joey adds as Juls wipes the tears under her eyes.

The driver spins around to face us. "Ladies. Oh, and gentleman, sorry. Where the hell am I going?"

"I'm closest. Dylan's Sweet Tooth on Fayette please." I fall back against Joey. "Oh, man, this was so fun. Juls, seriously, thanks for this."

She winks at me as we pull away from the club. "So fun. I love you three. AND I'M GETTING MARRIED TOMORROW!" We all laugh and cheer as we drive off down the road, the petty arguments of the night left behind along with Brooke's vomit that came shortly after we started out onto the dance floor. I called it though. The girl should really not be around hard liquor.

I'm dropped off a mere fifteen minutes later and say my quick goodbyes before I stumble inside and lock up behind me. After peeling out of my dress and removing my makeup, I open my dresser drawer and spot the University of Chicago T-shirt that I had stuffed into my duffle bag when I was packing up my stuff the day I ended things with Reese. I should have sent it back to him through Ian when I realized I took it, but a part of me, a part of me that nobody knows about, likes wearing it to bed some nights when I want to smell him. I don't wear it often for fear that my scent will overpower his. But I do decide on wearing it tonight. I slip it on and climb into bed, grabbing my phone and opening up my internet search.

While on the dance floor tonight, the Arctic Monkeys song pumped through the speakers and I let myself dance to it, not wanting to give away how badly it killed me to hear it. And as I moved my body to it, I remembered how I never looked up the lyrics and it's been on my mind the entire evening. So now in the privacy of my dark bedroom, I'm finally looking up the lyrics to the song that reminded him of me.

"Oh, God." I read the lyrics again, and again, letting them sink into me and cursing myself for even looking them up in the first place, and for the stupid club for playing this stupid song. "Fuck." I shut down my phone and roll over, burying my head into the pillow to soften the cries that are coming from me now. *Jesus, that song? Really? It's a song about wanting to be with someone so badly, thinking about them all the time, wanting more with them. Dreaming about them. That song? How could that song remind him of me?* I bury my face into his T-shirt and cry harder, trying to push the lyrics out of my head to give myself some relief. I inhale his scent, the scent that is slowly fading, and I finally calm myself down enough to fall asleep. And sleep I am definitely going to need if I'm going to survive the next forty-eight hours.

Chapter
TWENTY-TWO

I WAKE UP A LITTLE after eleven a.m. on Friday and prepare myself for the day ahead. I decide to go on a run by myself today, only wanting my own thoughts to occupy my head and not Joey's relentless ranting. After my five miles, I lock up shop and head upstairs to shower and get dressed to finish Juls and Ian's wedding cake. The shop is closed and will be until Monday since we've had her wedding to prepare for, and I'm grateful for the quiet. I slip on my apron and whip up the cream cheese icing she requested, admiring the sugared dahlias I've already created to cascade down the cake. I curse myself for thinking of Reese at the sight of them and whip faster. *Damn it. What guy pays attention to details like that? I'd put money on Ian not giving two shits about the flowers that took me hours to create.*

After icing the cake and cleaning up my mess, I glance at the time on the oven. It's three thirty p.m. and I need to be at the church in an hour, and definitely need another shower. I untie my apron and throw it on the worktop before I dart up the stairs. I've picked a black sleeveless dress and pumps to wear tonight, pinning half of my hair up and leaving the rest in loose waves down my back. My makeup looks elegant, but not too done up, and I smile weakly into the mirror as I gaze at my reflection. My dress is hanging off my body more than it used to, and

I know it's because I haven't been eating much. Besides my daily taste tests, I'm having to choke down my meals that Joey has been bringing me, or at least parts of my meals. But at least I *am* eating. After one last look, I grab my clutch and head toward the night I've been dreading.

St. Stephen's church was Ian's pick, as was the reception and mostly every other detail for that matter. I park along the side of the beautiful building and straighten my dress out as I make my way to the front steps. Stopping at the bottom and glancing up at the double doors, my nerves hit me in one hard rush and I want to turn right around and get back into the comfort of Sam, but I can't. I close my eyes and grip the handrail. "Come on, Dylan." I pick up my feet and move up the stairs, clearing my throat before I open one of the doors.

The church is beautiful, with dark wood furnishings and stained glass windows allowing the sunlight to shine through in all different colors. Even if you aren't religious, try stepping into a catholic church and not feeling the presence of something way the hell bigger than you. I glance up at the massive cathedral ceiling and admire the painted murals when I hear Juls screeching my name.

"There you are. Now if Brooke would just hurry the hell up, we can get started." She's at my side instantly and looks beautiful. Dressed in a deep plum dress and her hair pulled up sleekly, she's practically glowing. She leans in and hugs me as my eyes glance up toward the bodies at the front of the church. But of course, I don't need to look to know he is here already. I felt him the moment I stepped inside this stupid building. My eyes find his instantly as he stands with Ian and the other men. His lips part slightly and I watch his chest rise with a deep intake of breath. Before I can rake my eyes down his body, I pull back from Juls and break the contact.

"You look beautiful and ready to be married."

"Thanks. You don't look so bad yourself. Come on, my parents have been asking when you'd get here." She grabs my hand and pulls me up front as I keep my eyes fixed on anyone but him. Luckily, we stop a few pews short of the men where all the parents are congregating.

"Dylan, there you are. Wow, you look stunning, dear. How's the bakery business going?" Mrs. Wicks wraps me up in a hug. She was always like a second mother to me.

"It's great and thank you. You look amazing yourself. And how are you doing, Mr. Wicks? Ready to give your oldest daughter away?"

He pulls me into his arms and I'm immediately hit with the smell of cigars. "Fat chance. She'll never get rid of her old man. It's good to see you, Dylan."

"You too." At that moment, the front doors swing open and Brooke comes barreling through, looking like she just woke up and most likely feeling a lot worse. I hear Juls gasp behind me. "Excuse me," I say politely before I begin quickly making my way down the aisle toward a very stupid looking bridesmaid.

"Dylan. Remember that guy last night?" I grab her wrist and pull her behind a pillar as she tries to get out of my grasp. "Jeez. What's the big deal?"

"What the fuck? Are you still drunk?" I ask as Joey comes rushing up to us with Juls on his heels. I notice quickly that all talking has stopped at the front of the church and can feel a million pairs of eyes on us.

"No, I'm not drunk. I'm just hung-over. Ooohhh, which one is Reese?" I grip her harder and she yelps.

"Oh, for Christ's sake. Way to keep it classy, Brooke," Joey whispers harshly as the preacher walks over toward us. We all straighten up a few inches.

"Are we ready to begin, Miss. Wicks?" he asks and she smiles quickly and nods, glancing back at me with her panicky eyes.

"We're ready," I confirm, keeping my hand on Brooke's arm as we all follow the preacher toward the front. I glare over at her and she cowers beside me as we walk up to the front. "Pull your shit together. And if you act like this tomorrow, I will personally make sure you don't get laid. I will vagina block the shit out of you." Her mouth drops open and I hear Joey laugh behind us.

"What? You better stay the hell away from my vagina," she grunts and my grip tightens.

"Ha! I bet you've never uttered *those* words before, Brooke," Joey laughs.

We stop as the preacher turns and faces everyone, and I quickly glance up and over to my right, finding Reese's eyes on me and quickly dropping my stare back down. I let go of Brooke and she sighs in relief, massaging her reddened arm.

"Okay, everyone, we're going to do a quick run through of the ceremony, just to make sure everyone knows their places. So, if I can have the groomsmen, best man, and the groom all standing to my left right here," he motions down at the stairs below him. "And, ladies, and gentleman, if you would line up at the front doors and we'll get started." *Oh, good. I'll only have to walk with Reese at the end of the ceremony down the aisle. That's not too bad. What is it? Twenty-five, thirty feet of contact? I can handle that.* We quickly form a line at the back of the room as I stand in front of Juls, Joey in front of me, and Brooke, hopefully, leading the way. God, help her if she can't make it up to the altar.

"You ready for this?" Joey leans back and whispers.

"Yup. You?"

"Oh, please, have you seen my baby up there? Gorgeous." I giggle at his response and hear the preacher announce for Brooke to start walking, which she does after Joey gives her a right shove. "Asshole. She's going to be such a pain tomorrow," he says before he begins walking and I can't help but smile. My assistant as a bridesmaid. Of course.

"I love you," Juls says behind me and I feel my eyes water a bit.

"Love you," I say as I begin making my walk up the aisle. I don't want to. I really don't want to, but my eyes find his immediately and I finally get my first real look at him in eighty-four days. He's wearing a black suit, perfectly tailored to that body with a green striped tie and white dress shirt. His hair looks like it's been cut a bit, but still has its perfectly tousled look to it, and his eyes are piercing into mine, the green beaming out of them thanks to his tie color choice. I see them quickly drop and run down my dress before he flicks back up to meet mine, jaw set and tense. I take my spot on the same step as him and finally look away toward Juls who is with her father at the back of the church. She begins her walk up and I keep my eyes on her even though I can feel him looking at me. Studying me.

The preacher runs through the ceremony, going over the vows that Ian and Juls' picked out for tomorrow. I smile and laugh as they recite them and keep turning around to make sure Brooke is still upright and awake. Joey gives me a reassuring wink with each turn and I know he's got her covered. *Thank God.* After the mock exchanging of the rings and pronouncement of their marriage, the two of them begin filing down the aisle and I quickly clamp my eyes shut, knowing what's coming next. *Shit. He's going to touch me. He's going to touch me and I'm going to lose it.*

"Okay, now Dylan and Reese, you may walk down together. Billy and Joey, you can follow when they are about halfway down the rows." I open my eyes and step forward after the preacher finishes and see Reese already waiting for me, elbow out so I can easily slip my hand through it. I swallow loudly and grip the inside of his elbow as we begin walking silently down the aisle. I can hear his breathing, slow and steady as if he's unaffected by this entirely. *Figures. I wasn't sure what I was expecting here. The sight of me causing him to faint possibly?* But no, not even uneven, nervous breathing.

"You look beautiful," he says, low and throaty, and I gasp slightly, but don't respond. We reach the end of the aisle and I quickly drop my hand from his arm and move to stand next to Juls and as far away from him as possible. *Shit. Don't be affected by that, Dylan.* After the rest of the wedding party comes down the aisle, we all say our momentary goodbyes as we file out toward our vehicles. I quickly walk to Sam and scramble in, wanting to avoid any alone time with Reese as I see him walking out with Ian and the other men. His eyes fall on my delivery van fleetingly before he hops in his Range Rover and pulls away from the church. I drop my head on the wheel. "Okay. Half of the night is over. Now, you just need to get through the dinner and you'll only have to worry about tomorrow." After my little pep talk, I start up Sam and make my way toward Casa Mia's.

The rehearsal dinner is booked at a quaint Italian restaurant and a long rectangular table has been set aside for us in the very back. My place is next to Juls and three seats down from Reese who is sitting next to Ian. I'm immensely grateful that he isn't seated on the opposite side because I've done enough looking for one evening. Joey plops down next to me and let's out an exhaustive sigh.

"Problems with our favorite bridesmaid?" I ask, noticing she hasn't graced us with her presence at the table yet. I pick up my water and take a few sips.

"I'm going to kill her. She insisted on riding with me and then tried to feel me up in the car." Water shoots out of my mouth and covers the, thankfully, empty place setting across from me as I quickly bring a napkin up to my face.

"Jesus, Dylan. Are you all right?" Juls asks as I continue coughing. I glance over at her and see everyone is staring at me, and I mean everyone, as I quickly shake off my choke fest.

I turn quickly toward Joey. "Are you serious?"

"Do I *look* serious? I feel like I've been molested. She almost made me cause an accident on highway eleven."

My coughing turns into giggling as I lean my head onto his shoulder and we both crack up at the situation. "Oh, my God. That's amazing. I so needed to hear that right now." I laugh as he shakes his head at me, picking up his water.

"What's going on?" Juls asks softly as our dinner is brought out to us. I'm suddenly starving and the dish that's in front of me is about to be destroyed.

I eye her up mischievously. "Your lovely sister has been putting the moves on JoJo." Her fork drops.

"What? Oh, great. That's just great." On cue, Brooke appears and quickly claims her seat next to Joey who stiffens next to me. Juls leans across and snaps her fingers at her sister. "You're an asshole."

"Yeah, I'm sorry, Joey. That was a bit embarrassing. Although, was it just me or did something move?" She giggles and orders something alcoholic from the waiter, which Joey quickly cancels for her.

"Did something move? Are you fucking insane? And no booze for you. I can only imagine what would happen if you started drinking."

I shake my head and take a bite of my chicken picatta, moaning around my fork as a familiar face moves toward our table and stands across from me.

"Hey, Dylan. How's it going?" Juls' cousin Tony eyes me up and I quickly smile and wave at him from my seat. We've known each other for years and go way back, but never anything more than friendship.

"Hey, Tony. How are you?"

"I'm great. Get your sweet ass out of that chair and come give me a hug." I laugh and scramble out of my seat, walking down the side of the table that does not contain my ex-fling, and get quickly lifted into the air. "You look good, girl," he says into my hair as he gives me his usual bear hug.

"Thanks. Jesus, put me down already." He sets me on my feet and I shake my head at him, straightening out his tie. "So, what's new in the world of computer programming?" My eyes quickly flick toward Reese who is staring at me with daggers. *Oh, please. Like you have any right anymore.*

"Nailed it. Nice memory. It's good. How about you? Juls told me something about your bakery getting broken into or some shit a few months back? That's fucked up."

"Yeah, well, it's fine now. They caught the psycho who did it and there wasn't any permanent damage." Heather was apprehended by the police a few weeks after the break in. Her prints matched the ones on the brick and she admitted to everything, getting charged with breaking and entering and also getting moved out of the city by her parents. Juls had relayed the information from Ian when he found out about it.

"So, any man in your life or have I finally caught up with you when you're single?" I smile sweetly at Tony, but shake my head. He is definitely not my type and even if he was, I have no interest in dating anybody right now. Especially when the man who broke me is sitting no more than ten feet away from me, continually staring at my profile.

"Oh, please, like you could even handle me," I playfully respond and he nods in agreement. "It's good to see you. I'll catch up with you later, okay?" I turn to go back around the table, but see a major pile up of bodies at the end I want to walk down and grunt as I have to make my way toward the other end. I walk behind Trent and Billy's chairs, giving them both smiles, as I quickly move past Reese's and feel his hand grip my elbow, halting me at his side.

"What the fuck was that?" he growls up at me.

I snatch my arm out of his hand and scowl back down at him. "What the fuck was what?"

"You know what. Are you seriously going to blatantly flirt in front of me? Is that how this shit is going to play out?" *Is he serious? I am in no mood for any Reese style tirade and this is definitely not the place for it.*

I bend lower to get my face nice and close to his and see him back up a bit. "You think *that* was flirting? I've known Tony for ten years; he's like a brother to me. But if I *did* want to flirt with him, it wouldn't be any of your goddamned business, now would it?" My tone is clipped and I'm fuming, feeling Ian move quickly out of his seat.

"Okay. Wow, that didn't take long. Umm, Dylan, why don't you go over to your seat, and, Reese, just calm the fuck down, man." Ian ushers me past Juls. I quickly pull out my chair and plant myself down in it, glaring over in his direction as Reese narrows his eyes at me.

"Jesus, what the hell was that?" Juls asks as Joey leans in.

"Actually, I'm surprised it didn't happen sooner. I had money on you kicking him in the nuts at the church," he adds. I wave my hands at both of them to back them off me.

"Nothing. He accused me of flirting with Tony. Fucking prick," I say through clenched teeth. I was definitely not flirting with him. I've never seen Tony as anything other than an acquaintance, even though he's asked me out more times than I can count. My eyes glance down the table and I see Ian leaning in and talking to a tense looking Reese. *Ugh. Stupid men.*

"You and Tony? That's fucking hilarious," Juls says and continues cutting up her chicken. "And even if you were, he has no right to act like that."

"I know," I agree loudly and get quickly shushed. "Acting all holier than thou. I'm sure he waited a whole five seconds before he threw another girl into his bed after I left it." I shove a piece of chicken in my mouth and start chewing as Brooke leans across Joey's lap.

"I heard him tell you that you looked beautiful. That was really sweet," she whispers and earns herself the evil eye from all three of us.

"Shut up, Brooke," we all say in unison as we continue eating our meals. I don't look down the table again for the rest of the night and keep my conversations with anyone other than Juls and Joey to a minimum. This evening has been exhausting. I'm emotionally drained and unsure how the hell I'm going to handle tomorrow. I'm reassured that I'll only really have to deal with Reese during the ceremony, and once we're at the reception, I can stay as far away from him as I'd like. But it's the mere fact that we'll once again be at a wedding together, where this whole fucked up situation started that is going to have me in knots. I need to focus on making sure everything runs smoothly for Juls, so that's what I'll do. It's my job as her maid of honor and it will keep my mind off unwanted memories of falling into laps and bathroom sex romps. Speaking of bathrooms, I plan on avoiding the ones tomorrow at all costs.

Chapter
TWENTY-THREE

ULS AND IAN'S BIG DAY has finally arrived and miraculously, everything is running smoothly. I got up early and delivered the cake with Joey to the reception hall before we headed over to the bridal suite where we are all currently getting ready. Juls is glowing, Joey is routinely sneaking out to get a peek at the men who are dressing at the other end of the church, and Brooke is completely sober and has her wits about her. After slipping into my stunning chocolate brown floor length strapless dress, I help Juls into hers, along with her mother.

"Oh, sweetheart. This dress," Mrs. Wicks says, tears filling her freshly painted eyes as I try to hold mine back. My makeup is looking pristine and fabulous and I have no desire to ruin it with unwanted tears. We finish buttoning her up and step back. She's stunning, absolutely gorgeous in her wedding gown and I bite my lip to hold my emotions in.

"Damn, Juls. I have money on Ian losing his mind when he sees you at the end of the aisle," Brooke says as she smoothes out her dress. Joey comes bustling back into the suite and drops his jaw on the floor.

"Holy fuck. You look amazing."

"Joseph! You're in a church," Mrs. Wicks sternly informs him, both hands flying up to her hips. "Easy on the language today please, and that goes for all four of you. Especially you, Dylan." She flicks her daggers at me.

"Me? Please, I'm such a lady." I shrug and catch a wink from Juls in the mirror as the suite door swings open again, this time revealing a very handsome and slightly nervous looking Mr. Wicks.

"Oh my. Darling, you look so beautiful." He moves and stands in front of Juls, grabbing both of her hands in his and pulling her off her stool. "That's it, wedding's off. You're too pretty for that man."

"Daddy," she says through a huge smile and he softens in front of her. I move up to the mirror and take a good look at myself as they exchange a private father-daughter moment, Joey joining me at my side. My hair is pinned up into an elegant twist, a few pieces pulled out and tucked behind my ears, which are adorned with the amber stud earrings Juls gifted us with this morning. My makeup is sophisticated but subtle, a light dusting of rose lip-gloss that I'm somehow managing to pull off without looking like I belong on a street corner, and my dress is perfect, hugging me across my chest and showing a classy amount of cleavage if there ever was such a thing. I feel Joey's hand on my lower back.

"Look at us. We almost look *too* good for this wedding. I'm afraid we might just upstage the bride," he whispers as we both glance over at Juls who is hugging her father.

"Not a chance," I say and he nods in agreement. Mr. Wicks backs away from his daughter and turns toward all of us.

"It's time people. Let's move this along before I lock my daughter in this room and refuse to let Ian have her." We all giggle at his comment, hearing the hint of seriousness in his tone as we file out of the bridal suite and down the back staircase that leads toward a hidden area where we're supposed to line up. I haven't seen the inside of the church since we arrived here hours ago and I'm a bit nervous at the number of people in attendance who will be watching me walk up the aisle. My heels are insanely high, dark brown sling backs that I've scuffed the bottoms of to prevent any major slip up. But I'm still nervous about walking in them. Karma could easily give me a right shove in the back and send me falling flat on my face, given the amount of hate she's shown me lately. *All this animosity. And for what? Because I fell in love with a man who only cared about fucking me? Nice, Karma. Way to stick with your fellow woman.*

We line up in order behind the double mahogany doors and wait patiently for them to open, the soft sound of violins streaming through the air. Another decision on Ian's part. The man apparently loves classical music. I clutch my beautiful bouquet in my hands, grateful to have something to hold on to as the doors slowly open in front of Brooke. My view is blocked entirely by Joey's massive frame, but I feel him. I always feel him. And I know as soon as I start walking, my eyes are going to lock on to his and I'm going to give in to it. *Whatever.* I just have one more day to endure and then I can go back to my shitty life. I turn around and spot Juls who is smiling at me, eyes gleaming and hand tightly looped through her father's arm. I give her a quick wink before I turn slowly and step forward, seeing Joey make his way toward the middle pews. It's now my cue to start walking, but I can't. My eyes have locked on to the most glorious sight I've ever seen and he's standing, waiting for me at the front of the altar in a tux. *Holy fucking shit.*

I know I'm supposed to be moving; I've walked up this aisle before. I just accomplished the feat last night. But I'm stuck. My two feet won't budge an inch and I hear the muffled voices of people around me wondering what the hell is going on. Joey is up at the front, motioning for me to start moving and Brooke is trying desperately not to crack up laughing. Meanwhile, Reese is staring at me, eyes burning into mine and I'm melting on the spot. I've never seen him look this handsome before and I'm suddenly regretting everything. The break up, the fact I agreed to be a part of this wedding, the shirt I kept. Everything. I force out a shaky breath and glance quickly back at Juls who is trying to remain calm but coming apart slowly. Her father is staring at me and looks unsure what to do as I clutch my bouquet tightly and shut my eyes. *Jesus Christ, Dylan. You need to move. Just start walking and you'll be up there before you know it.* I shake my head and open my eyes, and if I was unable to breathe before I closed them, I've completely forgotten how to work my lungs now.

Reese is making his way down the aisle toward me, purpose in each step and eyes glued on mine as everyone watches him and who he's walking toward. My lips part and I shift on my feet as he reaches my side, grabbing my hand and looping it through his arm. And without saying a word, he begins walking me up the aisle, earning a few sounds of amusement from the crowd, and smiling politely at them. I'm deposited on my step and he drops my hand, leaving an emptiness inside me as he returns to his place across from me. Our eyes meet briefly and I smile weakly at him, seeing his lip curl up slightly as the wedding march song begins to play.

The rest of the ceremony plays out the way it's supposed to. Rings and vows are exchanged, and I keep my eyes on the bride and groom who haven't broken contact since Juls hurriedly reached Ian at the front of the altar. I manage to only shed a few tears but quickly wipe them away before my makeup is affected. And as the preacher announces to the congregation Juls' official title as Mrs. Ian Thomas, they kiss and everyone stands and cheers. Ian showers her with affection as they begin their walk toward the back of the church, and I move to stand next to Reese who is already waiting and watching me. Always watching. We follow the bride and groom to the doors, not exchanging any words this time, even though I wanted to at least thank him for what he did earlier. I'm not sure I would have made it up to my place on the altar had he not come and gotten me. I quickly release my hand from his arm when we reach the bride and groom and wrap Juls up into a massive hug.

"You're married," I squeal. Joey and Brooke come scurrying up behind us and wrap their arms around me and Juls.

"I know. And now, we get to go parrttaaayyy." I release her with a giggle and turn around, walking over to Ian and giving him a big hug.

"You hurt her and I'll cut you up into tiny pieces and bury you throughout the city." He lifts me up and spins me around, a muffled laugh escaping his lips. Trent, Billy, and Reese are all watching and I hear laughs coming from them after my declaration.

He sets me down gently. "Oh, don't I know it. I'm well aware of your capabilities, Dylan. Even though you sometimes manage to forget how to walk." He smirks at me and I roll my eyes. I don't linger with him since Reese is at his side, chatting it up with the other groomsmen. And after Ian and Juls walk down the church steps through a cloud of tiny bubbles, we all pile into a stretch limo and head over toward the reception hall.

૭⌒ᵒ

THE HALL IS BEAUTIFUL, IMMACULATELY decked out in fall colors and everything to Juls' liking. It's also massive and probably close to the size of the Whitmore Mansion, which pulls at my heart strings a bit. But it's somehow classier because if Julianna Thomas is anything, it's classy. I'm doing my best to keep some distance between Reese and myself as we all stand cramped inside a small room, waiting for the guests to make their way into the hall so we can all be introduced together. And that part, I fear is what I've been dreading the most. Reese and I will be publicly announced together as best man and maid of honor in front of everyone, and we'll have to make our way through the crowd and onto the dance floor, all eyes on us. This just might kill me.

"All right, everyone, line up. The DJ is about to make your introductions so pair up with your person and let's get this party started," the chipper older woman who had ushered us into the room says. I mumble a curse under my breath as we make our way toward the double doors, taking my place behind Billy and Joey who are all over each other.

"You two make me want to vomit," I say as Reese steps up beside me, grabbing my attention immediately. His scent is intoxicating, and I almost stumble as it fills the air around me. I shake my head quickly and regroup.

"Don't hate, Dylan. It's not a good look on you," Billy says through a teasing smile.

"And why the fuck can't you be single? Damn it, Trent," Brooke grunts ahead of us and I buckle over in giggles. She's been hitting on poor Trent all night and he hasn't paid her any mind. It's really perfect considering the way she's behaved the past several days. "Ugh. Reese, switch with Trent." She turns back toward us and my body stiffens, but Reese doesn't react at all. Billy and Joey make wide eyes at me.

"Brooke, turn your fucking ass around right now before I cut you," I growl at her and feel Reese's jacket shake against my arm as he tries to muffle his laughs. Billy and Joey crack up in front of me and Trent shakes his head in amusement.

"God, I've missed you." The voice next to me makes me go

completely rigid, as do Billy and Joey who turn around quickly. "Oh, um, sorry I didn't... fuck." My eyes meet his briefly, and before I can even think of a reaction to that, the doors swing open and the DJ begins announcing the wedding party. Brooke and Trent, followed by Joey and Billy are sent through as Reese and I move up and he slips my hand through his arm. My breathing is irregular, I'm nervous as hell, and he can sense it. "Dylan, relax. I've got you." I open my mouth to tell him to *stop* getting me when the DJ comes through the speaker system.

"And now please give a warm welcome to our lovely maid of honor, Dylan Sparks, and her handsome escort, the best man, Reese Carroll."

Cheers and whistles fill the room as I'm practically dragged behind Reese. We pass a table of women who hoot and holler at him and he gives them his perfect smile as we walk toward the dance floor. "Jesus Christ," I mutter under my breath at them and feel his soft laugh shake against my body. We stand next to Joey and Billy and watch as Ian and Juls are announced, my hand removed from his arm to allow me to clap along with the crowd of people as they walk joyously into the hall. They stop in the center of the dance floor and begin their first dance as husband and wife. The wedding party moves about, talking amongst themselves, and I glance over and see Reese make his way toward a table where a dark-headed woman is sitting, her eyes beaming at him. She stands and practically hurls herself up into his arms and he wraps her up, planting kisses into her hair. I immediately turn away. *Shit. Are you serious right now? He brought a fucking date?* The sound of the song is blurred out around me as I move toward Joey and yank him away from Billy, pulling him toward the opposite end of the dance floor.

"Jesus, what?" he asks as I finally let go of his jacket. I'm shaking and he eyes up my appearance, his hand coming up to grab my bare shoulder. "What's wrong?"

"He brought a date. A fucking date, Joey. I was *not* expecting that." My chest is rising and falling rapidly and I feel like I might just pass out right here in the middle of this thing. I see his eyes search across the dance floor and spot Reese, who is talking closely with the young and very attractive woman.

"Fuck. That's so not cool. Want me to say something? I can throw his ass out of here. Or hers if you want."

"Oh, please, like you would stand a chance against Reese. But her, maybe." He narrows his eyes at me and makes a face. "Fuck, this is awful. He's all over her. I figured Brooke would be the only bitch I'd be fighting today." The soft song dies down and everyone is told to take their seats so the meal can be served. I make an obscene gesture in the direction of Reese who is none the wiser as I walk up to the bridal party table and take my seat next to Juls.

I'm quiet during the meal, my only words to Juls being I'm so happy for her and she looks radiant. I pick at the food on my plate and keep finding myself glancing over at the table that Reese had been hovering over during the first dance. The woman is young, probably close to my age, and has dark brown curly hair that falls just above her shoulders. She's talking amongst the other guests at her table and having a blast, while my mind is eyeing up my utensils and deciding which weapon of choice I'd like to use on her if I get the chance. But really, is it her fault he asked her here as his date? She probably doesn't know about me, let alone the history we share. She's an innocent bystander who he's dragged into this mess like a complete fucking asshole. I'm gripping my knife tightly in my fist and feel Joey pry it out of my grasp, quickly putting it far away from me.

"Relax, please. I'd really rather not have the cops called at Juls' wedding reception," he says under his breath as I let out a forceful one. The DJ softens the music and talks through the speakers as I try and calm down.

"And now I will ask the wedding party make their way out onto the dance floor for a special number."

"Oh, great. Give me my knife back," I growl at Joey as we all stand up and he shoves it farther down the table. He grabs my waist and directs me down the stairs, the rest of the wedding party meeting us out on the dance floor, and finally letting go of me when he plants me directly in front of Reese. I cross my arms over my chest and refuse to look up and into his eyes. *Bastard.* I hear a small sound of amusement from above me as he steps into me and pries them down, wrapping his hand around my back, while his other holds mine against his chest. A song that guts me begins playing overhead and I flick my eyes up to his and see his soft smile. Of all songs the DJ could have picked for this stupid moment, he picks "Look After You"? *Perfect.*

"What the fuck is this? Did you ask for him to play this song?" I ask angrily as I try to wiggle free. His grip around me tightens.

"So what if I did? It doesn't mean anything to you anyway, so what's the problem?"

"Oh, you're so right, Reese. It means nothing to me. You're a fucking asshole, you know that? I can't believe you brought a date to this thing and had the nerve to accuse me of flirting with Juls' cousin." I glare up at him as he moves me around the dance floor, my anger level rising at the realization that he's also good at slow dancing. Really fucking good at it.

"What date? What the fuck are you talking about?"

I tilt my head in the direction of the pretty brunette who is staring at us, smiling for some weird ass reason. "That date. I saw you with her. Kissing her and talking all close and intimate. Fuck you. I would never do that in front of you."

He shakes his head at me. "*That* is my fucking sister, Dylan. Ian invited her *and* her husband who couldn't make it because he's away on business and I haven't seen her for months. That's why she got such a warm welcoming from me. But it doesn't really fucking matter if it's my sister or not, now does it? You ended things, remember? You fucking *destroyed* me."

I push away from him and take a step back. Staring, shocked at his admission. "I destroyed you? Fuck you. You completely broke me, you stupid shit." I slap him hard across the face because it's what I do and storm off the dance floor, pushing my way through the crowd of people who, I'm sure, have been focused on us since our heated argument started. I'm out the double doors and make my way down the long empty hallway, unsure of where I'm headed when I hear the doors swing open in the distance behind me.

"Dylan!"

I keep moving, picking up my pace but stumble forward once my heel catches on my dress, landing hard on my knees, my hands breaking my fall and hitting the marble floor. Falling back onto my heels, I drop my head into my hands and try to muffle my cries. I don't want him to see me like this, but it's too late. His body drops down and I'm lifted off the floor and onto my feet as he tries to pull me against his chest. I push away and pry his hands off my waist.

"Let go of me. I hate you. I fucking hate what you did to me." I wipe under my eyes and mentally curse myself for the mascara that appears on my fingertips.

His eyes widen. "What did I do? Dylan, goddamn it. What the fuck did I do besides everything you wanted?"

"Everything *I* wanted? How was what we did what I wanted? You're the one who wanted a casual hook up. You're the one who never did anything serious and only wanted it to be about sex. I *never* wanted that."

He steps closer and I back up, but I'm pressed against the wall, unable to put anymore distance between us. "What the fuck are you talking about?" His eyes search my face for an explanation. "*You* were the one who said this was just fun and nothing serious. You labeled it that when we were at The Tavern that night. *You* were the one who refused to let me get close to you, never wanting things to get too intimate between us. That was *all* you, Dylan. I fucking told you that you had all the control." He roughly rakes his hands through his hair and down his face. "This shit was never casual for me. Never. You've owned me since that fucking wedding."

"I fucking heard you with Ian. I came to your office the day I ended things to tell you I loved you, and I fucking heard you. You said you didn't do serious and you were just fucking me because you liked to. How could you say that about me? After everything. After your birthday and," my face falls apart in tears and I push against his chest, "and after you made love to me. How could you say that?"

His hands grip mine, holding them to his chest, his eyes widening and pupils dilating. "*That's* why you ended things? Fuck, love, if you would have just stayed and listened."

I pull my hands away from his. "Don't call me that. And listened to what? I heard everything I needed to hear. I meant nothing to you and you meant *everything* to me."

He shakes his head and grabs me by the waist, pulling me against him so our chests are touching. He sighs heavily. "Christ, Dylan, if you would have just stayed and listened for a few more seconds, you would have heard Ian call me out on my bullshit." His hand comes up and he pushes my hair behind my ears, his thumb lingering on my cheek. "I only said those things because I'd been desperately trying to convince myself that it was only about sex between us, because I knew that was what you wanted. I was certain that was what you wanted and the only way I could have you. But it was never just about sex. Not for me. After Ian called me out, I admitted how crazy I was for you. How you were the only woman who ever got to me and that drove me completely insane, and not just because you like to challenge me. Which you do so *fucking* well."

My breathing becomes labored as I stand pressed against him, unable to move or blink. His eyes are burning into mine and his hands are now softly squeezing my hips. I open my mouth to speak but he silences me with his words.

"I was so in love with you and I couldn't admit it, because admitting it meant dragging you out of your casual fucking comfort zone and into it with me. And I was scared you would pull away. And you pulled away from me anyway without me ever getting the chance to say it."

I'm shaking against him and don't know what to say, or if I can even speak anymore. He's admitted everything I've ever wanted to hear and I can only stare up at him through a tear stained face.

"I called you, every day and sent you messages. Begging, pleading for an answer from you and you ignored me." His hand comes up and strokes my cheek and I lean into it. "Why? Why wouldn't you talk to me? We could have fixed this, but now…"

My eyes widen in panic as he drops his hand and shakes his head. I'm frozen against the wall, unable to move as his body turns and he begins walking back toward the reception hall. *No. He loves me. And I love him. This shit can't end like this. Fuck that.*

"Seriously?" I yell and he halts, his hand on the door and his face down so I can't see his expression. I march over to him and rip his hand off the doorknob, pulling him away from it, and slamming his back against the wall. "You're really going to leave it like that? You said you loved me, do you not anymore?" My rapid breathing fills the air between us as he gazes down at me, clenched jaw and furrowed brow. But he doesn't speak. I grip his tux jacket with both hands and stare up into his soft eyes. *Fuck this. He's here. I'm here, and I'm saying it.* "I love you. I want you, Reese. Just you, and not at all in the stupid casual bullshit way. I want everything. Sleepovers and sex in beds. All kinds of beds. Yours, mine, whoever's. I want to introduce you to my parents and I want to bake your birthday cake every year while you sit and look at me the way only *you* look at me." I take in a shaky breath while he stands, watching me, studying me. "It fucking *killed me* to pull away from you."

I step in close to him and bury my face into his neck, not knowing or caring if this is appropriate. I need to be here right now, and as his arms slowly wrap around me and pull me close to him, I finally exhale.

He moans softly, his hand stroking my hair as I feel his lips curl up against my forehead. "You know, this shit could have been avoided entirely if you would have just stormed in and slapped the piss out of me after you overheard that bullshit." I pull my head back and see his perfect smile gleaming down at me and I tightly wrap my arms around his back. "I mean really, the one time I would actually *want* you to slap me, you don't. I would have scooped you up right then and told you how much I loved you. Where the hell was my hot-headed girl *that* day?"

I shake my head at the memory. "Broken on the floor. You're right though, that was very uncharacteristic of me."

He plants several kisses to my forehead. "Well, I've been a miserable piece of shit without you. Apparently, unbearable to be around, if you ask Ian. How have you been, love?"

I laugh my first real laugh in months and wipe under my eyes. "Bitchy and more hostile than usual. Poor Joey, he really has taken the brunt of our breakup."

"That sounds about right. Now, you have two options here." I smile big at his words.

"They better both involve your hands and mouth on me or I'm finding myself another groomsman."

He issues me a warning stare and I smirk. "Obviously, I've gone eighty-five days without touching you, and it's taken every ounce of strength in my body to not rip you right out of this dress, which you look absolutely beautiful in by the way." He plants a quick kiss to my lips as I back up and wait for my options.

"Option one, we can go back inside and you can let me dance with you some more, enjoy your company that I have greatly missed over the past grueling months, and, hopefully, witness you getting into it with Brooke again because that shit was fucking hilarious." I laugh at him as he pushes off from the wall and grabs my face between his hands, his thumb slowly tracing my bottom lip. The pull between us is stronger than ever and I'm about to say fuck option one without even hearing my other choice. But I let him give it to me anyway. "Or, we can go off somewhere and I can fuck you until you scream my name in that sexy way that you do, all throaty and raspy." His tongue sweeps across my lips and I pull him in, firmly stroking mine against his. I moan softly into his mouth, tasting and relishing in his flavor. "Christ, I'm so in love with you, Dylan. Insanely in love. Do you have any idea how much I've missed your face?" His finger slowly trails over my lips and along my jaw while he studies me.

I lean in and plant quick kisses on his lips. "Just my face?" My hand runs down the front of him and cups his length. His eyes widen.

"Option two then? Thank fuck, because if you would have picked one I would have taken you in front of everyone on that dance floor and not given a shit about who watched us." He bends down and I'm quickly hauled up onto his shoulder. I'm issued a firm slap on my backside as he takes me down the hallway. I squeal and laugh against him, admiring my own view of his perfect behind. I'm quickly slid down his front as we stand just outside the men's bathroom, his brow arched at me as his hand grips the handle.

"It is rather fitting, picking up where this whole thing began." He opens the door and peers inside as I jump around on my heels.

"Well, hopefully, this time you won't get all weird on me afterwards. I'm sure you're used to sex with me by now." I'm pulled into the restroom and the door is locked behind me as I'm lifted off my feet, legs firmly wrapping around his waist.

"Oh, I don't know, love, you always surprise me. Fuck, I don't ever want to leave this bathroom. Any issue with not returning to the reception?" His mouth latches onto mine and I'm quickly silenced, my answer not worth a damn anyway when I can be kissed like this. *The man can kiss better than anyone; I'm sure of it.* I'm pressed against the wall, my bare back stinging on the cold tile as his tongue roams freely inside my mouth. He licks along my lips, pulling my tongue into his mouth and softly sucking on it before he releases it and moves down my neck.

"I've missed you," I say as his mouth kisses and sucks on the top of my breasts, his hands gripping my ass and hiking up my dress. "Oh, God, I'm so wet for you."

He growls against my chest as his hand slides up between us, running up my inner thigh and meeting the fabric of my panties. "Shit. I need to taste you before I fuck you. I'm dying here." I'm carried over to a small leather bench that's on the opposite side of the restroom and laid out on it, my dress quickly hiked up to reveal my white lacy panties and matching garter. "Holy fuck," he says as he drops down to his knees and moves between my legs. The bathroom door rattles with someone's knocking. "Go away!" he yells and I laugh at his completely flustered state. He tucks my panties into his pocket with a smirk before he delivers his first lick. "Damn, I've missed this. So sweet." He hums against me, moving his face rapidly between my thighs.

"OH!" I cry out, my hands gripping his hair and holding him between my legs as he devours me like I'm his last meal. His tongue is all over me, his movements ranging from quick flicks to my clit to slow savory laps of my length. I'm not holding in my moans, my voice is echoing throughout the bathroom, but I don't care. I want everyone to hear me. I love this man and his mouth and everything he does with it. He teases my clit and sucks on it slowly, pulling it into his mouth as he slips two fingers inside of me. I arch into him.

"I fucking love this pussy. Tell me it's mine, Dylan."

"It's yours. Oh, God, Reese, I'm so close." His fingers move in and out of me, the pace quickening as my hands tangle in his hair and I pull it hard. My back arches off the leather as he grabs my hips, his tongue rolling in my favorite rhythm. I'm whispering, pleading with him to lick me, harder, deeper, right there and he grabs my orgasm that's his to command and pulls it out of me.

I come and scream his name, over and over until my voice is strained and my throat aches. He takes his time sucking up all of my arousal, lingering on my clit the way I like as I tremble against him. The tight grip he has on my hips is slowly lessened as he plants the softest, gentlest Reese kiss to my pussy. My breathing slows and I cover my eyes with my arm as he stands on his feet.

"Well then, that didn't take long. How have your orgasms been without me?" His smug voice makes me giggle and I gaze up at him, hair sticking out every which way as he licks his lips.

"What orgasms?" I reply and quickly get up and switch spots with him, pushing him onto his back and making quick work of his belt. "I'm going to fuck you so hard; you're not going to be able to walk out of here." He smiles wickedly at me, the lines that I've missed so much appearing on either side of his eyes. "That okay with you?"

His pants are quickly pushed down along with his boxers and I marvel at his erection. *Now, that I definitely missed.* "Fine with me, love." His hands grip my waist as I straddle him, reaching under my dress and positioning himself below me. I lock eyes with him, waiting to lower myself down.

"I love you," I say as his hands pull down my top and reveal my breasts.

"I love you," he replies without hesitation, his eyes flicking up from my chest and holding my stare. I quickly crash down, pulling a throaty grunt out of his throat.

"Fuck. Dylan."

Oh, God. This. I forgot how perfect he feels in me. The way my body forms around him, molds to him like he's made for me. Just me. I can't move yet. I'm too caught up in the way he feels just like this and the look he's giving me. Green eyes burning into mine with that intensity, his intensity that I've missed so much. He's looking at me the way only he looks at me, the way I only ever want to be looked at by the man I've chosen. I chose him.

I pull my lip into my mouth as I rock against him, sliding up and down his length. His hips move beneath me as his hands firmly cup my breasts. He moans, grunts, and growls as I move, and I know he's not holding anything back. He's letting everyone know what I'm doing to him as my hands grip his jacket. I can't stop staring at him. The way his head falls back when I slide out of him and the way his neck rolls when I take him in. His tense jaw and slightly swollen lips with my favorite slit running down the middle. The way his body looks in his tux, broad, built, and fucking powerful. *Christ, has anyone ever looked this good in a tux before? Doubt it. Seriously, it's ridiculous.* Our sounds fill the room and it's the hottest thing I've ever heard. I'm soaked, completely drenched from his expert mouth and the sheer sight of him. I feel him tense under me as I slide him all the way out before I slowly move back down. I know he loves that, the feel of entering me over and over again. Arching into him and throwing my head back, I grip his thighs and begin to move fast, then faster.

"Just like that, love. Christ, I'm not going to last long. You're so fucking good." He sits up and wraps his arms around my back, pulling my chest to his face and latching onto my left nipple.

"Reese."

He sucks it hard, flicking it with his tongue before releasing it and moving beside it to where his mark has completely faded off me. His mouth sucks the tender skin there and I moan against him, my hands grabbing his head and pulling him closer to me. "I hate how they faded. I cried for days when I couldn't see them anymore." He moves to my other breast and gives my other nipple equal attention before freshening up the mark next to that one as I rock slowly. Strong hands grip my back and move down to my hips, moving me at the speed he wants and needs. Our eyes are locked and I let him control me because I've missed it and he needs it. My orgasm isn't far, the familiar pull building between my legs and slowly spreading out in every direction.

"Yours didn't fade on me. It's still there," he says as I drop my forehead to his, our breath warming each other's faces. *My mark on him? What mark? The writing?* His bottom lip gets pulled into his mouth and I know he's close.

"How could it not fade? Have you gone without showering for three months?" He slows down my movements, letting me glide along his length and linger where I want. I shudder against him at the speed change, feeling him rub me the way only he does.

"Do I smell like I haven't showered in three months?" His hands come between us and he begins unbuttoning his tux jacket, pulling it off while I balance myself on my knees. I'm anxious, giddy as hell to see his naked body and watch in amazement as he quickly makes work of his dress shirt.

"No, you smell amazing like you always do." I lean forward, drop my head into his neck and feel him laugh. I inhale deeply as his shirt is removed, and my eyes go to his right arm where my handwriting is visible in dark blue ink.

"What the... you got it tattooed?" My fingers run over the words that clearly won't rub off as he studies me. Always watching me. "Holy shit. That's so hot." I lean in and trail kisses over the words, my words that I wrote on him, as he lovingly strokes my arm. "Oh, my God. I love that you did that." My mouth makes its way up his shoulder to the curve of his neck. Grabbing his face with both hands, I kiss and lick up to his face and latch onto his mouth, pulling his bottom lip and sucking on it. He groans loudly as I slowly release it.

"I took a shower the day you," he shakes his head at the memory, "and it was starting to wash away even though I tried to avoid any soap getting on it. I was so fucking pissed that it was fading, like it was pulling away from me too. Christ, I was mad. I went out the next day and got it made permanent." *He tattooed himself with a reminder of me.* "I love that it's in your handwriting and that you put it there, just for you." His eyes study mine as I blink rapidly, sending tears down my face. He quickly reaches up and wipes them away, and I bend forward and kiss him sweetly.

"Just for me," I echo and push him back down on his back and start moving again. His hands grip my hips and pull me up and down, quickening my pace as I roam over his bare chest. Trailing over every inch of exposed skin, my hands become reacquainted with the feel of him, his muscles, and his softness, just him. I run down his shoulders, his arms, his chest, and linger on his stomach, which clenches as I ride him. His gaze is locked on my breasts, driving me to bring my hands up and touch myself. Molding them, I watch his eyes widen as I play with and pinch my nipples.

"Fuck, yes. That's so sexy, love." His hips come up to meet me and I drop my eyes down, locking onto his. Harder and faster, I feel him moving through me and pulling my orgasm to the surface as his thumbs press into my hipbones. I tell him to press harder, to bruise me because I want his marks on me, all over me. My hands drop to his chest and I pant against him, feeling him pulse against my walls. "Come for me, Dylan." I obey, quickly coming apart on top of him and rocking my hips to pull out his orgasm.

I droop forward and sprawl out onto his bare chest, feeling his arms wrap around me as we gasp against each other. "I love slutty wedding sex with you," I force out through my ragged breath, feeling his body shake slightly.

"Same here. We should really make a habit of this."

We let ourselves stay like that for several minutes, holding each other and coming down slowly before Reese sets me to the side and grabs some toilet paper to clean me up with. After resituating ourselves in the mirror and making out against the door for several, totally worth it, minutes, he reaches up and unlocks it, allowing for a mad rush of young boys to come into the bathroom.

"Uh oh," one says through a crooked grin as Reese quickly brushes past him, my hand in his with his fingers laced through mine the way I love. *Total boyfriend move.* We stop at the door leading to the reception and he turns toward me, bringing my hand up to his lips for a quick kiss.

"You ready for this, Sparks? You're officially mine now and I plan on being very intimate with you, and often. Lots of sex in beds and sleepovers." He smiles behind my hand quickly before his face turns serious. "But just so you know, when I say you're mine, I fucking mean it. I will personally remove anyone and anything that stands in my way of you. Including your panties."

My grin bursts through my face and he laughs with me as I place my hand on the doorknob with him. "Please, Carroll, bring on the intimacy because I'm not taking you any other way. And just so *you* know," my eyes narrow in on his and I spy his wicked grin behind my hand, "*you* are *mine* and I will dismember any chick who looks at you twice. And I fucking mean it."

We walk hand in hand through the crowd of people and spot the wedding party on the dance floor who all begin to cheer and whistle at the sight of us. Juls and Joey move quickly and pull us into the group.

"Fuck, yes. Who had the reception?" Joey asks and Billy and Ian both raise their hands. Juls, Brooke, and Trent all start clapping as Reese pulls me against his chest and kisses my hair.

"Damn it, Dylan. I really thought you two would fix your shit at the rehearsal. You just lost me a hundred bucks," Juls scoffs as Joey shakes his head at her. Reese grins widely at the lot of them and Ian moves in and slaps him firmly on the back, issuing me a quick wink.

"I was way off. I pegged your rekindled romance to happen tomorrow after you two went home and sulked over one another all night. Oh, well, at least my baby won." Joey beams, giving me a quick kiss on the cheek and rolling his eyes at Reese.

"Thank fuck, Dylan. This man has been so miserable. I've barely been able to stand him around the office. He's fired three receptionists in less than three months. No one wants to work for him."

Reese glares at Ian and I gasp. "Three? Why? What happened to that one guy? I liked him."

"He annoyed the hell out of me, so fucking cheery all the time. Then the one girl didn't know how to work the phones properly and lasted about twenty minutes before I made her cry. And the last one used your shampoo. Shit drove me crazy." Ian bursts out laughing and walks away from us as I fling my arms around my boyfriend's neck. *Yup, that's right. My boyfriend.*

"Awww. I'm sorry, handsome. I do hope you'll lighten up on your staff now that you have me back. I plan on making frequent visits to your office and would hate to see you giving your poor receptionists a hard time." I kiss his lips quickly as he smiles against me, his arms wrapping tightly around my waist.

"Frequent office visits? Mmmm, I can't wait, love. Any chance we can substitute frequent for daily?" He spins me around as a song begins to play and we pick up where we left off with our slow dance.

"Could you even handle me on a daily basis? I would insist on multiple orgasms and get rather hostile when I don't get my way," I whisper against his mouth, relishing in the combination of his minty flavor and me.

"Hostile with a dirty mouth?"

I arch my brow at him and nod slowly, his grin spreading across his face.

"Fuck, yes. I love that girl."

His hand firmly grips my ass and pulls me against him as we move slowly between the other couples. Our eyes are locked, bodies pressed together, and my head is tucked in my favorite spot in his neck. This is where I want to be, with the person I want to be with, and now that I have him, there's not a chance in hell I'm letting him go. And I'd love to see anyone try and stop me. Seriously, I know exactly where Joey hid my butter knife.

Epilogue

"**C**UPCAKE, YOU HAVE A SPECIAL delivery," Joey sings, emerging in the doorway with the familiar white box.

I wipe the flour off my hands and set my measuring cup on the worktop. "Do I need to sign for it?" I try and look past Joey to spot Fred in the main shop, but Joey's massive frame blocks my view.

"Nope. I signed for it. Here you go." He places it on the worktop and steps back.

Sliding it across the wood, I pull the white ribbon and lift the edges, opening the top of the box. *Hmm.* I'm rewarded with the same white box, only a bit smaller, with the same white ribbon. "That's strange." I pull the ribbon and lift the top, only to reveal yet another white box. I chuckle and shake my head. *My boyfriend is crazy.* Going through the motions once more, I lift the top of the significantly smaller box, and gasp loudly. Sitting in the middle of the smaller box is a brown card, but that's not what makes my heart flutter. What's making my pulse race faster than it ever has is the tiny black box that's peeking out from underneath it. "Oh, my God. Joey, look." I turn and if I wasn't already hyperventilating, I'm definitely losing my shit now. Standing next to my sobbing assistant is Reese, decked out in a dark gray suit, and making it look better than any man every could. "Hi," I manage to choke out, but it's barely audible.

"Hi, love. Read your note."

I force my fingers to move and pick up the brown card, opening it slowly.

Dylan,

One hundred and thirty-two days. That's how long I've loved you. That's how long I've wanted to protect you, take care of you, and cherish you. I've known for one hundred and thirty-two days that you are it for me, that you are my forever. You've completely captivated me. My heart, my soul, my entire being. I can't imagine my life without you in it, and as long as I have you, I don't need anything else. Just you and me. Forever.

I love every single part of you, and I always will.

X, Reese

"Oh, my God," I cry, my tears dropping down on the card. I glance to my right and have to drop my gaze. Because my gloriously handsome boyfriend is now on his knee, holding the little black box that he delivered to me himself. Joey wails behind him, naturally, and I reach up and wipe underneath my eyes. "What are you doing?" I'm not sure anyone will make out my words through my shaky, sob filled voice, but I say them anyway.

"I'm doing what I've wanted to do since you fell into my lap." He smiles that killer smile, the one that melts me every time I see it, and opens the box. My jaw hits the floor. I've never seen a more beautiful ring, and he chose it just for me. "Dylan, I never knew I wanted this, until I met you. All of the love I have in me has been yours and it always will be." My hands cover my nose and mouth as I stare down at him, the tears rapidly falling onto my fingers. "You've given me everything, love. Will you marry me?"

I drop down to my knees and throw my arms around him. "Yes. Yes. Yes." He wraps me up, pinning me to his body and buries his face into my neck. "Yes." I look up, seeing Joey, holding his phone out in front of him, and crying like a baby above us.

"Mmm, I can't wait to make you Mrs. Carroll," Reese says against the sensitive skin of my neck. "Here, let me put this on you." I lean back and drop back to my heels, holding my trembling left hand in front of me. He takes the ring out and slides it on my finger, pressing his lips to the top of my hand. "Do you like it?"

"Are you fucking kidding me?" Joey squeals behind him. "She loves it. I love it. Goddamn it, Billy."

Reese and I both laugh as I stare down at my hand. "I do love it. It's perfect, just like you." I hold his face in my hands, bringing our lips together. And I don't let go.

◦ᴗ

The End

Acknowledgements

THANK YOU TO FAMILY FOR being so incredibly supportive. To my mom for reading my dirty little thoughts and not slapping me across the face. And to Jess for not looking at me differently after you read some of my smut. I know it was hard. :)

To my favorite little X-Ray bestie, Farin. I think you were just as excited about Reese and Dylan's story as I was. Thank you for carrying the pages of my book around and reading it at red lights. Your encouragement got me here.

To R.J. Lewis for being too badass for words. I'm so grateful for you and your countless emails. You've been the biggest inspiration to me, and my filthy soul found its match in yours.

Last and certainly not least, thank you to everyone who read Sweet Addiction. I hope I made you chuckle and gave you other tingly feelings. (You know what I'm getting at.) I loved writing this story and I sincerely hope you enjoyed it.

If you have a second, please leave me a review on amazon.com or goodreads.com. I'd LOVE to hear from you, so feel free to follow me on Facebook.

Thank you again,

J

Books by
J DANIELS

SWEET ADDICTION SERIES

Sweet Addiction

Sweet Possession

Sweet Obsession

Sweet Love (Coming Soon)

ALABAMA SUMMER SERIES

Where I Belong

All I Want

When I Fall

Where We Belong

What I Need

So Much More (Halloween Novella)

All We Want

Say I'm Yours (Coming Soon)

DIRTY DEEDS SERIES

Four Letter Word

Hit the Spot

Bad for You

Down too Deep (Coming Soon)

About the Author

J DANIELS IS THE NEW YORK Times and USA Today Bestselling author of the Sweet Addiction series and the Alabama Summer series. She loves curling up with a good book, drinking a ridiculous amount of coffee, and writing stories her children will never read. J grew up in Baltimore and resides in Maryland with her family.

www.authorjdaniels.com

Facebook
www.facebook.com/jdanielsauthor

Twitter
@JDanielsbooks

Instagram
authorjdaniels

Printed in Great Britain
by Amazon